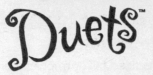
Duets™

Two brand-new stories in every volume... twice a month!

Duets Vol. #71

Talented Liz Jarrett takes us to Texas for Part One of the HOMETOWN HEARTTHROBS miniseries this month. Leigh Barrett is so-o-o *tired* of her three overprotective brothers! Her solution? Matchmake and marry 'em off one by one! Liz always writes "a passionate tale with delightful scenes and exciting characters," says *Romantic Times.*

Duets Vol. #72

Twice voted storyteller of the Year by *Romantic Times,* Silhouette writer Carol Finch never fails to "present her fans with rollicking, wild adventures...and fun from beginning to end." Jennifer Drew returns this month with another fun-filled BAD BOY GROOMS story. This writer "gives readers a top-notch reading experience with vibrant characters, strong story development and spicy tension," notes *Romantic Times.*

Be sure to pick up both Duets volumes today!

"You're an exceedingly attractive woman, Janna."

Morgan realized his hormones were in overdrive, but he didn't care.

Janna smirked. "Don't try to work your charm on me. I know what I look like."

"I'm just stating the facts, sweetheart. Are you telling me those big-city corporate types haven't noticed and panted after you?" he asked.

"Since I work ten-hour days, there hasn't been time for personal relationships." She plunked down at his table. "Besides, I learned my lesson about men twelve years ago—with you."

Morgan sighed heavily as he took his seat. "I was only eighteen years old then, Janna. You aren't going to hold me personally accountable for distorting your perception of men, are you?"

"I was sweet sixteen and never been kissed until that night with you. And you must have made a lasting impression on me because I'm still a virgin." Janna stared at him straight in the eyes.

The comment caused him to rear back in surprise—which wasn't a good thing since he was teetering off balance in his chair. Morgan yelped when the chair tipped back and crashed to the floor—with him in it.

For more, turn to page 9

Stop the Wedding!

"Thanks for coming to the zoo with me."

"Thanks for asking me. I enjoyed it." Stacy smiled at Nick, her face radiant. She had a fresh beauty that made his heartbeat erratic and his palms damp.

He started for her apartment door with leaden feet. After all they'd been through, their parting called for some kind of gesture.

She moved when he did, and the friendly peck he'd aimed at her cheek landed squarely on her lips with an impact that took his breath away.

Instead of resisting, she kissed him back. Emphatically.

The chemistry between them nearly floored him.

"We shouldn't..." she murmured.

"No," he agreed, but it wasn't in him to push her out of his arms.

She kissed him so hungrily he felt light-headed.

"Danger is a powerful turn-on," he muttered.

He didn't believe it, but he'd swear the sky was red to keep her where she was.

For more, turn to page 197

HARLEQUIN DUETS

ISBN 0-373-44138-X

Copyright in the collection:
Copyright © 2002 by Harlequin Books S.A.

The publisher acknowledges the copyright holders
of the individual works as follows:

THE FAMILY FEUD
Copyright © 2002 by Connie Feddersen

STOP THE WEDDING!
Copyright © 2002 by Pamela Hanson and Barbara Andrews

This edition published by arrangement with Harlequin Books S.A.

® and TM are trademarks of the publisher. Trademarks indicated with ® are registered in the United States Patent and Trademark Office, the Canadian Trade Marks Office and in other countries.

Visit us at www.eHarlequin.com

Printed in U.S.A.

The Family Feud

Carol Finch

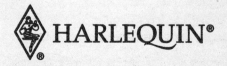

HARLEQUIN®

TORONTO • NEW YORK • LONDON
AMSTERDAM • PARIS • SYDNEY • HAMBURG
STOCKHOLM • ATHENS • TOKYO • MILAN • MADRID
PRAGUE • WARSAW • BUDAPEST • AUCKLAND

Dear Reader,

I'm delighted to be writing my fourth romantic comedy because love and laughter are the perfect combination for a story. In *The Family Feud*, Jan Mitchell is trying to reconcile her middle-age-crazy parents, but her old flame, Morgan Price, lands right smack-dab in the middle of the family feud. Ignoring him is about as easy as ignoring a rumbling volcano. Jan doesn't need a distraction during her family's fiasco, but there's Morgan, handsome and sexy as ever.

So what's a woman to do but fall head over heels for the first love of her life and hope she doesn't get her heart broken a second time.

Enjoy!

Carol Finch

Books by Carol Finch

HARLEQUIN DUETS
36—FIT TO BE TIED
45—A REGULAR JOE
62—MR. PREDICTABLE

SILHOUETTE SPECIAL EDITION
1242—NOT JUST ANOTHER COWBOY
1320—SOUL MATES

HARLEQUIN HISTORICALS
592—CALL OF THE WHITE WOLF

This book is dedicated to my husband, Ed,
and our children—Kurt, Jill, Christie, Jon and Jeff—
with much love. And our grandchildren—
Blake, Kennedy, Brooklyn and Livia.
Hugs and kisses!

1

"She's here, Morgan. I figured Sylvia would call her in to resolve the family crisis." Grimly, John Mitchell stared out the hardware store window. "Damn it, I didn't want my older daughter in the middle of this feud."

Morgan Price strode down the aisle of his store to halt beside John, who was keeping surveillance on the dress shop directly across the street. It seemed to Morgan that John spent an excessive amount of time staring at Sylvia's Boutique rather than simply hiking across the bricked street to work out his differences with his estranged wife. For Morgan, it was like being caught in the middle of a war zone during the Mitchell family feud, with one enemy camp keeping close observation on the other.

The Mitchell family feud had become the talk of this small hamlet of Oz that was located in the heart of Oklahoma's peanut country. Naturally, Morgan's mother, who delighted in being in the limelight every chance she got, wasted no time in fueling the fire by flirting outrageously with John.

Morgan's thoughts scattered like buckshot when Janna Mitchell slid one well-shaped, hose-clad leg from the low-slung car and rose to full stature. Wow! The shy, plain-Jane teenager he remembered from high school had obviously been a late bloomer. She'd blossomed into a strikingly attractive, curvaceous woman. Sighing in masculine appreciation, Morgan pressed his nose to the window to thoroughly appraise Janna.

Her chestnut hair was knotted in a tight, sophisticated something-or-other—Morgan had no idea what names applied to feminine hairdos. Despite Janna's streamlined navy blue silk business suit—that had *expensive* written all over it—Morgan could tell Janna had filled out in all the right places these past twelve years. The assertive way Janna held herself indicated she'd acquired the poise and self-confidence she'd lacked at shy, uncertain sixteen. That sweet, wide-eyed innocent teenager who'd been self-conscious about the metal braces on her teeth, and rarely smiled, had changed dramatically. She drew Morgan's marveling gaze and his fascination like a magnet.

"Five'll getcha ten that Janna hotfoots it over here to talk sense into me within fifteen minutes. Soon as Sylvia tells *her* twisted side of the story," John Mitchell muttered resentfully.

"Here's a thought," Morgan supplied helpfully, without taking his fascinated gaze off Janna, "why don't you hightail it across the street to intercept Janna and present *your* version of the feud *first?*"

John shook his head stubbornly. "Nope. I'm not going near that damn dress shop. I didn't want Sylvia to buy it in the first place. She openly defied me and that was the beginning of our problems."

Morgan slanted the older man a pointed glance. "That, and the fact that you purchased a Winnebago without consulting Sylvia first."

John snapped his head around to stare belligerently at Morgan. "Well, I couldn't let her walk all over me, could I? I've been giving in to my wife for thirty-three years. When I retired from teaching woodwork at the high school I decided my lifestyle and attitude were going to change.''

Morgan smiled in amusement when John refocused on the dress shop directly across the street. He'd lost count of the number of times the past month that John had stood as sentinel at the window, monitoring the comings and goings at Sylvia's Boutique. Yet, when Sylvia appeared John commenced muttering and scowling.

Since John had come to work part-time at the hardware store, he and Morgan had become close friends. Therefore, Morgan was well versed in the squabbles that had caused John and Sylvia's separation. As far as Morgan could tell, John had some legitimate complaints, but he suspected Sylvia had a few legitimate complaints of her own. However, according to John, there was supposed to be give and take in a marriage. John insisted he'd done the majority of giving for years—*he,* being the minority male in a household of a wife and two daughters. John had declared his independence now that he'd raised his family and put in his time teaching.

The feud was about to enter another dimension now that Janna Mitchell had arrived on the scene to resolve the rift between her parents. Morgan wasn't sure it would be easy because John and Sylvia were both stubborn and set in their ways. John was dead-set on having his terms met. Ditto for Sylvia. This feud could get ugly, especially since Morgan's mother had decided to work her wiles on John.

"I better round up the hardware I need for your mother's new kitchen cabinets so I can get the hell outta Dodge before Janna comes gunning for me,''

John grumbled as he glanced at his watch. "Soon as I get the door pulls, drawer sliders and hinges counted out and bagged up, I'm outta here."

When John wheeled like a soldier on parade and marched toward the cabinet hardware section of the store, Morgan followed on his heels. "I'll help you set Mom's new cabinets in place when I get off work this evening."

John smiled gratefully. "You don't know how many times I wished for a son to help me with my moonlighting projects and to take my side against my wife and daughters. It would've evened the odds. If I could pick a son you'd definitely be him."

"Thanks, John. The feeling's mutual," he said affectionately. "I would've liked having you for a dad."

"You could've used one as a kid," John agreed, then winked. "Maybe it isn't too late to make that wish come true, if you know what I mean."

Morgan didn't reply, just scooped up cabinet door pulls and then crammed them in another sack. If his mother had her way, John Mitchell would become husband number four. John thought he had marriage problems *now!* Morgan inwardly winced at the prospect of John getting tangled up with Georgina Price and her ever-changing whims.

Although Morgan loved his mother he was aware of her flaws. She was fickle and flirtatious by nature and by choice and she'd yet to remain in a relationship for more than five years—she'd only lasted three years with Morgan's dad. Marriage, as far as Morgan could tell, was worse than shooting rapids on a raging river. It was risky at best. He had firsthand experience at how divorce could cause upheaval in a person's life, since he and his mother had been through three of them.

Morgan wanted no part of it, and he sympathized with John's emotional pandemonium.

"Hurry up and help me gather the rest of the stuff I need for your mother's remodeling project," John requested, casting a wary glance toward the front door. "I'm not in the mood to deal with Janna right now."

Morgan quickened his pace, amused by John's determination to avoid his older daughter. If Morgan didn't know better he'd swear John was afraid Janna would grab him by the collar and drag him to the bargaining table to negotiate a compromise for the feud. Janna? That five-foot nothing of a female? Intimidating? Morgan couldn't satisfactorily link that characteristic to the timid, unassuming teenager he'd known in high school.

THE MOMENT Jan Mitchell entered Sylvia's Boutique her mother shrieked in delight and dashed forward to envelop her in a smothering hug. "Thank God, you're here! I knew you'd come!" Sylvia gushed. "You've got to do something about your father. He's driving me crazy and embarrassing me in front of my friends and customers."

When Sylvia stepped back, Jan appraised her mother's stylish linen dress and perfect hairdo. Except for the hint of tears in Sylvia's striking blue eyes she looked as vibrant, sophisticated and youthful as ever. The only thing missing was John Mitchell at Sylvia's side. Jan still couldn't believe her parents had split up. It was inconceivable there could be trouble in paradise after three decades of marriage. How did this happen?

Sylvia grabbed Jan by the shoulders and spun her toward the door she'd just entered. "Get over to the hardware store and talk to your father," she commanded. "He won't be there much longer."

"Why? Where's he going?"

Sylvia shoveled Jan out the door. "He's going out to Georgina Price's house to remodel her kitchen. Or so he claims," Sylvia said scornfully. "They're having an affair."

"What?" Jan chirped in astonishment.

"I told you that your father has gone middle-age crazy," Sylvia muttered sourly. *"I'm* the one who's supposed to be going through the change of life and *he's* the one who's impossible to live with!" She flicked her wrist to shoo Jan on her way. "Hurry over there and talk sense into him before he scurries off like the rat he is."

Resigned to a confrontation before she even had time to catch her breath after her long drive from Tulsa, Jan jaywalked across the yellow brick street the Chamber of Commerce had painted to draw tourists to this small town of Oz in western Oklahoma. Jan sorely wished there were a wizard in residence that could magically wave his arms and settle this feud.

Was it only yesterday that Jan had been holding a conference meeting with her staff at the corporate office to set up a new data processing system? Suddenly, here she was back in peanut country, walking the newly painted yellow brick road that symbolized the division line between her mother and father. According to her mother, neither she nor John would cross the street to confront each other. Someone else had to be the go-between and that duty fell to Jan. It seemed she'd played mediator in minor family skirmishes all her life. While living with a stubborn father and a flighty, emotional mother and younger sister, someone had to be the stabilizing force. Maybe that's why Jan had ended up as a troubleshooter for the corporate firm in Tulsa. She'd been troubleshooting problems for her family for years.

"Well, it's your own fault for landing in the middle of this mess," Jan chastised herself halfway across the yellow brick road. She'd always had a weakness when it came to her family. By nature she had an overwhelming tendency to fix things—hence her job at Delacort Industries.

The moment Sylvia called—wailing on and on about John storming off and camping out in his brand spanking new Winnebago camper that was parked at Price Farm—Jan had dropped what she'd been doing and come to save the day. Never mind that her younger sister Kendra lived here in Oz, managed the travel agency and should've handled the situation. However, Kendra possessed Sylvia's temperamental nature and was prone to panic first and then seek help from someone else, rather than solve the crisis herself.

Jan never had a flair for the dramatic—like Sylvia and Kendra, thank goodness. She prided herself in being calm, collected, organized and reliable in difficult situations. And so, here she was, back in the Land of Oz, hell-bent on mending family fences. Of course, Kendra couldn't be bothered because she was planning her wedding and had last-minute arrangements to make before the grand affair in less than a month.

Discarding her unproductive thoughts, Jan pushed open the door at the hardware store. A small electronic device overhead played: "We're Off To See The Wizard." Jan stopped dead in her tracks and her eyes popped when she spotted her father, wearing a trendy red polo shirt and cargo pants that had more pockets than Captain Kangaroo's. Even worse, her father could've been the poster model for Grecian Formula hair coloring. There wasn't a gray hair on his dark head and he'd used some kind of gel that made his hair shiny and stiff. Why was he trying to recapture his youth? He looked ridiculous!

"Daddy?" Jan croaked in disbelief.

John whipped around so fast that he knocked one of the paper sacks off the counter. Hinges skidded across the tiled floor. Hurriedly, he scooped them up and crammed them in the sack. "Hi, hon. I knew your mother would call you. I'm surprised that you didn't show up a month ago."

Jan strode down the aisle to give her father a greeting hug and peck on the cheek. "I only found out about this separation yesterday. Why didn't you call and tell me what was going on? I'd have been here sooner."

"You have your own life," John insisted. "I guess your mother decided to give me a month to come to my senses before she called you in. She's been treating me like I'm sixteen since the day I retired from teaching and I'm getting damned sick and tired of it."

Jan stared pointedly at John's youthful clothes, the new gold chain that encircled his neck and then focused on his dyed hair. "What's with this new image? Are we dressing like a teenager these days because we're in our second childhood, Daddy?" she asked him directly.

John puffed up like an inflated bagpipe. "No, we are not! We're trying to live life to its fullest, but your stick-in-the-mud mother has entrenched herself in that damn dress shop that I advised her not to buy. But did she listen when I told her I wanted to be able to pack a suitcase and drive off into the sunset on a whim?

Nope, she's got this marvelous career going, says she. Never mind that I've waited years for my retirement so we could travel.''

Jan smiled calmly at her red-faced father. ''Maybe we can have supper together and you can explain your frustration in detail. Then you and Mom can work out a satisfying compromise.''

John scooped the paper sacks off the counter. ''Sorry, hon, not tonight. I've got a hot date. You can come by tomorrow evening, but you might as well know, right here and now, that I'm not budging from *my* position, so your mother better give serious thought to budging from *hers*.''

Before Jan could reach out to snag his arm, John took off like a cannonball, leaving her to stare bewilderedly after him. For years, Jan had considered her father to be a reasonably adaptable man. Stubborn at the onset, but reasonably adaptable—until he went middle-age crazy on her.

''Janna?'' A deep, ultrasexy voice called from behind her.

Jan wheeled around to see Morgan Price ambling from his office. She steadied herself against a nearby shelf to prevent herself from staggering beneath the impact of Morgan's knock-'em-dead smile, his darkly handsome good looks and swarthy physique. He'd had the same effect on her back in high school. He'd dazzled her, fascinated her—until he'd committed the Queen Mother of all betrayals on a lovesick sixteen-year-old who idolized him. Her super-duper-deluxe crush on Morgan had transformed into hatred the night he'd made a fool of her and mortified her in front of her friends and classmates. He'd instantly fallen from grace and Jan had never forgiven his cruelty. Jan had learned her first lesson about love at his hands and she'd been careful never to commit the mistake again.

Morgan Price was the last man Jan wanted to encounter—she'd spent years avoiding him. But according to Sylvia, Morgan was responsible for John's stiff-necked stubbornness and his retreat into his second childhood. Now that John and Morgan were running buddies—so to speak—John patterned his appearance and lifestyle after Morgan.

"Hello, Morgan. Nice to see you again." *Not!* She tacked on silently.

Morgan folded his muscled arms over his broad chest, crossed his feet at the ankles and leaned casually against the counter. He flashed her another one of those killer smiles, and she steeled herself against his potent charm. She wasn't a lovestruck teenager anymore and she wasn't about to be taken in by those entrancing silver-blue eyes, shiny coal-black hair and that impressive athletic build that had won him all sorts of honors and recognition on high school and college basketball courts across the nation. For years he'd been hailed as the athletic wizard of Oz, but Jan's opinion of him leaned more toward the cruel, belittling devil incarnate.

"You look terrific, Janna," Morgan complimented in that smoky baritone voice that sent erotic chills shimmying down her spine. Willfully, she defied the devastating effect he had on her.

"It's *Jan* these days," she corrected as she tilted her chin to meet his appraising stare. Morgan might've won over her father with all that oozing charm, but she wasn't falling for it—ever again. "I came to see my dad, but since he's busy I'll go across the street to visit with Mom."

Turning on her heel, she tried to make a beeline for

the door, but Morgan was as quick and agile as he'd been during his heyday as reining Homecoming King, All-State superstar jock and Big Man on Campus. He grabbed her arm, halting her escape.

"Hold on a minute, honey," Morgan said huskily.

"Honey?" Jan jerked loose from his grasp and flambéed him with a glare as past resentment roiled inside her, seeking release. "Let's get something straight from the get-go," she told him sharply and directly. "I do not appreciate your negative influence on Dad during this marital crisis. I'm here to mend family fences and I'd appreciate it if you'd butt out and stop urging my father *not* to return home where he belongs!"

Morgan's thick black brows jackknifed in surprise. It did Jan a world of good to know she'd startled this hometown Casanova, who'd probably turned out to be as fickle as his mother. Morgan obviously expected to encounter the meek, lovesick teenager he'd mortified years ago. Well, he better think again! Jan had come into her own since she'd left Oz.

"Just calm down," Morgan said soothingly. "I'm trying to help straighten out this situation between your folks."

"Right," she said, then scoffed disdainfully. "You've got Dad dressing like he's half his age and dying his hair. And you call this *helping?*"

"You're holding *me* responsible for John's change in appearance?"

"Yes, I am. Considering that you hired Dad to help you part-time, and he's emulating your younger appearance and your frivolous lifestyle—"

"Hold it right there," Morgan leaped in. "You

haven't seen me in a decade, so how do you know I'm living a frivolous lifestyle?''

"Mother said," she flashed back.

Morgan let loose with a snort. "Pure gossip. I'm standing in line for sainthood and my certified documents should be arriving any day now."

Jan sent him a smirk that indicated she didn't find him the least bit amusing. "I'm asking you not to put any more juvenile ideas in Dad's head while I'm trying to get my parents back together."

"Look, Miss Family Fix-it, you've come barreling in here without knowing what's what. I suggest you get all your stories straight before you leap to erroneous conclusions and start hurling accusations. I happen to be an innocent bystander in the Mitchell family fiasco," he said hotly.

"Sure, just as innocent as you were the night of the Homecoming dance," she hurled impulsively, then mentally kicked herself for bringing *that* up at a time like *this*. She had to get out of here—pronto. Encountering the wildly attractive Morgan Price affected her more than she'd anticipated. She wasn't behaving in her customary calm, rational and controlled manner. Since when had she become so reactionary?

Morgan's dark brows shot up like exclamation marks and his jaw dropped on its hinges. "You're still holding that adolescent idiocy against me a dozen years later? Jeez, that's a little immature, don't you think?"

"I think," she said through clenched teeth, "that I'd like to avoid future contact with you while I'm in town. Instead of shoving my vulnerable father toward your mother for an affair that could destroy a solid marriage, I'd appreciate it if you'd stop playing matchmaker and let me handle this!"

Morgan glowered at her. She glared right back, matching him stare for formidable stare—though he was a good twelve inches taller and outweighed her by at least a hundred pounds. She wasn't going to be intimidated by this has-been athletic superstar, even if he was so sinfully handsome that her feminine hormones were spinning around like protons inside an atom. She wasn't going to succumb to Morgan's devilish charm. She wanted him to know she'd changed drastically and she couldn't be bowled over by his heart-stopping good looks and seductive voice.

"You've got it all wrong," he said sharply. "Just because I like your dad and hired him when he had so much idle time on his hands, and no one to share it with, doesn't make me the villain here. Your mother is so wrapped up in her la-di-da clothing store that she isn't giving John's transition in lifestyle the slightest consideration. She's too self-involved, inconsiderate and uncompromising, if you ask me."

"No one asked you," she sassed him.

He smirked derisively then shot her a critical glance. "I'm sure you can relate to self-involvement. You've been away for years, and suddenly you've come buzzing back to peanut country from the big city, expecting to snap your fingers and resolve this crisis overnight. Well, I've got a news flash for you, sugarbritches, it won't work that way. Your dad has some legitimate beefs that need to be addressed. Until you've heard both sides with an open mind, don't pass judgment on me or anyone else."

"Who are you to tell me how to deal with my parents, Mr. Nuts and Bolts?" she retaliated hotly. "You're an outsider!"

His thick brows flattened threateningly over his silver-blue eyes. "I'm the guy who can help or hamper your attempt to settle the family feud. So you don't want to make me angry. Got it, sugarbritches?"

"Just what, exactly, is your interest in this feud? Aren't you too old to be looking for a new daddy?" Jan asked sarcastically.

He bared his teeth and growled, "You're annoying the hell out of me, so if John's interested in my mother, then maybe that's fine by me. You're right, I never had the luxury of a father, just a string of men coming and going through the swinging door at my mother's house. Just about the time I adjusted to her latest boyfriend or husband she went hunting for a new one. Why do you think I spent all my time in the gym shooting hoops? My home life wasn't fun, but *you* probably took family stability for granted. Maybe you deserve to find out what I've put up with every day of my life!"

Jan stepped back a pace, surprised by the ferocity behind Morgan's words. Obviously, he was sensitive about the subject of his fickle mother. Jan hadn't given much thought to the upheaval and frustration he'd endured because of his mother's reputation in town. But still, she didn't want him stealing her father out from under her nose and more or less taking her place since she'd become the absentee sibling.

Morgan retreated a step, let out his breath in a *whoosh,* and then raked his fingers through his hair. "I'm sorry, Janna, I don't usually fly off the handle, but you managed to tick me off. The plain and simple facts are that, like it or not, I've become your dad's confidant and friend. If he won't open up to you about this rift with Sylvia or discuss his need to recapture his lost youth, then you can come see me and I'll give you John's perspective."

"Thanks, but I'll muddle through by myself," she insisted, tilting her chin stubbornly. "This is my family problem, after all."

He shrugged those impossibly broad shoulders. "Have it your way, Janna, but don't expect me to stop listening when John needs to blow off steam and discuss his problems with Sylvia."

With a curt nod, Jan turned on her heel and exited the store. It rankled that her father confided in Morgan and refused to talk to her—his oldest daughter who'd dropped her important project at work in her assistant's lap and had come running to solve the Mitchell clan's problems.

She supposed she was partly to blame for her parents' separation. She'd moved away to establish her own life and career and didn't get home as often as she should to ensure things ran smoothly. But she'd come home the instant she learned there was trouble because family was family, and they should stick together, stick up for one another, *not* confide in outsiders.

Composing herself, Jan stepped onto the sidewalk to inhale a breath of fresh air. Her encounter with Morgan hadn't gone as she'd hoped. She'd overreacted to seeing him again. She'd become spiteful and defensive and yes, damn it, a little juvenile. She supposed years of suppressed resentment had finally erupted. Now that she had the nerve to lambaste him, she'd let him have it with both barrels blazing. But she shouldn't have allowed Morgan to affect her because he was ancient history and she wasn't the teeniest bit attracted to him. She hadn't given Morgan a thought in years.

Right, Jan, since when did you become a pathological liar? said that taunting voice inside her head.

Okay, so maybe she'd given him a thought on occasion, but it didn't mean a thing. She'd just take a wide berth around Morgan and focus on reconciling her parents. The first order of business was to get her parents to *speak* to one another.

MORGAN HAD major difficulty concentrating while he waited on the three customers that arrived shortly after Janna stormed off. He hadn't been prepared for her hostility toward him. The moment he saw her up close all he could do was marvel at how attractive and assertive she'd become. He hadn't expected to feel an immediate flash of awareness and interest, but he had. Watching her pearlescent skin glow in the florescent light, staring at her petal-soft lips, and appraising the sculpted features of her oval face had drawn his undivided attention and inspired a few fantasies.

He hadn't expected her to walk in and flay him alive, as if *he* were responsible for the change in her father's appearance and behavior. Her verbal jabs had set fuse to his temper. Morgan rarely lost his temper. He'd learned to take life in stride and roll with the punches. But Janna had provoked him and he'd reflexively lashed out at her.

Some reunion that had turned out to be. She had her heart set on disliking him because of that kiss at Homecoming. True, he'd suffered a severe case of the guilts when the incident swelled out of proportion and she got her feelings trounced on. He'd tried to apologize about a half dozen times, but she had avoided him and wouldn't answer his phone calls.

Everyone in school had known plain-Jane Janna had a flaming crush on him. It was the worst-kept secret in Oz. Like a fool, Morgan had let his friends dare him into planting a juicy French kiss on Janna's lips that night after he'd shot the lights out of the gymnasium in a game against Oz's biggest rival. He'd been riding an emotional high after the victory, after his coronation as Homecoming King. Since his ornery teammates teased him about Janna constantly he'd decided to kiss her and appease his curiosity.

Truth was, there'd been something about Janna's shy demeanor and those wide-eyed innocent stares that appealed to him way back when. Even though she was two years younger and didn't run with his circle of friends, he'd kinda liked her. Even a dozen years ago, those enormous, deep-set, thick-lashed hazel eyes that were flecked with chips of gold had fascinated him. They were hypnotist's eyes and he'd been drawn to Janna on some level that an eighteen-year-old kid failed to comprehend.

And so Morgan had kissed her soundly that night, not just because of that idiotic dare, but because he'd *wanted* to. She'd been soft, incredibly sweet, yielding and giving in his arms. But by the time his knucklehead friends spread the word that they'd dared Morgan to kiss the skinny little self-conscious sophomore his potential friendship with Janna shattered in a zillion pieces. He'd made a stupid adolescent mistake and it looked as if Janna planned to hold it over his head for the rest of his life.

Ah well, no sense worrying about something that happened over a decade ago, he told himself realistically. Janna wouldn't be in town long enough for him to mend fences with her. She didn't want his input in the feud, didn't want his friendship... But damn, she looked sensational. The entire time he'd been arguing with her he'd had to resist the wild urge to reach over and unwind that sleek hairstyle that made her appear stuffy and unapproachable. He'd wanted to crack that cool, sophisticated exterior, hoping he'd find that sweet, moon-eyed teenager who'd idolized him.

Morgan smiled ruefully as he sacked up his customer's purchases and nodded his thanks. He hadn't meant to burst Janna's idealistic bubble all those years ago, but he had. Now she regarded him as an antagonist who had a vested interest in breaking up her parents' marriage. Chances were he'd only see her at a distance during her stay, which was probably for the best anyway. She wouldn't be around long enough for either of them to have an impact on each other's lives. And that was a damn shame because Morgan was definitely interested in getting to know her better.

Ironic, wasn't it? He was intrigued and attracted to the woman Janna had become and *she* wasn't interested in giving him the time of day. Who said there wasn't justice in the world?

2

WHILE LORNA MASON—Sylvia's assistant—dealt with the customers in the clothing store, Jan settled into the back office for an in-depth discussion with her mother. Through a steady stream of tears Sylvia confided the problems that arose after John retired. All his grand plans of going wherever the wind blew didn't appeal to Sylvia. After years of raising children, she'd purchased the clothing store—where she'd worked as a clerk for five years—and now enjoyed her success and a sense of accomplishment.

According to Sylvia, she and John wanted different things from life-after-fifty. He had a fanatical desire to see the world from behind the steering wheel of the new Winnebago motor home, living in RV parks on the American byways. Sylvia wanted to stay in hotels and dine out, not take her household duties on the road. While Sylvia listed her goals and aspirations Jan kept remembering what Morgan had said about hearing both sides of the story before she passed judgment in the feud.

A commotion erupted in the front of the shop. Jan recognized her younger sister's hysterical shriek immediately. She'd often heard that earsplitting wail during adolescence. Damn, Jan mused as she dashed from the office. She didn't need Kendra's theatrics right now.

Jan stumbled to a halt when she saw her sister standing in the middle of the floor, dressed in a baggy, banana-yellow sweat suit that Kendra usually wouldn't be caught dead wearing in public. But there was Kendra—her eyes puffy and red, her long blond hair in a wild tangle around her pale face—waving her arms in expansive gestures while she ranted and railed at Lorna who was having no luck whatsoever calming her down.

"Kendra, what's wrong?" Jan yelled to be heard over the wails.

Kendra whirled around and exploded in another fit of hysterics. "What's wrong, you ask? Only everything! My life is ruined! He humiliated me. Do you know what that snake did to me?"

The snake, Jan presumed, was Kendra's fiancé who usually went by the name Richard Samson. Apparently Rich had been demoted from the love of Kendra's life to the lowest life form to slither the earth. Jan never cared much for Richard because he'd been the first one to show up and taunt her after Morgan's mind-boggling, body-tingling kiss at the Homecoming dance. These days, the upstart lawyer couldn't carry on a conversation that didn't revolve around making money and the right connections. Jan had always suspected Richard dated Kendra because of her popularity and her stunning good looks. She'd been the trophy that complemented his prestigious position in the community.

"What did Richard do?" Jan asked as calmly as she knew how.

"He cheated on me!" Kendra screeched. "A month before our wedding he decided to have himself a little fling and I *caught* him doing it! I've already ordered the flowers, sent out invitations and hired the caterer."

"Oh, Kendra, honey," Sylvia groaned in dismay.

"We've already made the alterations in your wedding gown and I can't send it back!"

Jan rolled her eyes and sighed when her mother blurted that out. The careless comment added fuel to Kendra's fit-in-progress. Kendra wilted onto the carpeted floor and proceeded to bawl her head off.

"Please lock the door, Lorna," Jan requested as she knelt beside her blubbering sister. "This isn't a good time for customers to be arriving."

Lorna darted over to post the Closed sign and secure the door.

"Not a word about this, Lorna," Kendra wailed between gasping sobs. "Don't you dare tell a soul until I'm ready to publicly cancel the wedding…and I'm going to have to return all the gifts. Oh, my gawd!"

Jan did what she could to console her sister—which wasn't much because Sylvia plopped on the floor. Mother and youngest daughter wailed in chorus, cursed the male gender and sentenced all men everywhere to the furthermost regions of blazing hell.

Well, one good thing had come of this, Jan mused. The problem of John and Sylvia remaining civil to one another during the wedding and reception wouldn't be a concern. As for Richard Samson, good riddance. He was too full of himself and he didn't deserve Kendra.

"I'll show him, I swear I will," Kendra seethed as she wiped her eyes on the sleeve of her banana-yellow sweatshirt. "Two can play his cheating games. It would serve him right to find *me* with someone else!"

"That sounds a little rash," Jan cautioned. "I don't think rebounding to another man is a wise solution."

"Daddy's on the rebound. It worked for him. Why not for me?"

Jan could've clobbered her sister for the thoughtless

remark that set off Sylvia. They cried in each other's arms while Jan watched helplessly. In the midst of the most recent fiasco that was tearing the Mitchell clan asunder Jan's cell phone rang. She bounded up to fetch the phone from her purse.

"Hello?" she answered, distracted.

"Jan? It's Diane."

Jan sighed. Her assistant had called twice during the four-hour drive from Tulsa. Diane hesitated to make a decision without consulting Jan. She'd hoped this emergency leave would force Diane to become less dependent, but apparently Diane couldn't deal with her temporary position of authority.

"Diane, I'll call you back. I'm in the middle of a duel crisis here."

"But this is important," Diane whined.

"So were your first two phone calls, but I really have to hang up."

"Is someone crying? I think I hear crying. What's going on?"

"Yes, there's a lot of crying going on here, but I can handle it."

Jan switched off the phone to prevent another interruption. When she strode from the back office, mother and younger daughter were still sprawled in the middle of the shop, clutching at each other like the last two survivors of a catastrophic disaster.

"Men are pond scum," Kendra said on a shuddering sob. "Lower than pond scum, in fact. They're the bottom feeders in the cesspool of life."

"You can say that again," Sylvia howled. "You devote your life to your children and your husband and then he bails out on you, refuses to support *your* career and your dreams. I gave that man the best years of my life and this is the thanks I get! He leaves me for a floozy!''

Jan glanced at Lorna who was all eyes and ears. ''Lorna, why don't you go on home. You'll receive full pay, of course.''

''My, you Mitchells sure are having a run of bad luck, aren't you?'' Lorna murmured. She cast one last pitying glance over her shoulder at the twosome huddled together on the floor. ''First your dad walks out and ends up in Georgina Price's open arms. Now Kendra's fiancé fools around on her. Good thing you showed up when you did, Janna. Everyone knows you're the anchor of the family and they always call on you for help.''

She was the anchor all right…on a sinking ship. She was beginning to think Morgan Price was right. She couldn't waltz into Oz, wave her wand and work magic overnight. She definitely had her work cut out for her.

DESPITE THE King Kong-size headache hammering at her skull, Jan closed the boutique and transported her hysterical mother and sister home for a rousing pep talk—that had no effect whatsoever. Sylvia and Kendra broke open a bottle of wine and began another self-pitying tissue-fest that would probably last all night.

Jan's pounding headache couldn't tolerate another round of shrill, high-pitched wails so she piled into her car and headed to Morgan Price's farm where her father had parked his Winnebago camper during the separation. Driving past the wide expanse of peanut fields eased the tension roiling through Jan. The countryside was peaceful and serene, unlike the turmoil at home that triggered her high-level stress.

Jan parked beside the motor home that was hooked

to an electrical extension cord running from Morgan Price's garage. Mr. Nuts and Bolts had apparently done well for himself, she mused as she surveyed the spacious ranch-style brick home. Obviously his ability to manage the hardware store and tractor supply shop in Oz gained him financial success.

Her gaze drifted to the older compact brick home that sat two hundred yards farther down the graveled road. According to Sylvia, Georgina Price lived near her son, and it was there that John Mitchell was working part-time to renovate the kitchen. Also according to Sylvia, there was a little hanky-panky going on. The mere thought of her father having sex with anyone, even her mother, was enough to make Jan shudder. Her headache intensified and she absently massaged her throbbing temples. She didn't want to consider the physical aspect of her parents' relationship.

Jan dragged in a steadying breath, noted her dad's truck and headed toward the Winnebago. Although her dad informed her that he had a date, Jan hoped to catch him before he trotted over to Georgina's to do whatever it was that a fifty-eight-year-old man did when he was on the make and purposely tormenting his estranged wife—who was at home, consuming wine like it was going out of style and bawling in unison with their youngest daughter.

While Jan rapped on the door she asked herself why she didn't grab a bottle of booze and get soused. Certainly, this fiasco with her family was enough to drive a teetotaler like herself to drink.

When no one answered the knock, Jan hammered on the door again, then waited another impatient moment. "Be here, damn it."

"He's not there."

Startled by the husky baritone voice, Jan wheeled around on the narrow metal landing. The heel of her navy blue pump dropped off the edge, hurtling her off balance. She flapped her arms like a duck going airborne in an attempt to upright herself, but it was a wasted effort. Shrieking in alarm, she tumbled, pell-mell, down the steps, scraped her leg against the metal and landed in an undignified heap in the grass.

"Janna, are you all right?" Morgan asked as he sprinted toward her.

"No, I'm not all right," she muttered as she levered herself into a sitting position to survey the damage. What could be worse than coming off looking like a world-class klutz in front of a man you wanted to impress for only God knew what insane reason? "I've got a Godzilla-size headache from listening to my mother and sister bawling for three steady hours. I snagged my hose, ripped the heel off one shoe and twisted my wrist." She heaved a defeated sigh. "My family's falling apart right in front of my eyes and I can't seem to do anything about it."

Morgan hunkered down in front of her and flashed her a compassionate smile. "Definitely a rough day out here in peanut country." Effortlessly, he hoisted her to her feet. "I've got just the thing for you."

"What? A bottle of wine like the one Mother and Kendra are sharing? I don't drink. Or at least I usually don't drink," she amended as she took inventory of the gaping hole in the knee of her panty hose, her scraped shin and her aching wrist. "I'm thinking of making an exception."

Morgan chuckled as he plucked up Jan's de-heeled shoe. "I have wine in the house, but I had another kind of tension-reliever in mind."

Jan eyed him dubiously. "What? Forget-all-your-troubles sex? I'm not interested in that, either, thanks all the same."

Morgan snickered again, then scooped her effortlessly into his arms and carried her across the driveway. "Not sex, either," he assured her. "I'm not so egotistical to believe you like me enough for *that*."

Jan was surprised by his modesty. She'd pegged him as the Don Juan of Oz because women had fallen all over themselves to capture his interest since high school. If anything, Morgan's darkly handsome good looks had enhanced with age. A woman would have to be dead at least two weeks not to react to his masculine charm and sex appeal.

Even so, she scolded herself for finding comfort in his muscular arms. She wasn't accustomed to leaning on a man. She, after all, was the anchor for her family, the troubleshooter for her associates at work. People looked to her for solutions and encouragement. But, after the day she'd had, leaning on Morgan—even if he was the enemy—felt good, necessary even.

To Jan's surprise, Morgan deposited her on the seat of his hunter-green pickup, then strode around to the driver's side. "Where are we going?" she questioned. "I need to talk to Dad."

"John hitched a ride with me when I helped him secure the upper and lower cabinets in Mom's kitchen. She invited him to supper."

"Great, and you didn't stay to chaperone them?" she muttered, trying very hard not to notice how sexy Morgan looked in a plain white T-shirt and faded jeans that hugged his muscled thighs and lean hips like gloves.

He tossed her a wry smile. "I wasn't invited."

Jan sighed in frustration, but her gaze instinctively slid back to Morgan. She wondered if she'd ever get past the fact that she'd been wildly attracted to him as a teenager and was unwillingly attracted to him now. Damn, that's the last thing she needed, while in the middle of the family feud. Morgan was quartered out here in the enemy camp. Hell, he *owned* the enemy camp. Mr. Nuts and Bolts of the hardware world was aiding and abetting her father and making it easy for Daddy to dally with Georgina who had a reputation as a femme fatale.

Her headache roared back in full force.

Her sullen thoughts evaporated when Morgan drove over the metal cattle guard that led to a scenic pasture, complete with a tree-lined creek and herd of Black Angus cattle.

"This is where I come to escape the hassles and frustrations of the world," he confided as he climbed down from the truck. "Sit tight while I lower the tailgate and scatter the range cubes. Then we'll sit back and enjoy the peace and quiet of our surroundings."

Jan watched Morgan grab two three-gallon buckets from the truck bed. He ambled forward, whistled loudly, and then scattered cubes across the grass. In the distance, the cattle raised their heads, then trotted eagerly toward him. Jan smiled in spite of herself while Morgan gabbed conversationally with two dozen cows and their young calves. She wasn't sure what she'd expected him to do with his leisure time, but it certainly wasn't this. Having been raised in town, Jan hadn't had the chance to appreciate the wide-open spaces. Communing with nature, she decided, was good for the troubled soul.

Jan forgot to protest when Morgan swung her up in

his arms and settled her on the tailgate. Being pampered had its advantages, especially when she was one shoe short of a pair. "I see what you mean about easing the tension," she murmured as she surveyed the herd then breathed in a deep gulp of country air.

Morgan leaned over to gently massage the taut muscles of her neck and shoulders. Ah, the man had wonderful hands. She could only imagine how she'd feel if those magical hands were skimming over her naked body... What was she thinking? Damn it, the soft spot she'd developed years ago seemed to be spreading rapidly. That was not a good thing.

"So tell me what else went wrong today that has you knotted up like a rope," he murmured as he kneaded her stiff shoulders.

Jan hesitated, unsure she wanted to confide Kendra's fiasco. Then she decided Morgan would hear it through the grapevine because, no way, could Lorna Mason keep her trap shut. Likable and competent though Lorna was, her favorite hobby was gossiping and she was quite proficient at it.

"I came to tell Dad that Kendra's wedding has been called off."

"Yeah? How come?" he asked, continuing his marvelous massage.

"Because she found her fiancé in bed with another woman and now she and Mother are at home, drowning their troubles in wine. I told them that troubles have gills and fins and know how to swim, but their wounded pride wasn't listening."

"I'm sorry to hear it," Morgan commiserated. "Surprised? No. But sorry just the same."

"Richard Samson called the house twice while I was there, demanding to speak to Kendra," Jan confided.

''She told me to tell him to go straight to hell and never come back because she wasn't speaking to him as long as she lived—or he lived, whichever came first. In addition, she told me to inform him that she hoped he was the first to go so she could trample on his grave.''

Morgan chuckled. ''So, your sister is in phase one of the Woman Scorned Syndrome. She's put a death wish on the man she proclaimed to love and respect above all others till death do part. Quite the contradiction.''

''Yes, well, Mother and Kendra have a tendency toward melodrama,'' she said as she absently worked the stiffness from her tender wrist. ''But I wouldn't be the least bit forgiving or charitable to a man who supposedly loved me enough to marry me and then had a prewedding fling a month prior to publicly pledging undying love and devotion to me.'' She stared inquisitively at Morgan. ''Why do men do stuff like that?''

Morgan shrugged, then leaned back to brace his weight on his forearms. ''I'm not sure it's fair to condemn the entire male gender because of one idiot. Richard always had a roving eye to rival my mother's. He's handsome and successful, but he sees himself as a ladies' man.''

''But *you* wouldn't pull a stunt like that, right?'' she challenged him.

Morgan stared her squarely in the eye and Jan struggled valiantly not to get lost in those mesmerizing silver-blue pools that were surrounded with the kind of long curly lashes that women would kill for.

''If I was crazy in love with one woman? No,'' he declared. ''Or at least I don't think I'd be that stupid. But what the hell do I know? I was raised by a mother who was too busy chasing men to notice me.

"And the truth is," he was quick to add, "I'm not encouraging your dad to consort with my mother. She likes John because she needs a steady stream of male companions. She doesn't think she can function without a man in her life. I advised Mom to back off because John is vulnerable, but she doesn't listen to me. Never did."

"Parents," she grumbled. "You go off to have a life of your own, but you can't trust them to behave properly in your absence."

"Yeah well, Mom never behaved properly," Morgan replied. "I don't know a damn thing about family dynamics because my string of stepfathers weren't around long enough for me to figure out how a family is supposed to function. For me, turmoil and upheaval were a way of life."

One corner of Jan's heart melted. She never realized how good she'd had it, growing up in a loving household—even if that household had shattered recently and she was left to pick up the pieces. Life for Morgan couldn't have been easy, despite his popularity and athletic prowess.

Jan sighed audibly. "I want to apologize for coming down on you like a ton of bricks this afternoon. You just sort of got caught in the crossfire of my frustration with my parents. I'm sorry I took it out on you."

"And you never forgave me for the Homecoming incident," he put in perceptively. "I hurt and embarrassed you and I'm sorry as hell." Morgan reached over to curl his finger beneath her chin, raising her gaze to his. "For what it's worth, I took that stupid dare because I was curious about how it would feel to kiss that shy, unbelievably sweet sophomore who was in-

fatuated with me, even if she was caught up in the fact
that I was supposedly the superstar athlete of Oz.''

''That wasn't the reason I had a crush on you,'' she
blurted out, then withdrew into her own space. His
touch was seriously affecting her vital signs and her
thought processes. Plus, her emotions were already
spinning like a Tilt-A-Whirl carousel because of today's fiasco.

''No?'' he asked skeptically. ''In those days all the
girls I dated were caught up in my celebrity status. The
image is what attracted them.''

''Well, I wasn't looking to attach myself to the image,'' she insisted. ''I envied your outgoing personality
and your ability to make friends easily.'' She felt the
heat rush to her cheeks as she added, ''And okay, you
did have the dashing good looks of a heartthrob, still
do, but you were everything I wanted to be. Just working up the nerve to strike up a conversation with you
at school made my palms sweat and my pulse pound
in my ears. I was the little computer nerd with a mouthful of metal and the physique of Olive Oyl. You were
the high school stud muffin who inspired feminine
dreams.''

Morgan chuckled in amusement when Jan's face
turned a deeper shade of pink. Despite their initial argument at his store, being with Janna had a soothing
and yet arousing effect on him. He found himself wanting to touch her for whatever excuse he could dream
up. Staring into those lustrous hazel eyes, splattered
with shards of gold nuggets, left him wishing she'd be
in town long enough to make amends for his past mis-
takes.

Knowing she'd dropped whatever she was doing in
Tulsa to ride to her family's rescue impressed him. He

couldn't begin to imagine what it would feel like to have that kind of loyalty and devotion directed toward him. But Janna was here to resolve the Mitchell feud because she was fiercely loyal to those she loved most—and he wasn't included on that list.

According to John, Janna had always been the family peacemaker, the solid rock in a household of emotional and melodramatic women. Unlike Georgina Price, Janna had stability and stick-to-itness. Morgan admired that.

He hopped off the tailgate, then hooked his arm around Janna's waist to playfully tote her to the truck. She was a featherweight in his arms and he looked for any excuse to touch her. Plus, he didn't want her tramping around with one shoe off and one on and stepping in something gooey.

"Have you had supper yet?" he asked impulsively.

"No, I was too busy playing nursemaid and therapist to Mother and Kendra. But I've imposed enough on you already."

"It's not an imposition. I'd enjoy the company. I could throw together sandwiches and chips so neither of us would have to eat alone."

"Well, if you're sure I'm not intruding," she said hesitantly.

When they returned to the house, Morgan retrieved Jan's suitcase from her car so she could change clothes. He set her luggage by the door and watched her appraise his home. He didn't realize he was holding his breath, hoping for her approval, until she smiled in appreciation. It was that particularly radiant smile that hit him right where he lived. Her smile made her more appealing to him than she already was. God, she looked good and smelled alluring. He didn't know what fragrance she was wearing but it made him want to sidle closer and breathe her in.

"Nice place," she complimented as she walked unevenly into the living room. "I like your western décor."

"Your dad helped me with the construction. That's how we got reacquainted. I had him for a teacher in high school. Nice man, your father."

Jan wrinkled her nose. "I always thought so until he went middle-age crazy, bought a Winnebago motor home and walked out on Mom." She turned her questioning gaze on him. "Will you explain where Dad's coming from so I can get a better feel for the problems I need to address?"

"I'll tell you what he's told me over supper. Go change clothes while I grab the makings for sandwiches."

While Janna changed, Morgan rounded up supper. The phone rang while he had his head stuck in the fridge. One of the women from a nearby town that he dated occasionally invited him over for supper Saturday. Ordinarily, Morgan would've leaped at the chance for a home-cooked meal and romantic companionship, but he asked for a rain check. He suspected the reason was because Janna was underfoot. Not that he believed for one millisecond that this short-term truce was going anywhere, because it obviously couldn't. But he felt comfortable with her. Plus, he was inclined to compensate for hurting and humiliating her years earlier. He'd accidentally crushed what little self-confidence she'd acquired. She'd been a sweet, impressionable teenager and he'd trampled on her heart. He'd like Janna to realize that he wasn't the cocky, insensitive bastard she thought he was.

When Janna ambled toward him, wearing a powder-blue knit blouse and jeans that accentuated her curvaceous figure more than her streamlined business suit, Morgan's hand stalled over the slices of bread and ham he'd arranged on a plate. She'd let her hair down and a riot of shiny, spring-loaded chestnut curls tumbled over the rise of her full breasts and cascaded halfway down her back.

Damn! His male hormones snapped to attention in two seconds flat, reminding him that it'd been a long time between women.

Janna angled her head and stared inquisitively at him while he stood there immobilized by sexual awareness. "Something wrong?"

"Yeah," Morgan muttered. "You're an exceedingly attractive woman and it's hard not to notice, but I do apologize for staring."

"Right." She smirked as she tugged at her comfy blouse. "I grew up in a household with two tall, willowy blue-eyed blondes. I was the runt of the litter and Kendra attracted more boyfriends than she could count. I was overlooked constantly, the one given the second notice and second consideration. Don't try to work your charm on me, Morgan. I know what I look like."

No, he thought, obviously she didn't have a clue how appealing she was. "I'm just stating the facts, ma'am. I find you extremely attractive. Next you'll be telling me that none of those big city corporate types have noticed and panted after you," he added, then smirked. "Yeah, right."

Janna filled the glasses with ice. "First off, the majority of corporate types offend my independent streak. Second, romance in the workplace is ill-advised. Since I work ten-hour days there hasn't been time for per-

:onal relationships.'' She tossed him a surreptitious glance as she plunked down at his table. ''Besides, I earned my lesson about men twelve years ago.''

Morgan sighed heavily as he took his seat. ''If you're trying to make me feel like a world-class ass, you've succeeded. I was eighteen years old then, which is the equivalent of being a hormone-driven idiot. Jeez, Janna, you aren't going to hold me personally accountable for distorting your perception of men, too, are you?'' he asked as he rocked back on the hind legs of his chair—a habit he'd picked up during childhood, a habit his mother disliked. It had become his way of annoying Georgina whose lack of attention and constant string of men annoyed the hell out of him.

Jan leaned her forearms on the table, stared him straight in the eye and said, ''I was sweet sixteen and never been kissed until that night with you at Homecoming. And you *must* have made a lasting impression on me because I'm still a virgin.''

The forthright comment caused him to rear back in surprise—which wasn't a good thing since he was teetering off balance in his chair. Morgan yelped when the chair tipped back and crashed to the floor—with him in it.

3

MORGAN LAY THERE like an overturned beetle, his eyes bugging out. His body was vibrating like a paint mixer after the jarring fall. His brain echoed with Janna's shocking admission. A *virgin?* She was still a *virgin?* His forbidden, X-rated fantasies of getting to know Janna in the most intimate sense—on the couch, the dining table, in the shower and eventually on the bed—had just been shot all to hell.

Janna appeared above him, her glorious mane of hair tumbling around her face. She flashed him an impish grin, obviously delighted that she'd gotten his goat. Morgan just couldn't let it slide—maybe it was the natural-born competitor in him. "So, you're telling me you're still carrying a torch for me, hmm? Well, I'll be damned, sugarbritches."

She shot him a sour glower while she loomed over him. "Don't be a world-class ass, Morgan. I was just starting to like you again."

When she whipped around to return to her chair, Morgan lay there, wondering if he should apologize for ruining her love life. A *virgin?* Damn, he just couldn't seem to wrap his mind around that concept. He thought twenty-eight-year-old virgins were extinct. Apparently there was one on the endangered list and she'd returned to the Land of Oz.

When he stopped to consider how much he'd learned

about Janna in the course of one day it made his head whirl like the spin cycle of a washing machine. He'd dated and bedded other women and he hadn't been able to pin down their traits and characteristics as easily as he could define Janna.

She was a late bloomer who believed she was second-rate compared to her mother and sister's striking appearance—and boy, was she ever wrong about that! She'd learned not to trust the motives of men—his fault. She was well educated, devoted to her successful career and unfalteringly loyal to her family. She was honest and straightforward and had no delusions of self-importance. She impressed the hell out of him and she kept him off balance—which was why he was still sprawled in his upturned chair on the tiled floor, staring dazedly at the ceiling.

Being with Janna was like riding a roller coaster—blindfolded. Just when you caught your breath and got a grip you were plunging into another breathtaking dive and mind-spinning curve.

"Do you need help getting up?" she called to him.

No, he mused as he rolled onto all fours, then uprighted his chair. He needed help coping with the fact that *he* wanted to be the man who altered Janna's low opinion of men and introduced her to intimacy. After all, he was the one who provoked her to swear off men in the first place. Didn't it naturally follow that he should correct her misconceptions… *Whoa, down boy. Don't even go there,* he scolded himself. *You've done enough to influence her life. Just back off!*

Morgan sighed inwardly as he plunked into his seat. He'd already been dragged, unwillingly, into the middle of the Mitchell family feud. Getting involved with Janna would be the dumbest thing he'd ever done. Sec-

ond dumbest, he amended. Humiliating her and spoiling her perception of men twelve years ago was fast
becoming the curse of his life.

Morgan kept his gaze downcast and grabbed his
sandwich. After Janna's shocking announcement he
wasn't sure how to kick start conversation. He'd never
had that problem before. As she'd said, he was outgoing by nature and habit, especially after working
with the public for so many years. But damn if he could
think of a single, solitary thing to say.

"I'm sorry," Janna apologized. "I can't believe I
blurted that out."

"That makes two of us," Morgan mumbled.

"Maybe I've been subconsciously using your betrayal as a defense mechanism to prevent getting hurt
again, and for explaining the fact that I'm utterly lacking and inadequate in the romance department."

Damn, she was trying to apologize, but he was feeling worse by the minute. Glumly, Morgan bit into his
sandwich.

"So, now you know I haven't had any men. Have
you had a lot of women?" she asked flat-out.

Morgan sucked air—and the mouthful of ham sandwich stuck in his windpipe. While he choked and
gasped, Janna bounded up like a jackrabbit to whack
him soundly between the shoulder blades. After Janna
performed the Heimlich maneuver he managed to fill
his oxygen-deprived lungs. When his vocal apparatus
began to function properly he wasn't sure he wanted
to respond to that question, but she was staring at him
with persistent curiosity.

"Why do you want to know?" he bleated like a sick
lamb.

She shrugged nonchalantly. "I'm trying to revise the

bad impression I carried around for twelve years. Thus far, I've discovered you really aren't trying to urge Dad toward your mother, that your childhood was a constant adjustment to your mother's companions, that you have an honest affection for Dad and you aren't trying to undermine my attempt to mend family fences.'' She paused to wet her whistle with a sip of iced tea. ''I just wondered if you went through women to retaliate against your mother for giving more attention to her boyfriends than to her one and only son.''

''The answer to your last question is no. I'm not into transferring revenge against Mom to other women.'' He grinned rakishly. ''And how many women is a lot?''

She returned his smile and he felt another jolt of awareness deliver a one-two punch to his solar plexus—and body parts below the belt buckle.

''A lot would be ten in ten years,'' she decided.

''Less than ten, but not the right one, if there's such a thing as the right one,'' he qualified. ''After watching Mom operate I'm leery of marriage and the divorce that inevitably follows.''

''Understandable,'' she concurred. ''I've pretty much figured I'll be married to my job. I aspired to be the favorite aunt to Kendra's kids, but now, who knows how long before I reach exalted aunt status?''

Janna stood up to grab the pitcher of tea and filled his glass. It occurred to Morgan that Janna was the sort of individual who simply noted what needed to be done and did it. She was nurturing, efficient, competent and aware of what transpired around her, unlike many women he'd dated who were so caught up in themselves that they'd trip over a bomb in a posted minefield and be surprised when the ground exploded.

Damn, he liked Janna's style. He also liked the fact that she didn't play flirtatious games and that she wasn't aware of how appealing and attractive she was. He supposed that, being the plain goose surrounded by two elegant blond swans, Janna had accepted her lot in life and got on with it. Well, no plain goose, this, he mused, casting her a discreet but appreciative glance. She captivated him, bewitched him without trying.

The jangling phone sent Morgan's thoughts scattering like quail. He scooted his chair backward—carefully—to reach the phone. "Hello?"

"Morgan?" Sob, shudder and sniffle. "This is… S-Sylvia Mitchell. I c-can't find Janna so I need you to d-deliver a message to John. I'm sure he's out there somewhere, doing…whatever."

"Okay," Morgan said, his gaze fixed on Janna. His newfound protectiveness for Janna refused to let him inform Sylvia that her daughter was sitting across the table. The Mitchells had put Janna's emotions through the wringer today. She'd relaxed and he didn't want her stressing out again. Ask him, her family expected too much from her.

"Kendra disappeared," Sylvia went on shakily. "I dozed off after drinking too much wine. When I woke up Kendra was gone. I'm worried sick about her. The last thing I remember her saying was that she was going to have her revenge on her two-timing ex-fiancé by giving him a taste of his own medicine… Oops, I forgot that's not public knowledge yet."

"Mum's the word," Morgan assured her. "I'll send out a search party. Just try to get some rest and don't worry about a thing."

"Impossible!" Sylvia blubbered. "My whole world's falling apart!"

Morgan hung up the phone and met Janna's curious stare head-on. "How's your headache?" he asked.

"Bearable," she replied apprehensively. "What's wrong?"

Morgan grabbed the empty plates and set them in the sink. "Your sister has gone missing. As delicately as your mother knew how, she told me Kendra is out on the prowl to punish Richard for his infidelity."

"What!" Janna vaulted to her feet. "I've got to find her!"

Morgan expected as much. Janna was a one-woman rescue brigade. Her nagging headache and emotional exhaustion be damned. "We'll take my truck," Morgan insisted on his way to the door.

"You don't have to help." Janna grabbed her purse from the sofa. "I don't want to put you to more trouble. Thanks for supper—"

Morgan latched on to her arm before she barreled through the door. "I'm going along as backup, just in case things turn ugly."

"I can handle Kendra," she assured him confidently.

"Maybe so, but you might not be able to handle the jackass she turns to for comfort and validation. I can provide the muscle."

"That's sweet of you, but I've imposed too much already."

Morgan decided they could argue during their womanhunt. Time was wasting. "You aren't imposing. You're saving me from a dull evening of sorting socks. Besides, how am I going to learn about family dynamics unless I stick with you?" he said as he shepherded her toward his truck. "For curiosity's sake, I'd like to watch you operate, Miss Fix-it."

"Your significant other might not like it if we're

seen together,'' she said as she hurried to keep up with his long, swift strides.

"I'm not seeing anyone seriously." He cut her a quick glance. "But maybe *you* don't want to be seen with *me.*"

Janna shook her head, causing that mass of curlicue strands to ripple over her shoulders like molten flames, making him itch to bury his fingers in those silky tendrils. Funny, he'd never had a fetish for running his hands through a woman's hair before. Why *now?* Why *her?* Talk about your ill-fated attraction! He had a bad case of the hots and he needed to cool his jets.

"All I care about is rescuing my sister from a reckless fling she'll live to regret. How could she even think about sleeping with the first man who comes along? Surely she has more respect for herself than that."

"My guess is she isn't thinking clearly after that wine-fest," Morgan replied as he backed up the truck. "She's hurting and she's been betrayed. Her solution is to find a man who wants her on any terms and conditions." He stared surreptitiously at her. "Unlike you, who went to the opposite extreme after I shattered your adolescent illusions."

Janna placed her hand over his and smiled apologetically. "I shouldn't have unloaded on you earlier, and I'm sorry about that. Could we just forget I said that?"

Not likely. Morgan was fiercely attracted to this alluring virgin. Knowing he couldn't have her was slowly and steadily driving him crazy. As soon as they rescued Kendra, he'd keep his distance from Janna. As much as he enjoyed her company he couldn't let himself get too involved or attached. Resolved to that sensible notion, Morgan headed toward the local beer joint to find Janna's gone-wild sister.

Jan grabbed the door latch, intent on leaping from the truck the moment Morgan stamped on the brake. Her sense of urgency provoked her to find her moronic sister—pdq. Jan didn't bother to rake herself over live coals for blurting out her virgin status to Morgan. She supposed she only wanted to shock him, get a reaction from him and she'd derived wicked amusement watching him crash to the floor and gape at her in amazement.

Yet, none of that mattered at the moment, Jan mused as she bounded from the truck and hightailed it to Goober Pea Tavern. She had to save Kendra from sheer idiocy. Kendra wasn't accustomed to being jilted and now she was determined to soothe her feminine pride by reinforcing the belief that men still wanted her.

Jan cannoned through the door, momentarily disoriented by the cloud of smoke and dimly lit interior. She could only make out shadowy silhouettes at the tables and bar. Lord, she hoped she wasn't too late to rescue Kendra. If she'd come and gone, Jan wasn't sure where to search next.

Squinting, Jan panned the crowded bar and studied the couples that two-stepped around the dance floor while the jukebox played Garth Brooks's hit: "I've Got Friends In Low Places." Frantically, Jan tried to locate that mop of tangled blond hair that belonged to Kendra. She felt Morgan's reassuring presence behind her and she fully appreciated his towering height when his arm shot out to indicate the chummy couple nestled in a corner booth. Jan plunged forward, oblivious to the speculative male glances directed at her.

With Morgan hot on her heels, Jan strode up to the booth and stared disapprovingly at her inebriated sister who was half sprawled on her burly date. When the man stroked Kendra's arm and nuzzled her neck, indignation rose inside Jan. She swatted the man's wandering hand away from her sister.

"Hey, scram, will ya?" the blond-haired Romeo drawled. "I'm busy here. You'll have to wait your turn, darlin'."

"That's my sister you're pawing," Jan snapped. "Back off, bozo."

Behind her, Morgan leaned close to advise, "It's best not to provoke a drunk. Use some tact or let me handle this."

Before Jan could take a less-combative approach Romeo shoved her away and she stumbled against the rock-hard wall of Morgan's chest. Jan tried to remain calm and rational, but when Romeo's hand glided over the side of Kendra's bosom, which was accentuated by the shrink-wrap, passion-pink dress, Jan lost her temper in one second flat.

"Hands off," she growled. "I want to talk to my sister. Now!"

Kendra stirred sluggishly, her head lolling against Romeo's broad shoulder. "Janna?" She blinked dazedly. "Tha' you? Wha're ya doin' 'ere?"

"Saving you from disaster." She tugged on Kendra's limp arm. "C'mon. Let's go."

"Buzz off," Romeo snarled menacingly.

Jan was in the process of dragging Kendra off the seat when Romeo grabbed a fistful of her shirt and yanked her sideways. The movement caused their pitcher of beer to splatter on her chest and dribble on the crotch of his jeans.

"Damn it to hell!" he yowled. "Now you've gone and done it!"

"Hey, Sonny. How's it goin'?" Morgan asked calmly.

Romeo—or rather Sonny—blinked like an awakened owl, craned his thick neck and looked past Jan. "That you, Morgan?"

"Yep. Sorry about the interruption, but Kendra has to go home now."

Sonny cast a droopy-eyed glance at Kendra who could barely hold up her head. "We were making plans to go to her place."

"Some other time maybe, but not tonight. Now be a pal and unclench your hand from Janna's blouse so she can stand up. We don't wanna make a scene and get evicted, this being your favorite watering hole and all."

"Janna?" Sonny Blair blinked in disbelief as he appraised her. "Damn, this isn't the Janna I remember. The scrawny kid you French-kissed at Homecoming way back when?"

Jan inwardly cringed when Sonny snickered drunkenly. His grasp on her shirt loosened so she could upright herself. In dismay, she glanced down to see her knit blouse clinging to her like a coat of wet paint.

"Hot damn, girl," Sonny slurred as he leered at her. "You filled out in all the right places, didn't ya?"

"Get Kendra out of here," Morgan murmured against her ear. "I'll take care of Sonny."

Jan hoisted her sister from the booth, then steadied herself when Kendra staggered drunkenly. "Damn it, Keni," she growled at her sister. "You should have more sense than to pull a stunt like this."

"Don't care," Kendra mumbled. "Besides, I wasn't

gonna sleep with Sonny, y'know. I may be tipsy but I'm not stupid. I wanna show the dog that I don't need him. I hate men, all of 'em. Want 'em all dead.''

"Of course, you do, and for good reason," Jan agreed—anything to keep Kendra moving toward the door. "They're worthless, pesky creatures. I don't know why the good Lord saw fit to populate the planet with them."

"Me, neither," Kendra slurred out. "Hate 'em, hate 'em."

"Which is why hanging out with Sonny-boy isn't the answer—" Jan jerked upright when an unseen hand patted her familiarly on the fanny.

Instinctively, she whipped around to protest, but Morgan was a step behind her, frowning warningly at her. "Just keep moving," he advised.

"But, he—" she tried to explain.

Morgan glided his arm around her waist and clamped hold of Kendra who was wobbling like a bowling pin. "I'll come back and beat the living hell out of your groper if that makes you happy, but let's get Kendra home to bed first before we kick ass. Okay?"

Jan decided he was right. She wasn't reacting logically at the moment and inciting a barroom brawl over a pat on the butt wasn't worth the trouble. She'd be wise to take Morgan's advice and get the hell out of here while the getting was good. She'd deal with her righteous indignation later.

Once outside, Morgan hoisted Kendra into his arms and strode quickly toward his truck. "Hold it, Morgan," Jan objected. "I'll drive Keni home in her car and you can get back to your farm. I've inconvenienced you enough for one night, but I do appreciate all your help.''

He never broke stride. ''You'll need a hand putting her in bed and it'll be easier to haul her from my truck than from that piddling compact car.''

Jan smothered a ridiculous sensation of jealousy when her sister looped her arms around Morgan's shoulders and pressed a string of kisses down his neck. ''Kendra Rose Mitchell, behave yourself!'' she shouted.

''He smells so good,'' Kendra mumbled sluggishly. ''Feels good, too. Better 'an wha's-'is-name.''

''I know he does, but five minutes ago you wanted all men dead, so just keep your lips to yourself,'' Jan commanded.

Morgan propped Kendra on the seat, then turned back to Jan. ''Bring her car. I'll follow you because I don't know where she lives.''

Jan wasn't sure she trusted Kendra on the bench seat with Morgan. When Morgan closed the door, then pivoted toward her, she said, ''You shouldn't be within touching distance of Keni right now.''

To her surprise, Morgan bent to brush a light kiss across her lips. ''Thanks for your concern about my honor, but I should be safe. I predict your little sis will pass out during the drive. Lead the way to her place and unlock her door so I can carry her inside.''

Jan was still standing there, her lips tingling, her body pulsating, when Morgan strode around the truck. Why had he kissed her? And why'd she have to like it so much? She didn't need this on top of all else!

''Gawd, you're losing it, too,'' Jan muttered at herself. If she weren't careful she'd turn into a basket case like her mom and sister. She was *not* going to go ape over Morgan again. She was a mature, sensible woman these days. That was nothing but a harmless, reassuring kiss he'd bestowed on her. It just happened to pack the wallop of a heat-seeking missile because she was emotionally distressed and ultrasensitive to the man. The kiss was nothing special, so she'd forget about it—just as soon as her traitorous body stopped quivering and coiling with awareness and desire.

MORGAN GLANCED over at his unconscious passenger, then stared at the taillights that led the way to Kendra's place. He needed to get a grip. Unfortunately, visions of Sonny grabbing Janna by her shirt and dragging her across the table kept triggering his protective instincts. He'd wanted to punch Sonny in the chops. Then he'd wanted to kick himself in the keister when he'd ogled Janna's beer-drenched blouse that exposed the full swell of her breasts and beaded nipples. To top it off, he'd felt the vicious urge to peel a strip off Eddie Pender's hide when he swatted Janna's fanny. Damn, jumbles of emotions were surging through him with Janna's name attached.

Morgan cut Kendra another glance, surveying her long, shapely legs and the passion-pink dress that accentuated her curvaceous figure. By anyone's standards Kendra was a knockout, but she didn't do a thing for him, even when she'd been rubbing against him and slobbering on his neck. All he'd felt was resentment. If not for Kendra's wild escapade to get revenge, Janna wouldn't smell like a brewery and wouldn't have gotten her butt patted by a local joker who hung out at Goober Pea Tavern.

And why on earth had Morgan leaned down to kiss Janna, right there in the parking lot? He had no idea.

Maybe he wanted her to know that Kendra's breathy kisses had no effect whatsoever on him. Maybe he wanted to stake his claim after Eddie and Sonny put their hands on her.

"Don't get attached or involved," Morgan chanted during the short drive. "It's a dead-end street if ever there was one."

Excellent advice—too bad he forgot it the moment Janna climbed from the car and his headlights flooded over that clingy knit shirt, curvy jean-clad hips and glinted off that flaming chestnut hair. Damn...

Morgan sighed heavily as he walked around the truck to haul Kendra off the seat. He was ready for this evening to end. His forbidden attraction to Janna and the incident at the bar had him all worked up. He needed to sleep on his sensible advice and wake up with a clear head.

He glanced down at Kendra's limp form and grinned wryly. He was sincerely glad he wouldn't have *Kendra's* head in the morning.

"Right this way." Janna motioned him into the apartment bedroom.

Morgan watched Janna turn down the sheets—his gaze glued to her shapely derriere—then he deposited Kendra on her bed.

"Should I undress her, do you think?" Janna asked. "I haven't spent much time around drunks so I don't know the standard procedure."

"Take off her shoes and cover her up," Morgan instructed. "The first rule of thumb is not to cater to, or pamper, drunks. They get what they've got coming so don't waste much sympathy on them."

Janna chewed thoughtfully on her bottom lip.

"Maybe I should stay with her in case she gets sick. She might need me."

"No," Morgan contradicted. "*You* need your rest. Kendra brought this on herself. On rare occasions when I've drunk myself unconscious, I don't want anyone around when I wake up."

"You're sure?" Her worried gaze lingered on her sister's wan face.

"You wanna come back to my place, drink my bottle of wine and find out for yourself?" he asked, grinning. "Hangovers are hellish, believe me."

"No, I guess I'll take your word for it." Still, she hesitated, never taking her sympathetic gaze off Kendra.

Although Morgan admired Janna's concern for her foolish sister it was getting late. "I thought you wanted to speak to your dad tonight."

Janna sighed audibly as she cast another glance at Kendra. "I do, but I don't know if I can take knowing my dad and your mom might've been—"

When she slammed her mouth shut, Morgan smiled compassionately. "Yeah, I know. I've been through that before...wondering..."

"Parents," she muttered. "And they think their kids drive *them* crazy?"

"Amen to that," he seconded.

Janna's attention swung back to Kendra. "You've told me all the reasons I shouldn't stay with Keni, but I'd feel better if I were here."

Morgan opened his mouth to object, but his brain hit the skids when Janna pushed up on tiptoe to graze his lips in a soft, tormentingly sweet kiss.

"Thanks for all your help," she whispered.

At that precise moment, for reasons that utterly defeated him, he knew he couldn't let it go with that one wispy kiss. At least a hundred times he'd played that deep, searing kiss of long ago over in his mind. He wanted to know if the jolt he'd received way back when was as titillating as he remembered. He didn't wait to see if Janna would accept or reject him, just hooked his arm around her trim waist, pulled her up his torso until her feet were dangling in midair and he claimed her mouth.

Devoured her was more like it, he realized. The velvety texture of her lips lured him in. In less than a heartbeat he was plundering the soft recesses of her mouth with his tongue, pressing her body into his masculine contours—which had turned hard and aching in record time. Desire hit him so hard so fast that his head twirled like a pinwheel. Kissing Janna was everything he remembered—and then some. This experience had turned highly combustible in two seconds flat and he couldn't get enough of her!

Morgan wasn't sure where his next breath would come from and he didn't care because he was pretty sure he could survive on the pure unadulterated pleasure coiling inside him. He tried to ease his grasp on Janna, but his arms developed a will of their own and refused to let her go. It was as if he'd been suspended in a time warp of amazing pleasure and pulsating adrenaline. Hungry passion shot through his veins like electrical currents. One hand skimmed over the taut peaks of her breasts, savoring the feel of her, hearing her gasp of pleasure. The other hand clamped against her butt, pressing her against his arousal, and he groaned in unfulfilled need.

"Oh, gawd! I'm dying…!"

Kendra's gravelly voice jostled Morgan to his

senses. Reluctantly, he set Janna to her feet, then kept a grip on her arm when her legs wobbled unsteadily. The astounded look on her face, in those enormous, mesmerizing eyes, tempted him to start right where'd he'd left off. But Kendra was floundering on the bed and groaning in misery.

"I better help her," Janna wheezed.

"I better go home," Morgan said raggedly. "But you need to know there was no dare involved in that kiss. I kissed you because I wanted to. Hell, I *needed* to. If that offends you, I'm sorry. G'night."

Morgan got the hell out of there before Janna came to her senses and railed at him for practically giving her a tonsillectomy. Damn, as kisses went, that one was of the 220-volt variety. He was still sizzling from the shock of it when he climbed into his truck. He'd probably blown the makings of a friendship, but hell's jingling bells! That kiss between them had gone off the charts and touching her familiarly left him aching.

Morgan breathed deeply to get himself under control and tried to assemble rational thought, but it just wasn't happening. One devouring kiss and caress and wham! He wanted her—badly. But she was a—

He slammed the heel of his hand against the steering wheel and cursed inventively. He might not be a rocket scientist, but he had enough brainpower to figure out that if he was the reason Janna avoided intimacy, the chances of her ending up in his bed were about a billion to one. No, he amended, make that a gazillion to one. He'd damn well better cool his heels—and the other parts of his male anatomy that needed to cool off. If he didn't, what little headway he'd made today, hoping to compensate for hurting and humiliating Janna twelve years ago, would be blown to smithereens.

Morgan repeated all the sensible reasons why he should keep his distance during his drive home. Too bad his male body wasn't paying the slightest attention to the logic sent down from his brain. He was still on a slow burn when he walked through his front door—and aching need didn't go away after he crawled into bed—alone—either.

4

KENDRA'S TORMENTED MOAN prompted Jan to lurch toward her sister, though her body was still humming with sensual awareness. Good gracious! The impact Morgan had on her at sixteen was a drop in the proverbial bucket compared to the potent effect he'd had on her tonight. Their first kiss had been branded in her memory a decade ago, but it had been superimposed by tonight's mind-scrambling, body-sizzling, knock-you-off-your-feet kisses and caresses. For certain, what that man did to a woman's senses was worse than a drug overdose. It should be declared illegal in all fifty states!

Willfully, Jan tried to stop quivering like a tuning fork and focus absolute attention on Kendra who was struggling to gain her feet and moaning in nauseated torment. Janna grabbed hold of her sister and steered her toward the bathroom.

It was a long night that granted Jan only fits and starts of sleep. But she was there each time Kendra needed her, soothing her, consoling her. If this was Kendra's method of purging Richard Samson's memory and his betrayal it should be effective. She'd cursed Richard soundly and consigned him to hell with each agonized breath.

Bleary-eyed, Jan awoke and glanced at the digital clock. As near as she could figure she'd gotten a whopping two hours' sleep. Kendra was still oblivious to the world so Jan made use of the shower and tried to clear the fuzzy cobwebs from her brain. Jan glanced around Kendra's room, recalling that her suitcase and car were still at Morgan's place. The thought of going commando was a little unsettling, but Jan wasn't about to borrow anything more than a blouse from her sister. For certain, she couldn't wear her own beer-stained shirt.

Quickly, Jan rummaged through Kendra's overstuffed closet. She slipped on a black knit blouse and tiptoed from the darkened room. Since Kendra's apartment was only two blocks from Main Street, Jan hiked off, hoping the walk would invigorate her. She needed coffee—intravenously would be best. But she'd settle for a cup from the Peanut Gallery Café.

Janna walked into the busy restaurant and men's heads turned in synchronized rhythm as she ambled to the counter. Did she have her shirt on backward, or what? Why were men staring openly at her? Must be her wild hairdo, she decided as she slid onto the tall stool. Those untamable chestnut curls were probably in a wild tangle after her morning walk.

"Hey, Janna. Heard you were back in town."

Jan glanced up and smiled at Shirley Knott, the waitress. "Hi, Shirley, could I have a cup of coffee, please?"

"Black or blond and sweet?" Shirley asked as she champed on her chewing gum, and then fluffed her puffy platinum hair.

"Definitely doctored," Jan requested.

Shirley grabbed a cup and picked up the steaming pot. "So…how are you coming with that rift between your folks?" Snap, pop.

"Just getting started on the project," Jan replied.

Shirley smacked her gum and leaned her forearms on the counter. "Ask me, you need to grab them both by their shirt collars, drag them into the same room and knock their heads together a couple of times."

Jan took a cautious sip, then smiled. "I'll admit the idea holds certain appeal, but I was saving that for my last resort."

Shirley nodded her dyed blond head pensively. "Yeah, I s'pose that'd be best. I gotta tell ya though, I was shocked down to my skivvies when I heard your folks split up. My gosh, they've been married forever."

While Jan drank her coffee, Shirley commenced to explain—in detail—what went wrong with her marriage. From what Jan ascertained, reopening the lines of communication between her parents was essential. Shirley and her ex, it seemed, had relied heavily on shouting matches and juvenile retaliations.

Before Jan finished her second cup of coffee, two of her mother's friends walked over to add their two cents' worth. The female consensus was that, basically, men were insensitive, obtuse, unobservant idiots who required social and emotional training. The lists of improvements needed to bring the male of the species up to snuff went on—and on.

The threesome volunteered to teach Jan's dad how *not* to behave like an imbecile when he was obviously wrong. They offered to instruct John on how to do his share of domestic chores and how to combat the stupidity of walking out on Sylvia, who'd been devoted, steadfast and loyal forever. Since John was one hundred percent at fault—according to the women—he should hightail it to Sylvia's Boutique, throw himself at her feet and humbly beg forgiveness. Oh, and bringing a bouquet of flowers, along with a card that read "I'm so terribly sorry for being a fool," wouldn't hurt, either.

Jan exited the café, startled to find four men—who hadn't given her a second glance in high school—trailing her. Why was she—who'd been the opposite of popular and pursued a decade ago—suddenly the center of attention? Probably because she was braless and pantiless and male radar picked up on that sort of thing. Regardless of the reason for the unwanted attention, Jan was escorted to the hardware store. What she wanted, instead, was time to gather her thoughts before encountering her father.

"WHAT THE DEVIL is going on with Janna?" John Mitchell questioned.

The comment drew the attention of Morgan and five customers. They strode to the window to join John. Morgan frowned disapprovingly when he noticed who was vying for Janna's attention. Jealousy nipped at him like a rabid dog, but he restrained himself from marching across the yellow brick road to retrieve Janna. Word had obviously spread through Oz that Janna had transformed into a bombshell. Every skirt-chaser in peanut country had come to take a gander at her.

"What's this all about?" John demanded of Morgan. "First I find her car parked at *your* house overnight and now this!"

When the customers flung Morgan speculative glances he wished John would've kept his yap shut. "Janna came by to see you last night, but you weren't home. She drove Kendra's car to the apartment."

John muttered under his breath—something about his younger daughter going wild and the older one turning into a streetwalker. Morgan would've loudly objected, but his thoughts derailed when Janna wiggled and jiggled her way across the street. He couldn't take his eyes off her chest to save his life. Neither, he noted, could the other men who'd pressed their faces against the window. With that flaming hair framing her pretty face and that trim-fitting blouse that hugged her unbound breasts like a lover's caress, it was all Morgan could do not to groan aloud.

Damn, seeing her and wanting her were becoming synonymous. He had to get a grip before he embarrassed himself in front of John and the customers. Criminey, he'd been in a state of arousal most of the night—up to and including his erotic dreams that featured hers truly. The cold shower he'd taken this morning had lost its effectiveness and he was back to wanting her with what was fast becoming an irrational obsession.

The door chimed its musical refrain as Janna entered the hardware store. Morgan's gaze dropped to her breasts and he clenched his teeth when he noticed the other men—John excluded—were looking their fill. Morgan wanted to clobber his customers. Two of them were married, damn it.

Janna nodded a quick greeting, then focused her attention on John. "Daddy, I'd like to talk to you in private." Her gaze skittered briefly to Morgan. "Could we use your office?"

When John reluctantly followed Jan down the aisle, one unattached customer leered at the hypnotic swing of Janna's hips. "Man, did she turn into one hot tamale."

"Hubba, hubba," bachelor number two purred.

"Shezam!" Bachelor number three all but drooled on himself.

"Knock it off, fellas," Morgan snapped as unwarranted possessiveness roared through him and his traitorous gaze focused on her denim-clad fanny.

"I'd like to knock some of that off," bachelor number two said rudely.

Infuriated, Morgan grabbed the man by the nape of his shirt and propelled him out the door. At the moment Morgan wasn't proud to call himself a man because he didn't want to be lumped in the same category with these disrespectful, heavy-breathing Neanderthals.

"You guys wanna buy something? Fine. If not, take a hike," Morgan said discourteously. "On your way out the door, tell those other skirt-chasers across the street to get lost. I don't want them standing around, panting on my doorstep and fogging up the windows."

"Jeez, Morgan, don't get your shorts in a tangle," bachelor number one said, then snickered. "We're only scoping out the attractive scenery. Looking at a gorgeous, well-built woman isn't a federal offense."

Morgan's dark brows flattened over his narrowed eyes as his arm shot toward the door. "Scram. Janna Mitchell isn't a sex object."

"Couldn't prove it by me," bachelor number three said, smiling scampishly. "And since when did you turn into such a Goody Two-shoes?"

"Since I realized men degenerate into jackasses in the presence of beautiful women," Morgan muttered.

"Yeah, but this one's so hot she makes my—"

"Out!" Morgan snarled. "And don't come back until you can keep your eyes in your head and your thoughts out of the gutter."

"Sheesh, what a grouch," bachelor number one said as he exited.

Morgan sighed audibly. What the hell was wrong with him? He had no claim on Janna, but every protective instinct he possessed—plus about a dozen he wasn't aware he had—uncoiled inside him when his customers ogled and salivated over her. He was more than a little ashamed that he'd visually undressed her—which is probably why he'd taken out his frustration on his customers. He would've covered her with the shirt off his back if he hadn't been so focused on the taut nipples that pressed seductively against her knit blouse. Muttering at himself, Morgan stalked off to rearrange the stock on the shelves, while Janna conferred with John.

JAN EASED a hip on the desk when her father plunked sullenly into the chair. "Dad, I know this must've been a difficult month for you. I know it was hard on Mom because she couldn't get through the telling of her side of the feud without breaking down in tears. She really misses you."

John snorted. "Not enough to tramp over here to apologize."

Jan smiled faintly. "What things would you like her to apologize for?"

"For starters, she could admit that buying that blasted clothing store was a mistake of gigantic proportions," he burst out resentfully.

"You don't think Mom deserves the sense of accomplishment that comes from owning her own store?" she asked tactfully. "Did she begrudge your successful career as a teacher? Does she begrudge all the praise you receive from moonlighting as a carpenter?"

"No, but she certainly complained that I wasn't home to help raise you girls while I was moonlighting to make extra money when we needed it," John replied. "I couldn't win for losing."

Her dad was probably right on that count. Even so, he'd opened himself up for criticism. "By objecting to the time Mom spends at her store, you're guilty of doing the same thing *you* claim *she* did."

John flashed her a disgruntled frown. "Maybe so, but the situation is different now. We don't have babies underfoot. We're in our late fifties."

Jan swallowed a smile. Her dad wasn't dressed like he was over the hill. He was wearing another of his trendy shirts and slacks that were better suited for college students, not a man suffering a midlife crisis.

"This should be our time together. We should be seeing the world together, not chained to that damned dress shop," John muttered sourly.

"Couldn't you see the world from a car seat and stay at hotels?" she asked gently. "You could still sightsee to your heart's content."

John slammed his fist on the desk. "No, damn it. I knew you'd take *her* side. The Winnebago is my idea of a vacation!"

"And your idea of fun is dining with Georgina Price when you know you're humiliating Mom to no end? How'd you like it if Mom was seeing someone and inspiring gossip and speculation?"

John stuck out his chin stubbornly. "Fine by me. Maybe she'll entice her boyfriend instead of ignoring him the way she's been ignoring me."

Jan fought valiantly to prevent a blush from creeping into her cheeks. She was trying to tiptoe around the sexual aspect of her parents' relationship. "Er...let's bypass that issue and focus on other problems."

"Why? Don't you want to know she doesn't find me desirable anymore? Why do you think I've dyed my hair and bought these flashy clothes? I thought it'd gain her notice. But, you know what she did?" he asked bitterly. "She *laughed* at me. Well, other women have taken notice!"

Georgina Price again, Jan mused. No doubt, the woman gushed compliments to attract John's interest and he soaked it up like a sponge.

Jan leaned forward and got right in John's face. "Dad, what's the real reason for this second childhood and your desire to see the world?"

John opened his mouth, slammed it shut and then glared at her for a moment. "I don't want to talk to you about this stuff. Morgan knows how I feel and why. He's a man and he understands where I'm coming from."

"I'm trying to understand so I can explain your needs to Mom," Jan replied. "She's embarrassed about the separation and she's humiliated because you're lollygagging with Georgina. Mom wants you to support her new career, not force her to give up her store."

John shook his head—not a dyed hair moved. The shiny gel held it in place like superglue. "You're too biased and I can't discuss things openly with you because it makes you and me uncomfortable. Since your mother appointed you as her speakpiece I'm appointing Morgan as mine."

"Dad—"

He held up his hand like a traffic cop. "Nope, I've made up my mind. You girls aren't going to gang up on me anymore. You can talk to me about this separation *through* Morgan, or not at all and that's final. And by the way,'' he added. ''I heard gossip that your sister went on a binge last night after she cancelled the wedding. Tell her to get her act together. Now, if you'll excuse me, I'd like to earn my wages at the store.''

''But, Daddy—'' Jan's shoulders slumped in defeat as John marched from the office. Great, now she had to play he-said-she-said with Morgan. How was she supposed to concentrate on getting down to the basic issues that kept her parents apart when last night's mind-boggling kiss was right there between them? Just seeing him this morning, looking sinfully handsome, got her hormones all riled up again.

When Jan exited the office, Morgan and John were deep in conversation. Jan figured her dad was informing Morgan that he'd been appointed negotiator for the male side of the Mitchell feud. And here Jan had decided it was best not to spend much time alone with Morgan, considering her volatile reaction to him the previous night. Well, scratch that. For the sake of her parents' crumbling marriage she'd have to set aside her vulnerability to Morgan and focus on getting to the crux of the problems with her parents.

When Morgan ambled toward her, Jan battled the warm sensations that rippled through her and tamped down her desire. Her female hormones needed to take a chill pill, she decided irritably. She had a relationship to salvage and it demanded her absolute concentration. She wasn't going gaga over Morgan again.

''So,'' Morgan murmured, staring at the air over her left shoulder. ''I've been informed that I've been appointed as John's spokesman. Is that going to be a problem for you?''

''Not as big a problem as walking away and letting

a divorce take place," she replied. "Dad says…" Her voice trailed off when she noticed who'd entered the store. "Well, damn."

Morgan glanced over his shoulder and frowned darkly. "Gee, I wonder who Richard wants to plead his indefensible case to Kendra?"

Richard plastered on a high-voltage smile and moved steadily toward Jan. "Janna…" His gaze dropped to her chest. "Whoa. Word around town is that you've changed drastically. That's an understatement. You look—"

"Do you have a reason for being here?" Morgan cut in. "If so, state your purpose. Jan and I are in the middle of a discussion."

"Yeah, okay." Richard shifted awkwardly beneath Morgan's hard stare. "I want Jan to talk to Kendra for me." It was a command, not a request. "I dropped by to see her this morning. She looked like hell, by the way. I tried to talk to her, but she stormed out the door and told me she's going to see that country bumpkin rancher she was dating when I—"

"When you beat his time?" Morgan supplied helpfully.

The suave, Nordic-godlike lawyer winced. "Well, I wouldn't put it that way. But the point is Kendra went running to Evan Gray to punish me for something that didn't mean a thing."

Jan wanted to wallop Richard upside the head. "You could've talked all day without saying that," she snapped.

"Well, it *didn't* mean anything. I went a little crazy is all."

"Easy for you to say after a reckless tumble in the

hay,'' Jan said through her teeth. "I wouldn't be surprised to hear it wasn't the first time."

Richard had the decency—though not a lot of it, mind you—to blush sheepishly. "It's Kendra I love and want to marry. That was just sex—"

When Jan pounced Morgan roped his arm around her waist and held her back. Damn if he didn't admire her killer instinct. She went straight for the jugular. "You can't kill him," Morgan cautioned.

"Why not? He deserves to die!" Jan sputtered in outrage. She squirmed for release, but Morgan refused to let her go.

When Jan hissed and spat like an angry cat, Richard took a wary step backward. "Look, I know I made a mistake."

"What? Getting *caught* in bed with your secretary? You can say that again, Richie," Jan seethed. "Because of you, my sister was deathly ill all night. She's been humiliated, and you want me to intercept her and talk to her before she falls into that 'country bumpkin rancher's' clutches?"

"Well, yeah, I do," Richard said, undaunted.

"So, it's okay for you to have a premarital fling to sow your wild oats, but not Kendra?" Jan demanded hotly.

"Well, she's a woman. Women aren't supposed to—"

"Argh!" Jan, seeing red, launched herself forward, itching to claw out the man's eyes, pickle them and hand them back to him in a hermetically sealed jar. Unfortunately, Morgan's arms tightened around her like vise grips, leaving her clawing air.

"Richard, ol' pal," Morgan said calmly. "I advise you to skedaddle before I turn this little wildcat loose.

As you can plainly see, she's in attack mode, she's got attitude and she's ferociously protective of her family.''

"Just track down Kendra, okay?" Richard pleaded and retreated. "Make her talk to me so we can work this out, okay? Please? I love her."

"You sure have a strange way of showing it," Jan snarled. "Words are cheap and you betrayed her trust in the worst possible way. If you were my fiancé I'd have you castrated so you couldn't cheat again—ever!"

She could feel Morgan's massive body shaking in silent amusement, but still he wouldn't release her. If he'd been there all through the night, while Jan listened to Kendra wretch, sob and wail, he wouldn't think this was so damn funny.

Morgan didn't set Jan on her feet until Richard scuttled through the door. Huffily, she rearranged her shirt that had twisted sideways while she squirmed and wriggled for release.

"That went well, didn't it?" Morgan commented, swallowing a grin.

Jan skewered him with a glare. "You should've let me kill him."

Morgan cupped her chin in his hand and stared into her bloodshot eyes. "How much sleep did you get last night?"

"Very damn little," she muttered sourly.

"Breakfast?" he inquired.

"Two cups of coffee."

Morgan nodded in pretended thoughtfulness. "I still don't think we could've gotten you off a murder rap by pleading temporary insanity. Duress, insomnia, lack of nutrition and excessive caffeine probably wouldn't hold up in court."

Jan raked her hair from her face, sighed heavily and told herself to calm down. Morgan was right. She was weary and wired and just plain furious with Richard. Even so, she had to find Kendra before she repeated last night's idiocy and rebounded to her former boyfriend—who, by the way, wasn't a country bumpkin, not in Jan's book, leastwise. Evan Gray might've been too old for Kendra and not nearly as handsome and sophisticated as Richard, but he'd been good to Kendra.

"May I borrow your truck to track down Kendra?" Jan asked. "I'd ask Dad, but he won't talk to me unless I go through you."

Morgan turned her around and guided her down the aisle. "We'll both go. Your dad can mind the store."

"No." Jan put on the brakes, but Morgan uprooted her without breaking stride. "Really, Morgan, I can handle this. It's my problem."

"I told you last night that I'm making the Mitchells a study in family concept and interactions."

"I don't know why," she mumbled as he swept her alongside him. "We've turned dysfunctional."

"Regardless, I'm going along for the ride. It's my pickup, after all. I don't want you to run down Richard with it." Morgan waved his arm to nab John's attention. "I'll be back before you leave for lunch."

"You're taking Janna with you? Good." John smiled devilishly. "After lunch I'm going to test drive that flashy sports car I've had my eye on."

Jan groaned. "Dad—"

"Clam up," Morgan cut in. "He's only baiting you so you'll go running to Sylvia to tattle. Then she'll be upset and the feud will fester."

Jan swore she was near tears by the time she reached

the pickup. Frustration was building inside her like molten lava, threatening to blow sky high. She needed a nutritious meal, a good night's sleep…and a family that didn't drive her nuts! If she had a nervous break-down, they'd all be sorry. Who'd save them from them-selves?

"I wanna go back to Tulsa," she murmured as Morgan headed west.

"Wise idea," he agreed. "Despite the hype, Oz isn't the magical paradise we'd have tourists believe."

Jan's cell phone shrilled in her purse, contributing to the headache she felt intensifying behind her eyes. "Hello?"

"Jan, things are falling apart here," Diane whined in a voice that reminded Jan of a mewling Siamese cat. "Nobody knows how to operate this new software pro-gram. They keep grilling me and you know I'm un-comfortable leading a meeting. I can't do it!"

"Diane, just take a breath and calm down," Jan or-dered.

Morgan took his eyes off the road momentarily to toss her a grin that implied she shouldn't be calling the kettle black after her little scene with Richard. Child-ishly, she stuck out her tongue at him. He chuckled.

"When are you coming home?" Diane wanted to know.

"I'm not sure. I have another crisis to resolve," Jan reported.

"My gosh, boss, the company needs you. I need you. You have to come home. I'm not ready to command yet."

"Of course, you are," Jan encouraged as she mas-saged her pounding temples. The headache was in-creasing in intensity by the second. It felt as if elf-size carpenters were drilling holes in her skull. "You have the educational background and know-how. That's why I hired you."

"Well, you made a mistake. The staff keeps storming the office, firing off questions at me and interrupting each other. It's so noisy I can't think straight!" she yowled.

"Breathe, Diane," Jan instructed. "Now listen very carefully. Don't sit there making up excuses as to why you can't handle the situation while I'm talking to you. Just *listen* to me. Are you listening with both ears?"

"Yes, boss," Diane said dutifully.

Jan closed her eyes against the glaring sunlight that aggravated her headache and gave Diane the step-by-step procedure to follow, in hopes of pacifying the staff. When she finally convinced Diane that she could handle the situation, Jan disconnected and then slumped against the seat. Between her family and her assistant she felt emotionally and physically drained.

"So, maybe going back to Tulsa isn't such a hot idea," Morgan said.

Jan didn't open her eyes. It took too much effort. "I've decided to fly off to a deserted island in the South Pacific. No forwarding address. No phone connection," she whispered. "Nothing but uninterrupted silence."

"I'll help you pack."

"I haven't *un*packed," she reminded him, then pried open one eye to glance at him. "Now, if you'll agree to marry my sister and adopt my parents, I'll be indebted to you for life."

Morgan gave his raven head a shake, then smiled. "Sorry, but Kendra isn't my type and I already have an uncontrollable mother to deal with."

"Not your type?" Jan scoffed. "Kendra is every man's fantasy."

"I'm not every man," he clarified as he hung a left and drove down the graveled road. "I've gotten attached to a flame-haired fireball female who tells everybody else to calm down while she tries to take her sister's unfaithful fiancé apart with her bare hands."

"I wasn't going to take Richard apart," she corrected, lips twitching. "I was only going to jerk out his eyeballs and castrate him on the spot."

"Oh, pardon me. My mistake…Janna?"

"Yes?" She sighed tiredly and squirmed to find a more comfortable position on the seat.

"About last night's kiss, I—"

"I liked it," she broke in. "It was the only good thing in an otherwise hellish day." She glanced his way, wondering how he'd reacted to her honesty. Maybe she shouldn't have admitted any such thing, but she was suddenly wishing there was one person in Oz that she could be truthful and open with. She was tired of playing mediator for her parents, watching what she said and how she said it. She just wanted to be herself for a few minutes before she had to psych herself up to deal with Kendra's latest shenanigan.

"So, we're square then?" Morgan asked. "No hard feelings—except on my part, obviously. No regrets on either side of that kiss?"

Jan chuckled at his off-color play on words. "No regrets, except that I didn't listen when you warned me not to stay at Kendra's because I wouldn't get any sleep."

He waited a beat and then, without taking his eyes off the road, he said so quietly that she had to strain her ears to hear him. "You probably wouldn't have gotten much sleep at my place, either, despite your current status.''

Jan pondered the quiet comment during the drive to Evan Gray's ranch. Why, she wondered, was he suggesting that she could experiment with sex at his place? Because she was convenient? Because she was a challenge to him? Because one-night flings were the norm for him?

She closed her eyes, massaged her aching temples and decided this wasn't the time to puzzle out the answer to that question. She had a killer headache and a gone-wild sister to rescue—again. No sense borrowing trouble when she already had a truckload of it.

5

MORGAN WATCHED in admiration as Janna drew herself up to full stature, cut a quick glance toward Kendra's car, and then strode determinedly toward the two-story farmhouse. Despite the apparent exhaustion and emotional turmoil swirling around her, Janna was intent on dragging her sister from Evan's clutches and saving Kendra from a critical mistake.

What Janna didn't know was that Evan Gray was probably the one man in Oz who could handle Kendra and who loved her still, despite her engagement to slick Richard, the ladies' man. Morgan well remembered Evan's drunken binge after he'd lost Kendra to the smooth-talking lawyer. What Morgan didn't know was whether Kendra had lingering feelings for Evan or if she was just looking for vindication. Whatever her true agenda, Morgan didn't want to see Evan hurt again.

Morgan bit back a chuckle when Janna pounded both fists on the door, then grabbed her aching head. One look at her ashen face indicated she was operating on sheer will. When no one answered the insistent knock, Janna invited herself inside.

"That might not be a good idea," Morgan cautioned, then sighed when she flagrantly ignored him. The woman was hell on wheels, he decided.

Morgan grimaced when he heard country music and slumberous laughter wafting down the hallway. He snagged Janna's arm, but she shook loose and darted ahead of him. "No," he muttered as he clamped his hands over her eyes as she rounded the corner to the bedroom.

Sure enough, Evan and Kendra were exactly where Morgan predicted they'd be and they'd done exactly what he presumed they'd done. In between a raft of four-letter words, Evan more or less told them to leave. Not that the command had any effect on Janna. She clawed Morgan's fingers from her eyes and gasped in dismay.

"Kendra!" Janna yelped as her face turned a dozen shades of red.

To Evan's credit, he protectively shielded Kendra with his brawny body. As Morgan suspected, this was far more than a reckless tryst to Evan. The man was in it for the love, not just for the lust. Morgan had no way of knowing Kendra's motives, but he hoped like hell she didn't bring this rugged rancher to his knees, leaving him holding his heart in his hands and triggering another monthlong binge.

"I said get the hell out of here!" Evan roared furiously.

"Go away!" Kendra wailed, covering her head with the sheet.

"No. If you aren't in the living room in five minutes I'm coming back for you," Janna insisted, her face still pulsing beet-red, her back ramrod stiff. "I don't care if I have to go through Evan to get to you. Got it, sis?"

"Yes," Kendra simpered, still cowering under the sheet.

When Janna wheeled around and stalked off, Morgan tarried in the hall. After Kendra dashed past him, her blouse inside out, her jeans sagging on her hips,

Morgan stepped into the bedroom to meet Evan's menacing scowl. "Sorry about that. I tried to stop her, I really did."

Evan zipped his jeans and snatched up his work shirt. "Right, you couldn't manhandle that shrimp of a female," he bit off sarcastically.

"Right, just like you couldn't tell a rebounding blonde *no* and you couldn't fight her off when she had her way with you," Morgan retaliated with equal sarcasm.

Evan's hands stalled over the buttons of his shirt, and then he smiled wryly when Morgan arched a challenging brow. Evan's smile evaporated as he fastened his shirt. "I never got over her," he confided. "I'll take her back any way I can get her—in a red-hot minute."

"Obviously," Morgan murmured. "But what if she's only using you, Evan? What if she's here today and gone tomorrow?"

Evan crammed his shirttail in his jeans, refusing to meet Morgan's steady gaze. "Doesn't matter. I love her. Always have. Always will. You know that. Hell, who in town doesn't know it?"

"Fine, it's public knowledge," Morgan agreed. "But, damn it, I consider you a friend and I don't want to see you hurt again."

Evan smiled faintly. "Thanks, Morgan. I appreciate your concern. But Kendra needs me. She may be too distraught to realize it yet, but today was a milestone." He sent Morgan a meaningful glance. "Ever been in love so deep that you couldn't let a day go by without driving by her place, catching sight of her on the street and wishing she was still yours?"

"No, can't say that I have," Morgan admitted truthfully.

"Then don't judge me until you've stood in my boots and wanted someone so badly that you ache with it. Hell, I know I don't have Richard's cash flow, his social connections or his dashing good looks, but I'd sure as hell never do to Kendra what Richard did to her. I'm not gonna cower in the bedroom while her sister—and damn, does she look like a fox these days. When did that happen?"

Morgan shrugged and waited for Evan to finish his comment.

"Anyway, I'm offering Kendra moral support and I want Janna to know this isn't a fly-by-night fling on my part."

Morgan sighed as he followed Evan down the hall. Love, he decided, was hell—and then some. If he ever found himself in as deep as Evan Gray he might just shoot himself and avoid the misery.

By the time Morgan reentered the living room Kendra was blubbering in tears and Janna was trying to shuffle her out the door. Morgan intercepted the looks bouncing back and forth between Evan and Kendra and he rolled his eyes. He'd never had much appreciation for melodrama. How did Janna deal with this stuff on a regular basis while growing up in her household?

"I'm sorry if I embarrassed you, Evan," Kendra murmured as Janna tugged her toward the door. "Janna says I should leave now."

Evan nodded, his gaze locked on Kendra. "I'll be here if you need me. I'm just a phone call away…always…" Although Janna glared mutinously at him, Evan didn't flinch. "I mean it, Kendra. If you need me, just call me and I'll be there for you."

Morgan watched Janna haul her sobbing sister away, then turned back to Evan. "You wanna grab a beer tonight...oh say, eightish?"

Evan nodded his tousled brown head. "Yeah, thanks, Morgan."

Morgan ambled outside to see Janna, behind the wheel of Kendra's car, chauffeuring her sister home. Well, he supposed his mission here had been accomplished. He might as well head back to town. He wanted to be on hand to see how many more dragons Janna planned to slay in her quest to put the Humpty-Dumpty Mitchell family back together again. Damn, that woman was something, wasn't she? She'd go to amazing extremes to protect her family.

He couldn't believe Janna was the same bashful duckling he'd known in high school. No wonder the town was in an uproar and bachelors were crawling from the woodwork to take a gander at her.

JAN DROVE Kendra's car toward Morgan's home so she could retrieve her own car and suitcase. Kendra stared straight ahead, her arms crossed hostilely over her chest, her backbone rigid.

"I really wish you hadn't interfered," Kendra ground out bitterly. "You embarrassed Evan and me to no end."

"Well, excuse me for worrying about you," Jan snapped, then breathed deeply, wishing her hellish headache would ease off. No such luck.

"It's not what you think," Kendra mumbled. "You need to know that."

Jan's brows shot up at the absurdity of Kendra's remark. "Not what I think? Hello? You just stooped to Richard's level to retaliate."

"No, I didn't!" Kendra railed explosively.

Jan winced at the high-pitched shriek that blasted her eardrums and vibrated through her sensitive head. "You need to come to your senses and show some respect for yourself. Keni, these escapades have to stop."

Kendra half turned on the seat, her blue eyes shooting hot sparks. "For your information, Ms. Know-It-All and Fix-All, that was my first time and I'm glad it was with someone who cares about me."

Jan's jaw dropped to her chest. Her astounded gaze flew to her sister.

Kendra nodded affirmatively. "Despite what you think, I'm no more promiscuous than you. Do you think I'm so stupid and shallow that I don't know my outward appearance attracts men and I've been some kind of masculine challenge for years? I thought if Richard would wait until we married that he *did* want me for who I am not what I look like. But his betrayal spoke volumes. I'm just window dressing to him."

Jan sat there, thunderstruck. She and her sister had drifted apart the past few years. She'd erroneously assumed Kendra had been caught up in her own appeal to men and had become intimate with one or two of them.

"Having drinks with Sonny was all about revenge and inciting gossip for Richard's benefit. But Evan was always different from the rest. Caring and kind. Why I let Mom and Dad convince me he was too old I'll never know. I guess I was waiting for Evan to make a commitment to me, but he admitted today that he believed I was too good for him. I didn't understand where he was coming from until this afternoon. I discovered my feelings for him are as strong as ever. And then wham! Here you come to save the day, dragging the devil's advocate from Daddy's camp along with you and taking Daddy's side—''

"I most certainly have not!" Jan protested.

"Looks like it to Mom and me," Kendra flung back. "And worse, you interrupted a pivotal moment between Evan and me and I'm not sure I'm going to forgive you for that!"

Jan stopped Kendra's car beside her own vehicle and climbed out—as did Kendra who stormed around to plunk behind her steering wheel.

"Butt out of my life," Kendra demanded sharply. "I'm going to marry Evan, if he'll have me after I foolishly got engaged to Richard."

Jan's mouth fell open again. "You can't rebound to Evan at the snap of your fingers. You can't keep the wedding gifts, your caterers and your church reservation! Next you'll be telling me that you're going to scratch out Richard's name on the invitation and pencil in Evan's. *Are you insane?*"

"No, I'm thinking clearly for the first time in a long time."

Jan shook her finger at her sister's stubborn expression. "Now you listen to me, Kendra Rose. You go shower and change and go to work. You've already missed a full day at the travel agency. And you damn well better cool it with Evan. Don't you dare hurt him the way Richard hurt y—"

Jan didn't get to finish her sentence because Kendra shoved the car in Reverse and laid rubber. Kendra stuck her head out the window and yelled, "Leave me alone, Butinsky! You're not the boss of me, so there!"

Jan rolled her eyes and muttered, "Oh, now, that's mature."

Tired, hungry and exasperated to the extreme Jan stalked to Morgan's house to retrieve her suitcase, then cursed when she found the door locked. Reversing direction she approached her car and flung herself onto the seat.

No good deed, it seemed, went unpunished. She'd tried to rescue her sister from her own stupidity and had inadvertently, embarrassingly, interrupted the aftermath of her sister's initiation into passion. Who would've thought the much-sought-after Kendra, the gorgeous, well-built, blue-eyed blond bombshell had taken time to analyze the male psyche and realized she was a challenge and acquisition to her endless male admirers. Kendra had more depth and insight than Jan had given her credit. Yet, Jan still wasn't sure Kendra was thinking clearly, for she could've been motivated to give herself to Evan, just to spite Richard.

Jan put her car in Reverse and backed away from her dad's Winnebago. Although she was desperately trying to help her family, Kendra was furious with her. Her dad wouldn't speak directly to her and her mother thought Jan had joined the enemy camp. Worse, her family was turning her into a raving lunatic, who would've ripped Richard Samson to shreds at the hardware store, if Morgan hadn't kept her chained in his arms. No doubt, that little scene would be zipping along Oz's grapevine. The whole town would think she'd gone as bonkers as the rest of her family. Then Jan had burst in on her sister and Evan during their monumental tryst. Jeez, she just couldn't catch a break today.

Fighting the urge to bawl her head off, knowing it would aggravate her megaheadache, Jan drove to town. What she needed was the privacy and isolation to fall to pieces, then regroup. Unfortunately, she didn't have that luxury. She had to hightail it to Oz and assure her mother that she hadn't taken Daddy's side in the feud and that she was striving to find a workable solution to the separation.

Ten minutes later Jan pulled into the only available parking space, which happened to be in front of Dorothy's Hair Salon. The owner and proprietor's name wasn't Dorothy. She'd recently changed the salon's name to promote tourist trade in Oz. The town's original name was Oswald, but after that whole Lee Harvey fiasco, the name had been cropped off to Oz. Then someone had the bright idea to change the image to a magical city. In Jan's opinion—which obviously counted for zilch in her hometown—combining the tale of Oz with the peanut capital of the world didn't quite fit. But the Chamber of Commerce was advocating the transition for the sake of tourism. Next thing Jan knew the school system would be renamed Munchkinland, Goober Pea Tavern would become Wicked Witch's Saloon—or some such nonsense. If Morgan's two shops combined to become Tin Man's Supply Shop she would lose all the respect she'd recently gained for him....

The thought caused Jan's hand to stall over the door latch. It dawned on her that she'd gained tremendous respect for the man she'd held a grudge against for a dozen years. Through all her family chaos Morgan had been *her* anchor, the calming waters beside the whirlpool of emotional undercurrents that kept sucking her under. Well, except for the kiss—which carried the impact of a thermonuclear bomb—he'd delivered last night, she amended.

Jan climbed from the car and reminded herself that

she didn't have time to delve into these feelings for Morgan that kept ambushing her at inopportune moments. She had to speak to her mother before the poor woman's resentment festered up and exploded like Kendra's had.

Before Jan reached Sylvia's Boutique, three women, with their hair in curlers, scampered from the salon and bore down on her. Gina Thompson, owner and proprietor, led the brigade.

"Janna, hon, we want a word with you," Gina insisted.

Jan bit back a groan as she appraised Gina's dyed copper-red hair, thick coat of makeup, false eyelashes and trendy clothes that suited her age of fifty no better than John Mitchell's outrageous attire. She smiled faintly and nodded a greeting to the women. "Is there a problem?"

"Absolutely," Gina confirmed. "You aren't going about this business of getting your folks to kiss and make up the right way. The other girls—"

Jan presumed that anyone under the age of eighty qualified as a girl.

"—think that since John is flaunting Georgina in Sylvia's face that she should return the favor. We've selected a man to serve as the jealousy factor for Sylvia. We want you to approach your mom with the idea," Gina went on. The curler brigade nodded in perfect agreement. "We'll send Stanley Witham over to the boutique. He's a lonely widower and he could use some female companionship. This'll work splendidly."

"I don't know," Jan said dubiously. "I'm afraid a male admirer in Mom's life will complicate what is already a complex situation."

Gina flicked her plump wrist in dismissal of Jan's

concern. Gold bracelets jangled in the silence. "Nonsense. You've gotta have some motivation here and all the girls who've come and gone from my salon the past month agree this is the best solution. If John thinks Stanley is moving in on Sylvia and she shows interest, John will reconsider this ridiculous separation and come running home to protect his wife from the advances of another man. You know how territorial most men are."

Gina snapped her fingers, which boasted long acrylic nails, coated in glittering hot pink. "Presto! Problem solved. John and Sylvia are back together and the gossip dies down so we can concentrate our thought processes on making the necessary changes and improvements to draw tourists to the magical Land of Oz."

Three heads bobbed enthusiastically.

Jan smiled past the Queen Mother of Headaches that hammered at her skull. "I appreciate your help and I'll certainly give your scheme some serious consideration." Not damn likely!

"Just remember we're ready to turn Stanley loose."

That sounded ominous. Enter Sylvia's new love interest? Jan could no more picture her dad with Georgina than she could picture Sylvia with the red-haired, bewhiskered Stanley Witham who ran the recently renamed Magic Pill Pharmacy. My God, everyone in the Land of Oz had gone nuts and *she* right along with them! Jan was on the verge of a nervous breakdown, but she didn't have the time to invest in her own mental health because her family had gone over the edge—the whole bunch of them!

Composing herself as best she could, Jan headed for the dress shop. The minute she stepped inside, Sylvia and Lorna glowered at her as if she'd committed all seven deadly sins simultaneously.

"Ah, so the traitor shows her face at last," Sylvia said snidely.

"Mom—"

"Don't Mom me, young lady," Sylvia interrupted in a sharp tone. "Word has it that your car was parked in the enemy camp. I saw for myself that you came waltzing from the hardware store this morning with Morgan Price at your side. Furthermore, I knew you didn't leave with him against your will because you weren't being physically forced and you didn't look drugged, either!"

Jan eyed her mother curiously. "And how do you know that?"

Sylvia reached under the counter to retrieve a pair of high-powered binoculars and waved them in Jan's face. "Because I was watching you closely," she said. "I watch the goings on at the hardware store very carefully and I have for a month."

Jan gaped at her mother-turned-private-eye, and then glanced at Lorna who nodded confirmation. Things around this town were out of control!

Sylvia scowled as she swung the binoculars into place. "Here comes Georgina, sauntering toward the hardware store. Lord, would you look at that slinky outfit she's poured into? The woman doesn't have an ounce of style or good taste. Her overblown hairstyle reminds me of the mother on *Married With Children*."

Jan, Lorna and Sylvia approached the window to monitor Georgina's drumroll walk to the store. Jan grimaced when Georgina paused and waved to Morgan who exited the tractor supply shop. Georgina, Jan noted, made a big production of hugging her only son, as if she hadn't seen him in a couple of years. The false public display of affection made Jan grit her teeth.

"Just look at that Jezebel," Sylvia said, and scowled. "Her clothes are so tight I can tell which side's up on the quarter in the pocket of those painted-on pants. It's tails. No surprise there. And that skintight blouse! What second-rate store does she shop at, I wonder? And that ridiculous 'do. I swear she must cut and dye her hair herself!"

Jan made a thorough study of Georgina. True, the woman dressed to attract male attention, but she didn't look as sleazy as Sylvia let on. Honestly, Jan could see why Georgina drew her dad's interest, while her mother's conservative clothing style—though elegant and expensive—shouted stuffy and unapproachable. Jan was a little guilty of that herself, she realized. Ordinarily, she leaned toward streamlined business suits at work to give her a unisex appearance that her mixed staff related to. Georgina, however, went straight for sex appeal that had Available stamped all over the body-enhancing outfit.

When Morgan was a teenager, Jan knew he'd been uncomfortable with his mother's sexy wardrobe and her string of men. Morgan was fortunate, however, that he didn't have to endure too much razzing. If he hadn't been such a well-respected superstar athlete it might've been worse. Jan knew for a fact that other students discussed Morgan's mom behind his back, but no one dared to insult her for fear he'd pounce. Life with Georgina hadn't been easy or normal. Jan sympathized with Morgan because parents were still parents. You had to love 'em, even if they made you crazy.

"There's John," Sylvia muttered as she peered

through the binoculars. "I can see him at the window. He's grinning like a fool at Georgina. I'd like to march over there and pull that woman's hair out by the dyed roots. And John, look at him in those ridiculous clothes!"

Suddenly Sylvia jerked the binoculars away from her face and glared at Jan. "And you're promoting this affair by loitering in the enemy camp. How could you do this to me?"

Uh-oh, Sylvia was going melodramatic again. Jan steeled herself against the third lecture of the day from a family member. "No, I'm not," Jan replied. "I want you and Dad back together. Maybe it's time you changed your hairdo and dressed like Georgina to attract Dad's attention. You know, put some pizzazz back in your marriage."

Sylvia gasped, scandalized. "You want me to dress like a vamp?"

"Yes, maybe then Dad will think you still care enough to nab his attention, and realize *he* still appeals to *you*. Maybe he's dressing younger in hopes of attracting *your* attention. Ever think of that?" Jan asked.

"Don't try to sidetrack me with that rubbish," Sylvia snapped. "I called you to help and so far you've accomplished nothing but take your dad's side. Last night you were out running around only God knows where when Kendra went berserk and I needed you to find her. And I seriously doubt you were discussing our situation with your father because Georgina let it be known at Peanut Gallery Café, midmorning, that she was with John last night. I know for a fact that you didn't come home because I checked your room when I got up at two-thirty. Where were you and what in heaven's name were you doing last night?"

"I was tending Kendra while she tossed her cookies," Jan reported, trying to keep her temper under control. "I spent the night on the floor beside her bed, tending her when she was ill and swearing she was dying."

"Oh, well...uh...good." Sylvia relaxed a smidgen, but then she frowned suspiciously. "That still doesn't explain why you left the store this morning with Morgan. You should've been talking sense into your middle-age crazy father."

"I did try to reason with Dad," Jan said. "But he thinks I'm on your side of the feud. He insisted that I have to talk to *him* through *Morgan*."

"What?" Sylvia yowled. "That's preposterous!"

"No more preposterous than you sending me over to negotiate issues with Dad. If you won't meet him face-to-face, then he wants a mediator, too. If the two of you would agree to meet on neutral turf and discuss—"

Her voice fizzled out when Stanley Witham, wearing his blue pharmaceutical smock, carrying a gigantic bouquet of flowers, strode into the shop. Jan inwardly groaned. The busybodies at the hair salon had taken it upon themselves to activate their male-rival-and-jealousy-factor scheme without permission. Well, wasn't that just dandy? Jan was in the middle of defending her position to her suspicious mother. Enter Stanley, stage left, to complicate the situation.

Jan had no doubt that Dad was keeping surveillance at the hardware store window and witnessed Stanley's arrival. Anyone with half a brain in his head—middle-age crazy or not—understood the implication of Stanley arriving with a riotous bouquet of flowers in hand.

"Hello, Sylvia," Stanley said, smiling. At least Jan

presumed he was smiling. With that carrot-colored beard and mustache—which oddly enough, reminded her of the cowardly lion character in the *Wizard of Oz*—it was difficult to tell for certain.

"These are for you." Stanley thrust the bouquet at Sylvia who smiled appreciatively, and then took a whiff of the fragrant flowers.

"How thoughtful of you, Stanley. I haven't received flowers in years."

Note to self, Jan mused. *Tell Dad to send Mom flowers.*

"I thought we might have dinner tonight at Uncle Henry and Auntie Em's Restaurant," Stanley invited. "Will you join me, Sylvia?"

Sylvia took another sniff of the flowers and nodded. "I'd love to."

"I'll pick you up about six-thirty, if that's okay."

Sylvia flashed a dazzling smile. "Perfect."

"Well, I better get back to the drugstore. I have several prescriptions to fill this afternoon. I don't want to be late for our first date."

When Stanley exited, Jan turned on her mother. "How could you? Don't you know this will provoke Dad to retaliate?"

"Well, maybe it's time he discovers how it feels to have the shoe on the other foot. I've watched him dally with Georgina and heard the humiliating rumors about what's going on between them. Maybe *I* should be making rumors of my own for a change and he can see how he likes it!"

Sylvia glanced around, as if something had suddenly occurred to her. "Where's your sister? I thought you said you were consoling her."

"I sent her to work to get her mind on something

besides the…er…cancelled wedding." Jan omitted the incident at Evan Gray's ranch and Kendra's idiotic declaration that she was going ahead with the wedding by substituting another groom—provided the groom agreed to stand in.

Lord, what a mess, thought Jan. She was afraid to leave Kendra alone for more than an hour, for fear she'd concoct another harebrained scheme to retaliate against Richard's mortifying betrayal. Yet, Jan needed to stay here and talk Sylvia out of this idea of accepting a date.

"Mom," she said gently. "I think you should call Stanley and cancel."

Sylvia's chin snapped up rebelliously. "No. You march across the street and tell your father that I'll cancel my dates when he cancels his."

Before Jan could debate the issue, two customers strode inside and began oohing and aahing over the extravagant bouquet of flowers. Sylvia, darn her, announced they were from Stanley who'd invited her to dinner.

Defeated, exasperated, her stomach rumbling, Jan pivoted toward the door. Another ingredient of retaliation and revenge had been stirred into the mix of the Mitchell family feud, raising the stakes and the consequences. Jan knew she needed to devise a fail-safe plan to end this feud, but her thoughts were in such turmoil she couldn't think straight—especially when she was sporting this headache.

Once outside the boutique, Jan struggled to compose herself. She was having one hell of a day and it was only half over. She definitely needed to find a place to hide so she could fall apart, vent her emotions and then regroup. It couldn't be at her mother's house since Sylvia was perturbed with her. It couldn't be at Kendra's apartment because her sister didn't want to speak to her after the fiasco with Evan. It couldn't be at her dad's Winnebago because he didn't want to talk to her, either.

She, who'd come to save the day, had become the family pariah.

When her cell phone jingled, Jan thrust her hand into her purse to switch it off. Diane was probably calling with another corporate calamity. Frankly, Jan wasn't in the mood to deal with that on top of all else.

Before Jan could cross the yellow brick road three of the men, who'd trailed after her this morning, arrived on the scene— Was it just this morning? So much had happened that she'd lost track of time. When the men flirted with her and invited her to the bar for a drink this evening she tried to veer around them. They blocked her path, refusing to take no for an answer.

"Drinks at eight…maybe…if I have time," she hedged, anxious to get rid of them. She might need an excuse to return to the tavern so she could keep surveillance on Kendra. That was the *only* reason Janna would hang out with these casanovas.

Her mouth set in a grim line Jan strode across the street to determine how her dad reacted to Stanley Witham's arrival at the boutique—with flowers in hand and dating on his mind.

6

JAN ENTERED the hardware store and stopped short when she saw that Georgina had her arm draped over her dad's shoulder and he'd slipped his arm around her waist. "Dad!" Jan all but shouted in disapproval. Neither John nor Georgina unhanded one another. It was, she was sure, a display of defiance. "I need to talk to you *now*," Jan said as she stalked down the aisle. She grabbed her dad's arm and towed him into the plumbing supply department. "I suppose you observed that little scene at the boutique."

"Hard to miss," John muttered sourly.

"But not hard to figure out why Mom accepted the date," Jan pointed out. "How long do you and Mom plan to one-up each other? Until you've completely destroyed a thirty-three-year marriage?"

John's chin jutted out and he took a militant stance. "We aren't having this discussion. I told you to talk to me through Morgan. I'm busy at the moment. I'm on my way over to Georgie's to lay tile."

Now it was *Georgie?* Giving the woman a pet name couldn't be a good sign. And if he was laying anything besides tile Jan was going to have to murder her own father... Good gad, what was she saying? She was definitely skirting the edge, about to plunge off the deep end.

"Besides, I saw you talking to those clucking old

hens at the beauty shop," John said resentfully. "I know they're siding with your mother, same as you. Now, I've got places to go and things to do before my date tonight."

"Well, I hope you and Mom don't meet up at the restaurant at six-thirty with your dates. It could be awkward," she tossed out. Why? She had no idea, except maybe she'd reached the furthermost point of desperation in her attempt to resolve this feud.

John jerked back as if she'd slapped him upside the head. "Sylvia and Stanley are planning to parade around town on each other's arm? Well, hell, at least I've had the decency not to do *that!*"

"No? What do you call draping your arm around Georgina in the store and on the street? Maybe Mom is entitled to the same demonstrations of affection. Obviously she's not getting any affection and support from you."

John glowered at her and Jan could've kicked herself—repeatedly—when he said, "Fine, the gloves are officially off in this feud! As for you, little girl, don't talk to me again!" He wheeled around and stormed over to Georgina, and then half dragged her from the store in his haste to leave.

Jan watched in dismay as John cuddled Georgina closely to him and she hung on him like English ivy. Tormented to the extreme, Jan wilted onto the floor in the plumbing supply department. She scrubbed her hands over her face and remembered she hadn't applied makeup this morning, hadn't combed her hair and was still commando.

There was so much emotional upheaval whirling around her that she hadn't given much thought to her own appearance. God, how she wished the floor would open up so she could drop out of sight. Everyone was aggravated with her and none of her attempts to mend family fences were working. Plus, she looked like hell. She wanted to throw up her hands in defeat and walk away without looking back.

"Janna? Are you okay?"

"No, my entire family hates me." Through a mist of tears she glanced up to see Morgan squatting down in front of her. It took what little restraint she had left not to fling herself into his arms and bawl her fool head off.

"I don't hate you, sugar," he assured softly as he cupped her chin to appraise her wan face.

"Well," she said, "that makes you a minority of one."

He smiled reassuringly. "Everything's gonna be all right."

"Will it?" she asked, lips trembling, eyes flooding with unwanted tears. "I'd like to have your guarantee in writing, if you don't mind."

Morgan stared at her somberly. "I know you didn't get any sleep and skipped breakfast. Did you at least take time for lunch?"

"Lunch?" She stared at him blankly. "What time is it? I must've left my watch at Kendra's after I showered. I didn't have a change of clothes..." Her voice trailed off and her face flushed with heat.

Morgan grinned wryly. "No panties or bra. Yeah, I noticed." His gaze dipped momentarily to her clingy knit blouse. "I, and every other man with eyes in his head, couldn't help but notice you're braless."

Self-conscious, Jan crossed her arms over her chest. "That must be what drew those guys on the street," she mused aloud. "I wondered why they invited me to the tavern for drinks this evening."

Morgan said nothing, just got an indecipherable look on his face.

"I better shove off," Jan said as she came slowly to her feet. "I need to make sure Kendra went to work like I told her, instead of haring off in another attempt to ruin her life and her reputation."

Morgan leaned so close she thought he might kiss her. Indeed, she wished he would. That'd get her adrenaline pumping like nothing else could.

"You need to rest before you drop in your tracks," he murmured. "Go out to my place and catch a nap. I'll be home in an hour to fix our supper."

Jan shook her head, but smiled appreciatively. "Thanks, but I need to check on Kendra, then keep my eye on Mom and her date this evening."

Morgan's black brows shot to his hairline. "Her date?" he parroted.

She nodded grimly. "With Stanley the pharmacist. This is the last straw. I've decided to put my entire family up for auction to the highest bidder. Emotionally speaking, they're getting too expensive to keep."

"Janna, wait—" Morgan protested, but she didn't break stride, just waved at him before she exited the store.

Morgan sighed heavily as he walked back to the counter. He couldn't keep his mind off Janna. She'd looked so small, so pale, so fragile and vulnerable when he'd found her sitting cross-legged in the plumbing department. He'd wanted to scoop her into his arms, carry her home and tuck her in bed. And yeah, the man in him wanted to crawl in beside her and love away the torment he saw swirling in those expressive hazel eyes.

That mere wisp of a woman was running on fumes and he was worried about her. He didn't know where she'd spent the past few hours, but he sure as hell was going to keep his appointment to have a drink with Evan, just in case Janna decided to accept the invitation from the skirt-chasers who'd zeroed in on her twice today.

If he had to kick some butt to protect her innocence then he'd do it. No one was going to mess with Janna on his watch. Her family was driving her bonkers and if she snapped—like she did with Richard Samson this morning—Morgan wanted to be there to keep the situation under control.

Four hours later, fresh from the shower, Morgan towel-dried his hair, and then donned clean clothes. After devouring two ham sandwiches he checked his watch and grabbed his keys. He was to meet Evan Gray in ten minutes for a beer. Morgan fully intended to warn Evan to watch his step with Kendra Mitchell who was obviously in an emotional tailspin after Richard's unforgivable fling.

Morgan swore foully as he climbed into his truck. Richard hadn't been half bad in high school, but he'd turned into an egotistical ass after he passed the bar exam and hung out his shingle in Oz. Richard better not be pestering Janna to be his go-between to Kendra, either, he fumed. If Richard had an ounce of sense— and Morgan wasn't prepared to swear he did—he'd take a wide berth around the Mitchell sisters. Richard had screwed up—royally and literally. He needed to cut his losses and back off.

Morgan pulled into the parking lot at Goober Pea

Tavern and muttered when he spotted Janna and Kendra's cars. Great, both bombshells were gracing the beer joint with their presence. Kendra, no doubt, planned to be seen with Evan, just in case word hadn't reached Richard that she'd recently reconciled with her ex-boyfriend. Morgan was unsure of Janna's motive for accepting the invitation from the skirt-chasers. He was more than a little concerned that Janna might turn to the bottled variety of courage and moral support to deal with her family crises, while keeping surveillance on Kendra—just in case she did something rash, again.

The moment Morgan ambled into the darkened interior, his internal radar homed in on Janna who was sitting at a table with the very men he was compelled to warn her away from. Kendra, he noted, was snuggled up in the back booth with Evan. Morgan sighed in frustration as he zigzagged around the tables. He could use a relaxing evening himself, even if he wasn't facing the same kind of turmoil Janna was experiencing. He'd much rather be sitting in the pasture with his cowherd. His cattle didn't ordinarily cause him a lot of grief—like the Mitchell sisters. One in particular.

Morgan noticed the empty glass of wine sitting in front of Janna and he halted beside her table. "Let's dance," he requested abruptly.

"Hey, Morgan, we're kinda in the middle of a conversation here," skirt-chaser number one protested.

"Just mark your place and I'll have her back in a couple of minutes," Morgan said as he hoisted Janna from her chair. When they were out of earshot of her male admirers, he added, "I thought you didn't drink."

"I don't, but it's been a hellish day and I'm wallowing in self-pity. I can tolerate those bozos's company while I keep track of Kendra. The drinks take the edge off," she explained, smiling bleakly. "My family hates me. Kendra wouldn't speak to me when she sauntered past to park herself in the booth with Evan. My mom's flaunting her date at the restaurant and Dad's with your mother. I'm drinking to everything that could possibly go wrong—and did."

While George Strait's slow-tempoed song played on the jukebox Morgan took Janna in his arms and pulled her close. Suddenly, the other couples on the dance floor became invisible to him. He was aware of nothing but her enticing scent, the tantalizing feel of her body molded to his. Every frustration that hounded him throughout the day faded away. He could go on holding her close the whole livelong night and be content, but he reckoned her male admirers would object to his monopolizing her time.

"Did you have supper?" he murmured against her ear.

He felt her shiver in response to having his moist breath whisper over the column of her neck and he was relieved to know he affected her the same way she affected him—like a match set to a fuse of dynamite.

"I stopped by Scarecrow Quick Shop for gourmet crackers and a chilled bottle of Diet Coke," she informed him impishly.

"Mmm, that's nutritious. No wonder you look so healthy."

Janna leaned back to meet his disapproving frown. "You don't have to worry about me, Morgan. I'll be okay. My eating habits are the least of my concerns right now."

His palm splayed over the small of her back, fitting her intimately against him. A gnawing hunger prowled through him, putting all five senses on red alert. Maybe he'd only been reacquainted with Janna for a couple of days, but wanting her had become such a constant thing that he swore it'd hounded him for years on end. Damn, his body was reacting dramatically to the feel of her moving rhythmically against him. He knew she could feel him growing hard against her. Even worse, he was going to embarrass the hell out of himself when he made that walk back to the corner booth to join Evan and Kendra.

"Morgan?" she whispered, a hint of wonderment and surprise in her sluggish voice.

She knew he was aroused so there was no use denying the obvious. He bent his head to skim his lips against her earlobe and felt her shiver in his arms. He pulled her closer, feeling her breasts meshed against his chest, her hips gliding provocatively against the cradle of his thighs. Desire, hot and heavy, pounded through his veins, stirring his ultrasensitive male body to the extreme. Suddenly, dancing felt more like foreplay and the need to be horizontal rather than vertical was driving him nuts.

"You turn me on, Janna. That's the long and short of it," he whispered against her cheek.

Again, she reared back in his arms and smiled impishly. When Morgan realized what he'd said—and how it sounded—he chuckled. "That didn't come out quite right. Sorry."

She looped her arms around his neck and settled familiarly against him, her head resting on his chest. He wondered if she noticed that his heartbeat was pounding like a jackhammer against her cheek. He couldn't imagine how she could miss it. Damn it! If they kept dancing he was afraid he'd discard the good sense he'd spent thirty years cultivating and make out with her, right here on the spot, in front of God and everyone else.

Morgan was both relieved and frustrated when the song ended. No woman put him through an emotional meat grinder the way Janna did. He could list a dozen sensible reasons why he shouldn't pursue her—especially when the Mitchell family feud had her emotions in constant upheaval. But he wanted her, nonetheless.

As he walked Janna to her table, he angled his head toward her, inhaling the sweet fragrance of her hair and he nearly lost it—again. What this innocent female did to him should be a criminal offense. He'd been perfectly satisfied with his life until she'd shown up. And whammo! Nothing was the same as before. When Janna sank into her chair he gave her arm a firm but gentle squeeze and held on a moment longer than necessary. He wasn't even sure himself what the gesture implied, so when she peered inquisitively at him he couldn't do anything but shrug and smile lamely. Damn, double damn! He wanted to grab her hand and haul her away so he could have her all to himself.

Exasperated by the ravenous cravings buffeting him, and rigidly uncomfortable in all the wrong places, Morgan stalked over to the bar to order a beer. He had to give his male body time to cool down before making the conspicuous long walk to the corner booth.

Behind him he heard Janna's sultry laughter in response to whatever witty remark her admirers made. Morgan gnashed his teeth until he nearly ground off the enamel. He didn't want Janna hanging out with those clowns while she was so vulnerable, for fear she'd do something rash after one too many sips of wine. If he became any more possessive of her he might as well hang a sign around her neck stating she was *his* property and there'd be hell to pay for trespassing on his private territory. What the devil was wrong with him? He'd never been possessive of other women he'd dated.

Once Morgan had his unruly body under control—somewhat—he grabbed his drink and headed to the corner. Neither Evan nor Kendra looked particularly pleased by his intrusion, but that was too bad for them. Evan was his friend and Kendra was Janna's sister. Someone had to ensure these two didn't do something crazy—again.

"We've decided to get married next month," Evan announced as Morgan slid into the booth.

Morgan was so shocked that he accidentally clanked his glass against the corner of the table. Beer catapulted over his hand and dribbled onto the wooden floor. He whipped his head around to gape at Evan as if he had tree limbs sprouting from that chunk of wood he called his skull.

"Does Janna know about this?" was the first thing out of Morgan's mouth.

Kendra's chin tilted defiantly. "This is none of her business. I'm twenty-five years old and perfectly capable of running my own life."

Morgan smiled inwardly. Ask him, Kendra was capable of *ruining* her own life. Although he didn't want to offend Evan, he felt compelled to say, "Two days ago, Kendra, you were engaged to marry someone else. Or have you forgotten that already?"

"We know what we're doing," Evan said defensively. "If you can't be happy for us, then maybe you better take a hike. And that'd be a real shame because I was going to ask you to be my best man."

Oh yeah, that'd be just peachy keen, wouldn't it?

He'd already gotten himself tangled up in the Mitchell feud and his mother had cast her roving eye on potential husband number four. She had no objection to seeing the U.S. of A. from the passenger seat of a Winnebago motor home. Plus, if Morgan agreed to be a party to this hasty wedding, Janna would probably be furious.

"I'll have to get back to you on that, Evan," he said evasively, then took a long swallow of beer.

Kendra cast him a speculative glance. "Why can't you commit yourself now? Don't tell me you're afraid to cross my sister. Or will you be otherwise occupied, giving *your* mother away to *my* dad on the same day?"

If this was an example of the aggravation Janna had dealt with all day Morgan could understand why she'd looked frazzled and frustrated at his shop. Morgan had had about all the fun he could stand for one night. He was going home. Obviously, he was cramping the newly engaged couple's style and they weren't interested in his advice. Plus, Janna was at the table with her fan club, trying to distract herself from her mounting frustrations and Morgan hadn't been invited to join her.

Morgan guzzled the remainder of his beer and shot to his feet. "Congratulations on your upcoming nuptials," he mumbled. "If Kendra doesn't cancel her second wedding in the next couple of days, I'll be glad to stand up with you, Evan…if you think getting married is the thing to do."

He could feel duel glares skewering him as he walked away, but he didn't care. Evan and Kendra had lost their minds. Marriage didn't last—just ask his mother. This one was doomed from the onset. Kendra was on the rebound and Evan was so crazy in love—

and lust—that he wasn't thinking straight. Never could when it came to that willowy, blue-eyed blonde.

Morgan had intended to breeze from the tavern, but he found himself skidding to a halt when he noticed Janna had nearly polished off her second glass of wine. Worse, one of Janna's admirers had draped a bulky arm over the back of her chair and was leaning too close for Morgan's comfort. He bent down to whisper in her ear. "Kendra and Evan just announced their engagement. If you need me, I'll be at home."

Janna jerked upright in her chair. Her wide-eyed gaze shot to the cozy couple in the corner booth, then leaped back to Morgan. "Are they insane?"

"That'd be my guess. I've been asked to be the best man," he reported, then smirked. "Can life in Oz *get* more complicated?"

Morgan strode from the bar, wondering if he should hang around, in case it was necessary to break up a catfight between the Mitchell sisters. On second thought, Evan had gotten himself into this mess, so maybe he should be the one to handle whatever conflict arose. Besides, Morgan mused, he needed to hightail it back to the farm to ensure John Mitchell didn't rebound into his mother's bed to retaliate against Sylvia's date with Stanley Witham.

Criminey! Maybe *he* should take a long vacation to a deserted South Seas island. He was beginning to feel like a ricocheting pinball. No wonder Janna was so distressed. Getting caught in the crazed interactions of the Mitchell family would send you straight south to crazy-ville.

JANNA LEANED away when one of her male companions got up close and personal for the third time. Her gaze drifted to the corner booth, wondering if she should keep her nose out of her sister's affairs or jump in with both feet. She took the last sip of wine and discovered the buzz she received didn't compare to the erotic tingles she'd felt while dancing with Morgan.

If you need me I'll be at home...

His whispered words echoed in her mind. She needed him, all right, for a half dozen reasons. For moral support, for a sympathetic ear, to ease this gnawing ache of desire that'd tormented her since they'd danced and she'd discovered his reaction to her. She still couldn't quite believe it, of course, but the temptation of turning to him for consolation—and so much more—was dominating her thoughts and smothering her common sense. If she had to choose one man on this planet to initiate her into passion, Morgan Price would be her pick. But Jan wasn't sure she could handle a reckless, one-night stand with the very same man who'd become her standard of measurement for wildly attractive men. Plus, Morgan and the Homecoming Incident had distorted her perspectives of romance for years. Morgan was the only man who had the power to hurt her. And ironically, he'd become her one and only confidant and friend while dealing with her dysfunctional family.

Her gaze and thoughts shifted to the corner again, and she watched in helpless torment as Evan curled his finger beneath Kendra's chin, then bent his head to brush his lips over hers with such gentle affection that Jan felt a sentimental tug on her heartstrings. Morgan was right. Evan had the look of a man so deeply committed that he was willing to take whatever risk necessary to have Kendra—if even for a few days, a few weeks, as long as she was willing to stay. Janna couldn't even imagine what it would be like to have a man look at her with that kind of loyalty and devotion. Evan might've been ten years older than Kendra, but the expression on his rugged face indicated that he knew exactly what he needed to make his life complete.

Unfortunately, Kendra didn't know her own mind at the moment. Evan deserved better than a flighty female looking for validation and vindication. Impulsively, Jan vaulted to her feet. She couldn't stand aside and allow Kendra to devastate Evan again.

"Hey, where're ya goin', darlin'?" one of her companions crooned.

Jan didn't reply, just made a beeline to the corner booth.

Kendra's spine stiffened immediately and she tossed Jan a belligerent glance. "I told you to butt out," Kendra muttered.

Jan braced her hands on the table and leaned forward, teeth bared. "If you hurt this man, sis, I swear—"

Evan clamped hold of her forearm. "We're consenting adults. We know what we're doing."

"That," she countered, "is debatable." Her gaze homed in on Kendra, despite the pressure applied to her arm. "Don't we have enough problems with Mom and Dad squabbling without you stirring up more trouble?"

To Jan's astounded disbelief, her sister grabbed a glass of beer and reared back, prepared to toss the contents in her face. If not for Evan's quick reaction, Jan was positively certain she'd have been doused.

"Quit following me!" Kendra yelled, drawing entirely too much attention.

When Jan didn't budge from her spot, Kendra snatched up her purse and scooted off the seat. Jan's eyes bulged when she noticed the micro miniskirt her sister was wearing. Kendra might as well have had Take Me I'm Yours printed on her body in screaming red letters!

"Are you coming, Evan?" Kendra questioned, ignoring Jan as if she'd turned invisible. "I'll be waiting at your place."

Jan's shoulders slumped defeatedly when Evan released her arm to follow Kendra's dramatic departure.

If you need me, I'll be at home.

She needed, Jan decided as she gathered her dignity and pivoted to face the curious onlookers. My, but the Mitchells were providing plenty of fodder for gossip in Oz. Maybe she should retrieve her suitcase from Morgan's house and make the drive back to Tulsa. Her family didn't want her interference. They wanted to screw up their lives by themselves. And come to think of it, things had gone from bad to worse the moment Jan arrived to help.

Exasperated, Jan stepped outside to see Kendra and Evan's taillights fading into the distance. Well, no question as to what they'd be doing tonight. And what, she wondered as she plunked into her car, were John and Sylvia doing with their dates tonight? Probably having a sex-fest...she was the odd man out.

The thought intensified the off-again-on-again headache she'd battled all day. Several doses of pain relievers hadn't fazed the persistent throb behind her eyes. Her emotions were swinging like a pendulum and she was standing on the crumbling edge, with few options as to where to turn or even where to bed down for the night. For sure, she wasn't welcome with any family member.

If you need me, I'll be at home.

Jan switched the ignition and drove off into the night. She was pretty sure where she was going to end up and not at all sure if she wanted to delve into the hidden reasons why. But of one thing she *was* certain, for a couple of glorious minutes on the dance floor, while Morgan's arms were wrapped securely around her, she'd felt content, satisfied, at peace with herself. The memory of that moment—while their bodies swayed and clung together in perfect rhythm—was like a beacon calling out to her from the fog of frustration that engulfed her. She'd been fighting her way through a haze of emotion since she arrived in Oz to save the day—and failed miserably. The yearning to find herself back in Morgan's sheltering arms was almost more than she could bear.

JAN PULLED into Morgan's driveway and sat there for a long moment, arguing with herself. Reason versus hungry need with all its tantalizing trimmings. The scale was definitely tipping in favor of bending to reckless desire. If she had a lick of sense she'd retrieve her suitcase and go…somewhere else. A motel maybe. Yeah, that was the sensible thing to do. Jan had been the personification of sensible—wearing her sensible shoes, her sensible business suits and making sensible decisions. Was she willing to trade years of sensibility for one devil-may-care night to revisit *puppy* love? Maybe it was better to kill the *dog* it had turned into and get the hell out of here—fast.

The porchlight flickered on and the front door opened invitingly. Jan sighed appreciatively when she

saw Morgan's muscular silhouette in the backwash of
light. It was as if he were welcoming her, as if he'd
been waiting for her to come home.

Jan frowned pensively. This wasn't home—though
it felt like it tonight. Well, if nothing else, she needed
to grab her suitcase. Ah, and what she wouldn't give
for a warm, relaxing shower to wash away her frustration.

Afraid she couldn't trust herself to be alone with
Morgan, she climbed from the car. His bedeviling silver-blue eyes monitored every step she took, as if trying to assure himself that she was all right. She could
feel the tension knotting inside her, the sexual awareness pulsating as she approached him. She halted on
the front porch and her gaze collided with his pene-
trating stare that sought to probe the secrets hidden in
her soul.

Run for your life! Self-preservation instinct shouted
in alarm.

Take what comfort he can give you for the night,
another voice whispered in her head. *Let him send your
topsy-turvy world spinning into oblivion. He was your
first love. Why not let him be your first time, too?*

"Janna?" His gaze never wavered from her face.
She wondered if she looked as vulnerable and unsettled
as she felt. Probably.

She swallowed uneasily, fidgeted from one foot to
the other and wrestled with the nearly overwhelming
temptation humming through her.

"What's wrong?" he asked softly. "Tell me,
Janna."

After a long moment Janna arrived at her decision.
She inhaled a deep breath and said, "Morgan, would
you do something for me if I asked you?"

"Anything for you, sweetheart. I thought I'd made that pretty clear," he murmured. "Whatever you want, whatever you need. I'm here for you."

He sounded so sincere, looked so utterly tempting that she couldn't resist the forbidden yearnings swamping her. With a wobbly cry that was acceptance and defeat in one, she walked straight to him. She tucked her head against the solid wall of his chest and sighed at the comforting feel of his brawny arms closing firmly, protectively around her. He held her, nuzzled his chin against the top of her head and she felt sentimental tears welling up in her eyes.

"I was on my way to find you when you drove up," he confided huskily. "I was afraid you and your sister might've gotten into it. Afraid your male admirers—"

"I was only killing time with them," she cut in, snuggling closer. "It's been an awful day. But could we not talk about it right now? I could use a shower and a place to unwind…or fall apart…whichever comes first."

Morgan ushered her inside without releasing his grasp on her. He guided her down the hall to the master bedroom. "Make yourself at home, Janna. I'm gonna toss a frozen pizza in the oven. You haven't had enough to eat today to sustain a damn bird."

"I'm fine. I—"

When he kissed her into silence Jan was truly surprised she didn't melt in a puddle at his feet. This was exactly what she'd needed, she realized. His kisses revived her—among other things. When his lips touched down on hers heady sensations channeled through her weary body, regenerating her failing energy and flagging spirit.

She wrapped her arms around his neck and pulled

him close, tasting him thoroughly, pouring all her conflicting emotion and churning frustration into the kiss. Forget the hot shower and pizza. She could survive quite nicely by feasting on him, feeling his muscled contours blending perfectly into hers. Ah, he was her port in the storm, her anchor in troubled waters.

Before she was ready to let him go Morgan set her away from him. "Hit the shower," he insisted gruffly.

Jan glanced over her shoulder at him, hurt and confused by his brisk tone. "Are you mad at me?"

Morgan shook his dark head, muttered under his breath, then said, "Nope, I'm mad at *me*." When she frowned, puzzled, his arm shot toward the private bathroom. "Don't ask, just go bathe."

She went, unsure of what had gone wrong between the beginning and end of that incredible kiss. Well, she'd make him tell her later, she decided. He was turning out to be the best friend she had in Oz and she needed someone to turn to when her entire family turned against her.

Sighing tiredly, Jan peeled off her clothes, stepped into the shower, and moaned contentedly when the warm pulsating water sluiced over her. This wasn't anywhere near as satisfying as kissing Morgan, but it was the next best thing.

7

MORGAN STALKED down the hall, wishing he could kick himself all the way into next week. He knew, as surely as he lived and breathed, that if Janna offered him the slightest invitation he was going to take advantage of her fragile, vulnerable emotions. He resented his own weakness for her, but he was through denying that he wanted her.

He shouldn't touch her, he told himself as he ripped the plastic wrap off the pizza, then tossed it in the pan. Forgoing the instructions to preheat, he shoved the pizza in the oven and set the timer. He wanted Janna here so he could ensure she was safe and protected, but at the same time he didn't want her here because he wasn't sure he could protect her from himself.

He had the hots for a woman who didn't know diddly about being intimate with a man. How could he even think what he was thinking? He was a jerk, a sexual vulture, a predator waiting to pounce on innocent prey.

Scowling ferociously at himself, Morgan plopped into the chair, drummed his fingers on the table and told himself he was going to do the honorable thing, even if it killed him. He'd feed Janna, put her to bed, and then he'd walk outside, throw back his head and howl at the moon in tormented sexual frustration. An ice-cold shower wouldn't hurt either.

Resolved to his plan of action, Morgan waited for Janna to reappear. When she did emerge from the bedroom, dressed in one of his white T-shirts—and nothing else, damn it to hell!—his honorable intentions took a kamikaze dive, crashed and burned. His breath sighed out of him as his gaze drifted over the nearly transparent shirt that hit her midthigh and erotically outlined and accentuated the full swells of her breasts, their beaded peaks and the faint shadow at the juncture of her shapely legs. Gawd! His body hit instant boil and he groaned inwardly.

Janna halted ten feet away and said, "I took the liberty of borrowing your shirt."

"So I see," he bleated, then cursed his faltering voice.

"I felt the need to wear something loose and comfortable. I hope you don't mind."

She took another step toward him. The air stirred and he picked up the tantalizing scent of soap and alluring woman. His gaze raked helplessly over her and his body coiled, clenched and hardened painfully. Damn!

"I want to know why you're mad at *you*," she said, venturing closer.

"Because," he muttered, trying to look everywhere except at erotic temptation standing barefoot in his kitchen.

"That's no reason." She took another step toward him. "Why?"

Frustrated, Morgan slammed his fist against the table. "Damn it, woman, you found out what you do to me while we were on the dance floor. Do I have to spell it out for you?"

"I arouse you," she said, pondering his admission.

Morgan snorted. "That's putting it mildly. You set me on fire, but—"

"But I don't do one-nighters and you know it," she finished for him. She smiled as she reached out to comb her fingers through his tousled hair. "You've turned out to be my best friend. I can confide in you, turn to you when the chips are down. I never want to be anything but honest with you."

Her words humbled him; her touch devastated him. He was a quivering mass of conflicting emotions. Wanting her was eating him alive. His need to protect her was torturing him to the extreme. "Janna—"

She eased onto his lap and curled trustingly against his chest. Reflexively, his arms roped around her. He breathed her, absorbed the feel of having her cuddled familiarly against him.

"I want to make love with you," she murmured.

He not only heard her request but felt it vibrating through his mind and body. It was what he wanted— oh, how he wanted!—but it was the last thing he wanted because he'd never touched a virgin and wasn't sure he wanted to start now.

"Morgan, did you hear me?" she asked, tilting her face to his.

Oh, yeah, she was coming through loud and clear, all right. He tried to speak, but his tongue was stuck to the roof of his mouth. The air, so thick with her tantalizing scent, clogged his lungs. When her hand brushed tentatively over his chest, his heart slammed forcefully against his ribs and he swore one cracked.

"You said you'd do anything for me," she reminded him softly. "'Whatever you want, whatever you need,' you said. That's what I need tonight. I'm not what you're used to, but I swear I'll try to satisfy you—"

He pressed his forefinger to her velvety lips and closed his eyes momentarily, summoning the ability to speak. When he opened his eyes she was staring at him with those thick-lashed, hypnotic pools of golden hazel. He knew he'd lost the battle, but he felt compelled to say, "You might regret this in the morning and I'll lose the best friend and confidante *I* have."

She shook her head in contradiction. Curlicue stands of chestnut hair caressed his arm as she smiled playfully at him. "The only one here who's going to lose anything is *me,* but you're the one I want to do the honors, because I trust you, respect you."

"I wouldn't if I were you," he muttered darkly. "Our budding friendship aside, I'm still a man and I'm the one who hurt and humiliated you, even if unintentionally, a dozen years ago."

She arched up to brush her lips over his in a featherlight kiss that nearly drove him nuts, then she shifted in his lap, deliberately moving against the rigid flesh straining against the fly of his jeans. "Then you owe me—big time," she teased. "Pay up, Morgan."

The oven timer blared in the electrified silence. Morgan jerked reflexively and nearly catapulted Janna onto the floor. When she yelped and tilted off balance he hauled her upright. "Pizza's done," he croaked.

"So am I." She looped her arms around his neck and stared directly at him. "Pizza or me, Morgan. Your call."

The ultimatum rang in his ears as she rubbed up against him like a kitten. "Well, hell, that's no choice at all," he said as he rose from the chair with Janna's legs clamped around his waist. In the time it took to blink Morgan switched off the buzzer, removed the pizza and headed for the bedroom. "Okay, sugar-britches, you asked for it."

"Sure did. I put on your T-shirt with nothing but me beneath in hopes of seducing you so you can check your guilt at the door."

His guilt maybe, but not his caring concern about the threshold she was ready to cross with him as her guide and instructor. The instant he laid her on his bed, he promised himself that he was going to be tender and gentle and be there for *her,* even if it killed him—and he could think of worse ways to die. Disappointing or disillusioning Janna was *not* an option.

Jan stared unblinkingly at Morgan as he shed his shirt and tossed it recklessly aside. Her admiring gaze swept over his masculine chest, washboard belly and muscled arms. Her breath struck in her throat when he unzipped his jeans and shoved them over his hips. His dark brows arched questioningly, as if giving her time to change her mind. She wasn't going to. Her attention focused on the obvious bulge in his briefs and her face went up in flames. Her gaze leaped upward to see him grinning rakishly at her.

"It's not too late to change your mind," he rasped. "But you also need to know it's now—or forever hold your peace."

Jan gulped. "Maybe you should turn off the light."

He chuckled. "Brave, but not quite *that* adventurous, huh?" When she nodded he hit the switch, plunging the room into darkness save the glow of the night light that illuminated his enticing physique. "Better?"

"Yes, for this first time at least," she squeaked.

There was a pregnant pause. "The first time? Uh...how many times are you planning on doing this?'' he asked as he dropped his briefs and eased down beside her on the bed.

Jan reached out to trail her fingers over his broad shoulders and his hair-matted chest. "As many times as it takes for me to get it right."

"Mmm." He snickered softly as he stretched out beside her. "A perfectionist, are you?"

"Must be, I picked you over everyone else on the planet, didn't I?"

"Ah, Janna," he whispered before his mouth slanted over hers and she lost the ability to think straight.

In less than the time it took to breathe what little reservation she had left flitted into oblivion. The taste of him, the feel of his naked body half-covering hers swamped her senses. She gave herself up to his skillful kiss and surrendered to the erotic feel of his hands gliding downward to cup her breast. Sensations burst inside her like fireworks, making her sizzle and burn with anticipation and pleasure. Modesty fled when he scrunched up the hem of the shirt and drew it off, leaving her as naked as he was. And when his tongue flicked at her nipple, Jan helplessly arched upward, wanting more of the tingling sensations that expanded through every fiber of her being.

Her body was on fire and Morgan's kisses and caresses were fanning the flames. When he took her sensitive nipple in his mouth, laved it with his tongue, then suckled her, Jan moaned aloud. She practically melted into the mattress when he plucked at one nipple with thumb and forefinger, while flicking and suckling the other with his tongue. And then, when she was positively certain foreplay couldn't get much better than this, his free hand skimmed over her belly, making nerves jump beneath his languid caress. When he cupped her, his thumb gliding against her most sensitive flesh, Jan gasped for breath—and found none. Her feminine body quivered with wicked anticipation. She ached for more but wasn't sure she could endure more of his maddeningly deliberate seduction. She could barely draw breath because her heart was thundering in her chest like a thoroughbred. If she hyperventilated and passed out she'd never forgive herself!

As he teased and stroked between her legs sensations converged so rapidly that her overheated body went into nuclear meltdown. His hands and lips were everywhere at once, playing on her flesh like a skilled pianist hitting every note on a keyboard. There was nothing in her sphere of existence but the incredible, indefinable sensations provoked by his masterful kisses and caresses. Mercy! They hadn't even done the deed and she swore she was already coming apart in his arms...

Her body exploded with yet another round of ineffable sensations when his finger glided inside her, stroked her over and over...and sent her cartwheeling into a mindless abyss. "Ah...no!" she wheezed, clutching desperately at Morgan.

"Ah...yes," he whispered against the rigid peak of her breast. "Stay with me, sweetheart, there's more."

An incredible sense of wonder flooded through Morgan as Janna climaxed around his fingertip. Liquid fire bathed his hand as he held her suspended in pleasure. The satisfaction of making her come for him, of devoting absolute concentration to pleasuring her was an unprecedented experience. He knew he could ease his own aching need by sliding over her, into her, but he was too fascinated with her reactions to his lovemaking. He wanted to taste and touch every satiny inch of her luscious body before he lost himself to his own passion. He wanted to know her by heart, to feel her lose control against his lips and fingertips.

Although Janna clutched desperately at his shoulders, he shifted his weight and slid between her thighs. When he caressed her with thumb and fingertip, he felt her tremble, heard her panting for breath. He draped her legs over his shoulders and bent his head to skim his lips over her sleek, hot flesh. When he flicked out his tongue to tease her, arouse her, again and again, she cried out his name, over and over.

When he felt spasms of pleasure ricocheting through her, searing through him like sensual lightning, he shifted again and reached for the protection he kept in the nightstand drawer. He braced himself above her, fumbling to cover himself as he stared into her shadowed face, wishing for more light so he could see those expressive eyes of hers. He wanted to watch her accept him, take him inside her so he could stop at the first sign of discomfort.

Right, lover boy, like you could stop when you want her so badly you're shaking with it.

Morgan pressed forward, feeling the slick heat of her body welcoming him, enticing him to bury himself to the hilt. With a groan of impatience he thrust forward, then felt Janna flinch in an attempt to adjust to the unfamiliar pressure of his intimate invasion.

Well, hell, so much for finesse. Gritting his teeth, he forced himself not to move, giving her time to adjust and accept him. "Janna?"

"What?"

He smiled at the tension in her voice, in her body. Although she'd been all in favor moments ago, he could tell she wasn't so sure this milestone was going to be everything she'd expected. "Are you okay?"

"If you say so."

He chuckled as he reached between their joined bodies to tease the sensitive nub of passion. With each gliding stroke of his fingertip he could feel her responding, relaxing. When he thrust forward, her arms came around his waist and she held on to him like a drowning victim. He moved inside her, slowly at first...until she matched him thrust for thrust, giving herself over to the pleasure they created in one another.

And suddenly, they were gliding in magical rhythm, as if they'd been together their whole lives and were made to fit together perfectly. He could feel the pleasure expanding, intensifying so rapidly that he lost his grasp on self-control. And where his attentive concern for Janna had gotten off to he didn't know. He was rocking against her like a wild man, clutching her to him so fiercely he was afraid he'd squeeze her in two.

This wasn't supposed to be happening! This was supposed to be all about *her,* not about *him.* But suddenly, there was no he or she, just they—one living breathing entity lost to infinitesimal pleasure.

He heard his name tumble from her lips as she convulsed around him, taking him with her into shudders of ecstasy. Like a blazing comet, he caught fire, burned and disintegrated like scattered ashes.

Sweet mercy, he thought as every ounce of strength abandoned him. What the hell had just happened? A man wasn't supposed to fly apart like shrapnel...was he? He never had before. Oh certainly, he'd had loads of fun in the sack, but tonight went so far beyond physical and familiar that it was damn scary. For a minute there, he thought he remembered reaching some transcendental state of existence that was as close to intergalactic space travel as he'd ever hope to come.

About a century later Morgan recovered enough energy to raise his head, then impulsively dropped a kiss to Janna's lips that were parted in what he was pretty sure was a satisfied smile. Good. That answered the $64,000 question about whether she'd enjoyed lovemaking as much as he had—a little *too* much, to his way of thinking.

He should say something witty. Too bad his brain was still stuck in neutral. When Janna reached up to trace his lips, his eyebrows and cheekbones with her index finger, he decided not to bother with clever witticisms. Everything was right with the world when he was nestled deep inside her and they were as close as two people could possibly get. And so, he just kissed her again, and she kissed him back. They lay together for the longest time, stroking each other, nuzzling, and perfectly content with their intimate knowledge of one another.

When Morgan finally eased away, he felt the damnedest sense of loss he'd ever experienced. To compensate for that empty feeling he hooked his arm around Janna's waist and held her spoon fashion. He felt Janna go lax against him and he was glad she'd finally relaxed enough to sleep.

Carefully, he inched away, grabbed his briefs and jeans and dressed on the way down the hall. He'd let Janna catch a few *Z's,* and then he'd wake her up and feed her pizza. First thing in the morning, he was going to fix her breakfast and make her eat that, too. While she was dealing with one family crisis after another she needed a keeper to ensure she slept and ate and talked out her frustration. And by damned, he was the man for the job.

After nuking the pizza Morgan padded barefoot to

the bedroom to kiss Janna awake—a service he'd gladly perform without pay while she was in Oz. Oh, and she could have the fringe benefits of unbelievable sex whenever she wanted that, too. He was feeling exceptionally generous when it came to his duties as Janna's keeper and protector.

JANNA MOANED softly as Morgan switched on the light then bestowed one gentle kiss after another on her lips. Although there was an unfamiliar tenderness between her legs, the rest of her body was so relaxed she wasn't sure she could rise if her life depended on it. What she'd experienced with him might be old hat to him, but for her? Wow! Morgan knew exactly how to touch a woman and make her come completely unraveled in his arms.

"Hey, Sleepyhead," he murmured as he sank down beside her.

"Is it morning already?" she groaned.

"No, I let you catch a catnap, but I insist you eat. If we don't keep you at your fighting weight you can't go another round in your family feud."

"I'm not hungry," she mumbled, distracted by his kisses.

"Tough, you're gonna eat and like it, so don't give me any lip."

Jan levered up against the headboard and accepted the steamy pizza he thrust at her. "Damn, you have your way with a woman then you think you're the boss," she teased, then smiled graciously. "Thanks, Morgan."

"Anything for you," he replied wickedly, reminding her of the conversation that landed them in bed together.

Jan munched on the pepperoni pizza and grinned wryly. "I don't think this would've been as much fun a decade or so ago, fumbling around with some half-baked amateur. I'm sure glad I waited for a real pro."

Morgan sucked in his breath so hard he choked. Jan pounded him on the back. "Thanks," he wheezed.

Jan took another bite of pizza and frowned ponderously. "What do you suppose forms the foundation of a solid relationship?" she mused aloud.

"You're asking me? The by-product of three divorces?" He swallowed a bite of pizza, then said, "I guess commitment would be vital. If you say till death do you part, then you ought to mean it."

Jan nodded in agreement. "Attitude is important, I'd say. You don't put yourself in a position to betray your spouse and you honor your commitment, through the ups and downs of daily living. You should care enough to be supportive and cooperative and think in terms of *we,* not *I.* In addition, the relationship should be as close to fifty-fifty as it can get. I like the fact that you let me be *me,* and I want you to be yourself around me. I think a person has to like and respect their significant other if a relationship is going to last."

"Agreed," Morgan put in as he reached over to retrieve the two glasses of iced tea. "You should talk out your frustrations so they don't swell out of proportion."

"Because you should be the best of friends, confidants and you should be able to communicate," she tacked on thoughtfully.

"Right, like we do," he added. "I opened up to you about my inner feelings for Mom when I don't ordinarily let anyone know how exasperated I am that she never loved my dad or anyone else enough to stick it out.''

''Exactly,'' Jan said. ''If you can't tell your spouse how you feel after you've given him your body, been naked with him in every sense of the word, then you don't really have a relationship.''

''Which is why I can't figure out my mother,'' Morgan said between bites. ''Why say 'I do,' if you just want sex without strings attached?''

Jan stared pensively at the expensive bedroom furnishings and munched on another slice of pizza. ''So, my folks must've been able to communicate at some point in time. Physically, they must've been compatible. So why did they drift apart emotionally and physically?''

Morgan considered her question for a moment, then shrugged. ''Maybe when you and Kendra left the nest they started thinking in selfish terms about what each one wanted from life.''

Jan snapped up her head and smiled. ''I think you're on to something, Einstein. Mom got self-involved with her career about the time Dad geared up to retire from his career. They no longer consider what's best for the family unit, but rather for themselves.'' She frowned curiously. ''Just what made Dad so determined to travel and change his appearance?''

Morgan lounged against the headboard. ''He told me that a good friend of his was always yammering about how he was going to see the world when he retired, but he didn't live to spend the money he saved for traveling. I think that got to John. He's afraid it'll happen to him if he waits until Sylvia grows tired of minding the shop. As far as reclaiming his youth, I think he looked in the mirror and saw the older version of himself. He figures he no longer appeals to Sylvia and he's trying to gain her attention.''

"Are you telling me that when a man's body goes he thinks his sex appeal goes with it?" Jan asked.

"Pretty much." Morgan stared at her somberly. "If you dare tell another man what I'm about to tell you, I'll deny it."

He looked so serious that Jan slapped her hand over her chest. "I solemnly promise not to reveal a word of what you say."

Morgan shifted awkwardly, then said, "Fact is, a man's ego is fragile. Sure, we strut and boast, but deep down, we want to believe we've got the body of Greek gods that appeal to women. When it's gone our confidence is shot and we feel insecure."

"Well, you don't have to sweat it," Jan was quick to assure him. "I'd never get tired of looking at you—" She slammed her mouth shut so fast she nearly clipped off her tongue.

Morgan cocked a dark brow. "Yeah? You like my bod, do you?"

"Yeah, definitely Greek-god caliber," she confirmed.

"Now, maybe, but what about thirty years down the road? What if I lose all my hair, half my teeth and pick up a spare tire? Are you gonna have the hots for me then, sugarbritches?"

Jan was very much afraid she would because she was very much afraid—terrified, actually—that she'd somehow managed to fall in love with her old flame. It was illogical, inconceivable, but there you had it. Morgan had become everything she needed when she needed it—supportive, concerned, honest and let's not forget the mind-boggling passion he'd introduced her to. If you created her personal image of Mr. Perfect his name would be Morgan Price.

"Well?" he prompted. "If you have to give the question that much thought, then—"

"I don't," she cut in. "Truth?"

"Yeah, that's kinda what I'm going for here. I've come to expect it from you."

"Truth," she told him, "is that it wouldn't matter how many false teeth you needed to fill in the gaps so you could eat. I'd still look at you and think I'd made off with the grand prize because you were prettier than I was to begin with. Plus, I like what's in your heart and in your personality, so—"

"Whoa, darlin'. Rewind and play back," Morgan interrupted. "This in-depth discussion of what it takes to form a lasting relationship goes no further until we agree on one vital point." He stabbed a finger in her face and shook it. "You're a knockout…and don't give me that look of disbelief again. It's the truth. You are." When Jan snorted indelicately Morgan framed her face in his hands, leaned in close and said, "You are, damn it. You're smart and loyal and you're so attractive that I've been in a permanent state of arousal since you showed up in Oz. And before you start thinking that what we did, right here in this bed, was just about sex, let me tell you that it's the whole irresistible package that brought me to my knees. You got it, sugar-britches?"

Jan stared at him, amazed by his insistent need to convince her that she was something special. Although she had confidence in her talents and abilities, she'd never considered herself ravishingly attractive, especially compared to her mom and sister. To her, they were the epitome of beauty and she'd accepted that years ago.

"Got it?" he demanded when she didn't reply immediately.

"Okay, if you say so."

"I do say so, *emphatically*. Are we clear here?" he grilled her.

Jan's lips twitched. "Crystal."

A wicked smile pursed his lips as his hand strayed over the sheet that covered her bare breasts. "We better be, because I'm prepared to make love to you all over again and hold you in sexual captivity until you admit that you're more woman than I can resist."

"That prospect is supposed to be a threat?" she asked impishly.

His grin was pure devilry and it sent wicked chills down her spine. "Maybe not, but I'm having a hard time concentrating on the topic of conversation. I'd rather start where we left off, just to see if it was as good as I think it was."

"Was it?" Jan studied him intently. "I did okay for my first time?"

Morgan kissed her soundly and said, "If you were any better, darlin', I might not have survived." He settled back against the headboard, cleared his throat and tried to figure out where the Mitchell marriage went sour and how to fix it. He knew that was important to Janna so it was important to him. "Now that we have that issue settled and out of the way, we need to figure out how to unite your folks so they aren't running in opposite directions. Got any bright ideas?"

Janna frowned thoughtfully, then sipped her drink. "We need something alarming that will force Mom and Dad to ignore their differences to join forces. You know, some sort of emotional shock therapy.''

Morgan jerked upright when an idea struck like a bolt from the blue. ''I've got it!''

''What is it?'' she asked excitedly.

Morgan slumped against the headboard and glanced at her. ''Never mind. It wouldn't be good for your reputation, for one. And secondly, it would involve role-playing. You could get hurt or embarrassed. I've put you through that already. I don't want to do it again because I felt guilty as hell the first time. Nope, it's a bad idea.''

Jan launched herself at him, forcing him to his back, and leaned over him. ''I'll make the decision on whether your idea has merit. What is it?''

He loved it when she got feisty. He'd never forget that scene with Richard. Janna was all fists, bared teeth and flying fur when she was in attack mode. She might've been a shrimp of a female, but she had the kind of spirit that wouldn't quit.

''Tell me,'' she commanded, ''or I'll work my newly discovered feminine wiles until you're begging to tell me what I want to know.''

Grinning, he tossed her words in her face. ''This prospect is supposed to be a threat?'' Then he added, ''Lady, you can have your way with me as many times as you please. You won't hear me whining about it.''

''Mmm, I like the sound of that,'' she murmured as she melted over him. ''I think I've gone from abstinence to addiction overnight.''

Morgan was primed to lose himself in her steamy kiss—until someone pounded on his front door. He and Janna sprang apart in one second flat.

"Morgan! If Janna is in there with you I'm going to take you apart!"

"Dad!" Janna gasped as she bounded, naked, from bed to retrieve some clothes. "What was your grand scheme?" she asked hurriedly. "Now's the time to put it in motion before Dad comes unglued."

"He already is." Morgan vaulted from bed to scoop up Janna's jeans. "Here's the deal," he said quickly. "You and I suddenly have it so bad for each other that we've decided to tie the knot the same day as Kendra and her substitute groom get hitched. You think that won't stand John and Sylvia on end and get them together to talk sense into the four of us?"

Janna's hand stalled over the black blouse that she'd borrowed from Kendra. Her look of stunned disbelief transformed into an elfish grin. "Mom and Dad will freak out, certain Kendra and I have lost our minds. I love it!"

Morgan smiled. "John and Sylvia are going to hate Evan and me for taking advantage of their crazed daughters. You're gonna have to let your folks, and everyone else, know you're so hopelessly in love with me—"

"Because I never got over you, even after that mortifying Homecoming incident," she embellished as she threw on her blouse and shimmied into her jeans.

"Nice touch," he complimented on the way to the door. "We ought to be able to get good mileage out of that carrying-a-torch thing. And everyone in Oz knows Evan never got over Kendra. As for me, I took one look at you and lost my heart, which is why I've been dogging your heels to make sure none of the local yokels beat my time with you. You game, sugar-britches?"

Janna nodded as she followed him down the hall. "If this scheme gets Mom and Dad back on the same side, I'll even run naked down the yellow brick road to celebrate."

Morgan pulled up short, causing Janna to tail end him. "Nope, you can scratch that. No one gets to see this gorgeous body of yours except me."

"Spoilsport," she teased as she veered around him to take the lead. "I was *sooo* looking forward to streaking through Oz in my birthday suit."

"Morgan! Open this damn door or I'll break it down!" John Mitchell roared at the top of his lungs.

Morgan grabbed Janna's arm and situated her protectively behind him. "I'll handle your dad. If he decides to go for someone's throat I want it to be mine. Psych yourself up to pretend you're crazy in love with me or we'll never pull this off."

8

JAN KNEW full well she wouldn't have to pretend she'd fallen hard for Morgan. Furthermore, she had to agree his idea was perfect, especially since Kendra planned to announce her engagement to Evan. But Jan sincerely hoped her dad didn't have a seizure before he stormed home to inform Sylvia that their daughters had taken leave of their senses and planned to marry in a fevered frenzy.

"I'll give you to the count of three!" John boomed. "One, two—"

Morgan jerked open the door. Jan glanced around his broad shoulders to note her father had his booted foot raised, prepared to kick the door to splinters. John slammed down his hiked leg, jerked upright and took inventory of Morgan's bare chest, bare feet and tousled hair. His furious glare shot to Jan, noting her wild tangle of hair, and bare feet. He exploded like a volcano.

"What the *hell* is going on here?" His murderous glare swung back to Morgan. "Damn you, boy. You told me this morning that Janna's car was in your driveway, but she stayed with Kendra. You lied to me."

Morgan didn't dispute him because his silence contributed to their charade.

John's gaze rocketed toward Jan, radiating disapproval. "And *you*, what the hell are you thinking, shacking up with him like this?"

Although Morgan tried to shield her from John's seething tirade, Jan stepped up beside him, glided her arm around his bare waist and hugged him affectionately. "I'm in love with Morgan and I plan to spend every spare minute with him," she announced.

John's eyes shot open like a disturbed owl's, then his gaze narrowed reproachfully. "You've only been in town a few days, damn it!"

"Yeah well, when ya know, ya just know," Jan countered, then reached up to pull Morgan's head to hers. She kissed him zealously. All the while, John sputtered and hissed like an overheated teapot.

"And I'm crazy in love with Janna," Morgan declared as he raked his fingers affectionately through her spring-loaded curls. "We just clicked. There's more chemistry between us than you'll find in a science lab."

"You're both insane!" John spouted off. "That's not the way it works. You just don't…do the things you've obviously been doing together in a small town like this!"

"Doesn't matter who knows," Jan said with an unconcerned shrug. She hugged Morgan for effect, then dropped the live grenade in her dad's lap. "We're getting married in a month."

John staggered back, as if she'd slugged him in the jaw. *"What!"*

Morgan nodded confirmation. "Yup, we're tying the knot in a double ceremony with Kendra and Evan Gray."

John grabbed the doorjamb for support. The color

drained from his face like a flushing toilet. His legs wobbled unsteadily. *"What?"*

Jan bit back a giggle, amused that they'd shocked John so thoroughly that he'd been reduced to one-syllable-word sentences.

"Haven't you heard yet?" she asked her thunder-struck father. "Kendra is going through with the wedding since all the arrangements are made. She's going to scratch out Richard's name and pencil in Evan's. Plus, it'll save you and Mom a bundle on the ceremony if Morgan and I get hitched at the same time. How's that for economizing?"

John's mouth opened and shut like a dresser drawer.

"I'm going to become Mrs. Nuts and Bolts of the Hardware Dynasty and Keni is going to be Mrs. Cattle Baron," she added, smiling happily.

"Janna's going to update my computer system and accounting," Morgan put in as he tugged Jan in front of him, then pulled her against his bare chest. "Fifty-fifty partnership. What's mine is hers."

"But your job's in Tulsa," John chirped.

Jan shrugged nonchalantly. "A job's a job, Dad. Morgan is all I want and need. If he decides to sell his house and pitch a tent I'll be right there beside him, through thick and thin, because I love him and he makes me deliriously happy. I want to be with him permanently."

"You two are nuts!" John blared. "You're acting irresponsibly and so is that airheaded sister of yours." He glowered pitchforks at Jan. "She's obviously on the rebound and I have no idea what the hell *you're* thinking!"

"Then I'll tell you," Jan offered, all smiles. "I'm thinking I've made the wisest decision of my life. I get to move back to my old stomping ground and be with my family and I get the grand prize himself for a husband. Morgan was my first love, after all. Everybody in Oz knows that. I've carried a torch for him for years and I've measured every man up to him and found them all lacking.''

"And I always regretted that I never had a chance with Janna before I went off to college to play ball.'' Morgan gave her a loving squeeze as he nuzzled his chin on the top of her head. "I knew the moment she walked in my store that the reason I never married was because I'd left unfinished business in my past. The timing wasn't right for us then, because we were too young. Now it's perfect. You know, like destiny, fate, that sort of thing.''

John braced both hands against the doorframe to prevent his legs from folding up like a lawn chair. Clearly, the story they were feeding him had thrown him completely off balance.

"And you don't need to concern yourself about whether Evan is devoted to Keni,'' Jan added cheerfully. "It's public knowledge that he never got over her when Richard swept her off her feet. Oh sure, Keni's on the rebound and is out to show Rich that she doesn't need him after he cheated on her. But hey, Evan's who she ran to for consolation, so that suggests she feels secure and comfortable and safe with him. He'll make her happy.''

"And those things are important in a relationship,'' Morgan put in helpfully. "Take us, for instance. We share our feelings with each other. We have similar backgrounds, similar values, similar wants and needs. I'll do my part to help raise our kids and I'll be there the way my dad and stepdads were never there for me.''

"Yeah well, wait until those kids of yours go off the deep end like you have!" John spluttered in frustration. "This won't work, I'm telling ya. You need more than a few days to decide your future!"

"We have almost a month," Jan said confidently. "After living with Morgan for a few weeks, we'll have our relationship working like a well-oiled machine.''

"You are *not* living with him," John protested loudly. "I forbid it. I intend to tell your crazed sister the same damn thing! You aren't living in sin, not if I have something to say about it.''

"You don't," Morgan countered. "I'm thirty and she's twenty-eight. We're consenting adults and we're in love. We know our own minds.''

"No, you're *out* of your minds and *in* lust," John growled ferociously. "And furthermore, I'm quitting my job, as of now. No one in town is going to think for one darn minute that I approve of this absurdity. I don't want to be at the store while you're crawling all over each other like a couple of dogs in heat!''

Jan inwardly winced, but she refused to react to the insult. After all, she and Morgan were going for effect here and he'd warned her this scheme might obliterate her reputation. It was worth the price if this shock-therapy ploy prompted John and Sylvia to join forces to save their daughters from what appeared to be rash irresponsibility.

Jan sighed audibly, then nuzzled against Morgan's neck. "Dad, it's getting late. I'm tired and Morgan and I want to go back to bed.''

"No!" John's hand shot out to grab her wrist.

Morgan's reflexes were faster. He snagged John's

forearm and held it fast. "Nobody touches my future wife or forces her to do something she doesn't want to do, not even her father."

Morgan was good. He almost had her believing he was fiercely protective and she knew this was just a charade. His narrowed gaze, glittering silver-blue eyes and clenched jaw made a believer of John and he retreated into his own space.

"She belongs in our house, in our bed and that's where she'll stay," Morgan went on determinedly. "What's mine I keep and I protect, even from you, so leave...now."

John stared bewilderedly at Morgan. "You've gone as berserk as Janna. I thought you had more common sense than most folks I know." He looked them up and down disdainfully, then turned a one-eighty. "I'm going to talk sense into Kendra. Maybe *she'll* listen to reason."

When the door slammed shut, Jan slumped against Morgan. "I better call Keni and warn her to expect a hostile visitor."

"No, you crawl in bed and I'll talk to Evan," Morgan insisted. "I'll explain our plan in detail."

"Thanks," she murmured. "But one thing, Morgan."

"What's the one thing?" he asked as he led her toward the bedroom.

"If the whole town's going to know I've shacked up with you, then I get all the fringe benefits, don't I?"

Morgan felt his body clench at the mere thought of repeating the incredible interlude of passion. A roguish grin twitched his lips. "Anything for you, sugarbritches, but I would've thought you'd be..." His voice fizzled out, but then he reminded himself that the makings of a solid relationship began with honesty and communication. "I thought you'd be sore after that first time. You might want to wait until tomorrow."

Janna pressed a kiss to his bare shoulder, then grinned playfully. "I appreciate your concern, but I've waited twenty-eight years. I plan to practice until I'm as good as you are. That is, if you agree to be my tutor. I like to be good at what I do, you know. It's one of my traits, after all."

Morgan halted at the bedroom door, noting the telltale signs on the sheets. He expected guilt to hit him between the eyes. Instead, he felt an unprecedented sense of possessiveness. She was his, if only for a month, if only as part of a scheme to reunite John and Sylvia.

Janna followed his gaze and she squeezed his hand. "It's okay. No regrets. I'll strip the bed and hop in the shower while you make the call."

Morgan hugged Janna close, feeling a swirl of emotions he couldn't separate and wasn't sure he wanted to identify.

"What's wrong?" she asked.

He stared into those mystifying eyes and heard the words tumbling off his lips before he could stop them. "I don't want to see you hurt or embarrassed. I know your reputation will suffer more than mine because men never catch as much flack as women. I'll come off looking like Mr. Macho who swept you off your feet, but you—"

She flung up her hand to shush him. "I'm fine with all this, Morgan. Really. I get to be with you for a while. And hopefully, Mom and Dad will band together long enough to realize they still need each other."

He studied her for a long moment. "Okay, if you're sure you can handle the gossip. But promise me that if anyone harasses you that I'll be the first to know so I can modify their bad behavior."

Janna grinned impishly and his heart all but melted in his chest. "Evidently you weren't paying attention when I encountered Richard Samson. I can stand up for myself and have for years. If it'll make you feel better, you can have a turn with my hecklers when I'm finished."

"Deal." He dropped a kiss to her forehead. "I'll make the call."

He headed for the kitchen to call Evan who was none too pleased with the untimely interruption. But that was tough. Evan had an irate future father-in-law gunning for him. Forewarned was forearmed. When Morgan hurriedly explained the plan that he and Janna were going to say their vows with Evan there was dead silence on the line.

"Hello? You still there?" Morgan demanded.

"Yeah, I just needed to pick up my teeth after they fell to the floor. Are you serious?" Evan questioned.

"For all intents and purposes, Janna and I are engaged and that's the story we're sticking with."

"And you're playing it to the hilt, I suppose," Evan murmured speculatively. "Interesting."

"Our engagement and prospective marriage is going to look as real as it can get," Morgan confirmed. "And yours better, too."

"Oh, mine's for real. You know that… Uh-oh, I see headlights coming down the road. I better fill in Kendra—fast."

Morgan hung up and headed for the bedroom. As of now, he was engaged and in love and he was going to play the role for all it was worth. He grinned devilishly, knowing he was getting the best end of this deal, even if this shocking scheme didn't permanently reunite John and Sylvia.

When Morgan entered the bedroom, Janna had just pulled the spread into place. Impulsively, he grabbed her hand and towed her behind him. "C'mon, sugar-britches, I wanna show you my shower."

"I've already seen it, remember?"

He waggled his eyebrows suggestively. "Yeah, but you haven't seen it with me in there with you, teaching you things you claim you want to know."

Janna stared at him warily. "Are we going to leave the light on?"

"Definitely," he replied as he peeled off her blouse and made a visual feast of her creamy breasts. "No secrets between future husbands and wives, you know. Everything has to remain in the open."

"But we aren't—"

When Morgan dropped his briefs and jeans without an ounce of modesty, her voice dried up. She stared at him, her cheeks flushing with heat. "It has to feel real to look real," he reminded her, amazed at the sense of pride he derived when she studied him, as if he was a living, breathing work of art. "We're in this together, after all."

"Even if this plan blows up in our faces?" she chirped, still staring at his nude body.

"*Especially* if that happens because I'm the only person on the face of the planet who knows the frustration you've gone through to reconcile your folks. That makes us confidants and friends who share all."

Janna raised her gaze to his face and grinned. "Does

that mean I have free license to touch whatever I want, whenever I want?''

''I'm all yours—''

His voice broke when she folded her hand around his rigid flesh. She gave him a look of pure feminine mischief as she discovered the feel of him with palm and fingertips. Her caresses altered his breathing, left him throbbing with need. He groaned aloud when his legs wobbled unsteadily.

''You like?'' she questioned, stroking him from base to tip.

''Mmm,'' was all he could get out.

''Then let's hit the showers, Ace.''

By the time she led him beneath the spraying mist Morgan was so hot and bothered that his breath came in gasps and spurts. For a novice, Janna learned fast what he liked and how to torment him with pleasure. She couldn't seem to keep her hands off him. She discovered every inch of his sensitive body, and he returned the favor. In mindless urgency, he pressed her against the tiled wall, her legs anchored around his hips. He thrust against her with a hungry impatience that astounded and bewildered him. Feeling her silky body surrounding him, arching against him in wild abandon was almost more than he could endure. Any thought of tenderness drowned in the shower as they came together in a breathless frenzy of need.

And that business about a man needing time to recover before he could repeat a performance? You could forget that. That must've been a wives' tale, if ever there was one. From the shower stall to the freshly made bed was all the time he needed to recover. He and Janna were rolling and tumbling around on the quilts like long-lost lovers reunited after an eternity.

It was the damnedest, most incredible thing he'd ever experienced. It was as if Janna had been saving up her entire life and had directed all her pent-up passion to him. Not that he was complaining, mind you. He'd found a woman who could match him in bed and out. A woman with sass, spirit and a powerful craving to compensate for years of abstinence in one wild, indescribable night of rapturous lovemaking.

Damn, she was gonna wear him plumb out, he decided as he collapsed on top of her in exhaustion. Neither of them was likely to sleep a wink. He knew it for a fact when Janna glided sensually against him and said, "Ya know, if Mama would've told me, when I was a kid, that playing house was gonna be this much fun, I would have looked you up every time I came home for the holidays."

He chuckled softly. "Stop squirming. You need to rest."

When she kissed him and said, "I need *you* more," he knew for sure there'd be no shut-eye tonight. Janna Mitchell was no longer the shy, bashful sophomore with braces on her teeth. She was one hundred percent woman. Being the gentleman he was, he'd never tell a lady *no* when she stated, in plain words, what she wanted to do to him, with him. Suddenly they were so hot for each other, so lost in each other that they rolled off the end of the bed and landed, laughing, in a tangle of entwined arms and legs.

They burned down the night and tried to put out every fire of passion blazing between them but their need seemed insatiable. If Morgan hadn't checked off every X-rated fantasy he'd ever dreamed up he couldn't imagine what he'd left out!

JAN MOANED and groaned as she struggled from the depths of a short doze that couldn't have lasted more than two hours—tops. She was achy and sore...and getting that way was more fun than she'd ever had. Discovering passion, with Morgan as her guide and tutor, just didn't get any better than this. She'd have blushed at the memories they'd made if he hadn't insisted there'd be no secrets and modesty between them because their relationship—in order to be convincing— needed to look and feel realistic. They'd listed aspects of a good relationship and were testing them out.

"Good, you're awake."

Jan pried open one eye, raked the tangled hair from her face and sighed appreciatively at the sight of Morgan striding to the side of the bed with a greeting smile that made her heart flip-flop. He held a cookie sheet that served as an improvised tray. She stared gratefully at the steaming coffee and toast he'd thoughtfully prepared for her.

Morgan sank down on the bed, balancing the tray. "Starting now, I'm going to see to it that you get three squares a day," he announced, then flashed her a stern glance. "Eat and drink, woman. I mean business."

She cocked a brow as she levered up against the headboard, then plucked up a slice of buttered toast. "Do you plan to be this pushy every morning until we've gotten my parents back together?"

"Absolutely," he said, undaunted. "If *I* go into emotional shakedown at some future point in time and I don't eat and sleep you have permission to make me take care of myself. That's mutual support, as I see it."

Jan nodded agreeably, then sipped her coffee. "That's something my folks have disregarded in favor of chasing individual dreams."

"Exactly," Morgan replied. "But you and I are going to become the sterling example of how to conduct the perfect relationship. Each time your folks bombard us with all the reasons why this whirlwind engagement is headed for disaster—just like Evan and Kendra's—we're going to spout off all the positive things we have going for us."

Jan nodded pensively. "Subtle, thought-provoking hints." She smiled at Morgan, then impulsively leaned over to press a kiss to his sensuous lips. "You, my darling, are an absolute genius. I love the way your mind works."

"Thank you, honeycakes," he murmured. "We'll go heavy on the endearments and displays of affection when we encounter your folks. By the way, the Winnebago is no longer beside our driveway."

Jan's alarmed gaze shot to Morgan. "Is it at your mom's?"

He shook his raven head and munched on his toast. "Nope. I'm hoping John parked in his own driveway and is plotting with Sylvia, as we speak, to stop the duel wedding."

Jan slumped against the headboard and sighed whimsically. "Ah, if only that were true. That'd be the first step in reconciliation. But we can't make this easy for them. They have to fight a battle against Keni and me long enough to realize they're on the same side and want to stay there."

"And meanwhile, we'll be learning all there is to know about each other. Such as, I'm financially stable." He glanced at her curiously. "Are you a spendthrift?"

"Nope. Definitely not. I pride myself in being a sensible money manager and I've stashed away cash for a rainy day.''

"Ditto. Morning person or night owl?" he asked abruptly.

"Usually morning," she said, smiling wryly. "Except when someone prevents me from getting my minimum nightly requirement of sleep."

The grin he flashed made Jan want to hurl herself against his bare chest and start right where they'd left off a few hours earlier. It was a sexy, playful, all-knowing smile. "Same goes, sugarbritches, but I couldn't tell which side of the bed you prefer since we were every which way on it."

Jan blushed profusely, remembering how she'd discarded every inhibition with Morgan. She didn't recognize herself these days. When Morgan touched her she went up in flames—repeatedly.

Morgan arched a brow and grinned into her blushing face. "Yeah, I agree, last night was incredible, but which side of the bed do you prefer?"

"Left," she informed him. "You?"

"I'm a right-hand-side kind of guy... Food preferences?"

"Italian, Mexican and thick, juicy steaks. You?"

"Ditto, but in reverse order."

"Fine, I'll stop by the market and pick up steaks for supper," she volunteered. "It's my turn to cook. If you don't mind, I'd like to make use of your washer and dryer. I'll do your laundry while I'm at it."

"Deal." He sipped his coffee. "Medium rare. No starch."

Jan snickered. "No starch? Does that mean I can't serve baked potatoes with your steak?"

He grinned back. "Cute, darlin'. I was referring to my laundry."

Morgan went on to list his personal preferences in meats, casseroles, veggies and desserts. He also listed his preferences in reading material, TV sit-coms, and naturally, televised sporting events.

"Uh-oh," Jan broke in. "We might hit a snag here. I like the History, Discovery and Art and Entertainment channels."

"Ah, time to compromise," he declared. "We'll tape one or the other on the VCR, but I gotta tell ya, when the college where I played basketball is playing live, I'm on the couch with popcorn and Coke...is that okay?"

Jan looped her arm around his shoulders and smiled good-naturedly. "No problem, sweetums. After watching you play ball in high school, basketball has become my favorite sport..." She winked provocatively. "Until last night, that is."

Morgan choked on his bite of toast and sputtered for breath. Jan whacked him on the back. "You seem to have a reccurring problem with choking," she teased. "Is this a medical condition I need to know about?"

"No, you delight in startling me when my mouth's full," he wheezed. "Cut that out."

"Fine, next time I'll make sure you've swallowed before I hit you with total honesty."

Morgan took a sip of coffee and glanced pensively at Janna. He'd never known a woman so forthright...so right. The thought jarred him. He kept telling himself that he'd volunteered to help her resolve her family crisis because he felt he owed her a debt for old hurts and he was compensating for humiliating her years ago. But this relationship they were projecting felt so real that he kept forgetting it was a charade. He'd told Janna that her reputation might suffer the worst damage, but he suspected that having her underfoot in his home, living like a real couple, doing things together that couples did, was going to be hard to forget when she packed up and returned to Tulsa. Would she, like he, be wishing this wasn't make-believe? How would she feel about making this arrangement permanent?

Permanent? Morgan inwardly winced. Thanks to his mother, he didn't know the meaning of the word. In addition, he'd never dated a woman more than six months. Of course, he'd never gone into a relationship, making a checklist and compatibility comparisons, either. But still, what if he turned out to be as fickle and unreliable as his mom?

Well, he wouldn't allow himself to be like her, he decided resolutely. He was going to focus on making Janna happy and comfortable and he'd think in terms of *them*, not himself. Resolved, Morgan tugged Janna to her feet and headed to the shower. He forced himself to concentrate on the day ahead of them, not the arousing tingles of seeing her naked and alluring and tormentingly irresistible. He had to get ready for work, he reminded himself sternly. A man couldn't survive on wild, mind-boggling sex alone.

You would've thought last night would've tided him over for a few hours. But when he pulled Janna beneath the warm mist he had the unmistakable feeling this shower stall was going to get thoroughly steamed up before they rinsed off and dressed for the day... Sure nuff...

JAN VEERED into the travel agency, relieved to see her sister manning the computer and not one potential traveler on hand. Good, she and Kendra needed time to get their stories straight before encountering their parents.

"How'd it go with Dad last night?" Jan asked without preamble.

Kendra eased back in her chair and shrugged. "Probably the same way it went for you. Dad kept spouting off about how neither of us had any sense, same for you and Morgan." Kendra frowned curiously. "Do you honestly think this scheme is going to get Mom and Dad back together?"

"Plan A was trying to talk sense into them separately, but it didn't work. Plan B is fighting insanity with insanity."

Kendra titled her chin upward. "I know what I'm doing. You may be putting on an act, but I intend to marry Evan because I love him."

Jan studied her sister astutely. "You're okay with living out on a farm and facing the gossip that won't die down for a while?"

Kendra nodded in absolute conviction. "I like the wide-open spaces. Evan's going to do renovations on the old house. I love that old house with its tall windows and bright sunlight. Furthermore, I love Evan and I made a disastrous mistake when I broke up with him the first time. He cares what *I* want, how *I* feel—unlike Richard who centered our future plans on his goals and aspirations of running for mayor then state legislator and probably president. Gad, perish that thought!"

Jan flashed a smile, convinced that Keni did indeed know what she wanted from life and that Evan was it. "Fine, you have my full support. I always thought Richard was a cocky jerk and you were too good for him."

"So, you're on my side now?" Kendra asked hopefully.

"Yes, and all systems are go for our double ceremony. If anyone asks, I'm as nuts about Morgan as you are about Evan."

Kendra stared at her for a long, contemplative moment. "Are you?"

"Are I what?" she said teasingly.

"Nuts about him."

Jan shifted from one foot to the other, then met Kendra's probing stare. "'Fraid so. And don't tell me I'm crazy because I'm thinking the same thing myself. But there you have it. When you know, you just know."

"Amen to that—" Her gaze shot to the door. "Oh, hell."

When the bell chimed, Jan lurched around to see Richard Samson barging inside, a furious frown stamped on his handsome face.

"Have you two lost your damn minds!" he all but shouted. "I just heard about this ridiculous double wedding!"

Although it was second nature to leap to her family's defense, Jan held her tongue when Kendra vaulted to her feet and faced down Richard. "There's nothing ridiculous about it," Kendra told her fuming ex-fiancé.

Richard smirked arrogantly. "Well, don't come crying to me when you realize you made a mistake and need the best divorce lawyer around. I'll make sure that country bumpkin takes you for all you're worth."

Kendra's arm shot toward the door. "Beat it, Richard, and never come back unless you want me to book you on a one-way flight to hell!"

"You'll be damn sorry you didn't marry me," he muttered spitefully.

"No, I'm damn glad I came to my senses in time," Kendra countered.

When Richard, sputtering and cursing, spun on his well-shod heels and stormed out, Jan gave Kendra the high five. "Well done, sis."

Kendra drew herself up proudly. "I was pretty good, wasn't I? No hysterics, no tears, no melodramatics."

"Obviously Evan has a settling influence on you."

Kendra grinned impishly. "Not entirely."

Jan knew exactly what her sister meant because she felt the same way about Morgan, even if their engagement wasn't real…Jan squelched the thought immediately. As Morgan said, and it was true, they had to make their relationship *feel* real if it was going to *look* real. For as long as it took to put her parents on the same side, Jan was going to think and react like a woman in love, a woman determined to wed in less than a month.

"Why don't you and Evan join us for supper?" Jan invited.

"Sounds great, but I'll have to check with Evan."

"Gook thinking. I'll do the same with Morgan," Jan said. "We believe that strong relationships depend on consideration and cooperation. You shouldn't make plans without notifying your significant other, unlike Mom and Dad who bought a dress shop and Winnebago without the other's approval. Selfishness has no place in a good relationship."

Kendra arched a perfectly sculpted blond brow. "You and Morgan have outlined and detailed the makings of a good relationship?"

"Absolutely," Jan affirmed. "In order to figure out where Mom and Dad went wrong, we figured out what made a relationship work right. We've discussed our likes and dislikes, character traits and living habits.''

"Wise idea," Kendra murmured. "Evan and I need to do that."

"Communication and honesty are tantamount," Jan said with great conviction. "Oh, and let's have lunch at the diner around noonish. We need to be seen together so Mom and Dad will realize we're a united force and they'll have to confront us as a united force."

On her way out the door her cell phone shrilled at her. She rooted into her oversize purse to answer the call. It was Diane with another crisis to resolve. Jan tried to reassure her assistant while she drove to the service station to fill her car with gas. Unfortunately, Diane didn't respond well to the pep talk and Jan felt herself tensing up. Then she reminded herself that she'd be going home to Morgan tonight, which made her long-distance problems easier to bear.

MORGAN WAS ASHAMED to admit he wasn't the least bit disappointed that neither John nor Sylvia approached him to announce their reconciliation because that was one more day he'd get to spend with Janna. When she resolved her family crisis she'd leave Oz. The thought caused unsettling feelings to churn in the pit of his stomach. Knowing their days were numbered made him want to make the most of every moment.

When Janna hiked off to have lunch with her sister he was glad she was eating regularly, but disappointed he couldn't be with her. What the hell was wrong with him? He knew Janna had arrangements to make. It wasn't as if he hadn't seen her for several hours during the day, for she'd taken a look at his accounting program to determine needed updates. She'd even waited on a few customers while he ran next door to the tractor supply shop to check orders and inventory.

He did, however, enjoy being a couple that invited Evan and Kendra to supper. Watching Evan stare at Kendra, as if the poor man couldn't believe his good fortune, reminded Morgan of his own pleasure of having Janna to come home to.

"I stopped by the service station for fuel this morning and Roger Preston cornered me," Janna said while they were gathered around the supper table. "That grease-monkey-turned-psychologist had a good idea.

He suggested that we pool our resources and send Mom and Dad on a second honeymoon in a romantic setting.''

"Not a bad idea," Evan agreed.

"But *not* in the Winnebago," Morgan put in. "No sense asking for trouble when that RV is still a sensitive subject."

"Has anyone seen John or Sylvia today?" Kendra asked.

Janna shook her head and Morgan had the damnedest urge to reach over and slide his fingers through those shiny chestnut curls. Their guests hadn't been there an hour and already he was craving privacy.

"Lorna said Mom didn't come to work today," Janna reported. "I haven't talked to Dad, but I drove by the house to see the Winnebago parked in the driveway. I'm taking that as a good sign. At least he didn't hightail it out of the county in his house on wheels."

When the doorbell chimed Morgan surged to his feet. "Maybe that's John now… Hi, Mom. What's up?"

Georgina Price, dressed in one of her flashy ensembles, invited herself inside and halted abruptly when she noticed the guests seated at the table. "So, the wild gossip is true?"

Four heads bobbed. Georgina rounded on Morgan. "You really are getting married?"

"Yep, sure am," he confirmed.

"But you and Janna just—"

He waved her off. "I know what I want and this is it. She's the one."

Morgan got a warm, fuzzy feeling in his chest when Janna bounded up and strode over to loop her arm around his waist, offering a show of support and giving him an affectionate hug.

"Hi, Georgina, I haven't had the chance to say hello properly," she said in a cordial tone. "I know Morgan and I are rushing things, but we know what we're doing." She pushed up on tiptoe to kiss his cheek, then cuddled close. "I hope you and I can be friends as well as relatives."

Georgina stared at them ponderously, then glanced at Evan who had his arm draped protectively around Kendra and smiled adoringly at her. "So...I guess I need to buy a dress for the ceremony. Any particular color?"

Morgan tensed, but Janna smiled cheerily. "Our signature colors are mauve and seafoam," she said without missing a beat. "Anything you choose will be fine. If there are guests you want to invite let me know and I'll put them on the list."

Morgan commended Janna's acting ability. Apparently his mom was convinced because she nodded agreeably. "Well, I'll go and let you finish supper." Georgina glanced back at Morgan. "I haven't seen or heard from John. Is he going to finish installing the cupboards and gluing down my Formica tile?"

"I'll take care of it," Morgan volunteered.

"I'll help," Evan said. "I was going to ask Morgan to help me with some remodeling at the farm. We can trade off labor."

"Well, okay," Georgina murmured as she sauntered out the door. "Just as long as my kitchen's put back together soon."

Morgan was glad to have that conversation out of the way. Not that he expected objection from his mother. After all, she'd been through three weddings and she knew the drill. What she didn't know was how to make a relationship last, but Morgan sure as hell did. He and Janna had put their heads together to pinpoint potential problems and find workable solutions.

Morgan was halfway through his steak when the doorbell chimed again. "Hell, what is this place? Grand Central Station?"

"It better not be Richard again," Kendra muttered.

"I hope it is," Evan growled spitefully.

Janna popped up like a jack-in-the-box. "I'll get it."

Morgan's hand stalled halfway to his mouth when the door swung open. To everyone's surprise—and secret delight—John and Sylvia stood on the porch, glaring at Janna. Also to their surprise, Sylvia was dressed in slacks and a knit sweater that accentuated her figure. She was sporting a sassy new 'do that complimented the shape of her face. John had discarded that awful gold chain that Morgan had secretly thought would've been more befitting as a collar for a bulldog. Furthermore, John was back to wearing normal clothes. That, Morgan decided, was a good sign.

"Hi, Mom and Dad. Come in," Janna invited, despite the mutinous glares directed at her. "We're having supper. You can join us for dessert."

John stalked forward. Sylvia was one step behind him. They halted beside the table. "Have the four of you gone crazy?" he blurted out.

"Now, calm down, Dad," Janna said as she swerved around her parents. "No need to burst a blood vessel. We know what we're doing."

"No, you don't," Sylvia put in. "You've got the whole town standing on its ear. Everyone thinks the Mitchells have had a collective breakdown. Your dad and I intend to let it be known that this double wedding is a hoax.''

''But it's not,'' Kendra contradicted. ''Evan and I love each other.''

''Ditto for Morgan and me,'' Janna put in.

John snorted. ''Hell, you hardly know each other. We raised you better than to make rash decisions. We might expect this from Kendra—''

''Hey, watch it,'' Evan snapped. ''That's my future wife you're bad-mouthing. I resent it.''

''Oh, hush up,'' Sylvia snapped right back, then looked down her nose at Evan. ''We'll get to you and Kendra in a minute. We know she's flighty and high-strung, but Jan is the sensible, dependable one—''

''Well, maybe I'm tired of solving everyone's problems. I want a relationship of my own,'' Janna cut in. ''I want to marry Morgan.''

''And I resent being called flighty and high-strung,'' Kendra flared, then glanced at Evan for support. ''Tell them, Evan.''

''You're extremely sensible and dependable,'' he confirmed.

''See?'' Kendra said proudly.

Sylvia ignored her and turned back to Janna. ''You have a fine career in Tulsa and you can't give it up for a man you've only known a few days.''

''I've known Morgan forever,'' Janna contradicted heatedly. ''Besides, quantity of time doesn't compare to the quality time we've spent together lately. I'd much rather have Morgan than my job in Tulsa. And for your information, it isn't the world's most perfect profession. I work long days and there's no time for a social life. I want a husband and family—''

''When you end up with two ditzy daughters like

we've got, then you'll deserve it,'' John broke in sarcastically. ''You think you've raised 'em properly and have them out on their own and poof! They go ballistic and insane.'' He wheeled to shake his finger in Morgan's face. ''And you, I treated you like the son I never had and you fooled around with my daughter and then flaunted it in my face! I ought to strangle you!''

Morgan opened his mouth to defend himself, but Janna beat him to the punch. Suddenly he knew what it was like to have her feisty, unswerving brand of loyalty directed to him. True, he could stand up for himself, but watching her in action was pure pleasure.

''Hold it right there, Dad.'' Janna got right in John's face. ''Morgan was the perfect gentleman. Truth is, *I* seduced him.''

All eyes swung to Morgan. Evan grinned wryly, Kendra bit back a smile and John and Sylvia smirked in disbelief.

''It's true. I saw him after all these years and I knew, instinctively, intuitively, that he's the reason I never settled down. He's the real deal. He makes me laugh. He makes me happy and I love being with him. My life in Tulsa was the time I killed, awaiting my destiny. He's it, so you better learn to accept that.''

''Are you through lecturing your own parents?'' Sylvia muttered.

''No, as a matter of fact.'' Janna inhaled a deep breath and plunged on. ''You have no right whatsoever to tell Kendra and me how to live our lives because yours is a disaster. Just look at the two of you. After three decades of marriage and sacrifice, *you* split up over a dumb Winnebago and a stupid dress shop. You call that mature? I don't think so!

''What happened to the love?'' she ranted on. ''Did

it die out because you stopped making an effort? Where are you going to find two other people on the planet who share your history, the ups and downs, the joys and frustrations you've faced together? Plus, can you imagine how complicated holidays are going to be when we have to watch what we say, for fear of upsetting one of you? How are we going to juggle time so one of you won't be left out? And what about your future grandchildren? How are you going to explain your divorce to them after you finish telling them you'll love *them* forever and ever, but you couldn't make the same promise to each other?''

Morgan sat there, amused and amazed, while Janna grabbed a quick breath and proceeded to rake her parents over live coals for behaving so childishly that they refused to cross the yellow brick road to parley and kept spying on each other like military reconnaissance.

Finally John waved his arms in expansive gestures to shut Janna up. "This is about you and your crazed sister," he blustered. "There's not going to be a wedding in three weeks and that's final. I'm the head of the Mitchell family household and what I say goes!"

"You listen to your father," Sylvia chimed in. "He said no weddings and he means no weddings!"

At that point Kendra bounded up to join the melee. Morgan leaned back in his chair, watching the Mitchells go at each other, nail and tooth. They were yammering all at once. He heard Janna tell John to send Sylvia flowers—whatever that was about. Morgan grabbed his fork and bit into the cold baked potato. Evan followed suit. They ate while the Mitchells squabbled.

"So, how are cattle prices?" Morgan asked. "I have some steers ready to sell. Is the market up or down?"

"Up," Evan reported. "I hauled a dozen steers to the stockyard this morning. If you want to borrow my trailer, let me know."

"I'm *not* melodramatic!" Kendra shrilled suddenly. "And you have no room to talk, Mom. You bawled your head off over Dad during our wine-fest, blubbering about how he was playing footsie with Georgina—"

"That's enough!" John roared. "I never touched the woman, damn it!"

"Oh, really?" This from Janna. "I saw your arm draped around her."

"That was just to infuriate your mother," John shot back.

Morgan inwardly winced. He really wished his mom hadn't insinuated herself in the middle of the feud. But that was Mom, through and through. She liked turmoil and attention. Always had.

Eventually, Janna shouted, "Enough! You're spoiling my appetite and Morgan insists I eat regularly."

"So what's he now? Your nutritionist?" Sylvia smarted off.

"No, he's the love of my life. And if you try to cancel the weddings we'll just fly off to Las Vegas and tie the knot… If that meets with Morgan's approval. I don't make plans without consulting him because his opinion is important to me and we're considerate of each other."

Morgan smiled around a bite of steak and winked when Janna glanced at him. "Sounds like a plan to me, sweetheart. Just give me a couple of days' notice to get someone to run the store and I'm there with bells on."

"There? You see?" Janna said to her parents. "We

communicate. We compromise. We consider each other's wants, needs and feelings. It doesn't get better than that. You two should try it and see if it works for you.''

Janna grabbed her parents by the elbows and shepherded them to the door. ''Thanks for dropping in. We have plans to make. Good night.''

When she locked the door and slumped against it, Morgan's admiration rose another notch. This was one hell of a woman.

''Well, that was tons of fun,'' Evan said dryly. ''Are all our family gatherings going to be a real hoot?''

Kendra plunked down in her chair. ''Lord, let's hope not. But at least Janna gave them enough food for thought to choke a horse. Hopefully, they'll get their act together soon.''

Again, Morgan found himself selfishly wishing it would be later so this charade would last. He glanced over at Janna who was still holding up the front door. ''You okay, sugarbritches?''

The question snapped her out of her momentary daze and she smiled—forced though Morgan knew it was. Funny, it hadn't taken him long to interpret her facial expressions. Maybe because he'd been so intensely attentive, attuned and aware of her. As she'd said, they'd spent quality time together, learning each other's moods, whims and traits. Hell, you might say they'd taken a crash course in building a sound relationship.

''I'm fine,'' Janna said as she strode to her chair. ''It just amazes me how quickly I develop a headache when I confront our parents.''

''Really? I don't know why you let them get to you,'' Kendra said.

"Because she's made it her life's mission to fix things," Morgan said in her defense.

Kendra's brows shot up, then she frowned curiously. "Is this part of the relationship analysis you two are conducting?"

"Yup," Morgan said. "Ask me anything about Janna's habits, characteristics and preferences."

"What's her favorite color?" Kendra grilled him.

"Sunflower yellow," he said without the slightest hesitation.

"Favorite food?"

"Other than chocolate chip cookies that she'd kill for, you mean? Easy, that'd be chicken Alfredo." Then Kendra asked, "Favorite holiday?" And he said, "Fireworks on the Fourth of July." She said, "Favorite song?" He said, "Bryan Adams's 'I'd Die For You.'"

Evan and Kendra were obviously impressed because they peered at him in astonishment, then glanced pensively at one another. Morgan said, "So...how about you two? Are you experts on each other?"

Evan grinned slyly. "Ask me that tomorrow and there won't be a single, solitary thing I won't know about Kendra."

"Éclair anyone?" Janna offered as she set the rectangular dish on the table. "It's Morgan's favorite, you know. Hunter green's his favorite color, hence his flashy pickup truck. I'm partial to the color myself." She leaned over to kiss him, then cut into the dessert. "Mom and Dad could take lessons from us. And *they* think *our* generation is clueless? Not hardly!"

That warm, fuzzy feeling that ambushed Morgan several times during the evening kept intensifying during dessert. By the time Kendra and Evan shoved off,

Morgan was more than ready to have Janna all to himself.

When the door closed behind their guests, Janna turned to him with a seductive smile. "I thought they'd never leave," she murmured as she peeled off his polo shirt and tossed it recklessly over her shoulder.

"You and me both, babe," he rasped, instantly aroused.

"I want you."

"You've got me," he assured her the instant before his lips slanted possessively over hers and his hands drifted over her luscious body.

A string of clothing, like Hansel and Gretel's breadcrumbs, formed a path to the bedroom. By the time they were naked on the bed Morgan was so needy he could barely draw breath. When he reached out to caress Janna she shook her head and pushed his hands away.

"It's my turn tonight," she said. "I told Kendra and Evan I knew everything there was to know about you, but that's not quite true…yet." Her hazel eyes danced with mischief as her palm splayed over his laboring chest, swirled across his belly…and ventured lower.

Morgan swallowed a groan when she discovered the various textures of his skin, the contours of his body. When her adventurous hand glided over his aching flesh and stroked him tenderly, he moaned aloud.

"You like?" she whispered, then bent to flick her tongue against the ultrasenstive tip of his sex.

"Careful," he wheezed, clutching the sheet in his fists. "I don't have much self-control where you're concerned."

"I'll be sure to enter that in my journal of All There Is To Know About Morgan Price," she teased playfully. Her soft lips skimmed over him. "What about this? Do anything for ya?"

Hot chills skittered down his spine. "Keep that up and we'll be finished before we start," he warned through clenched teeth. "Seriously, sweetheart, maybe you should save your experiments until another night. I'm not sure I have the willpower...aw, geez..."

Morgan gasped, then groaned when her silky hair slid over his abdomen in a tantalizing caress and she took him into her mouth and nipped him gently with her teeth. Her hands wandered everywhere—over his hips, thighs and calves, tormenting him with immeasurable pleasure. She stroked him with thumb and fingertip, suckled him, and he wanted to throw back his head and howl in unholy torment, but he could barely draw breath.

"More, you say? My pleasure," she murmured against his throbbing length. "Your wish is my command."

"No...you're killing me," Morgan rasped, then groaned when she kissed and caressed him all over again. "Damn, woman, I'm dying here!"

He decided, there and then, that he might have gotten tangled up with more woman than he could handle. Janna was a quick study when it came to inventive lovemaking. Every kiss and caress dragged him closer to the crumbling edge of restraint. And damn it, he'd planned to have his hands and lips all over her by now. But she seemed to be having so much fun having her way with him that he didn't want to spoil her enjoyment, even if she was driving him crazy with pleasure. What was a guy to do?

The thought spiraled into oblivion when Janna straddled him, guided him to her and welcomed him into her dewy warmth. He was pretty sure he was chanting her name while he clutched her hips and arched upward, thrusting into her, again and again. Her breath broke and she quivered around him, sending him catapulting into mind-scrambling ecstasy. Like a wild man, he clutched her to his chest and shuddered in helpless release.

In the aftermath of passion too incredible for words Morgan gathered Janna close to his heart and let his sweet dreams take up where reality left off.

As THE WEEK passed Morgan settled into the satisfying and comfortable routine of working at both stores and spending every spare minute with Janna. She spent a great deal of time devising a software program to make his accounting program user friendly and more effective.

Morgan caught himself glancing toward his office at regular intervals, watching her poised at his computer, her head bowed in profound concentration. Her presence in his life seemed so natural and necessary that he forgot what it was like not to have her nearby, not to see her on a daily basis. It was as if she'd become an extension of his own life and somehow completed a part of him that had gone missing.

He and Janna made it a point to appear in public together every chance they got—holding hands and sharing brief kisses that added credence to their charade. As promised, John boycotted the hardware store, but he and Sylvia left messages on the answering machine, asking if Morgan and Janna had come to their senses yet and called off the wedding. Of course, Morgan and Janna didn't back down. Each day they played the masquerade for all it was worth to ensure John and

Sylvia remained a united force in their effort to halt the double wedding.

Ah, but the nights, Morgan thought, grinning rakishly, were the most fun of all. Janna was fulfilling every secret fantasy he'd ever conjured up and their passion for each other never failed to astound him.

He and Janna had fallen into the enjoyable habit of tumbling into bed early every night and rising every morning with barely enough time to shower, dress, grab a bite to eat and dash off to work. Morgan loved their daily routine....

Which was why he was totally unprepared—after another interlude of mind-numbing lovemaking—when Janna nestled against him and said, "Mmm, I'm going to miss you like crazy, Morgan."

His eyes popped open and he angled his head to peer into her passion-drugged eyes. "Miss me? Where are you going?"

"I have to go to Tulsa tomorrow," she said drowsily. "My assistant is freaking out. She called three times this afternoon, threatening to quit if I didn't come work out the glitches in the software program."

Morgan felt as if she'd sucker-punched him. "Leaving?" The concept seemed so foreign he couldn't grasp it, didn't *want* to grasp it.

"Just for a couple of days. Three at the most. I told Kendra to tell Mom and Dad I'm off buying a wedding gown and subrenting my apartment. That'll give credence to our wedding plans. Plus, I put her in charge of monitoring Mom and Dad's activities to determine how close they are to reconciliation."

Morgan reminded himself—repeatedly—that this relationship was a sham, a means to an end. But it felt too damn real. If he didn't watch it, he wouldn't be able to tell reality from fantasy. That was a good thing if you wanted to convince John and Sylvia, but it was hard on the heart. Playing house had fantastic advantages, but there was one drawback. Morgan was going to be lost when Janna gathered her belongings and went home.

Damn, he didn't want to think about that now. He'd just live in the moment, keep Janna with him, play the charade and hope the Mitchell standoff lasted for weeks, months maybe.

"Morgan? You okay?" Janna questioned as she propped herself on his chest. "You're awfully quiet. Are you upset that I'm just now telling you about my plans? It's just that it's been a hectic day and—"

He pressed his fingertip to her petal-soft lips and strived for a light tone. "It's okay, but if you're gonna be gone a couple of nights we've no choice but to make up for lost time. Quality time is our motto." He managed to flash her a smile that concealed the edgy desperation roiling inside him.

She drew figure eights on his chest and grinned mischievously. "You wanna make up for lost time now or wait till I get back?"

Morgan rolled her onto her side without releasing her from his arms. "Better make a note in your journal that I'm not a procrastinator. Unless, of course, you don't think you can keep up with my pace."

She raised an eyebrow in challenge. "Just try me, stud muffin, and we'll see who cries uncle first."

Morgan claimed her lips and felt her immediate and willing surrender. She might be gone a couple of days, but he'd make damned sure that his memory was branded on her mind.

And when all was said and done, neither of them

had the strength to cry uncle. They simply drifted off to sleep, content and sated in each other's arms.

JAN MADE the drive to Tulsa without pit stops and arrived to find the office in turmoil. The personnel treated her as if she'd gone AWOL, but she pasted on a smile and assured the staff that she'd have things running smoothly in no time at all.

Diane was so relieved to see Jan that she broke into tears, dashed forward and nearly squeezed the stuffing out of her. The poor woman was so eager to hand over the reins of control that she asked for two days of vacation to recover from stress.

Throughout the day, Jan kept expecting the buzz of satisfaction and accomplishment to hit her while she worked to pinpoint the problems with the new program. It just wasn't there. Furthermore, she had a devil of a time keeping her mind on business because her thoughts kept straying to Morgan. This, she realized, was how she was going to feel when her parents resolved their differences and returned to normal. She'd be here and Morgan would be there and she'd feel empty and dissatisfied with a career that once occupied most of her time and all her thoughts.

Fiendishly, she worked on the software program to make it staff friendly, hoping to create shortcuts that would alleviate the complaints and simplify procedures. Jan was still in the office at ten that evening, knowing she preferred work to her empty apartment. If Morgan wasn't there—and he wouldn't be—she didn't want to be there, either.

Concentrate, damn it, Jan lectured herself when her mind wandered for the umpteenth time. Her stomach growled, reminding her that she'd eaten crackers for lunch and skipped supper entirely. Morgan wouldn't be pleased. He fretted when she didn't eat decent meals. Morgan...with those mystifying silver-blue eyes that she could get lost in so easily, with that ultraseductive grin that made the lines around his eyes crinkle. His sizzling touch, the feel of his masculine body gliding over her...under her...beside her...sending her spiraling in mindless, indefinable pleasure....

"Stop it!" Jan blurted out in the silence of the abandoned office. She'd never get the modifications made if she daydreamed about Morgan. Besides, their relationship was a temporary charade. It wasn't real. It wasn't permanent. Just because she'd dummied up and fallen head over heels in love with him, just as she'd done a dozen years ago, didn't alter reality. But this was a trillion times worse than the infatuated puppy love of days gone by. This was soul-deep affection that couldn't be duplicated.

She wanted the fantasy to be real. She wanted the intimacy and emotional commitment she and Morgan had formed to understand where her parents had gone wrong and to make things right again. He'd been there every time she needed him. He'd listened when she needed to talk. How was she going to give that up when she liked it so much? Wanted it so much?

Jan raked her fingers through her hair, scrubbed her hands over her face and stared at the computer monitor that blurred before her eyes. Suddenly, Morgan's handsome face became the screen saver that bleeped across her mind and she couldn't get past him. Gawd!

She definitely needed a break, an injection of caffeine and then she'd get back to work. Tiredly, Jan scooted away from the desk and ambled down the empty hall to shove quarters into the vending machine.

Lights flashed. A can of Diet Coke thudded into the metal bin. She grabbed the drink, popped the top and chugged the drink. It fizzed in her empty stomach while she paced the hall to stretch her legs and work the kinks from her back.

This is your life, Janna Renee Mitchell, so how do you like it now? She didn't. She felt like a robot going through the programmed paces.

Determinedly, Jan returned to her desk and went to work. Her only motivation was to fix the glitches and streamline the program so she could hightail it back to Oz.

Four Diet Cokes and a Mr. Goodbar later Jan gave up for the night. Her eyes felt like they'd been coated with sand granules and her spine had fused together in a temporary hunch. She had to get some sleep.

Wearily, she took the elevator to the parking garage and discovered she'd been locked in for the night. Fantastic! She'd have to sleep in her back seat—which didn't do a blasted thing for her aching back.

10

MORGAN WANDERED around his home and his pasture like the soul survivor of a nuclear holocaust. He felt lost. It stupefied him to realize how quickly he'd grown accustomed to having Janna underfoot. Not having her to come home to, not seeing her feminine paraphernalia in his bedroom and bathroom made him feel as if his world was out of kilter.

Reaching for the phone, Morgan dialed her apartment for the tenth time. Still no answer. She'd told him she'd have to work late at the office, but he'd called her at home at midnight and again at seven in the morning. It was as if she'd dropped off the edge of the earth and he was worried as hell about her. What if she had car trouble or some psycho had abducted her? What if she'd decided she really did belong in Tulsa with her high-paying job that was more fulfilling than pretending to be in love with him?

No, Morgan assured himself. Janna was open and honest with him. If she were tired of playing charades she'd tell him flat-out...wouldn't she? An uneasy sensation skittered around his belly as he slouched in his recliner, grabbed the remote control and surfed the TV channels. Pensively, he contemplated the emotional roller coaster ride and whirlwind affair that landed Janna in his bed. She'd been surviving on adrenaline and very little else while she darted hither and yon, trying to reunite her parents and keep Kendra out of trouble. Morgan, hoping to compensate for hurting Janna years earlier, had become the shoulder she leaned on during her emotional meltdown. He was the only place she had to turn when her family turned against her. She'd turned to him in desperation, seeking comfort.

Then there was the day she discovered Kendra had maintained the same status of virginity and landed in Evans's bed after rebounding from Richard. Morgan frowned thoughtfully. Could it be that Janna wanted him to make love to her because her sister had turned to Evan? The thought made him grimace. He wasn't sure, being an only child, what sibling rivalry might provoke the Mitchell sisters to do. Maybe Janna had turned to him for validation and compassion. Maybe she simply got caught up in the excitement and newness of sex. For sure, he'd been a willing tutor and she'd been in an emotional frenzy.

And, of course, he's the one who devised this scheme to shock John and Sylvia into joining forces. What if Janna returned to her own world and realized her escapade in the Land of Oz was just a lifelike dream, triggered by the emotional trauma of her parents' separation? And what if all these feelings *he* had for Janna were just part of *her* fantasy world? Maybe the reason she hadn't called was because she'd come to her senses and realized she'd made a mistake with him and that she wanted to keep distance between them so she could clear her head.

Is that why she hadn't called? Where the hell was she? Living at that damn office, solving everybody's corporate problems and loving every minute of it? Well, what about him? Didn't he count for anything?

Did she think life in the Land of Oz went on hold, like pushing the pause button on the VCR?

"Damn," Morgan muttered. Sitting at home while Janna was out of town wasn't his idea of fun. It gave him too much time to deal with the rising tide of insecurity and frustration that swamped and buffeted him.

Morgan tossed aside the remote control and paced from wall to wall. He glanced at his watch. Janna had been gone two days and not one word. How considerate was that? Had she spoken with Kendra and learned that John and Sylvia had moved in together? Morgan knew that for a fact because he'd kept surveillance on the Mitchell home and he'd seen John and Sylvia drive off together to eat at Uncle Henry and Auntie Em's House of Fine Dining. He figured it was a public display of reconciliation. Whether their mended fences included the horizontal hokey-pokey he couldn't say because he drew the line at sneaking up to the bedroom window.

So, if Janna had been informed of this new development she might think there was no rush to return to Oz. That left Morgan in frustrated limbo. Hell! He was going nuts here! He wanted Janna with him, in bed and out. The citizens of Oz kept bombarding him with questions about his upcoming nuptials, razzing him that Janna had gotten cold feet and whizzed off. Then there was Evan and Kendra who couldn't keep their hands off each other in public. They looked so hopelessly in love that it made Morgan want to throw up because he was so damn envious and unbearably lonely.

Swearing foully, Morgan glared at his watch. It was two in the morning. He reached for the phone, got the answering machine for the forty-eleventh time and refused to leave another message. What the hell was he supposed to say? Are you alive or not? Have you forgotten about me or not? Are you coming back or not? Is this your way of paying me back for mortifying you a dozen years ago? Is this your idea of retaliation?

Morgan jerked upright when headlights flashed across the living room wall and he heard the crunch of gravel. When Morgan heard a car door slam, he strode to the front door and whipped it open. Every ounce of frustration turned to alarm and concern when he saw Janna weaving unsteadily toward him. Damn, he'd never been so glad to see anyone in his life, even if she looked like a staggering zombie.

"Janna?" he whispered when she all but fell into his arms. "What's wrong?" He scooped her up and made a beeline toward the bedroom, alarmed by the lack of color in her face, the unnatural glaze over her eyes.

"Exhausted," she whimpered as her head lolled against his arm. "Missed you... Couldn't call because the sound of your voice would be too distracting. Had to get my work done..."

Suddenly, two days and nights of concern, second-guessing and insecurity went up in a puff of smoke. She'd come back to him. He should be railing at her for working herself into exhaustion. But she missed him, she said. Ah...all was right with the world again.

Gently, he laid her on the left side of the bed. It was her preference, after all. Then he peeled off her sensible black jacket, blouse and bra.

"Need a shower," she mumbled, groping for the zipper of her skirt.

"You need sleep more," he insisted as he tugged off her clothes.

She sighed audibly, curled up in a fetal position and nuzzled against the pillow. "Love you..."

Morgan froze to the spot. "What did you say?"

He received no response. Janna was down for the count. He knew she'd made that claim several times to convince her parents their charade was real, but she'd never said those words directly to him. Did she mean what she said or had she simply slipped back into her role the moment she landed in Oz? Well, it didn't matter, he told himself. Janna was back for now and they'd resume their charade. His life wouldn't be so empty.

Resolved to that plan, Morgan shed his clothes and climbed into bed. He gathered Janna in his arms, tucked her cheek against his chest and asked himself at what point in time had this charade become reality. It didn't matter really, he supposed. It just *was*. Somehow, the time they'd spent pinpointing the foundations of a strong relationship had become what he had with Janna. The passion—and boy, was that incredible! The caring, the concern, the need for her companionship, the need to have her involved in his life. The honesty, the friendship, the sound of her laughter, the togetherness that went way beyond physical. It was all right here, steeped in reality.

Somehow he had to convince her this wasn't a game that ended when John and Sylvia realized their marriage wasn't over—just entering a new phase. He'd have to tell Janna that he loved her, of course, because he'd realized it for certain the moment he'd come home to this empty house where her memory filled every corner to overflowing. Problem was, how could he make her believe his heartfelt confession wasn't part of the act?

Well, he'd worry about that tomorrow, he decided

as he nuzzled his face against Janna's fragrant hair. Right now he had Janna exactly where he wanted her and he could relax and fall asleep—and he did immediately.

JANNA ROLLED to her back and grimaced. She'd slept like the dead and she had a crick in her neck, a backache and her brain was clogged with fuzzy cobwebs. Where was she?

Reluctantly, she opened her eyes to stare at the ceiling. The haze of exhaustion parted and she remembered she'd worked nonstop to resolve the software glitches and oversee sessions to ensure the personnel could operate the software without going into full-scale riot.

Jan glanced sideways to see the empty pillow beside her. She smiled when she noticed the wilted wildflower and a note. When she looked at the digital clock she was amazed to see that it was nearly noon. She shouldn't be surprised since she'd forgone sleep for nearly forty-eight hours.

Jan plucked up the note, rubbed her blurry eyes and read, *There's a sandwich and fruit in the fridge. Veg out today, sugarbritches. I've got everything under control so don't worry about a thing.*

Jan smiled contentedly. Real or not, her relationship and the supposed engagement felt right, necessary and vital. There was nothing she'd like more than to lounge in bed, but she needed to check the status of her parents' marriage. That, after all, was the purpose of her return to Oz, wasn't it? This was all about her desire to see her parents reconciled.

Jan levered onto her elbow then heaved herself to her feet. Sluggishly, she wobbled to the shower. Dressed in jeans and a T-shirt, she rooted around in the fridge to find the sandwich and fruit Morgan prepared for her. Her heart squeezed in her chest when she spotted the oversize chocolate chip cookie on the counter. He remembered, bless him. She could do with a cookie fix to get her inner juices pumping.

After she polished off her lunch, she strode outside, inhaled a breath of country air and plunked into her car. She'd talk Kendra into closing down the travel agency for an hour so they could present a united front when they confronted John and Sylvia. If they hadn't figured out by now that they belonged together, Jan would simply knock their heads together until they came to their senses.

JAN WAS RELIEVED to note that the Winnebago was still parked beside the driveway when she and Kendra reached the house where they'd grown up. Kendra reported that Sylvia had left the boutique around eleven. That meant that John and Sylvia had either murdered each other during lunch or they'd arrived at a workable solution to maintain a show of force against their daughters' whirlwind weddings.

"Ready?" Jan asked as they climbed from the car. "Operation Reconciliation begins and ends here and now."

"Ready," Kendra affirmed.

Jan arched a surprised brow when Sylvia answered the door, looking mussed. Sylvia, however, recovered in time to pin both daughters with a disdainful stare. "I hope you dropped by to inform us that you've reconsidered the hasty wedding."

"Nope." Jan breezed past her mother to see her dad half sprawled on the couch. His polo shirt was twisted sideways and the hem dangled from the waistband of his jeans. Hmmm… Interesting.

"Oh, swell, our daughters from loony-tune land have come to visit," John said, then smirked. "Called off the weddings, I hope?"

"No." Kendra tossed her purse on the end table and took a determined stance beside Jan. "Are you two officially back together or not?"

John and Sylvia exchanged glances. Then they stared at Jan and Kendra. "Doesn't matter," Sylvia said loftily. "Whether we've kissed and made up, we still aren't attending your weddings. The marriages can't possibly last. We aren't throwing our good money to bad. You can pay the florist, the caterer and minister if you intend to go through with this idiocy."

"Fine, no problem." Jan crossed her arms over her chest and stared down her parents. "We've decided to send you on an all-expense-paid second honeymoon to the Bahamas. You're going. This is not negotiable."

"I already booked your anniversary cruise," Kendra added. "You'll be back in time for our weddings, if you change your minds and choose to attend. Janna will man the dress shop during your absence. Evan and Morgan will complete Georgina's remodeling project."

"We, and our fiancés, have spent our time comparing our likes and dislikes, our habits, our characteristics and our goals to ensure our relationships don't go sour like yours almost did," Jan declared. "Now, we'll ask again. Is your marriage up and working again or not?"

Again, John and Sylvia glanced at one another. Finally, John said, "Yeah, we've talked things through. We're keeping the dress shop and the Winnebago motor home. Sylvia agreed to ride in the RV and stay at the campground as long as I treat her to dinner. We'll fly to the East and West coasts for long-distance sight-seeing trips from time to time.''

"Good, a workable compromise," Jan complimented.

"But I'm still not giving you girls away at those weddings," John said stubbornly.

Jan didn't clue in her dad that she wouldn't be a bride and that the charade was a scheme to get the results they wanted. No matter how she wished otherwise, she knew in her heart of hearts that Morgan had only agreed to help her because he wanted to compensate for hurting her years ago. He'd said so at the onset. Of course, being the hot-blooded man he was, he hadn't objected to the fringe benefits of playing house.

Be that as it may, marriage was a serious commitment and Morgan hadn't actually asked her to marry him. He hadn't actually said he loved her, either. Wanted her, yes. He'd made that clear often enough, but she knew he wasn't keen on marriage after life with Georgina.

But no matter, up till the last minute, John and Sylvia were going to have to stick together, believing both loco daughters were tying the matrimonial knot. How she and Morgan were going to break up at the last minute so he wouldn't look jilted, she didn't know yet. She supposed it would be best if he was the one to call off the wedding. She'd leave town and not show up until the holidays and avoid contact with Ozians.

After all the time and effort Morgan had committed to this charade, Jan refused to let him look the laughingstock. She knew what that felt like and she wouldn't wish that on anyone—except Richard Samson, the jerk.

"Fine, Daddy, be your stubborn self and don't take that walk down the aisle with Janna and me on each arm,'' Kendra spoke up. ''But you need to know I love Evan for all the right reasons, not because I'm retaliating against Richard. Evan cares for me the way Richard never did and never will. Since you approved of Richard and his social status, and disapproved of the age difference with Evan, I let myself be dragged along. I tried to tell myself that I could marry Mr. Going Places and it'd be enough. But I don't want to settle. I want Evan because he makes me happy and he needs me to make him happy. I'm not his prize and that's all I ever was to Richard.''

Dead silence. Sylvia and John stared at Kendra for a long moment.

Good for her, Jan thought. Kendra was telling it like it was without going into an emotional frenzy. Evidently, Kendra knew what she wanted and was prepared to fight for it. Jan's opinion of her sister escalated several notches. Now, if John and Sylvia would realize this wasn't a rebound engagement, things might simmer down.

''Well?'' Kendra prompted impatiently. ''Do I have your blessing?''

John threw up his hands and let them drop limply against the couch. ''Well hell, I never could win an argument against you girls,'' he muttered. ''Fine, marry the rancher.'' He glanced at his wife. ''What's your vote, hon?''

''Oh, all right,'' Sylvia gave in. ''But during the first five years of adjustment to married life, don't come crying to us. We expect you to stay and work it out.'' She glanced at Jan. ''Same goes for you, too, young lady. If you're going to be all over us to work out our differences then you darn well better invest the effort in your own marriage.''

Jan nodded, wondering if now was the time to announce that Kendra and Evan were for real and that she and Morgan were for show. Maybe not. After the hubbub died down and things were running smoothly she'd fess up. Best not to risk more turmoil, Jan decided. She gave her mom and dad a hug and told them she was relieved the family feud had ended favorably.

On her way to the car, Kendra tossed Jan a curious glance. "So…what's going to happen with you and Morgan?"

Jan slid behind the steering wheel. "You'll be the first to know after I tell him that Mom and Dad have reconciled."

"You should just marry him, loving him as you do," Kendra advised.

"Great idea," Jan said with mock enthusiasm. "One problem though. I don't know if he loves me back."

Kendra's baby blues shot open wide. "You've been boasting about being honest and communicative and you don't know for sure?"

"That was for show," Jan grumbled as she backed from the driveway. "We had to look and sound convincing, didn't we?"

"Sure as hell looked real to me," Kendra said.

"Feeling the way I do about him, I didn't have to try as hard as he did. He's an exceptional actor."

"Then he should be on the silver screen with Surround Sound technology because he made a believer out of me," Kendra replied. "You go find out for sure because I need to contact the caterer and florist."

"Don't push," Jan muttered.

"Don't stall," Kendra countered. "Look at me, I went straight to Evan, didn't I?"

"No, you didn't," she pointed out. "You went to that bozo named Sonny Blair."

"No, Evan wasn't home so I ended up at Goober Pea Tavern, hoping he'd show up, *then* I ended up with Sonny. Now you go straight to Morgan, tell him how you feel and find out if he wants to tie the knot. If he doesn't, then I'll close up the agency and go murder the big lug for you."

Jan smiled past her apprehension. "Thanks, sis, you're swell."

"What are sisters for? You were there when I needed you so I'm returning the favor. *Go talk to him,*" Kendra ordered emphatically.

Jan stopped in front of the travel agency to drop off Kendra, and then she inhaled a courageous breath and headed for the hardware store. It was time to lay her heart on the line and hope she didn't get it trampled. The irony of being jilted by the same man she'd had her first flaming crush on did not escape her notice.

An uneasy feeling settled over Jan when she didn't see Morgan's hunter-green truck and noticed the hardware store was closed in the middle of the afternoon. What was that all about? Where was Morgan?

Jan drove around the block, then headed for Morgan's ranch, unsure where else to look. Driving past the wide-open spaces didn't ease the tension coiling inside her. She wanted this encounter over and done so she could hotfoot it back to Tulsa to nurse her broken heart.

Jan scowled when she saw Morgan's and Evan's pickups parked at Georgina's house. Evidently, they were finishing up the remodeling her dad had left undone. Damn, she'd have to postpone the confrontation with Morgan.

Hoo-kay, she had some time to kill. She might as well use it to spiffy up Morgan's house. She'd wash, fold, put away his laundry and cook his third favorite meal of lasagna. It was the least she could do after all the time and effort he'd contributed to her parents' reconciliation. She owed him—big time.

MORGAN TOOK OFF his work gloves, stuffed them in his hip pocket, then loaded the tools in his truck. "Thanks, Evan. When you're ready to remodel your house let me know. I'll give you a discount on materials and help with the labor."

Evan smiled gratefully. "Thanks. By the way, I called Keni while you were gathering tools. She has good news. John and Sylvia's marriage is back on track. They agreed to a second honeymoon and gave their blessing to our marriages."

Morgan felt as if he'd been gut-punched. The charade was over. He glanced north to see Janna's car in his driveway. Was she packing up to head to Tulsa for good? The thought caused his heart to lurch painfully.

"You okay, man?" Evan asked worriedly.

"Not very okay," Morgan mumbled as plunked into his truck. "I guess I better go see what my future holds."

Evan propped his forearms on the open window of the pickup. "What do you want your future to hold?"

Morgan smirked at the brawny rancher. "Who are you? My fairy godmother, here to grant three wishes?"

Evan snickered. "Could be. What's your first wish?"

Morgan stared into the distance, wishing Evan would drive to the house and ask Janna if she'd stay for good.

But that was the burning question he needed to ask himself. "Just *wish* me luck," he murmured.

"You've got it, three times over, friend. Go find out where you stand."

Yeah, that sounded easy enough. Just drive home, walk inside and say... His thoughts stalled. Say what? *Don't leave me? I love you?* That was honest and straightforward, just the way Janna liked things. Him, too.

Okaayy, he could do that, though he'd never made that declaration to another woman. His mom had bandied the words around for years without meaning them in a permanent sense. She could say *I love you* in one breath and her affection fizzled out in the next. Morgan had been careful not to blurt out the words, even in the heat of passion. But now, when it really mattered, when he wanted to speak from the heart, he wondered if the words would stick in his craw and come out sounding insincere.

Grimly, he drove home, switched off the engine and stared at the house. He could do this, he encouraged himself. He'd just walk through the door, find Janna and spit out the words before he lost his nerve. Good plan.

When he stepped inside, he smelled food cooking and grimaced apprehensively. If this was a fare-thee-well supper he wasn't a damn bit hungry. In fact, apprehension was tying his stomach in knots.

"Janna?" he bleated, amazed his voice had practically abandoned him.

Nothing, just the sound of laundry flopping around in the dryer.

He glanced left, then right, noting the house had been vacuumed and tidied up. Morgan felt panic rising.

He knew dozens of things about Janna's habits, but he didn't know if she was one of those individuals who liked to have everything spiffied up and put in its place before she left. Metaphorically, no clutter left behind, nothing left undone when you put your car in goodbye gear.

"Janna!" This time her name came out loud and clear. Hell, his mother could probably hear him yelling from her house.

"Morgan?"

He half collapsed against the back of his recliner. "Where are you?"

"Cleaning the bathroom."

That couldn't be good, could it? No one cleaned toilets and sinks for the fun of it. No, she was disinfecting his house and making a clean sweep before she skedaddled. Panic put a stranglehold on him and he charged down the hall in fanatic haste. He found Janna on her knees, rinsing the shower stall. Her head was bowed, intent on her chore. Uh-oh, another bad sign. She wouldn't meet his eyes. Damn it, he had to do something—fast!

"Don't do that," he ordered gruffly.

Janna rocked back on her heels and stared warily at him. Why was she looking at him like that? It was the same look she'd given him when he offered a method of relaxation for her hellish headache and she presumed he meant sex. Damn! The expression in those luminous hazel eyes indicated she wasn't sure what to expect from him.

"The charade's over," she blurted out, staring at his kneecaps. "Mom and Dad are officially back together. I'm cleaning house and cooking supper to repay you for everything you've done to help me."

She was leaving. This was it. All of a sudden Morgan remembered what Evan had said about being so deeply, so hopelessly in love that you ached with it, that you couldn't stand the thought of a day going by without seeing the one you loved. He had to tell her how he felt. Now.

Instead, like a coward, he burst out with, "You said you loved me."

Her gaze leaped to his face. "What?"

"Last night when I tucked you in bed you said you loved me."

"I did?" A blush scaled her neck and bled across her creamy cheeks.

"Yeah, you did. Did you mean it or was that part of the act?" He was dying to know that very second.

He was acting so weird that Jan wasn't sure what he expected her to say in response. He just loomed over her, his gaze bearing down on her as if he were agitated. And what was that business about not cleaning his shower? Did he think she'd made herself too much at home or something?

"Well?" he demanded impatiently. "Did you mean it or didn't you?"

For sure, she wasn't going to bare her heart while crouched at his feet. She'd meet him face-to-face. Jan surged up, dried off her hands, swallowed the knot of apprehension clogging her throat and said honestly, "Yes, I meant it, plus everything I told my folks, up to and including that part about you being the ideal I used to measure all other men. There. Happy now?"

He just stared at her for what seemed an hour. She wanted to scream at him for keeping her in suspense. "Well, good," he said finally. "I'm glad."

To her disbelief, he spun around and walked from

the bathroom. That really got her riled up. She stormed after him. "What is that supposed to mean?" she demanded sharply. "I tell you I love you for real and all you have to say is, 'Well, good? I'm glad'?"

"Are we having our first spat as a couple?" he asked as he shed his sweaty work shirt and slam-dunked it in the laundry hamper.

When he grinned at her she wanted to kill him, never mind Kendra's generous offer to do the dastardly deed. "Apparently so," she snapped.

"Well," he said as he unzipped his jeans, "I don't know what you're so het up about because I love you and I meant all the stuff I said to your folks, too."

Eyes popping, Jan stood there like a tongue-tied doofus. It was a moment before she recovered her powers of speech. "You do? For real?"

The Morgan she'd come to know and love finally smiled at her. It wasn't that tense expression that flattened his sensuous lips, but that one that made his eyes twinkle like polished sapphires.

"Yeah, for real," he confirmed. "You aren't cleaning house in preparation for leaving, are you? Because if you are, sugarbritches, I gotta warn ya that you won't get far. I wanna play for keeps." He stared at her directly. "And now for the million-dollar question—how much do you love me? How far are you willing to stick your neck out? Enough to marry me in a couple of weeks?"

Jan nearly collapsed in relief and delight—and couldn't find her tongue to save her life.

"I need your final answer," he said as he shed his jeans. "You won't mind being Mrs. Nuts and Bolts, will you?"

Her eyes filled with so many tears that he became a

blur and she really hated that because he peeled off his briefs and she wanted to memorize every glorious inch of him. He really was all hers now? Forever and ever?

"C'mon, sugarbritches, let's get down and dirty in that clean shower," he said as he reached for her hand. "Then I'm gonna make love with you until neither of us can see straight."

"I can't see straight right now," she blubbered, appalled that she'd become as melodramatic as her mother and sister.

Morgan pulled her into his arms and made short work of her clothes. All those tears and sobs were really starting to worry him. "Hey now, hon. Loving me isn't such a bad thing, is it? If this is about leaving your job—"

"No," she broke in. "I only care about you. I love you like crazy!"

She flung herself, naked, at his chest. Morgan felt every last ounce of tension fly off in the four winds. He clamped his arms around her waist and hoisted her off the floor. "I'll do anything for you," he promised sincerely. "I love you so damn much that life without you would be intolerable."

Jan looped her arms around his neck and her legs around his waist. She tilted her head up and smiled through the tears spilling from her eyes and streaming down her cheeks. "Then let's get married and show the citizens of Oz what an everlasting relationship looks like."

Morgan chuckled as he stepped beneath the pulsating mist. "If it *feels* real and *looks* real, then it *is* real, I always say. Grab your ruby slippers, sugarbritches. We're off on an adventure that'll last the rest of our lives."

When Jan kissed him, putting her heart, body and soul into it, Morgan returned the favor. He knew he'd been Janna's *first kiss* and her *first heartbreak,* but she was the love of his life and she'd never doubt how he felt about her. What he and Janna had discovered was the real deal. He wasn't going to let the best thing that ever happened to him slip away or go stale. Fifty years down the road he wanted to look into Janna's hypnotic eyes and see that same sparkle of love that glowed up at him now.

This was good—the very best—and it was forever. He *knew* it, *felt* it all the way to his soul when they blended into one and went up in flames in each other's arms.

Stop the Wedding!

Jennifer Drew

HARLEQUIN®

TORONTO • NEW YORK • LONDON
AMSTERDAM • PARIS • SYDNEY • HAMBURG
STOCKHOLM • ATHENS • TOKYO • MILAN • MADRID
PRAGUE • WARSAW • BUDAPEST • AUCKLAND

Dear Reader,

Wedding jitters are natural, but bride-to-be
Stacy Moore has more than her fair share. With a
little over six weeks to go before the big day, she
still can't find the perfect dress and her beloved
aunt hates the groom-to-be. To make matters worse,
she's kidnapped by two bumbling bad guys and her
rescuer turns out to be the man of her dreams!

Hunky Nick Franklin is cooling his heels on an errand
when he plays knight-in-shining-armor to rescue the
wedding-gown-clad blonde he's been admiring.
Soon he wants to rescue her from her stuffed-shirt
fiancé.

What's a girl to do when the real Mr. Right
waltzes into her life after the invitations are sent,
the mints molded and the caterers consulted? We
(Jennifer Drew is the pseudonym for the mother/
daughter writing team of Barbara Andrews and
Pam Hanson) hope you'll have as much fun finding
out as we did!

Enjoy!

Jennifer Drew

Books by Jennifer Drew

HARLEQUIN DUETS
  7—TAMING LUKE
18—BABY LESSONS
45—MR. RIGHT UNDER HER NOSE
59—ONE BRIDE TOO MANY*
     ONE GROOM TO GO*

*Bad Boy Grooms

For Jennifer Tam, with gratitude for saying,
"Why not give Nick his own story?"

1

IF HE HAD TO hang around a shop like Lenora's Bridal Salon, at least he was only waiting for his mother, Nick Franklin consoled himself. He didn't ever plan to get married, but he was bemused by his widowed mother's whirlwind courtship. Who would've guessed she'd meet a great guy and start planning a wedding in eight months?

He shifted his weight from one leg to the other and crossed his arms over the flaking sports-team logo on his faded navy T-shirt.

"Wouldn't you like to sit, sir?" asked Joyce, a middle-aged clerk, dressed as though she were twenty in a miniskirt and clunky wooden platforms.

Looking at the few scattered chairs upholstered in cream satin with fussy gold-and-white carved legs, he politely declined. He felt idiotic enough waiting here for his mother to have a wedding suit fitted without plopping down on one of the pretentious little seats.

He couldn't be happier it was his mother, not him, getting married. Sue Bailey Franklin had been lonely since Nick's father died a few years ago, and being CEO of Bailey Baby Products wasn't compensation enough for putting up with her crotchety father, Marsh Bailey.

Her fiancé, David Gallagher, was a nice guy. Nick liked him and so did his twin half brothers, Cole and

Zack Bailey. What he didn't enjoy was being the designated flunky for his mother while she ran around putting together the wedding. Ordinarily she didn't need or want a chauffeur, but unfortunately she'd taken a bad fall from a horse a month ago. She and David had met taking riding lessons, but the romance had gone a lot better than the riding. After two surgeries, her broken right ankle was still wrapped up too much for her to drive.

Nick restlessly shifted position again. Considering how much he hated to stand around doing nothing, he could cross being a bodyguard off his list of potential careers. In fact, he wasn't even close to zeroing in on what he wanted to do with the rest of his life.

His mother popped her head through a curtained doorway, cell phone propped under her ear as she leaned on her crutches.

"Sorry, Nicky." She managed to cover the mouthpiece. "I have to talk to a sales rep. Trouble with distribution on the tub safety seats. I'll be in Lenora's office if you need me. Then just a few more tucks in the jacket, and we'll go."

He couldn't imagine the ivory silk suit fitting any better than it did now on his still-slender mom, but he sighed with resignation. Glancing around the shop for the umpteenth time, his attention turned to the door as a tall, willowy blonde entered the shop. Waiting would go a little faster with a gorgeous woman like that in the place.

Female companionship was what he'd missed the most last year when he'd worked on a Great Lakes ore freighter. On the other hand, there hadn't been any women onboard to tempt a confirmed bachelor to give up the freedom of single life.

Not that working for his brothers was an improvement over life on the boats. The men on the freighter had given Nick a hard time as the college-boy newcomer until he proved how adept he was at anything mechanical. Unfortunately, he had a lot more to prove to his bossy brothers, who still thought he was a slacker for deciding not to finish college until he had a firm career goal. Right now, he wasn't much more than a gofer for their construction business.

Both Cole and Zach had changed since he first went away to school. Once they'd been wild and single, definitely his role models. Now Cole was a diaper-daddy since the birth of his twin sons, and Zack, of all people, was besotted with his wife, a local TV personality. Nick still couldn't believe they both had become so—so domestic.

At least their grandfather, Marsh Bailey, wasn't pressuring him to get married the way he had the twins. It wouldn't do any good if he did. Nick knew he wasn't the marrying type and never would be. He liked variety too much! All he wanted to do was get Marsh off his back about getting a life, which to the old man meant settling on a career.

He still smarted remembering what Marsh had said about his shaky college career. Addle-brained jackass had been one of his more complimentary terms. To his mother's credit, she didn't add much to the criticism coming from the males in the family, but she had been disappointed. It made Nick doubly glad she had David to distract her.

Meanwhile, he was working on the career thing. Nick liked construction work well enough when one of his brothers wasn't using him as an errand boy.

The shop's other customer had pulled a wedding

dress from one of the racks and was holding it at arm's length studying it. Her hair was short, revealing the back of her neck in a way that made her look vulnerable.

"That one's nice," he said.

He'd startled the blonde as she examined the voluminous dress under the watchful eyes of the clerk—or maybe here salespeople were called bridal consultants. Nick practically shuddered at the thought of ever being trapped into a wedding of his own and had absolutely no opinions about the dress other than thinking she'd look great in it. He was just too bored to ignore a looker like the pretty shopper.

"I guess it is," she said uncertainly, handing it over to the older woman. "I might as well try it on."

Weren't brides supposed to be enthralled by those big swishy tents called wedding gowns? At least his mother had too much taste to try to look like a cake ornament. He approved of her simple ivory silk suit, even though he was seething with impatience to get out of there.

All he had to do while he waited was think, so he welcomed the distraction. He had a lot on his mind, mainly what he planned to do with the rest of his life. If he had it to do over, would he still blow off his business degree at Michigan State? Probably. He'd only been a semester or so away from graduating when he dropped out, sure he'd never make a go of it as a suit. His grandfather had gone ballistic, but he'd pulled some strings to get him into Alvirah College in central Michigan. Nick went reluctantly and made sure he didn't last a semester there.

He grinned. It hadn't been hard to get expelled from the conservative liberal arts school, which had been his intention as soon as he realized how wrong the place was for him. For the sake of keeping peace in the family he gave the place a chance. Not that he was afraid of Zack and Cole, even when they threatened to kick his butt so hard he'd land in the next state. In his short stay at Alvirah, he felt as if he were back in high school getting in trouble for cutting classes and making out with his girlfriend in the janitor's closet.

His education came to an abrupt end when he led a protest against a strict new curfew. It was bad enough they locked up the girls at night, but he hadn't had to be in at ten since middle school. Marsh hadn't been sympathetic to his grandson's protest for civil liberties, and Nick's ears still burned when he thought about that lecture.

But it sure had been fun taking the college president's Cadillac apart and reassembling it in the lounge of the girls' dorm. Nick had had to bribe a local mechanic to help and borrow his dolly to get it done in one night since his college buddies were mechanical klutzes. To Nick's credit, he'd taken full blame and refused to name his accomplices.

Okay, it was a dumb stunt, he thought, looking at his watch for the hundredth time. Working on a lake freighter with some really rough characters had convinced him he did need to get a life. He just hadn't figured out what he wanted to do. Cole and Zack had struck out on their own in spite of all the pressure to go into the family baby-products business, but he didn't see construction as a permanent niche for him.

The blonde came out of the dressing room trailing enough gown to hide six men under the skirt—not a bad place to be now that Nick thought of it. She posed in front of a really large three-panel mirror, but he could tell by her frown she didn't really want to walk down the aisle in a satin tent.

"It is so becoming on you, Ms. Moore," the salesperson gushed.

"I don't think so."

Good for her. He hated to see a customer intimidated by a snooty clerk. Even his mother, who headed a corporation and held a couple hundred jobs in her hands, wavered a little when she came eyeball-to-eyeball with a bullying salesperson.

Ah, he saw the problem. Blondie was fiddling with the neckline. It was a little low, but he thought she filled it out just fine. She wiggled the top, obviously not satisfied with it.

"It is so lovely," the clerk purred.

"I think I'll try the eyelet," she said decisively.

He liked a woman who could make her own decisions.

"I agree. I don't think that one is you," he said.

"Really?"

Was that a flash of anger in her bright blue eyes? Was she annoyed by his comment or with the whole process of trying to imitate a fairy-tale princess?

"Definitely not the style for you." He flashed her a big smile, but she didn't seem impressed.

"I think you should reserve your comments for your own fiancée," she said.

"I don't have one."

"You hang around bridal salons for kicks?"

The girl had a tongue. Even though she was an engaged woman, he was glad she wasn't a wimp.

"I'm waiting for my mother to get fitted. She's the bride," he explained.

"Oh."

Not much she could say to that, and she flounced off with the clerk trailing behind her carrying another dress.

STACY LET the saleswoman help her out of the voluminous skirt, but getting it off didn't make her feel less prickly. This was the fifth shop she'd been to in three weeks, and she was still no closer to finding the right dress. In the big stack of bridal magazines cluttering her apartment, there were so many choices she mistakenly thought the job of finding the right gown was easy! Ha! Maybe it was easy if she wanted to blow a couple thousand on an outfit to wear for one day, but her parents simply couldn't afford a dress that expensive. They insisted on giving her a wonderful wedding, but she wasn't going to let them go overboard.

She caught a glimpse of the discreet little price tag on the eyelet gown and winced. She loved the simple lines and delicate spaghetti straps, but even this modest gown was twelve hundred dollars. Her parents were urging her to get whatever she liked, but she didn't want them to go into debt for a pricey item she'd only use once. Maybe she could make a gown herself.

Yeah, and maybe she'd be the next Vera Wang, too. Her sewing skills hadn't improved much since she'd put the zipper in backward on a dress for her middle-school graduation. Aunt Lucille, her father's aunt who lived with the family, had saved the day on that. She wanted nothing to do with a wedding dress, though. Aunt Lu was the one person Stacy knew who really, really didn't like Jonathan, her fiancé. She said his smile didn't reach his eyes, whatever that meant coming from a nearsighted woman in her mid-seventies.

Dad kept assuring her price was no object. He did

have a good job at the bank, but financial institutions were stingy employers, much like preschools. Even though Stacy was assistant director of Happy Times Early Learning Center, her salary just about met expenses. And it wasn't as if she were an only child. Her two older brothers still qualified as newlyweds, and the younger two were in middle school and high school.

"Now this is really dreamy on you," Joyce said dramatically.

Stacy endured having the saleswoman enthuse over the dress, knowing the bridal consultant wasn't the one really annoying her. Her whole family, except for Aunt Lucille, and most of her friends, were just so darn pleased she was marrying Jonathan Mercer. Sure he was a lawyer and his family had old money. She had been lucky to meet him when he came to pick up his niece from the learning center. And yes, lots of women would kill to be in her shoes—never mind at the moment her feet were painfully pinched in the pumps the salon loaned for trying on gowns. She was just tired of hearing how fortunate she was. She was marrying Jonathan because she loved him, not because he had an impressive résumé!

She *was* fortunate to be engaged to a man like him. It was just that constantly being reminded of it was getting on her nerves. A big believer in knights in shining armor and fairy-tale endings, Stacy had been swept off her feet by him. She loved hearts and flowers and declarations of undying love, and her fiancé seemed to delight in pleasing her that way.

Jonathan was the most romantic man she'd ever met. Before he proposed, he practically filled her little apartment with huge baskets of spring flowers, yellow roses and daisies and all kinds of delicate blooms. Then he wined and dined her as though she were a princess, brought her home and proposed on bended knee. Corny maybe, but it still made her smile.

Maybe he was a little old-fashioned, not wanting her to work after they were married, but there was a lot to be said for a man who respected her and wanted to take care of her. And darn it, he was cute, too. Aunt Lucille called him a male Shirley Temple, but Stacy liked his curly blond hair and baby-blue eyes, not to mention the adorable little dimple in his right cheek. He never made her uncomfortable like, say, the hunky guy who'd commented on the dress. She didn't know why the stranger made her uneasy, except maybe because he exuded masculinity and had larger-than-life good looks.

But who knew planning the wedding could be such an ordeal? Was she ever going to find an affordable dress that was her?

The delicate cotton eyelet over a stiff lining was appealing, but she couldn't decide without getting a better view in the huge reception-room mirror. Unfortunately that meant parading in front of the gorgeous hunk in faded jeans, not that Mr. Muscles's opinion made the slightest bit of difference to her. She'd deliberately come alone so she wouldn't be influenced by her mother or one of her friends. No way would she pay any attention to his opinion, but the close scrutiny of those dark brown eyes did make her squirm.

She hesitated before leaving the dressing-room area, angry at herself for being intimidated by that guy. Her reaction to him was probably a throwback to her high school days when she'd been so shy her older brothers had arranged her first date. She'd been seventeen and the guy had taken her to a G-rated cartoon movie.

Maybe she was a little quieter than her friends and sometimes a tad bit reserved with strangers, but at twenty-four she'd outgrown the painful shyness of her younger days.

At least she was pretty sure she had.

She put on her Mona Lisa smile, hoping she looked mysterious, not vacuous, raised her chin a couple of notches, and pretended she didn't care about a stranger's reaction. He wasn't the groom, and his opinion didn't matter. She liked the way the bodice hugged her torso in a princess style and flared out, without making her look hippy. That was what counted. The only person she wanted to impress was Jonathan, and it would please him if the partners in his prestigious law firm approved of her.

There was nothing wrong with Jonathan being proud of her, she told herself. She wanted to be a good helpmate and hostess to his friends and co-workers, even though she wasn't convinced she wanted to be a stay-at-home wife, at least not until they had children.

Maybe it was so hard to pick her wedding dress because Jonathan seemed to think she was perfect. She didn't want to disappoint him by looking anything but her best at their wedding.

The whistle was long and low-pitched as she walked out, a vote of approval if she'd ever heard one. Stacy wanted to scurry back to the dressing room, but part of her was pleased by Mr. Muscles's reaction. It confirmed her opinion that this was the best of the many gowns she'd tried on. Maybe she owed it to her fiancé to buy a dress this expensive. After all, he was paying for the reception. Jonathan insisted the two hundred or more guests on his list were too many to expect the bride's parents to foot the bill.

She'd suggested a smaller wedding. Her own list of seventy-five included all her close relatives and friends, but Jonathan wouldn't hear of it.

Turning around in front of the mirror, she tried not to imagine the church with the guests on his side outnumbering hers by more than two to one.

"That's a big improvement," her self-appointed critic said.

"Thank you."

Why was she thanking him? She didn't design the dress, and she was still a long way from deciding on whether to buy it. There were maybe a hundred other bridal shops in the greater Detroit area. She hadn't checked any in Grosse Pointe or in St. Clair Shores or...

"Are you having a big wedding?" he asked.

"Bigger than I'd like."

She hadn't meant to say that. It just slipped out.

"I thought the bride decided all the wedding stuff."

"It can be a mutual decision," she said stiffly.

Ordinarily only Aunt Lucille made her feel this defensive.

"It's not mutual if you think it's too big."

Hunk or not, this guy was too much!

"Do you have a professional interest in other people's weddings?"

"Do I look like a wedding planner?" He laughed softly.

"More like the guy who carries boxes for the caterer."

He snorted and twisted his lips into an evil little half grin.

"An angel who plays hardball."

She didn't know whether to feel complimented or

insulted. Either way, she wished those dreamy dark eyes would go contemplate his own navel. How could she make a sensible decision when he curled his full lower lip, making her want to nibble on it.

Good grief! An alien had burrowed into her brain. She had a fiancé and a future. She couldn't think about Mr. Won't-Mind-His-Own-Business that way.

Stacy glanced around for the saleswoman, but there was no help there. For a woman old enough to know better, she had her eyes riveted on the hunk with a goofy expression that said "Take me" in about twenty languages.

"I think your mother is calling you," she said, intending to cut off any more chitchat from him.

She was dueling with words, eager to deflate his male ego. All he'd done was register approval of the dress, but the way he did it was challenging.

She was losing it for even considering doing battle with a man she didn't know. Maybe she did need her mother's help to pick a wedding dress. No, scratch that! Mom was so thrilled to have her only daughter getting married, she'd like to outfit her in enough ruffles, bows and lace to weigh down a circus elephant.

"I wish my mother *would* hurry up." He grinned broadly, making it hard to resent him. "I'd rather unload a boxcar of lumber than hang around here."

"Is that what you do? Unload lumber?"

She was curious in spite of her common sense saying, "Don't talk to strangers. Especially such a sexy one!"

"I work in construction—temporarily. And I bet you're..." he pursed his lips, giving her a few more thoughts she didn't want "...a dance instructor."

"A what?"

He did come up with some surprising comments. That had to be why she was still standing by the mirror listening to him.

"You're graceful, willowy, artsy-looking..."

"Artsy!" she laughed. "I have trouble drawing trees for my preschoolers."

"A teacher! I was close."

"Not even."

She turned her back to him, pretending to study the triple images of herself in the mirrors, but secretly looking at his image behind her. He had nice ears, flat against his head with little lobes. Enough of this! She turned her attention back to the business at hand. The dress did feel right. She smoothed the fabric over her waist, beginning to think she should buy it before she changed her mind again. She liked the spaghetti straps, the absence of a long, awkward train and the scoop neckline, demure and revealing at the same time.

"I vote for that one. Are you going to consult with your fiancé?" he said.

"No. I mean, I'm sure he trusts my judgment."

"If he doesn't, he's an idiot."

"He's not an idiot, he's a lawyer."

He grinned and opened his mouth to say more when an attractive older woman stuck her head around the heavy gold brocade curtain that separated the front of the shop from the back rooms.

"Nicky, I'm still trying to straighten out this mess." She wobbled on a crutch and gestured with her cell phone. "Maybe you should feed the parking meter. Do you have any change?"

Stacy would bet his mother was the only one who called him "Nicky." She was sure it didn't fit the big he-man image he had of himself. She tried not to notice when he patted a front pocket of his worn but snug jeans, producing the clink of metal on metal.

"I'll take care of it," he said.

He walked out, the door tinkling musically when he opened it. She wasn't the least bit interested in his firm, muscular buns, but the saleswoman's tongue lolled so far out of her mouth it nearly hit the floor.

Now she could think about the dress without nonstop commentary from *him* confusing her. Eyelet cotton looked so sweet, so innocent, so right for her. Would she wear gloves with it? Maybe little short ones that buttoned at the wrist. And an airy headdress, just a band with some netting. She liked her hair cut in a short, breezy style. She didn't want it overwhelmed by a large production number on her head. Unfortunately her last haircut needed to grow out some more. The choppy layers definitely didn't resemble the gamine look she'd been hoping for. The picture-perfect wedding got more complicated every day, and it was only two months away.

The door chimed again. She turned expecting to see "Nicky," and would have laughed out loud at the two arrivals if she wasn't so startled.

The clerk made a strangled little noise, but Stacy giggled, a nervous, startled sound that didn't seem to come from her.

Two men in masks barged into the shop. The tall one would have been ominous in black pants, black T-shirt and a black knit ski mask if he hadn't overdone the whole man-in-black thing. What was the point of black on a bright sunny day in June? Stacy felt panicky and made another funny noise when she realized he could be a genuine bad guy.

The other guy was chunky and looked sloppy in raggedy jeans and a blue long-sleeved workshirt. The cartoon-character neon-orange ski mask pulled over his head flattened his nose into a lumpish blob.

Why come in here with their faces covered? Robbers robbed banks! What were they doing in a place that probably did all their business with checks and credit cards?

"It's not Halloween yet," she blurted.

She hadn't meant to say anything to call attention to herself, but it slipped out. At least she didn't see any guns or knives or whatever robbers used. This had to be a joke, a very bad joke.

The pudgy one grabbed her arm, and that was no joke. He yanked her so hard, it hurt. She stumbled forward on the three-inch heels she was wearing, and the man in black, scarier than his partner, got an iron grip on her other arm.

"Stop! Let go of me!" She tried to hang back, but he hauled her toward the door as though she were weightless.

"Keep your mouth shut!" The man in the black mask spoke through a slit, his lips looking thin and mean through the narrow opening.

They pulled her outside and dragged her across the pavement. She tried to dig in her heels and sit down, but the men were too strong.

"You're making a terrible mistake! There's no reason to kidnap me. I'm not rich. I can't even afford this dress! You must have the wrong person."

"Shut up!" The voice coming out of the orange mask practically squealed.

They wanted her to be quiet? She screamed!

A dirty green delivery van was backed over the curb to be close to the door of the bridal salon.

"You can't park on the sidewalk," she cried out. "You are in so much trouble!"

Parking? She was worried about *parking!*

The round one released her to open the rear door of the van, but the man in black grabbed her from behind and put one grubby hand over her mouth. She thought of trying to bite, but who knew where that disgustingly hairy hand had been? Instead she kicked, landing a hard one on the soft rump of Orange Mask. He swore at her, but the door was gaping open ominously, revealing an area with dusty rubbery flooring. The only seats were the two in front, and litter and lawn clippings were strewn everywhere.

"Don't hurt her," the tall guy warned as he pushed her headfirst onto a pile of dirty blankets on one side of the van's floor.

She landed on her stomach with the air knocked out of her. She couldn't think, let alone react. Things like this didn't happen at an elegant suburban bridal salon! Jonathan even approved of her shopping there.

Suddenly she wasn't alone in the back of the van. Another man lunged through the driver-side door in front, and scrambled past the heap of wedding dress engulfing her body. He grabbed at one of the two rear doors to prevent it from closing.

Stacy rolled onto her side to see what was happening. Her rescuer was the man from the shop. He took a couple of hard swings at the bobbing orange mask, but couldn't move the kidnapper's bulk away from the opening. The chunky man kept trying to crawl inside, and Stacy couldn't see where his partner had gone. Then a shadow came out from nowhere. She screamed, but her warning came too late. A six-pack of beer came smashing down on Nicky's head.

He sprawled across her legs, knocking her flat, and the rear door banged shut with a dull thud. Black mask had come through the front and coldcocked him.

She couldn't get out from under Nicky's prone body, and the van was moving, going over the curb with a nasty bump, then driving sedately down the leisurely suburban shopping lane.

Didn't these idiots know they were supposed to speed away from the scene of a crime? They'd just committed a major, really serious, felony, and they were poking along slower than her Aunt Lucille. Did they expect to win points with the police for good driving?

All her defiance drained away in one big *swoosh*, and she was suddenly very, very frightened. She was pinned down by an unconscious, maybe dead, man.

He moaned. Okay, not dead, but maybe concussed. He was a cheeky rascal—her aunt's terminology—but he had tried to save her from the bad guys. "My hero," she whispered.

She wiggled desperately and heard a sickening tear. The dress would be ruined. If she got out of this alive, she'd have to pay for it, and who knew what was staining it even as she lay helpless under six feet of muscle and bone with hardly an ounce of fat if her thighs were sending the right message.

"Ohh."

"Are you all right? Please move if you are! Oh, that sounds so unsympathetic, but you have me pinned. No, don't move! I don't think you're supposed to move with a head injury."

"I thought you were the quiet type," he moaned.

Suddenly it occurred to her he was grinding her bottom, her cool, panty-covered backside, against a scratchy wool blanket. The skirt of the dress was bunched around her waist and poofed up everywhere but where she needed it most.

"I hate it when people say I'm too quiet! Does a person have to chatter all the time? Ouch, you're squashing my legs!"

"They're very nice legs," he said, sounding alarmingly groggy. "And other very nice parts, too. What did he hit me with?"

"Beer, well, a six-pack actually. Where does it hurt? No, don't move—head injury. Yes, do— Ouch!"

He sat up, and so did she, struggling to put some skirt between herself and the dirty blankets on the van floor. She hoped the sprinkling of black hairs on them had come from a dog, not that it mattered much in the big picture.

"Maybe you should lie still," she warned him.

He looked pale, as pale as a sun-bronzed face could, and she wanted to touch him to see how badly he was hurt. On second thought, running her fingers through his unruly locks was too intimate for comfort.

"I'll be okay." He cautiously moved his head. "He clobbered me with beer?"

"Yes. You should see a doctor."

"No, I have a hard head. I just need to rest a minute."

"Right, and we're just out for a little ride with friends."

"Who are these guys?" he asked in a whisper.

"I don't have a clue."

"Didn't they mention why they grabbed you and threw you in here?"

"No. It's not like my parents are rich or something. Thanks for trying to stop them."

"Trying," he said sullenly.

He crawled to the other side of the van and slumped against it. This was not good.

"This man is hurt!" she yelled to the pair in front as the driver slowly pulled away from a stoplight. "You have to take him to the emergency room!"

"Shut up!"

"He could be badly hurt." He'd risked his life for her. She couldn't just let him suffer without trying to help.

"Maybe I should tie them up, Perce?"

"And maybe you should give them our addresses and phone numbers, you idiot."

"Sorry, forgot about the no-name part."

The van hit a bump, and Nick groaned.

"You have to let this man go!" she said in her firmest playground voice. "Let me go, too. You grabbed the wrong woman!"

"Shut her up!" the driver ordered.

She closed her eyes, terrified of what Orange Mask would do, then peeked through her fingers because she couldn't stand the suspense.

The big silver roll of duct tape her kidnapper held made her gulp.

2

"MUST BE ITCHY under that ski mask, Perce," Nick said mildly, after a long drive that climaxed in a boat ride to a remote island.

The tall kidnapper gave him a shove between the shoulder blades, and Nick walked a little faster up the rutted path toward a dilapidated shack at the edge of the woods. He and Stacy had been taken to an island in the middle of an inland lake somewhere in north-central Michigan, but beyond that, Nick didn't have a clue where they were.

If his hands weren't taped behind his back, he could have taken both of the inept thugs with a couple of chops and kicks. They didn't seem to be armed. What kind of idiots pulled off a kidnapping using nothing but a six-pack?

His head ached where he'd been clobbered and his hands were getting numb, but Stacy had it worse than he did. Harold, the name of the other kidnapper according to his partner, who yelled at him a lot, had his beefy paw wrapped around her upper arm like a vise, half dragging her as she stumbled along on spike heels. The long white skirt of the wedding dress tripped her every few steps as she tried to keep her balance.

The orange mask was floating somewhere on the lake, snatched off when the porky man succumbed to seasickness. His clothes got soaked when he stumbled getting out of the small boat to get on the island, and he grumbled constantly without getting any sympathy from his partner.

"My gut aches," Harold complained. "You didn't tell me about the boat."

"Think I wanted you to blab about the plan?" his partner snapped. "Cretin! I never heard of anyone tossing his cookies in a rowboat with a one-horse motor."

"There were waves," Harold whined. "I feel like I'm gonna die."

"I should make sure you do. Moron, how could you forget the cell phone?"

"Sorry!" His voice quivered. "I musta left it on the counter when I took the beer out of the fridge. You gotta admit the six-pack came in handy."

"Until you guzzled five cans and upchucked them in the lake."

"Ain't there a phone somewhere on this island?" Harold asked sullenly.

"No, there ain't a phone somewhere on this island," Percy mimicked. "I been here lots of times with my uncle Rudy."

"It's locked." Harold rattled the metal doorknob of the shack with his free hand, and looked back at his partner with malevolent eyes nearly engulfed by fat bulging up from his cheeks and overhanging his brows. Who said Neanderthals were extinct?

"Of course it's locked, stupid. You think Uncle Rudy wants just anybody using the place? The key's on the ledge above the door. Get it."

Harold found the key but knocked it into the weedy grass bordering the corrugated tin wall of the shack.

"Pick that up," he ordered Stacy, apparently forgetting her hands were taped behind her.

She shook her head vigorously, which was all she could do with duct tape still muffling her.

Nick admired her nerve considering her captor could snap her arm with his big meaty hands.

"I ain't putting my hand in there," Harold complained. "Could be snakes."

"Get the damn key!" his partner roared.

"Why do I have to do the dirty work?" Harold's face scrunched up like a giant baby's, and he looked about to bawl.

"Because you've got the brain of an orangutan! I can't turn my back on this guy to hunt for a key you dropped."

Nick gauged his chances of taking out both men while they were arguing, but without the use of his hands it was a bad idea. He didn't want Stacy to get hurt, and it wouldn't be smart to get bopped on his aching head again. So much for his superhero status.

After Harold got the door open and yanked his prisoner inside, Percy pushed Nick's shoulder to get him to move forward. One quick turn and a kick in the right place would take care of him, but lunging at Harold would be like colliding with a big rubber balloon. He'd bounce off the pudgy buffoon without hitting anything vital.

Nick stepped gingerly into the musty-smelling cabin, one small room probably intended to serve as a fishing shack. In the dim light from two small front windows he could see an antiquated iron stove in one corner, a table with a chipped, orange Formica top, two mismatched wooden chairs, a rust-stained sink and an old-fashioned kitchen cupboard with flaking green paint. A lumpy naked mattress lay on a painted white-metal bedstead. A couch with faded flowers on a black slipcover so threadbare it showed patches of mottled brown upholstery underneath, completed the furnishings. One corner served as a utility closet with a rusty lidless box of fishing lures, odd pieces of rope and other small bits of debris.

"I gotta go back to the mainland and phone in," Percy said. "Tie their feet with that rope." He pointed at the dingy gray strands in the corner.

Since their hands were already secured behind their back with duct tape, Harold mustered enough courage to push them down on the unsavory striped mattress to truss their ankles. Stacy made little strangling noises to suggest they take the tape off her mouth, but both of them ignored her.

"You stay here and keep your eye on them," Percy ordered his partner, as Harold began tying up Nick.

"No way! This place stinks."

This from a man who reeked like garbage, Nick thought. He kept quiet with great effort so they wouldn't think of slapping duct tape on his mouth, too.

"They're tied up. What can they do?" Harold cajoled, too.

"I'll be back as soon as I get to a phone," Percy said.

"You ain't leaving me here." He folded his massive arms across his chest. "You stay here. I'll go call."

Percy scratched his cheek and chin under the ski mask, then yanked on the rope around Nick's ankles to test it.

"I guess they'll stay put," he grudgingly admitted.

Yes, both of you go, Nick silently urged. Nothing would suit him better. The kidnappers' first mistake was bringing him along. Their second was not searching him.

"I don't see why we gotta call," Harold complained. "Like we ain't trustworthy or somethin'."

Percy cussed at his partner for talking too much and walked out the door, yanking off the mask as soon as his back was turned. Nick got a glimpse of sweaty red hair and not much else before Harold blocked the doorway and trailed after his partner.

Stacy made throaty little noises as soon as the pair was far enough away not to hear.

"If you don't mind me getting up close and personal, I think I can rip off the tape with my teeth," he said, trying to sound upbeat.

She started wiggling to the edge of the bed.

"No, don't try to stand. Lie flat. That way I don't have to worry about knocking you over."

She muttered something that sounded like chimp chatter.

Her breasts flattened the way women's did when they were on their backs, an observation he hadn't had the opportunity to make lately. The neckline of the dress gaped enough for him to see one smooth creamy swell of flesh, and he thought of how soft it would feel under his fingers. At the moment, though, he wanted to hear her take on this crazy kidnapping more than he wanted to check out her assets.

Two wide strips of silver tape had been slapped over her mouth from cheek to cheek. Fortunately, the lower strip was wrinkled on the left side giving him a starting place to fasten his teeth.

"This will be a little uncomfortable," he warned, pretty sure it would hurt like hell.

Without the use of his arms, he couldn't brace himself. He had to half lie on her and hope he wasn't too heavy.

"Sorry about the weight," he said, only too aware of her upper torso crushed under his.

She mumbled something that could have been, "Hurry up."

"Let's try it on our sides," he said after a minute or two, frustrated by his attempt to loosen the tape with his teeth. "That way I don't have to worry about hurting you."

He rolled on his side, and she wiggled against him, not a maneuver calculated to keep his mind on the job at hand. The old mattress sagged in the middle, and they rolled together in spite of his efforts to put distance between their lower extremities. He was heating up in more ways than one, but he didn't have time to squirm into a less provocative position.

Damn! All he had to do was pull the tape off with his teeth, but getting a hold of it wasn't as easy as it sounded. He bit at the slippery strip and accidentally nipped her chin below it.

"Sorry," he muttered, all too aware of the soft tickle of her breath when he got close to her nose.

The next try he managed to hook his lower teeth under an edge of the tape. He wanted to rip it off fast and get the pain over with, but the best he could do was nibble at the silver strip and use his tongue to further loosen it. He was making progress when a little whimper stopped him.

"Hang in there. I'm almost there."

At last he had an end firmly secured between his teeth. He yanked hard. She trembled from the pain but didn't jerk away. One piece was off, but unfortunately, the top strip stayed firmly in place. He had to repeat the process, nibbling away until he freed enough to pull it off. He hated hurting her—really detested the necessity of it.

"Ouch! That smarts!"

Her eyes were teary, but she was taking it pretty darn well.

"We don't have much time," he said urgently. "Now it's your turn. My jackknife is in my left front pocket. You've got to get it out for me."

"Out of your pocket?"

Her skin was bright pink where the tape had been, but she sounded pretty calm for a kidnapping victim. For that he was immensely grateful.

"Roll over me so you're on my left."

"Roll?"

"Unless you can fly." He remembered that somehow she'd gotten him into this mess.

"Well, okay."

He flattened himself against the mattress, but it was still a production for her to wiggle, squirm and inch her way across his body to the opposite side. After what seemed like an agonizingly long time, she managed to lie spoonlike beside him, her bottom and a few dozen yards of dress tucked against him so her bound hands were level with his pocket.

"I didn't know jeans had such deep pockets," she said after a couple of tentative attempts to retrieve the knife.

He could tell she was trying not to get too personal. He was torn between welcoming her intimate probing and not wanting her to start something he couldn't in good conscience finish.

She managed to get her fingers inside the slit, but they weren't long enough to extract the knife.

"I'm afraid I'll…" she said, hesitating.

He knew what she was afraid of. Those busy little fingers were going to embarrass both of them.

"That's not a knife!" he gasped when she squeezed more than cloth trying to work her way down to the knife.

"Sorry! I can't..."

"No choice. I'll try to scoot up a little."

"I feel like a worm wiggling on a sidewalk," she said. "Oh, I'm touching something hard. I nearly have it!"

She was touching more than his trusty knife.

"Oh, dear."

Oh, dear was right. She was on target in more than one way.

"Close, but no cigar," he quipped, trying to pretend he wasn't aching for her to go farther.

"Why do you have such deep pockets?" she complained.

"Just standard size," he assured her.

They weren't talking about jeans, and he wasn't the only one who was squirming in discomfort.

"I have it! Yes, I can get it!" she cried out excitedly. "Why do you carry a knife?"

"My dad gave it to me. Sometimes it's handy on the job. Leave it on the mattress between us, and I'll free your hands first. Don't worry. I'll go slow and put my finger under the tape before I cut."

"Can you do it without looking?"

"Sure." This back-to-back business was awkward, but he didn't see where he had a choice.

How long would it take those two morons to putt-putt across the lake and find a phone? Would they return immediately or blunder around for awhile? It probably depended on orders from the mysterious boss they were calling.

"Why kidnap you?" He asked the number one question, even though she hadn't seemed to have a clue before they taped her mouth in the van.

"Don't you think I've been racking my brains trying to think of a reason? My parents aren't at all wealthy, but…"

"But what?" He finished carefully slicing through the duct tape on her wrists. "Now cut mine."

She started cutting, but stopped talking.

"If you have any ideas, tell me. I'm not in the mood for games."

"My fiancé is well-off."

"Ah."

"Not him, exactly, but his family. He's a Mercer."

"One of *the* Mercers?"

Nick was no great admirer of the wealthy Mercer clan, but his grandfather moved in their circle thanks to the success of Bailey Baby Products.

"Yes. There, your arms are free," she said with satisfaction.

He took the knife and made quick work of the rotting ropes on his ankles and hers. Except for a sore head and stiffness in his shoulders and arms, he felt okay. He flexed his fingers and watched while she got up and moved around to restore circulation.

"Are you okay? How's your head?" she asked.

"Just a headache."

"Maybe I can find something for it. Everyone has aspirin."

"Don't worry about it. Let's get out of here."

He wasn't worried about the unarmed kidnappers,

but there was always the possibility they'd come back with something more lethal than a six-pack.

She was rummaging in the sorry-looking kitchen cupboard.

"Look. Cups, canned soup, a kettle." She pulled open a drawer and held up a small packet. "Told you! Everyone needs a painkiller once in awhile. Let me get you some water."

"Don't worry about it. We've got to go."

"You better take it," she said in a tone he was sure she usually reserved for four-year-olds.

"Okay." He took the packet and opened it, dry swallowing the tablets. He was too busy calculating their next move to worry about the thudding pain in his head. He and Stacy would probably be okay if they went into the woods behind the cabin. Percy and Harold had obviously never earned a Boy Scout badge in rope tying. He doubted they were any more competent in the woods.

Stacy was leaning over the stained old sink getting a drink from the dribble of water coming from the cold water faucet. He watched patiently until she was done, then leaned his head toward the faucet to catch some of the rusty-tasting trickle in his mouth.

"Nasty," he said, as he wiped his mouth and grabbed her hand, accidentally running his thumb over the big rock on her left hand. He didn't stop to admire the engagement ring, but he did wonder why those jerks hadn't taken it. Weren't they tempted by its obvious value? Couldn't they use it as proof they had her? He didn't know much about kidnappers, but Percy and his partner were one dumb pair of crooks if they thought they could pull this off.

STACY WASN'T at all sure she'd get far in the woods wearing the torturous heels, but waiting around for the creepy crooks to come back wasn't an option.

Imagine, she'd liked this wedding gown because it wasn't as elaborate as most. In the store she'd thought of it as simple elegance. Tramping through dense underbrush on an island that might or might not be deserted, she hated the voluminous skirt that constantly tripped her and the delicate spaghetti straps that left her arms vulnerable to scratches and bug bites.

"You doing okay?" Nick turned his head to check on her, but didn't slow down.

"Just dandy."

She gave him an ear-to-ear smile calculated to let him know how dumb his question was, then felt guilty. It was her fault he was in this mess. He was only here because he'd tried to help her. But why the heck was she here? How did Percy and Harold know where to find her? What did they expect to gain by bringing her to this briar patch of an island?

She was out of breath, and her sense of direction had totally deserted her.

"Do you know where we're going?" she called out, trying not to lose her breath.

"Straight into the woods for fifteen minutes, then we'll go left at a ninety degree angle. That should bring us back to the shore. Think of it as cutting a slice of pie."

"You're assuming this island is round. What if it's shaped like a one-legged elephant?"

"We landed on the eastern shore, so the sun should…"

"Oh, never mind! We're in lower Michigan, not the

Canadian wilderness. No one gets lost here.'' She
hoped.

''Do you need to rest?'' He stopped and waited for
her to catch up.

''Of course not. This is nothing compared to recess
with forty-two preschoolers.''

At least at work the kids did the crying and she
soothed. She was two blinks away from bawling, and
it didn't help to realize how worried her parents and
brothers would be. And, of course, there was Jonathan.

''Come on.'' Nick took her hand and guided her
over naked tree roots protruding through the ground
like giant tentacles.

She tripped anyway, going down on one knee with
a sickening rip. She was going to be stuck paying for
this dress, and it wouldn't even be fit to wear.

''Are you hurt?''

''Tell me we're playing a survivor game, and I'm
the next one to be voted off the island.''

She stood and balanced unsteadily on the big mama
of all roots.

''Maybe if you lose the shoes,'' he suggested.

''So I can step on prickly thorns and sharp stones
and things that crawl on their bellies?''

''Maybe I could carry you piggyback.'' He made the
offer with ill-concealed doubt.

''Thanks, but no thanks.''

She trusted him not to drop her, but how could she
ask it of him? She stepped gingerly over the rest of the
exposed roots and realized she didn't have a clue where
the shack was anymore.

''We'll angle back to the lake now,'' he said. ''With
any luck we'll come out of the woods too far away to

be seen from the shack when those two idiots get back.''

He found a path of sorts, and walking became less treacherous. She followed behind him, lifting her skirt to avoid falling over it.

The adrenaline rush of their getaway had subsided, and she had time to think. Unfortunately she wasn't focused on their escape. Her most vivid memory was more up close and personal, specifically wiggling the knife out of Nick's pocket.

She'd never think of him as a ''Nicky'' again. This was no little boy tramping ahead of her. In fact, the more she thought about touching him so intimately, the more uncomfortable she was. She kept her eyes averted when he looked back to check on her.

Actually, Nick was easy to watch as long as she didn't have to go eyeball-to-eyeball with him. Rusty-brown tendrils curled on his neck, and the sculpted muscles of his back were awesome even under his shirt.

Too bad Jonathan didn't have buns like his.

She regretted the thought as soon as it popped into her head. A firm enticing backside and thoroughbred thighs had nothing to do with a person's goodness. A man could be built like a Greek statue from the neck down and still be a bad candidate for happily ever after.

Jonathan was…nice. Really nice. She was ashamed of herself—well, a little bit anyway—for ogling the seat of a stranger's jeans.

Of course, men checked out women's bodies all the time. She knew that from overhearing her brothers' boy talk. So there was nothing wrong with a woman admiring a well-proportioned male. It meant absolutely nothing, but it did distract her from her problems. For a minute or two, she'd almost forgotten her feet were in agony and her knee smarted from falling.

"Wait here a minute," Nick suddenly warned.

She froze while he went ahead.

"It's okay," he called back. "Come on."

She followed, surprised by how spacey she'd been. If she hadn't been preoccupied, she would've heard water lapping along the shoreline. What she saw wasn't exactly a sandy beach, but the ground did slope gently down to the lake.

"Don't look at me," she said.

She stepped out of the painful shoes, pulled off her ruined panty hose, hoisted the skirt of the gown above her knees, and stepped into the shallow water. The muddy bottom seeped between her toes, and icy water lapped at her ankles, but it felt wonderful. For a few minutes she was so absorbed in the delicious numbing sensation in her sore feet, she didn't notice Nick watching her.

"Nice legs," he said lamely when she caught him staring.

He'd picked up her hose and shoes and was wiggling one heel.

"This is loose. Want me to snap them both off for you?"

"Sure, why not?"

They were ruined anyway, and it gave him something to do besides watch her walk out of the water.

She shivered a little from her icy footbath. It was dusk, the end of a long June day. The air fanning her cheeks was still pleasantly warm, but lake water was slow to heat up after a long Michigan winter. She'd had enough wading.

"How's the water?" Nick asked.

"Cold."

"Too far to swim anyway." He was staring across the blue expanse at the mainland. "I could make it if I had to, I guess, but I don't want to leave you here alone."

"I earned my Red Cross lifesaving," she said, miffed by his assumption she couldn't swim.

"It's farther than it looks," he warned. "Think I'll pass. If you want to strip down to your undies and give it a try, I'll be glad to watch."

"Not likely!"

He tossed the broken heels into the woods, handed her the remaining parts, and stuffed her shredded panty hose into the pocket with his knife.

"No sense making it too easy if those idiots try to find our trail."

"What do we do now?"

"Follow the shoreline. It seems to be a pretty big island. There may be some summer cottages. At least, we may find a boat."

"We could try to signal the mainland or something."

She looked longingly at the opposite shore.

He knelt over the lake's edge and scooped up a swallow of water in his hands. "Water seems pretty clear if you're parched."

She wasn't *that* thirsty.

"Is your head okay? Do you feel dizzy? How many fingers am I holding up?" She thrust three digits in front of his face, but he covered her hand with his and pushed it away.

"You don't need to play doctor with me, not that it wouldn't be fun in the right circumstances. Let's get going. I thought I heard a motor while you were frolicking in the lake.''

Sometimes his spin on things was downright annoying, but she padded behind him, barefoot, carrying a ruined shoe in either hand.

''Hey, lights ahead,'' he said, rounding a curve a few yards ahead of her. ''I think we're saved.''

3

"THEY HAVE electric lights," Stacy said, relieved to see spotlights mounted near the roof of a large log cabin, the first sign that the island was inhabited.

"Must have a generator," Nick said. "Maybe they'll have a cell phone we can use."

A barrel-chested guy in jeans, flannel shirt, leather vest and a wide belt that pushed his stomach up into a beach-ball shape, was dancing on a picnic table, trying to get a girl to join him. The other men hooted and squirted the contents of their beer cans at him.

They were all into facial hair. She spotted a guy who looked like Fu Manchu with a long dangling mustache, two versions of Blackbeard the Pirate and a braided beard with bits and pieces of what she hoped weren't bones woven in.

"It's a party," she said, the picture slowly coming together. Other words came to mind: melee, riot, orgy. "I hope they're friendly. They look like refugees from a 1960s motorcycle movie."

"Wait here," Nick cautioned. "Stay hidden in the trees."

"Like no one will spot me wearing a white tent."

He gave her a sigh of disapproval, but took her hand to guide her over the bumpy ground.

"Hey, here's another bride!" one of the Blackbeards yelled.

Between the bonfire blazing in a brick barbecue pit and the profusion of spotlights, the area in front of the substantial log dwelling was almost as bright as it would be in the light of day.

"Howdy," the big man said. "Looks like you two just got hitched."

A petite woman with flaming fuchsia hair sidled up to him and stared at Stacy curiously.

"This is Cindy. I'm Josh. Maid of honor and best man, although I can personally attest Cindy is no maiden." He roared at his own quip. "Didn't know there was another wedding reception on the island tonight."

"Oh, we're not married," Stacy said.

"Not yet," Nick quickly said. "We have a situation here."

"Do tell?"

"I love situations," Cindy said.

She had daisies woven in her hair like a hippie flower child and a filmy gauze garment clung to her. They both seemed friendly, so why didn't Nick ask if they had a phone?

"Stacy's daddy wanted her to marry a rich jerk, but she didn't go for the idea," he explained in a lazy drawl.

Good grief! Did he get that accent watching *Beverly Hillbillies* reruns?

"A girl's got the right to choose who she wants," Cindy said indignantly. "Did you steal her away from the wedding? Tell us all about it."

Here is a woman who loves a good soap opera, Stacy thought.

"The bottom line is," Nick said, "her daddy and the uptight suit he wanted her to marry have sent a couple of goons after us. You wouldn't have a cell phone I can use to call a friend of mine to come for us, would you?''

"No phones on the island," Josh said in the tone of a braggart. "Billy John won't have 'em. He comes here to relax, not worry about his business."

Stacy was pretty sure she didn't want to know what his business was.

"He's the groom," Cindy piped in. "He and my sister, Miranda, just got hitched."

Josh squeezed her behind.

She giggled and swatted his hand. "You behave tonight."

"Anyway, we need to get back," Nick said. "Any chance we could get a ride?"

"Could, but Billy John let his crazy brother take some chick out for a spin. He could be gone an hour or ten hours."

"How will you get back?" Stacy asked.

"Reckon we'll have a sleepover. Cabin can sleep fifty if they're all good friends. But if a person really had to leave the party, there must be an old fishing boat somewhere." He gestured at the shoreline in the opposite direction to the one Stacy and Nick had already covered. "If you don't mind rowing."

"Would it be okay if I borrow it?" Nick asked.

"Sure, but how the hell did you get here?"

"Leaky old boat. I abandoned it near a crappy cabin back there." He gestured. "Thought I could put her daddy's goons off the trail, but they're bloodhounds."

"Hey, stay and party with us!" Cindy said. "Plenty of beer, and Josh has a stash…"

"Hell yes, man, we're good for another twenty-four hours at least," Josh said expansively. "I'll introduce you to Billy John. He'll be tickled. There's the happy couple. Come on over.''

His huge plaid arm circled Cindy's shoulder like a boa coiling for the big squeeze, and propelled her toward the newlyweds.

"Come on, you two," Cindy called over her shoulder.

"Why?" Stacy whispered when they were out of hearing. "Why tell them that preposterous story?"

"Did you want me to explain you've been kidnapped? In a wedding dress? By two idiots who can't find their own feet? I'd really like to tell ol' Josh and Billy John I was decked by a six-pack!"

"I guess your story makes more sense than the truth," she admitted. "Who would believe what really happened?"

The newlyweds were looking at them, so Nick steered her over to meet them.

"That is so romantic," the tiny bride gushed when they approached. "A runaway bride! I love it!"

She was maybe five feet tall, and Stacy doubted she weighed more than ninety pounds. She was wearing the most elaborate wedding dress Stacy had ever seen. Yards and yards of a beaded-and-sequined skirt with a train that looped over her shoulder and trailed on the ground. Her headpiece was a foot-high creation of silk flowers and pearly vines, and the crowning touch was a pearl stud in her nose. Her hair cascaded down in burgundy curls like those of a fairy-tale princess, a look she managed to pull off in spite of the heavy black military boots laced on her feet.

If the bride was queen of the fairies, her groom belonged at the top of a beanstalk. He was maybe six and a half feet tall and three hundred pounds with a booming voice that made the ground underfoot vibrate. Or maybe it was the heavy metal music blasting out of the cabin. He was wearing the uniform of the day: jeans, plaid shirt and black leather vest, which made him resemble a lumberjack.

"Join the party!" the giant boomed. "We're gonna cut the cake pretty soon. Sixteen sheet cakes side by side with a genuine bigger-than-life frosted Elvis head. You folks ain't never seen anything like it. Had it made special by a little Italian bakery in De-troit."

"I'm having a piece of his lips," the bride giggled. "But first I want to hear all about your wicked daddy. 'Course, my daddy loves Billy John since he paid him a cool thou not to come to the wedding."

"Worth it. The guy's a noisy lush," her groom said.

"I have a wicked stepmother," Miranda said in a mock whisper. "She's always trying to put the make on Billy John. The old hag!"

"We'd be mighty honored to have a piece of your cake," Nick said, "seeing as how we didn't stay to sample my sweetie's. Then we'd better get moving. Would it be okay if I borrow a boat?"

"Take any you can find," the groom said magnanimously. "What'd you say your name is, you gorgeous gal?"

"Stacy." Maybe she should have made up a name. Priscilla came to mind.

"I'm going to look for a boat...sweetheart," Nick said. "Maybe you want to come with me."

"You don't wanna do that, Stacy." The groom put one arm around his bride and the other around her. "Miranda wants to hear all about your wedding. Never saw a gal so wedding crazy. I bet she dragged me into fifty of those salons before she found the dress she wanted. It was enough to make a grown man cry. But I surely do admire your gown. Exactly what are you wearing under it?''

"None of your business! You're a married man now." Miranda punched him in his protruding belly for emphasis, but he didn't even seem to notice.

Stacy gave the couple a toothy smile, but inside she was screaming *help*. She stood there numbly as she watched Nick head toward the shoreline.

A FEW HUNDRED yards or so from the partyers' cabin, a steep bank jutted out to the water. Anxiety made the distance from the party seem longer. Damn, he hated leaving Stacy with that mob, but he could search for a boat a whole lot faster without worrying about her tripping on that dress.

"Who appointed you her guardian angel?" he grumbled aloud as he cautiously climbed down from the bank to a level stretch of land.

Sure, she was cute bordering on beautiful. And it was true she had more than her share of assets. It was hard to look at her lips and not imagine kissing them. And legs like hers showed up on maybe one out of ten thousand—make that a hundred thousand—women.

She was also engaged. To be married. Soon.

He whipped out his arm to push back a clump of bushes blocking his way, and winced when a branch snapped back and stung him. He didn't want to get married, so why should it annoy him that a woman he'd met this morning did?

What he needed was a double cheeseburger and a phone, not necessarily in that order. Checking his watch, he saw it had been almost five hours since the two stooges grabbed Stacy and him. His mom must be frantic with worry, and by now his grandfather would be on the horn with the governor trying to get him to call out the National Guard.

He found a boat by walking into it. Add one skinned shin to what he owed the bungling kidnappers—and whoever put them up to it.

It was a wooden rowboat with an inch or so of water sloshing around in the bottom. He wouldn't trust it on Lake Superior, but it should get them to the shore across this lake. He tipped out the water and made sure the oars were in place.

The easiest way to get back to the party was to row there, but he had a bad feeling about Percy and Harold. He was pretty sure he'd heard a motor earlier, which meant they were probably blundering around trying to find them. If they were anywhere near, they'd likely spot the rowboat on the water.

Nick flexed his shoulders. He'd rowed for his high-school team, getting up at dawn morning after morning to train on the swift current of the Detroit River. This lake was placid, so he should make good time getting to the mainland. Trouble was, the kidnappers had a motor. Even with a good lead, they could cut him off. His and Stacy's best chance was to sneak away.

He dragged the boat to the edge of the woods and concealed it behind some bushes. Then he ran, scrambling up the rise on all fours in his haste to get back. If the party got rowdy, he wanted Stacy long gone.

WHEN HE GOT back to the cabin, everyone had momentarily lapsed into silent awe. The cake was coming.

First Billy John and Miranda reverently laid a cloth on the log picnic table.

"It's a genuine bedspread from a room at the Trail's

End Motel in Kalamazoo where Elvis is reputed to have spent a night in 1957," Cindy whispered to Stacy. "Just think, he may have propped his boots on that cloth. His hand may have pulled it off the bed. I get shivers just thinking about it."

Stacy stood at one end of the table, released at last from Billy John's bear hugs. The spread looked old enough to be an Elvis memento, but she was no expert. It was soiled tan with western symbols like hats and lariats woven in. One fringed end hung on the ground, and Stacy instinctively backed away. No doubt the bride and groom wouldn't take kindly to anyone tramping on it.

"Let's have a moment of silence while the boys bring out the cake," Billy John announced in a subdued rumble.

Stacy was fascinated despite her anxiety about when Nick would return. Four burly men walked from the cabin with the slow, measured pace of pallbearers. Each supported one corner of a large tray, and sure enough, Elvis smiled up, his face surrounded by mounds of red, yellow and purple flowers.

Fu Manchu wiped a tear away with the cuff of his yellow-and-black plaid shirt. Cindy sniffed, and Josh kept saying, "Awesome, awesome, awesome," with the cadence of a steam engine.

Stacy was so wrapped up in the moment, she was startled when Nick came up behind her and put one arm around her shoulders.

"I found a boat," he whispered. "Let's go."

"As soon as they cut the cake." Even if they were uninvited guests, they owed their hosts a few moments of rapt attention. "Elvis slept on that spread they're using as a tablecloth."

"No kidding? Did he cut his toenails on it?"

She elbowed him in the solar plexus and heard a muffled grunt.

A willowy brunette wearing a purple leather halter offered them plastic cups from a tray.

"Licorice, the bride's favorite flavor," she said in a hushed tone. "To toast the happy couple..."

Stacy took one and handed it to Nick.

"We'll share. More romantic," she explained.

"Black," he said when the girl moved away. "Spiffy."

"Spiffy? There's a word I haven't heard since never."

"To the bride and groom!" someone called out.

"To the bride and groom!" the guests shouted, raising their cups and gulping the contents.

Stacy put her hand over Nick's and brought the cup to her lips. She took a tiny sip, but when it was his turn, he only pretended to drink, subtly pouring the rest on the ground.

"Anything you drink here will have you seeing dog-size spiders," he warned.

"Do you think the cake is safe? I'm famished."

Using what looked like a bayonet, the bride was slicing into the middle of the cake.

"We get the lips," she said again with excited giggles.

"Time to go," Nick urged.

Stacy put her hand on his arm. "In a minute."

"Yeah, better not to offend," he reluctantly agreed.

Miranda freed her chosen square of cake, pushed it into her new husband's beard, and stood on tiptoes to finish the ritual.

''Gross,'' Nick said softly. ''We can sneak away now.''

''You're certainly not romantic.''

''We want another happy couple to get the second piece,'' Miranda announced loudly, wiping her mouth with the back of her hand. ''Stacy, since you couldn't stay for your cake, you can choose whatever part of Elvis you want.''

''Oh, I couldn't…''

''It's your cake. We shouldn't…'' Nick said, apparently trying to sound humble.

''Yes, you should. My sweetie wants you to have the next piece,'' Billy John insisted. ''Name your part.''

''Maybe a little bit of chin?'' Stacy hesitantly suggested.

''Close to the lips! Good choice!'' Miranda approved. ''Come cut it, honey.''

''You might as well,'' Nick said, sounding resigned.

Stacy lifted her skirt, careful not to step on the edge of the bedspread. Miranda was licking her new husband's sticky fingers as the guests shouted encouragement and X-rated comments.

''Trouble,'' Nick hissed. ''Look, but don't look like you're looking.'' He motioned subtly toward the trees.

She squinted at the darkness by the edge of the woods. One glance was enough.

''They've found us.''

''Yep.''

''What do we do?''

''Cut a chunk of cake and work your way behind Billy John. We'll make a run for it and hide in the woods until it's safe to use the boat.''

"Not the woods again!" She didn't want to sound whiny, but...

"Not much choice."

"They'll help us," she said feeling inspired by their new "friends."

"I don't want you getting hurt," Nick said with a sincerity she found touching.

They moved in close to the happy couple, and Stacy made the cut. Miranda dug the piece out and thrust a chunk their way using the wicked-looking blade as the server.

Stacy took it, thanked Miranda with an enthusiasm that wasn't at all playacting, and broke off part of it to stuff into Nick's mouth. The excitement all around her was contagious, and she was having a good time.

He took the cake from her, held it to her lips, and gave her a glob of almost solid frosting.

"You have to kiss!" the real bride insisted.

"Yeah, kiss," Nick agreed.

"Oh, my...." she managed to gasp as his lips came down on hers, warm, sticky and insistent. She was expecting a quick peck, but he was doing a thorough job. His mouth covered hers in a series of kisses far sweeter than cake. Her lips tingled, and she leaned forward on tiptoe, enjoying his lips pressing harder and harder against hers.

She opened her mouth without conscious intent and forgot this was supposed to be a pretend kiss. Was it her fault her mouth was open? She didn't invite his tongue to lick the frosting from hers, did she?

He was doing such a good job of making the on-lookers think they really were runaway lovers, he earned a barrage of raunchy comments.

"Well..." She planned to let him know what she

thought of men who took unfair advantage, but he didn't leave her enough breath. "Well…" This had gone too far.

He kissed her again, a quick, hard smooch that made her wonder how much of it was acting—and how much was pure pleasure.

"Billy John, we have a little problem," Nick said, when he finally pulled his lips from hers. "Those goons Stacy's daddy sent, they're skulking around in the woods over there like the skunks they are. We gotta go."

"Did you find that old fishing boat?" The big man was all serious now.

"Sure did."

"We'll hold those boys up a bit."

"We would surely be obliged. Sorry we have to leave the party." Nick sounded as if he meant it. "Sure is a good one."

"Thanks. You can trust me, buddy." Billy John walked over to confer with a couple of his friends, and a whole different kind of buzz went through the party.

"We'll fan out and try to smoke them out of the woods," he said.

"No need to hurt them," Nick suggested. "Just slow them down awhile."

Nick took her hand, but she seriously doubted they could get away. Percy and Harold had disappeared into the woods, and it wouldn't take many smarts on their part to double back to their boat and catch up with them on the water.

The whole wedding party was moving toward the woods, but they were having too much fun for Stacy and Nick to expect any real help from them. Cindy was riding on Josh's shoulders, and another couple imitated them and started trying to unseat her.

Two more people splashed into the lake while a third stood on the shore encouraging them to dunk each other.

"Let's go," Nick insisted.

Now everyone was racing toward the lake to enjoy the water fight. Billy John rallied a few of the men to head into the woods, but the delay had given the kidnappers plenty of time to run behind the cabin and get away. Or more likely, lie in wait to stop them when they tried to get to the rowboat.

This was only a game to the wedding guests, but Stacy had an idea how to raise the stakes.

"You'll never get us now, Percy!" she screamed at the top of her lungs, almost certain the kidnappers weren't far away.

"Are you crazy?" Nick pulled on her arm, but she dug in her heels—what was left of them.

"You're too slow to catch us!" she shrieked for Harold's benefit. "Better get your mother to do it for you!"

She didn't enjoy sounding like a schoolyard bully, but she was desperate.

"It worked! They're coming," she said jubilantly.

The two men were streaking directly toward them from the woods. Just as she'd suspected, they'd hidden behind the cabin to escape the mob of wedding guests.

"Now would be a good time to leave," Nick suggested. "We don't know for sure they're not armed."

"No, no, no." She grabbed his hand and used her body as an anchor. "Not yet."

"When I get my hands on you..." Harold puffed, lumbering toward them like a winded buffalo.

He was ten yards from the table, then five, with Percy practically on his heels.

Percy went to one end of the table while Harold stumbled against the other, bending over and leaning on the edge to catch his breath. Paranoid Percy was wearing the ski mask again, still afraid he would be identified, no doubt. She could see the evil leer of satisfaction through the mouth hole. They thought their victims were trapped, and it wouldn't be hard to drag her into the woods before the pack of bearded giants got there. She didn't know what they were planning for Nick, but it would probably hurt. A lot.

The timing was everything. Just as Harold straightened to close in for the capture, she yanked on the Elvis bedspread with all her strength. The frosting face slid to the ground, and she screamed with all she had.

"The cake! He ruined Elvis!"

Looking for Percy and Harold had been a half-hearted lark for Billy John and the others, the women trailing along in wedding finery for the fun of it. Now the bride's shriek of indignation was echoed by a blood-chilling roar. The giant groom streaked toward the table with the power of a speeding locomotive.

Stacy couldn't hold back. She broke off a sizable corner of the fallen cake and hurled it at Harold.

"Good throw!" Nick said, getting into the spirit of it.

He blinded Percy with a big chunk of black-frosting hair, then spun around to push Harold down into the remains.

"Evidence. Frosting on his hands to prove he did it," he said, as the kidnapper demolished an eye and an ear trying to get up. "Time to go."

Nick grabbed her cake-covered hand and pulled her

toward the boat's hiding place. They left behind the
sound of sweet vengeance. Stacy glanced over her
shoulder to see a beer can bounce off Percy's head.
Harold was trying to crawl under the picnic table, but
the bride had retrieved the metal cake tray and was
swinging it at his posterior. She heard a lot of boisterous laughter and a few pathetic whines.

Maybe later she'd feel guilty for wrecking the cake,
but at least the happy bride had had a taste of Elvis's
lips. It was a bang-up way to launch a marriage.

4

"WE HAVE TO FIND a phone," Stacy said, as she trudged wearily along the edge of a blacktop road leading away from the lake.

"And food." Nick pointed at a rusty sign barely legible in the dark. "Cairo Casbah Cabins straight ahead."

"I wonder what time it is."

"It's a little after eleven. Oddly enough, I still have my watch. And my money and credit cards. You'd think ol' Perce would have taken them. Once you've kidnapped someone, petty theft hardly matters."

"Seems like ages since I put this dress on. I won't be getting married in it. Purple and red frosting is sure to leave a stain.

"When's the wedding?"

"Second Saturday in August. That's..." she counted on her fingers "...eight weeks."

"So soon?"

Was it just her or did he sound upset? She didn't have time to think about it further because he took her hand in his. She welcomed the contact. Although the moon was bright, the deserted road still seemed spooky.

"Marriage is a big step," he said, giving her hand a little squeeze. "Have you given it a lot of thought?"

"We've been engaged for more than a year, so it's not as if we're rushing into it."

"Guess not."

"Haven't you ever thought about getting married yourself?"

"No, not me," he protested vehemently.

"You make it sound like some terrible fate."

"I'm sure it's great for the right people, but what makes you so sure Mercer is the right guy?" He put his arm around her shoulder. "I don't want you to get cold."

"I've never heard of Cairo, Michigan," she said to change the subject. "Wonder exactly where it is?"

She had the strangest feeling, as though this was happening to someone else. The closest she'd ever had to an adventure before this was getting tipped out of a canoe at Girl Scout camp. Everything in her life was orderly and unexciting compared to walking along a dark tree-lined road with a sexy man like Nick.

"My guess is we're about a hundred and fifty miles northwest of Detroit. Of course, I might have lost track of some time in the van."

"I hope your head will be all right."

"It's fine now. No more finger tests." He squeezed her shoulder but not hard. "I gotta say, that was quite a wedding reception."

She giggled in agreement. "I'd like to do something memorable for mine, but Jonathan is pretty conservative. He'd never go for an Elvis cake."

"How about a cake shaped like Cobo Hall? Frosting cars instead of flowers since they have the big auto show there."

"What a good idea!"

"Or Tiger Stadium with plastic players?"

"The important thing is not to be ordinary." She laughed and skipped ahead with a surprising burst of energy.

"Nothing about you is ordinary. The way you set up Harold to take the blame for the cake was brilliant."

"Thank you, kind sir. Do you think they've gotten away yet?" She looked back at the dark stretch of road.

"Doubtful, but I'll be glad to hole up somewhere. This area must be part of a state park. It's unusual not to have a lot of cottages on such a nice lake."

"Unusual to be kidnapped by a pair of crooks who make the Three Stooges look sophisticated."

"I sure wish I knew who their boss is," Nick said thoughtfully. "But I guess the police will find out. They shouldn't be hard to track down."

"We never did get a good look at Percy."

"No, but I could pick Harold out at a convention of sumo wrestlers."

"Or a herd of walrus." She was walking backward, her skirt bunched under one arm.

"I see lights."

She spun around to look.

"Hurray!" No more kidnappers, no more Billy John bear hugs! She could soak the frosting out from under her nails.

She'd also be saying goodbye to Nick. He was Huck Finn to her Tom Sawyer, the only other person she knew who'd experienced being kidnapped. It sort of made them a support group of two.

They reached a pink neon sign in a few minutes.

The Cairo Casbah Cabins must have been built eons ago to accommodate motorists who came north to visit the country in their Model Ts. They looked like log dog houses.

"Looks like all the cabins are dark. Either everyone's gone to bed, or they don't have any guests," Nick said, taking her hand and guiding her up a rutted drive.

"Maybe the place has been abandoned. We could go into Cairo."

"Do you feel like walking more? Those blinking red lights are probably on the water tower to warn away small planes. I bet the town is still miles from here," he said.

"I guess it couldn't hurt to knock on the door of the biggest cabin."

They walked up to a larger building and saw an office sign over the door.

Nick rapped on the wooden door frame.

"It's pretty dark inside." Stacy peered through a square, bare window.

Nick was persistent even though it had to hurt his knuckles to knock so hard. She was ready to give up when a yellow bug light went on over their heads.

"Got no vacancies," a crackly old-man's voice said from behind a dark screen door.

"What we really need, sir, is a phone," Nick said.

"I'm in the business to rent cabins, not loan phones," the crotchety little man said. "I already told you, I don't rent out cabins this time of night."

"Then you do have a vacancy," Stacy said.

"Don't matter if I do or not."

"If you do, maybe you could make an exception just this once," Stacy said, coming as close to purring as she could. "Our car broke down, and we just got married. See, I'm still wearing my wedding gown."

Nick snickered. She knew if he did that again, she was going to—to what?

What would Miranda do to six feet of muscle and attitude? She'd be afraid to find out! The old man made a comment about dragging in riffraff off the road, and Nick snorted. Stacy poked her elbow into his ribs.

"Are there phones in your cabins?" he asked. "If there are, we'd be much obliged if you'd rent us a room. I can pay cash."

"'Course there are phones. Electric lights, space heaters, indoor plumbing. My cabins got all the amenities you city folks can't live without."

"You got me wrong, sir. I'm a country boy. Daddy raises sugar beets up in the thumb."

"Do tell?"

The wispy-haired man stepped closer to the screen. He seemed to be wearing an old-fashioned red nightshirt partially tucked into a pair of jeans.

"Of course, my little bride is from De-troit." He said it the way Billy John had with the accent on the first syllable. Now she was pretty sure he watched *Hee Haw* reruns.

"Well, come on in," the cabin manager said grudgingly. "Guess I got one left."

"For cash," Nick reiterated.

The front room ran the length of the roomy log cabin, and had a maple living-room set and a ten-inch TV. At the far end, a floor lamp with a low-watt bulb was on, probably so the man could walk to the door without stumbling. A small counter divided the living room from the official check-in area. The owner stepped behind it and flicked on an overhead light.

"I can let you have unit three. That'll be forty-five dollars for the night. What's left of it."

Nick counted out three twenties. "A little something

extra for yourself. I don't want anyone disturbing our honeymoon.''

He gave the man a lewd wink and took the key, an antique-looking iron one hanging on a piece of wood the size of a Ping-Pong paddle.

"I hope the honeymoon ain't as rough as the wedding,'' the old man commented, looking at Stacey with knowing eyes.

They managed not to giggle until they were behind the locked door of cabin three.

Elvis could have stayed there. The bedspread didn't exactly match the Trail's End memento, but it was the same drab tan with ratty fringing. The motif was mythical Mexican with slumbering men in huge sombreros improbably leaning against saguaro cacti. The headboard, nightstand, and three-drawer dresser were vintage mission oak, and the door of a bathroom the size of a phone booth stood open.

"It feels like a coffin,'' she said. Her short-lived burst of energy on the road had ebbed away.

"I have to admit I've never seen knotty-pine walls and ceiling,'' Nick said. "It's like being inside a box. But here's the phone.''

A dial phone wouldn't have surprised her, but this was a vintage Touch-Tone model the color of dried mustard.

"My parents must be worried sick,'' she said.

"You call first.''

"Your mother saw the kidnapping. She must be frantic. You can call first.''

He shook his head and gave her the receiver, his hand warm when it brushed against hers.

She smiled her thanks. How could she have gotten through this without him? She owed him so much for trying to rescue her, for getting her off the island unharmed, for bolstering her courage by being so brave himself. Words failed her.

"I'll call my parents. They can tell Jonathan and everyone else I'm okay. I won't talk long—not longer than I have to."

He nodded. "I'll wash up a little."

He was giving her privacy, at least what was possible in the tiny cabin. Suddenly she felt all weepy, and it wouldn't do to be emotional with her parents. They'd think she was hurt or hysterical or something.

She dialed the familiar number, and her dad picked up on the first ring.

"Dad, it's me. I'm okay."

"Thank God! Where are you? Are you sure you're all right?"

"I'm sure about being all right—not so sure where we are. Have you ever heard of Cairo?"

"Egypt?" Her mother had picked up the extension.

"No, Mom. Cairo, Michigan. Oh, please don't cry!"

She started getting questions from both of them at once.

"I don't know why they kidnapped me... No, I'm not alone. Nick is with me.... Yes, Nick Franklin... I'm not hurt. I'm perfectly fine, but the dress I was trying on is ruined. I feel terrible about it.... Yes, I'll talk to Jonathan."

"I'll be right there to get you, darling," her fiancé said, sounding even more panicky than her parents.

She told him the name of the nearest town, but he'd have to rely on a road map to find it.

"I'm in a little cabin. I can stay here all night if I have to, so you don't have to break any speed records getting here," she told him.

Jonathan wasn't ready to let her hang up.

"Yes, I can use a knight in shining armor about now," she agreed with him, not pointing out that Nick had already filled that position. "Yes, the man who tried to stop the kidnappers is with me now."

Jonathan wanted to know everything about the kidnappers and their escape, but she didn't want Nick's family to worry a moment longer than they already had. Jonathan promised again to get there as quickly as possible.

"Yes, me, too," she said before she signed off, too self-conscious to say the three words to Jonathan now that Nick had returned from the bathroom.

She hung up and looked into Nick's dark brown eyes, noticing for the first time how they seemed to radiate warmth.

"Jonathan's coming. Sorry I talked so long."

"You didn't."

"He's on the way. You can ride home with us, of course."

She handed him the phone and gave him the same courtesy he'd given her by going into the tiny bathroom and closing the door.

YEAH, THE THREE of us can ride back together, Nick thought wryly. There was a plan. Already he didn't like her fiancé, and he hadn't even met him.

His mother had been hovering by the phone. When she heard his voice, she did something Sue Bailey Franklin never did. She cried.

His brother Cole came on the line.

"You okay for real?" he asked.

"I'm fine."

"Gramps used to worry one of us might get snatched

when we were little and cute,'' his older half brother said. ''Don't know why they'd kidnap a pug-ugly guy like you now.''

''I was in the wrong place at the wrong time.''

Nick was so not in the mood to go over the whole thing now. He glanced at the bathroom door, wondering if Stacy was as calm as she seemed.

''You were all over the six o'clock news,'' his brother said. ''The clerk at the bridal salon must have called the TV stations, then the police. At least, they arrived in that order.''

''Just what I need.''

Now that he thought about it, he did have a headache.

''Where are you? Zack's here. Marsh, too. They want to come get you.''

Did he want to spend two or three hours in a car with his grandfather pumping him for details?

''Cairo, somewhere in north-central Michigan. All I know is it's near a lake with an island. Maybe in some kind of wildlife preserve or state park since there's not much population. I have a ride home with Stacy. I'll tell you all about it when I get there.''

''Ah…'' Cole hesitated. ''Her fiancé has been in and out of the house. Volunteered to deliver the ransom money.''

''Did you get a ransom demand?''

''No, but he volunteered anyway. Hey, it's no trouble to come pick you up.''

''Thanks, but I'll get there okay. Convince Mom I'm fine. We were never in any real danger. The kidnappers were idiots.''

He said goodbye, pretty sure he'd made the right decision by not letting his family come for him. This would give them time to calm down—especially Marsh. After getting expelled from college, he hated sending his grandfather into a tailspin. He'd probably gone ballistic over the kidnapping. Nick was in no hurry to lay all the details about the kidnapping on him, not that he understood them himself. The two morons hadn't even taken his money. In fact, they were so incompetent they couldn't get away with shaking down little kids for lunch money. So who planned the abduction and sent those fools to carry it out?

Stacy came out of the bathroom, her face pink-cheeked and clean, her hair honey-blond where she'd slicked it down with water. She moved with a natural grace he was pretty sure couldn't be taught. Even in the stained and torn dress, she made a beautiful bride.

"Is your mom okay?" she asked.

"She will be now that her youngest son is off the hostage list. I will take you up on the ride, though. Otherwise my grandfather will insist on coming."

"It's the sensible thing to do. Where do you live?"

"Livonia. My brothers own a duplex there. I'm their temporary tenant. Beats living with my grandfather."

"Yeah, there comes a time when it's nice to be on your own. I have a little apartment in Royal Oak. My roommate got married at Christmas, so it's all mine. It's kind of nice not accounting to anyone."

"Until you tie the knot."

"Well, yes, of course."

"Are you hungry?" Silly question, he knew. She didn't even get her fill of Elvis's chin.

"Yes, but I'm more tired. Do you mind?" She gestured at the conventional-size double bed. "I'll just close my eyes for a few minutes."

"Go ahead. I'll see if there's such a thing as pizza delivery in the backwoods."

She pulled off the grimy spread and the tan all-weather insulated blanket and dropped down on the top sheet, her skirt fanning across the bed. He couldn't be sure, but she may have been asleep before her head hit the pillow.

The cabin had a single chair, probably leftover from an old kitchen set. The plank seat was solid wood painted pondscum green. He sat and picked up the thin phone directory.

Cairo had two restaurants. The first didn't answer the phone. The manager of the second had a good laugh when Nick asked about delivery, but promised a great pastie, Northern Michigan's version of a meat pie, if Nick came there. He was tempted until he asked how far it was from the Cairo Casbah Cabins. Three miles there and three back meant a six-mile trek. He decided to pass.

He hung up and tried to get comfortable on the chair, even taking off his shoes and propping his feet on the end of the bed. It didn't take long for his butt to go numb and his legs to feel stiff.

Stacy made a soft whimpering sound in her sleep. He watched the back of her neck, slim and white below the blunt edge of her hair. It was a spot made for nuzzling and...

And this kind of thinking really made sense! He shifted uncomfortably and gave up on the chair. He paced, but could only do a cramped two-step on the green linoleum floor.

"Man, this is silly," he groused to himself. What would it hurt to nap for a little while on the other side of the bed? He was pooped, and Stacy wouldn't even know he'd shared the bed if he woke up first.

He stretched out on his side, back to her, and checked his watch. Plenty of time for a short nap.

Damn! She'd been in a smelly van and a fishing shack, but she still reminded him of fresh rainwater in a spring garden. What was it about this woman that made a prosaic guy like him feel poetic? Crazy, but the soft rhythm of her breathing was keeping him awake.

He wanted to snuggle against her. They'd be a good fit. She was a perfect size for him, maybe six inches shorter and convex where he was concave. Or was it the other way around? He did know for sure he'd like to pin her with one leg and close the distance between them in all the important ways.

Rolling over, he lay watching her. She couldn't object to sharing the bed if he kept six inches between them. He forgot about being hungry and wished he could rip away the bedraggled skirt. From what he'd seen of her legs, it was practically criminal to keep them covered.

He flipped over again so his back was to her, but unfortunately out of sight didn't mean out of mind. He tried to imagine lying in his bunk on the ore boat, letting the waves of Lake Superior lull him to sleep. Eventually he got drowsy.

The phone jarred him awake, and he leapt out of bed to catch it on the second ring. Stacy didn't stir.

"Who is this?" a petulant voice asked.

"That's what I should be asking you."

"Jonathan Mercer. Is Stacy Moore there?"

"I think she's probably asleep."

He made it sound as though he were guessing. No

doubt she wouldn't thank him if he told her fiancé they were sacking out together on the same bed.

"Well, I guess I shouldn't wake her. Poor kid is probably exhausted after her ordeal. I'm calling from my BMW."

Hurray for you, Nick thought, liking her fiancé less and less.

"I've run into some road construction. Apparently they're using a night crew because there's too much traffic during the day. If Stacy wakes up and you see her, tell her I'm delayed. I'll get there as soon as humanly possible. She's had a terrible ordeal."

Nick wanted to say it hadn't been all bad, but nothing suggested Mercer had a sense of humor.

"Will do," Nick said, hanging up before the pompous ass could.

Stacy was still totally out of it. He eased down beside her and thought of turning off the dim overhead light, but didn't bother. He was more tired than before his short catnap. Leaving it on was simple laziness. It had nothing to do with wanting to look at her as she slept.

When he awoke again, a man was standing in the doorway, and Stacy was snuggled against Nick's back with her arm across him. It was the granddaddy of awkward situations.

"AHEM!" THE SLIM man cleared his throat.

"Jonathan!" Immediately awake, Stacy yelped as if someone had pinched her, and scrambled off the other side of the bed. "I was so tired—I didn't even know Nick was beside me."

"How did you get in? Did the old man give you a key?" Nick swung his legs to the floor, mad enough to stuff the key, paddle and all, down the skinny owner's throat—or maybe Jonathan's. "I bribed him not to tell anyone we were here, and he gives away the key."

"Why? Did you have something to hide?"

Jonathan was wearing pressed tan cotton slacks, a starched white shirt open at his throat with the long sleeves rolled up two turns, and Italian loafers with tassels but no socks.

"There was a possibility the kidnappers would find us," Nick said angrily. "Do you think I'd leave Stacy alone and unprotected while they're still on the loose?"

If that didn't defuse the arrogant wimp, nothing would.

"No, I guess not," her fiancé said grudgingly. "But you can imagine how this looks to me. I didn't expect to see Stacy…"

"Jonathan…sweetheart, you wouldn't be seeing me at all if it weren't for Nick," she said. "He's the one who got me off the island."

She traipsed barefoot over to her fiancé but neither of them initiated any smooching. At least Nick was spared that—not that it mattered to him.

"How much did you give him for the key?" Nick asked.

Common sense told him to drop it, but he was still mad. A better question would have been, Why not just knock?

"Twenty dollars. Are you ready to go, darling?"

"There's nothing to get ready," she said. "Oh, I promised Nick a ride home. Seemed silly for his family to drive all this way."

"If it's not too much trouble," Nick chimed in, almost hoping the curly-haired jerk would refuse him a ride.

"Of course," Jonathan said stiffly.

"Stacy hasn't eaten since— When?" Nick asked.

"Noon yesterday."

"I think I passed an all-night convenience store about fifty miles back," her fiancé said.

"That'll do, let's go," Nick said, hoping he could sleep on the way home—all the way home. He didn't want to see and hear a mushy reunion.

5

STACY HURRIED HOME at noon on Friday to make a tuna sandwich, but found she couldn't force herself to eat. Knowing she had an appointment at the police station zapped her appetite even though she very much wanted the kidnappers caught.

All week she'd been besieged by curious people. Parents picking up their children at the learning center, shoppers at the supermarket, even neighbors out for a walk pumped her for details about the abduction. Her fifteen minutes of fame had lasted from the Saturday-evening news through the week to Friday, and she'd had more than enough. She wondered if Nick was going through anything like it.

Her parents were urging her to move back home until her wedding. Her brothers hovered so protectively, she practically fell over one of them every time she opened her door. The older two, Kirk and Paul, tried to persuade her to stay with one of them. When she refused, their wives, Nancy and Emma, tag-teamed her, trying to "baby-sit" her when she wasn't at work. Sam, soon to be a high-school senior and busy with girlfriends and a summer job mowing at a golf course, checked on her every night after work. Jason, still in middle school and usually supremely indifferent to everything not involving a ball, was angling for an overnight stay with his big sis.

Thank heavens for Aunt Lucille! At least she didn't see any need to put Stacy in a protective bubble.

With a few minutes to spare, she belatedly made her bed. She was going to miss her little bedroom after the wedding. She'd painted odds and ends of cast-off furniture a cheery yellow and stenciled kids in sunbonnets on the dresser drawers and the single headboard. Aunt Lucille had braided a three-foot oval rug for her using yellow, black and red scrap material. A collection of framed hand-cut silhouettes hung on the wall, and discount-store lace curtains finished off the room.

Of course, nothing in her apartment was sophisticated enough for Jonathan's Grosse Pointe home. He bought antiques at places like Sothebys and Christies auction houses. She smiled at the idea of putting her couch with its flowered chintz slipcover in his formal living room.

The tea-kettle-shaped clock on her kitchen wall warned she had to get going. When the phone rang, she was tempted to let the machine get it. Then, for some irrational reason, she thought it might be Nick. She picked it up even as she acknowledged it was dumb to expect a call from a man she'd known for one day.

"Darling, I'm glad I caught you. I have to be in court in a few minutes. I just wanted to wish you good luck at the police station," Jonathan said.

"I'll be fine. All I have to do is look at some pictures."

"Of course, you'll do splendidly. Anyway, there's not much chance they'll catch the kidnappers. They're probably in Canada by now."

She thought Harold would stand out like a zit on a beauty contestant's chin anywhere on the planet, but

Jonathan was only trying to minimize her nervousness about looking at mug shots. She did appreciate the support he'd given her this week.

Of course, he had pouted all the way home from the Cairo Casbah Cabins, but she understood why. He'd wanted to be the hero. He'd even been willing to pay a ransom and deliver it himself, but there'd never been a demand. Then he wound his way through summer road construction only to find...

"I should leave now," she said, uncomfortable talking to Jonathan while thinking about Nick. She knew how fortunate she was to have a wonderful man like her fiancé. She loved him. She really did.

"First one piece of good news," Jonathan said. "I've been working closely with Lenora at the bridal salon. Her insurance will definitely cover the loss of your gown."

"Thank heavens!"

"All it took was a little legal finesse."

"Then I thank you. I should go back to her shop to see if she has something else I could wear."

"Oh, darling, I really don't think that's a good idea. My mother knows a lovely place..."

"Lenora doesn't want to sell me a dress?"

"I wouldn't exactly say that, but you being kidnapped did upset her."

"It upset *her!*" Well! She'd get married in her learning-center painting smock before she went back there.

"I'm sorry you had to take off work this afternoon," Jonathan said. "I know you wanted to save all your vacation time for the days before our wedding. Of course, afterward it won't matter. Remember, I'm picking you up at eight-thirty tomorrow morning for your tennis lesson, then we'll hit a few balls to practice what you learn."

"I remember."

Her job wouldn't matter? They had to talk about that soon.

"I love you," he said.

"Me, too."

She hung up and wondered whether "me, too" meant "I love me, too" instead of "I love you." Maybe she should stop saying it. Now that she thought about it, she never had said "me, too" until that time at the Cairo Casbah Cabins.

What else could she have done there? It felt too awkward saying "I love you" in front of Nick.

She was nearly out the door when the phone rang again. Running back to the kitchen, she snatched it up. Probably a telemarketer, but it could be...

"Hi...Mom."

It was a courtesy call, her mother politely checking to be sure Stacy had made it safely home for lunch. It must be her turn to play guard dog.

Their conversation was short. Mission accomplished, Mom could go back to her job as an executive secretary at a color-printing firm.

Stacy hurried down to the car from her second-floor apartment so she wouldn't be tempted to pick up the phone again.

There was one good thing about the Elm Park police station. No crime need go unreported for lack of a parking space. The long, squat brick building, a relic of the suburban building boom of the 1950s, had an ample number of spots. Sharing space with other government offices in the town hall, it was conveniently located a few blocks away from Lenora's Bridal Salon. Who besides Percy and Harold would kidnap their victim practically in the shadow of the law?

She knew where to go in the station—two right turns then check in with a uniformed clerk. The institutional tan floor and walls were adorned only by arrows and signs. The place was uncomfortably quiet as if everyone who passed her had weighty problems. Her throat was dry when she reached her destination. The officer behind the counter probably thought she was clearing it because she was nervous.

Who me? Nervous? she thought, carrying on an imaginary conversation with the policeman after he took her name. Why should I be nervous? I'm cradled in the arms of the law. Of course, cradles could rock and dump baby out.

When it came time to do the identification, Stacy was surprised the police didn't use big fat books full of hundreds of faces. A shame. She loved movie scenes where the victim pointed at a mug shot and cried out "That's the man!"

What really happened was another officer handed her printouts of five suspects. There were no statistics, no heights, weights, eye colors or names, just stark head-and-shoulder photos downloaded from a computer.

"No," Stacy said, shaking her head and repeating herself for the third time because a weary-looking droopy-lidded cop wanted her to be sure. "None of these is the Harold who kidnapped us. I'm really sorry."

He grunted, obviously short on comforting skills.

"His partner has red hair," she reminded him.

"Yes, ma'am."

On the way out she passed a couple more somber-faced uniformed officers with intimidating weapons

She felt like one of her preschoolers awed by the big guys. Of course, it was silly!

She'd smashed Miranda's Elvis cake knowing Billy John might toss her in the lake or worse if anyone saw her. Percy and Harold hadn't scared her on the island, so she certainly wasn't going to let herself be spooked now by this kidnapping business.

She couldn't help wondering whether Nick had seen the printouts yet.

Oh, be honest, she thought. She couldn't stop thinking about Nick—period. She had a full-blown schoolgirl crush on him just because he'd been there for her during the kidnapping. It was the same as being infatuated with a movie star or a rock musician, fun while it lasted, but nothing of substance. After all, she was engaged to a wonderful man.

NICK SAW Stacy go into the police station just as he was ready to pull out of the parking area to go back to work. She must be going to look at the same mug shots he had. It wouldn't take her long. One quick glance was enough to know none of those suspects was Harold. As for Percy, a glimpse of red hair on the back of his head wasn't much help to the cops.

Impulsively he killed the motor and decided to wait for her. He didn't see her hotshot fiancé with her, and she might need a friendly word after traipsing to the cop shop for nothing.

He settled down behind the wheel of the black sports car his grandfather had given him for his high-school graduation. Someday he'd have to replace it, but he had more important things on his mind right now, namely a career choice.

Working for Cole and Zack was a dead-end drag.

He'd grown up thinking his twin half brothers were the ultimate in cool, but what they did now wasn't what he wanted to do. He was trying, but he couldn't get excited about building one more bank, one more apartment building.

He was parked in the sun, and the black upholstery was heating up. He got out and stood by his car rather than toast his buns, hoping Stacy would make quick work of not identifying the fulsome five the police computer had spit out.

He fiddled with one sideview mirror, then the other, not that anything was wrong with either. He just loved tinkering, the one trait he definitely got from his grandfather. Marsh had retired from running the company he'd started, but he couldn't stay away from the lab and workrooms where employees of Bailey Baby Products came up with new ideas for toys and baby stuff.

Since his stint on the ore boat, Nick had been trying to figure out what to do with his life. He'd rather be celibate for six months than admit it, but maybe he did belong in the family business. The management part was a bore, so he wasn't executive material as his parents had hoped. But working with his hands, inventing new products, sounded better every day.

One thing was sure. Construction work bored him. Cole and Zack contracted for skilled laborers like plumbers and electricians, and they had some really good carpenters on the payroll. This left him doing mostly routine stuff. He didn't mind the manual labor, but he did hate the monotony. So far, his greatest challenge had been to design and build a dog house for a well-heeled client.

Trouble was, he'd tack on another six months of celibacy before he'd ask his grandfather to hire him.

Marsh was not a ballgame, pat-on-the-back type of grandpa. He was a stubborn, opinionated, crusty tyrant who loved to manipulate people, especially his own family. Nick's mother was a saint for putting up with him so well, especially since he'd scared away the twins' father with jail threats when she was a pregnant teen.

Nick shelved his own problems the instant he caught sight of Stacy. She looked perky and confident in white walking shorts, a red-and-white striped tank top and red canvas shoes, but he had a hunch she might welcome a familiar face after the institutional coldness of the town hall.

He moved fast, calling her name as he approached.

"Stacy, how are you doing?"

He should've thought of something clever to say, but all his usual lines failed him when he focused on her baby blues.

"Oh, Nick, are you here to look at mug shots?"

"I've done it. I saw you go in. Knew it wouldn't take long so I waited. Thought we could compare notes." He was overexplaining, but she had that effect on him.

"Well, I looked twice at the bald guy, but even with hair he couldn't be Harold. His nose was too pointy."

"Our boy's snout is the envy of all clowns. Plum-shaped and bright red."

She laughed even though it was a lame joke. She had a great sense of humor except when her fiancé was around. Nick knew polite laughter when he heard it, and that's all Mercer got on the ride back to Detroit. The self-important ambulance chaser wouldn't know when to laugh at a comedy club without a prompter.

Of course, he could be prejudiced, Nick admitted to

himself. Stacy deserved a man, not a weasel in wingtips.

"I'm disappointed, actually," she said. "I keep hoping they'll get caught and confess. I don't care about
long jail sentences, but I really want to know why they
picked me. Jonathan would have paid a ransom, but
how did they know who I was and where I'd be? Did
they follow me to Lenora's? Why did they have to call
someone if it wasn't to demand ransom money?"

"I guess it's wishful thinking to hope they'll get
caught and tell all."

She grinned, and he felt like a pit bull on a leash
because he didn't feel free to hug her. Damn, there
ought to be a law against marriage before age thirty.
Once a woman got a diamond, life got complicated.
He'd missed her like crazy all week, but his free-and-
easy attitude didn't include poaching on another guy's
turf. She was engaged, therefore she was off-limits. It
was a simple equation. It also stank.

"Can I buy you a cup of coffee? Just a quickie. I
have to get back to work."

She frowned.

She was going to say no.

He held his breath expecting her to do the sensible
thing and tell him to get lost.

"Will you throw in a Danish? I was too keyed up
to eat lunch."

"Anything but wedding cake."

She laughed, but he wanted to kick himself. Why
remind her of the upcoming nuptials? He certainly
didn't want to hear anything about her plans.

He did have a legitimate reason for taking up some
of her time. After what they'd gone through, they
needed to talk about the kidnapping and their escape.

Maybe together they could remember something that would help catch those idiots.

"My car's over there," he said.

"I'd better follow you. If I leave it here, I'll worry about tickets and towaways."

"I noticed an old-fashioned ice-cream parlor about a block down from Lenora's on the other side of the street."

"Sounds like fun. I'll meet you there."

STACY COULDN'T find a parking place. Maybe fate was telling her something. For instance, engaged women shouldn't date.

But she was famished, and they did need to rehash the kidnapping to see if they'd forgotten to tell the police anything important. If she paid for her own snack, it wasn't a date, was it?

She took it as a positive sign when a big van backed out of an angled parking spot just ahead of her. Her little red compact eased into it as though the car was programmed for nooners with handsome hunks. She'd worry about feeling guilty later.

Nick was waiting.

It was well past the lunch hour and the parlor wasn't very busy, so they could sit at any of the little round tables with twisted wire legs, each surrounded by three or four wire-backed chairs. The walls were festooned with old-time advertising signs and tin trays. Lovely ladies in Edwardian gowns and huge hats were still smiling after a hundred years. Or so Stacy liked to believe.

"Look at those flavors!" Nick whistled softly, and guided her over to a glass-fronted freezer where open tubs of ice cream were two deep in a rainbow array of colors. Next to them, another case held syrups, whipped cream, candies, fruit, nuts and sprinkles.

"I skipped lunch for a reason," Stacy said. "What's your favorite flavor?"

"Whatever's on my plate. I've never met a dish of ice cream I didn't like. What are you having?"

"Butter pecan with hot fudge sauce, and I'll hate myself in the morning."

"Make it two," Nick told a young girl with a dark braid down her back and brown saucer-size eyes totally focused on him.

The young soda jerk giggled, flirted and made a huge production out of recommending all kinds of extra toppings.

He's not a movie star, Stacy wanted to say. Instead she said, "My treat."

"I've got it." Nick pulled out a money clip made of an old silver dollar.

"No, I insist. I owe you."

"You don't owe me."

"Yes, I do." She pushed a bill across the counter to a second clerk who manned an ornate old brass cash register. "You're the only one who ever took a six-pack to the head for me."

"Don't even think of asking me how my head is!"

She wiggled two fingers in front of his nose to tease. He grabbed them, gently bent her fingers down, and kissed her knuckles.

He looked as surprised as she was.

She didn't realize how small the tables were until they were sharing one. Nick sat with his legs spread wide, so she had to keep hers locked together to avoid rubbing knees. His jeans were practically threadbare, and they strained over his muscular thighs like a second skin. She tried to focus on the gooey treat in front of her, but Nick's blue-cotton workshirt was open three buttons more than necessary.

Okay, so it was only open three buttons, but the slit of sun-bronzed skin was sprinkled with dark, eminently caressable hair. Her knuckles tingled. Her spine was relaying messages she didn't want to process. Her toes kept trying to curl. Worse, she was too keyed up, too turned on, to look directly into his eyes.

Nothing like this had happened on the island, except maybe when Billy John made them kiss. Or did he have to make them? She couldn't remember.

Nick had a little smear of hot fudge on his Cupid's bow. It was driving her wild. Didn't he feel it? She could imagine wiping it away with one quick flick of her tongue—or maybe several.

Good grief! She was sucking on an empty spoon. Had she made a disgusting noise? Had he noticed?

"I haven't had anything this good in years," he said.

"Me, either."

Was he talking about the ice cream? Was she? She'd lost her sense of taste. What was she eating? She looked down at her dish, shaped like a cone only flat on the bottom. Two of the three scoops were gone. She must have inhaled them while her mind was otherwise occupied.

Nick had hardly started his. She squirmed, knowing he must have been watching every bite she took.

"I don't usually wolf down food like that," she said, mortified by her pigginess.

"You have an interesting tongue movement. The tip flicks out a little after every bite."

"I didn't know..." She covered her lips with two fingers.

"No, don't be embarrassed. It's cute."

"You're cute with a chocolate mustache." She had to choke back a giggle.

"I forgot napkins," he said. "I'll get some."

"Never mind. I have a tissue," she said, but he was already on the way to get some from the holder on the counter.

His shoulders were even wider than she remembered, his waist slimmer, his buttocks rounder and tighter. She was fascinated by everything about him, but didn't want to be. She was engaged to a wonderful man, and she wanted to fondle Nick's bottom. She wanted to hear him moan the way men did when they were really turned on—at least the way she thought they did. Jonathan was always pretty subdued. Thinking about him while she watched Nick walk back was making her squirm with guilt—or something.

It was all Nick's fault! He should wear loose, pleated trousers, not jeans that bunched and wrinkled and bulged suggestively.

"Napkins." He handed her several, but didn't keep one for himself when he was the one who needed one.

"Thank you." And please sit down so I can't see so much of you.

He sat, the smear of chocolate giving him a rakish look. She couldn't stand it. She peeled off one of the napkins, reached across the tiny table, and wiped away the hot fudge.

"Thanks."

He gave her a thousand-watt grin, and part of her melted.

She struggled not to watch while he slowly finished his sundae. She wanted to brush his hair back from his forehead, run her finger along his eyebrows to make them smoother, and rub the back of her hand on his lightly bristled cheek.

She wanted to touch him, and the greater the urge became, the more guilty—and excited—she felt.

"Did you take the whole afternoon off to look at mug shots?" he asked.

"Yes, I have lots of vacation time coming."

"So you're free for the rest of the day?"

"I guess." She was venturing into dangerous territory here.

She assumed Jonathan would call later, but he rarely left his office before six. And she really did need to vent about the kidnapping with the one person who been through it with her.

"Let's go to the zoo," Nick suggested.

"What?"

"The Belle Isle Zoo. I haven't been there since I was a kid."

"Oh, I don't think I can."

No question, that would be a date.

"We haven't talked about the kidnappers yet. Maybe we can jog each other's memories, remember something they said or did."

"Don't you have to go back to work?"

He frowned. "Cole's out of town, so Zack's in charge. But what's the worst he can do? Fire me? I'll take the risk."

"I really shouldn't." She wasn't being coy.

"Have you picked out your wedding dress yet? I could tag along and give you my expert opinion."

"Be serious!"

"The zoo then?"

"Okay, the zoo, but only for a little while."

6

_____

"WE BRING OUR preschoolers to Belle Isle every spring," Stacy said. "It's a treat to be here without counting heads every two minutes."

"Ever lose any?" Nick asked, wondering who was watching the swarms of juveniles milling around on the elevated boardwalk that looked down on animal exhibits.

"No, but I'd hate to bring them here today. It looks like a Cub Scout convention."

She moved aside to avoid being mowed down by a trio of ruffians.

"Hard to believe I was once that young—and probably even wilder," he said.

"Oh, I don't know. I can still see the little boy in you."

"You think I'm still a kid?"

His pride took a hit, especially since Zack had told him just last week it was time to grow up. His brother didn't hurt his feelings, though. He knew his struggle to find a career didn't have anything to do with lack of maturity. It had everything to do with his grandfather being a control freak—and the stubbornness Nick had inherited from him.

"No! I didn't mean that at all," she said apologetically. "You just have boyish enthusiasm..."

"Boyish?"

He gave her a look meant to intimidate, but she went eyeball-to-eyeball without flinching.

"*Spontaneous* is a better word. You're not afraid to do something on impulse like coming here."

"When I should go back to work." He grinned ruefully.

"Everyone needs a break once in awhile."

She smiled, and his heart skipped a beat. But the last thing he wanted was to discuss his motives for goofing off this afternoon.

"Anything special you want to see?" he asked.

He took her hand and pulled her out of the way as a pack of Cubs surged by, more or less led by a perspiring, red-faced woman. There didn't seem to be any reason to release it after.

"I love the wolves. They look like big dogs looking for a hug, but they're so dangerous they make me shiver."

"I'll take the big cats any day."

"Lazy old lions. The male sleeps all day and makes the female do the work."

"Sounds like a good system to me," he teased.

The sun was hot, giving a pink flush to the cheeks of her heart-shaped face. She had one of those perky haircuts that fell into place and never look mussed, but one stray lock had fallen over her forehead. He flicked it aside. Touching her felt so right he wanted to rail at her for getting herself engaged to Mercer. He also wanted to ask her why, but he didn't have a right to go there.

He shouldn't be with her now. Even if he could mess up her wedding plans, which he doubted, he wasn't marriage material himself. He couldn't offer her what she seemed to want.

"A friend of mine had her wedding reception at the casino here," she said, leaving her hand in his, but not responding when he tentatively squeezed it. "Of course, casino isn't a very descriptive name for the old building. There's no gambling, but it's a nice place for events. My aunt Lucille went to a health fair there."

Wedding! He knew she knew she'd said a taboo word, but she tried to cover up by chattering about the senior-citizen stuff her aunt had done in the old Spanish-style building.

"A friend of mine got married at the conservatory here," he said when she fell silent.

Talking about weddings with Stacy was like pinching a sore spot, but he was having a hard time believing she'd actually marry Mercer.

"No need for a lot of flowers there," he went on. "Can you see yourself tying the knot among the cacti?"

"Jonathan wants a wedding just like his parents had. Same church, same flowers, same country-club reception. Guess I'm lucky I'm too tall to wear his mother's dress."

Why the hell did she want to get married? She was twenty-four, one year younger than he. He could understand his mother wanting to marry for companionship now that her three sons were grown up, but why did a smart, attractive, witty, resourceful, sexy woman want to spend the rest of her life with that jerky lawyer? More to the point, how could she crawl into bed with him? It went against the natural order for a beauty to end up with a toad.

Nick dropped her hand and tried to focus on the excuse he'd given for spending the afternoon with her.

"I've been trying to remember if the kidnappers gave any hints about where they live," he said.

"No."

"When they talked about forgetting the phone…"

"They refrigerate their beer. Big clue."

Apparently the wedding talk had made her cranky. It didn't do much for his disposition, either.

They swerved to avoid an especially boisterous bunch of Cubs, and Nick caught a glimpse of red hair to the left and slightly behind them.

"Is there any possibility…" He started to ask if she could've been followed this week, but decided not to worry her. "I can stop to tie my shoelace?"

He moved over to a railing and stooped down quickly, hoping she wouldn't see that both his workboots were firmly tied. When he stood, he had a chance to look behind him. A slender red-haired man built almost exactly like Percy was hovering a few dozen yards behind them, but he looked to be all of fifteen and had a busty little blonde glued to his side. That kid was no threat to Stacy, but until Percy and Harold were in custody, Nick would worry. They'd stolen nothing and hadn't had a chance to demand ransom. What was to stop them from trying again? With thousands of kids chasing around Belle Isle, who would notice one more scream if they tried to grab Stacy?

"It's hot today," he said, catching her hand again. "How does the aquarium sound to you?"

She smiled up at him, and it was all he could do not to wrap his arms around her and kiss her until she forgot Jonathan Mercer existed. But she'd made her choice, and Nick didn't want her to hate him for interfering.

"I love the aquarium," she said. "Real live sea monsters!"

"Earth's own aliens."

"I'm glad you suggested coming here. I feel so free. It's the first time all week my family hasn't hovered over me. Even my little brother wants to stay overnight and protect me. I'm getting claustrophobic."

"They're only worried about your safety."

Her family had a right to worry about her. He probably didn't. This protective feeling was new to him, but he wasn't sure how to deal with it. He did know how to take care of Percy and Harold if they got anywhere near Stacy when he was around, though.

But for now, he'd better be subtle. She wasn't in the mood for a bodyguard. At least he wouldn't lose her in the mob of people at the zoo, not with her hand firmly locked in his. They walked slowly toward the aquarium and didn't mention weddings again.

He liked watching her as she edged through the crowd inside the aquarium and stood face-to-face with a glassy-eyed monstrosity so improbably ugly it didn't seem real.

"I'm glad he can't survive on our turf," she said with a mock shudder.

A trio of Cubs squeezed in front of her trying to steam up the glass with their breath.

To avoid having his toes stomped by overzealous scouts, Nick backed up. He was still edgy enough to glance around the crowded room. Unfortunately, not everything ugly was swimming in a fish tank. A slender man who matched Percy's description in every detail except for the ski mask, was trying hard to be inconspicuous beside a tank of less popular freshwater fish.

Nick caught his eye for an instant, and the guy bolted toward the exit.

Nick struggled through the crowd trying to catch the sallow-faced man with sweat-plastered red hair. This time he wasn't spooked by a kid, and the guy's actions were suspicious as hell. Before Nick could confront him, the guy doubled back into the aquarium and tried to lose himself in the crowd.

Nick followed after checking to be sure Stacy was close behind him.

"What's wrong?" she asked.

"Nothing. Just thought I saw someone..."

He spotted the redhead wiggling his way through a bunch of Cubs who were making faces at the electric eels.

"Hey, Percy!" he shouted loudly, hoping the guy would give himself away by responding.

Instead the red-haired man sidestepped through the Scouts and made a dash for the exit again, holding up a dripping ice-cream cone.

"Hey, don't I know you?" Nick yelled, racing to head off the guy.

He charged and had to jump over a blob of melting chocolate ice cream that spilled from the soggy cone and hit the pavement.

"Gosh, mister, I'm sorry! I didn't know taking ice cream into the aquarium was such a big deal!" the man cried.

His voice was high-pitched, nothing like the masked kidnapper's.

"I thought you were following us," Nick said lamely, all too aware of Stacy a few paces behind him.

"Hell, no, why should I follow you? I thought I was

in trouble for taking the cone inside.'' He looked down and scowled at the remains of his ice cream.

''My mistake,'' Nick said. ''Sorry. Here let me buy you another one.'' He reached into his pocket, but the man walked away in disgust.

''You didn't make a friend there,'' Stacy said, arching one eyebrow.

''Guess not.'' He was embarrassed, but not ready to scare her with talk of being followed. ''Seen enough fish?''

''Yes, but what was that about?'' she asked.

''Red hair.''

He liked her too much to concoct a lie even though he didn't want to be grouped with her overprotective family. Not that they didn't have good reason to worry about her.

''You got a quick look at the back of Percy's head, and you thought that man was him?''

''Something like that,'' he grumbled, not liking the way this was going.

To his immense relief, she laughed.

''Hey, we may have been kidnapped by clowns, but there was nothing funny about them,'' he protested mildly.

''I'm laughing,'' she said a little breathlessly, ''because I've been doing the same thing all week. Every time I see red hair, I start playing P.I. At the supermarket I stalked one poor man from the produce department to the checkout counter just to make sure he wasn't stalking me. He must have thought I was coming on to him. He streaked out the door like his pants were on fire—right into a car where his wife and three kids were waiting.''

"I never thought about Percy being married," Nick said.

"Believe me, the man with the cone was not our kidnapper. Percy's probably hiding out until the heat is off."

"The heat is off? You've been watching too many old cops and robbers shows," he said with a laugh. "Want something to drink?"

"I'd love a lemonade, then I have to…"

"Don't say go. We haven't seen the spiders yet."

"Yuck!"

"You're afraid of them?"

He put his arm across her shoulders, but she shrugged it off.

"Not when they're behind glass, but maybe we should go over everything we told the police instead. See if we left out anything. That is why we came here," she reminded him.

"I told them Harold had a funny voice. He snorted between sentences. Did you notice that?"

He took her hand again, and she didn't pull away.

"The police weren't impressed by my description. I said if every human had an animal spirit, his was a pig."

"I've heard pigs are smart animals," Nick said, "which eliminates Harold. I compared him to a wrestler gone to seed, only not smart enough to learn the moves. Bulk without brain."

"They'll probably catch him eventually because he's a klutz. It's Percy who worries me."

"I'm more concerned about their mysterious boss," Nick said glumly.

"You know, I'm tired of thinking about all of them," she said. "Let's—"

She stopped and let a dozen or so Cubs flow around them on either side.

"Look behind you to the right, but be sneaky about it!" she whispered. "Red hair."

His stomach lurched. They could joke about phantom redheads, but he was sure Percy could still be a threat.

"Walk slowly and don't look behind you," he whispered back.

They were headed toward the exit and the old casino. If the redhead with his back turned to them was Percy, he'd probably follow them to a place not overrun by kids.

"I think I can recognize his voice if I hear it," Stacy said in a hushed voice.

"Is he following? Don't look!"

"I'll pretend to drop something and look back between my legs."

There was a trick he'd like to see her pull off. In fact, he'd like to watch any antic involving her gorgeous legs, bare today from midthigh to ankle.

"He has his nose buried in a zoo map. Maybe he thinks we've spotted him, and he's using it as a cover." With Stacy doubled over, and her shorts pulled tight over her sensational butt, it was all Nick could do not to...

"Nick! He must have spotted me looking at him. He's trying to get away!"

She straightened and grabbed his hand. "Let's get him!"

Right ahead of them, two harried-looking Cub Scout mothers were trying to gather stragglers into a big pack of shuffling, wrestling, yelling boys. They blocked the entire walkway, and the only way to get past them was through the middle. That's what the mysterious man did, and they followed.

Nick's workshirt sleeves were rolled above his elbow, so clothing didn't help when he connected with something cold and wet. Stacy fared even worse in their push through the unruly boys. She tripped over a rubber snake one of the hellions was trying to wrap around her ankle.

"Get out of my way, or I'll make you eat that fake reptile!" she threatened in an ominous voice too low for the chaperones to hear.

"I think you'd do it, too," Nick whispered as they broke free of the mob.

"Are you kidding? I hate snakes. I wouldn't even touch a rubber one."

"The kid believed you. He was so scared, he probably wet his pants."

"Don't be silly."

She grabbed his arm then quickly dropped it.

"You're covered with pink stuff!" She held up sticky fingers.

"Stuck my elbow in an ice-cream cone."

"More ice cream! It's our day for it."

She laughed while he tried to wipe it off on the edge of his shirt without slowing his pace.

"As long as your shirt is sticky anyway..."

She reached for the tail he'd pulled out from under his belted jeans.

"Be my guest. I love being used as a towel."

The backs of her fingers rubbed against the bare skin above his waist, and he nearly forgot they were in hot pursuit of a man who could be Percy.

"There he is! I can see him!" she cried out excitedly.

"Let's get him!"

Grabbing her hand, he raced toward a red-haired figure in dingy jeans, workboots, and a plaid shirt hanging out of his pants and rolled above the elbows much as Nick's was.

"Stop there, Percy!" Nick shouted grabbing the guy's shoulder.

It was a surprisingly slim shoulder.

Stacy stepped in front of their prey and gasped.

"Whoops!"

"Are you people crazy?"

The voice was shrill but very, very feminine. Nick let go while Stacy launched into a breathless explanation to the woman they'd all but tackled.

"Your hair is cut so short we thought you were a man—an acquaintance of ours—and we are so sorry," she blurted out. "Please, please, please, forgive us. Believe me, my fiancé doesn't go around accosting strange women. He is absolutely harmless, and we're both terribly sorry."

"Your fiancé?" she asked angrily.

Stacy held up the ring Nick hadn't given her. It was an impressive rock, and it did distract the woman.

"Maybe you'd better keep him on a leash," she said as Nick mumbled his own apologies. "Now, if you don't mind, I'm short two Cubs, and our bus is waiting."

"Oh, wow," Stacy said when the woman walked away. "I was afraid she'd scream for the police."

"Your fiancé?" Her explanation had shaken him up more than grabbing a strange woman had.

"I didn't want her to think you were just a garden-variety molester. Women never believe anything bad about a guy who gives away a diamond."

''Very clever,'' he said dryly, trying to sound cool and disinterested.

The shock of being called her fiancé nearly knocked him over. He was still shaky, and hot blood was pooling in sensitive areas. Was this why guys took the plunge?

STACY HATED Friday-afternoon traffic. That was the main reason she'd agreed to leave her car in a lot in Elm Park and ride to the Belle Isle bridge and zoo with Nick. Now, even though it was slow going on the expressway, she regretted it. The outing had been a disaster, and she shouldn't be sitting so close to a man who wasn't her fiancé.

''You should have seen your face when you saw we'd caught a woman,'' she said, because silence between them was not good, not good at all. Casual friends chatted. They didn't sit in gloomy silence with secret thoughts.

''Glad you enjoyed it. I felt like an idiot.''

''It was my fault, too. Funny how we saw red hair everywhere.''

''Probably because Percy was on our minds.''

She wished! How could she worry about a kidnapper when Nick was by her side, his soft brown hair tousled by the breeze that swept over the island from the Detroit River? How could she ignore his sun-bronzed forearm and the way his hand curled around hers? His dark brown eyes made her spine tingle, and his strong, square-jawed face was the stuff of erotic dreams. Good thing they were only fellow adventurers, pals, casual acquaintances.

''Your family is right about being cautious,'' he said.

"I know. Now that it's over, though, the whole thing doesn't seem real."

They didn't talk much on the way to where her car was parked. She felt safe with him, protected in a way her family couldn't provide. Their well-intentioned hovering had gone beyond concern and become an annoyance.

Nick understood the sudden shock of being abducted. He was doing a positive thing in looking out for redheaded men. He didn't make her feel smothered.

Of course, Jonathan had been very supportive. He didn't understand the trauma of being kidnapped, but he was willing to walk down Lake Shore Drive on his hands if it would keep her safe. She smiled to herself remembering how cute her fiancé was. When he wanted to come to her place and make out, he'd invent little excuses and show up with a florist's box or a bouquet from his Grosse Pointe garden.

When they first got engaged, they'd agreed to make their wedding night special by not having sex before then. But sometimes she wondered if that was a mistake. If they were…compatible in that area.

"There's your car, hubcaps and all," Nick said when he stopped his car a short distance from hers in the Elm Park lot behind a row of stores.

"Thanks, Nick. I had fun."

She opened the passenger door and slid out, leaning over once she was out of the car to say a few more words. "I hope you're not in trouble with your brother for skipping work."

"The last time Zack got physical, I was twelve years old. I spray painted girls' names all over his car. All he can do now is fire me, and I'm afraid Cole won't let him."

"Sounds like you have great brothers."

"I do, but sometimes they try to be my father."

"Well, bye…"

"I'm going to follow you home."

"Why?"

"Just to make sure you get there okay," he quickly said.

"Nick, I really don't need a bodyguard. How many redheads do you think I'll see between here and home?"

"Indulge me. I know I'm going overboard on this, but once I see you inside, I'm history."

"You're going to follow me even if I tell you not to, aren't you?" She grinned.

"Yep."

He gave her a smile that scored too far south for comfort.

"Maybe I should follow you home," she said. "Redheads come in both genders."

"I'm well aware of that, sweetheart."

Okay, so maybe he was doing a Cary Grant impression, but the endearment was too much. She slammed his door and hurried over to her own car before she admitted the butterflies in her stomach weren't from anxiety.

7

HE WAS ONLY following her home to be sure she got there safely.

By the time Nick pulled into the parking area behind Stacy's apartment, he almost believed that whopper himself. Then he remembered how it felt to have her hand tucked into his, her soft fingers entwined with his.

Darn those kidnappers! If they'd been a little more efficient, he might have spent days, even weeks, in the little shack with Stacy.

He was losing it! He liked women—always had—but he didn't come on to other guys' fiancées. Didn't need to. Give him a phone, and he'd have a date in five minutes.

Stacy parked a dozen or so spots from the back entrance of her complex. He pulled in beside her ignoring the Residents Only sign and got out of his car. He wouldn't be long. Once he checked out the security in her building, he'd get out of her life.

"You can't park there," she warned, confronting him with the hood of her car between them.

"I won't be here long, just long enough to check out your apartment."

"There are no red-haired men under my bed."

"Indulge my boyish whim." He flashed what he hoped was a winning smile.

"There is nothing boyish about you."

He knew that, but was glad to hear her admit it.

"One quick look, and I'm history," he promised, walking to the entrance with her.

"Residents have to open the door with a key," she said, using hers.

"What about visitors?"

"We can buzz them in."

"So if your neighbor lets someone in, they can end up at your door?"

"I suppose. It's never happened."

"No elevator?" he asked when they entered the rear lobby.

"By the front entrance, but the stairs are quicker. I only live on the second floor."

The steps were open. No one could hide under them and not be seen. He followed her up a short flight to a landing, then up to the second-floor corridor, noticing for the first time that her waist was small enough to span with his hands.

"Assuming Percy or some other low-life could talk a neighbor into letting him into the building, would you open your door for him?" he asked.

"Be serious!" She was beginning to sound really annoyed.

"How about a florist? Would you refuse delivery of flowers?"

"I'd tell him—or her—to leave them outside my door. I can hear whether the person goes back down the stairs."

"Good."

"And my dad talked the landlord into letting him have a second lock installed. It's all I can do to get into the place myself now."

She made slow work of unlocking the door. He knew

he was pushing it, but he followed her inside and closed the door behind him.

"Cute place."

He meant it. The room was light and uncluttered, just the way he liked his space.

"Thanks. The bedroom and bathroom are through that door. You can see the kitchenette. That's all there is. Now you really should go."

"Don't you want me to look under your bed or check the shower?" He was kidding, but couldn't help worrying about her.

"The place was locked up like a fortress!"

"There's the sliding-glass door." He pointed at a tiny plant-filled balcony.

"I keep a stick there so no one can slide it open from the outside. My father insisted even before the kidnapping."

"Good," he said again.

She didn't need or want his approval, and he was running out of excuses to stay near her. He didn't like making a nuisance of himself. In fact, this was an entirely new situation in his experience with women, but the prospect of leaving her appealed like ripping off adhesive tape from his neck to his knees.

"I guess you have a date with Mercer tonight," he said.

"Nothing definite."

He caught her glancing toward a phone on the kitchen counter. Her answering machine wasn't blinking.

"We're playing tennis at his club tomorrow morning," she hastily added. "Jonathan has me signed up for a lesson, then he'll go over the finer points with me."

Nick just bet he would. From what he could see of Stacy's finer points, no normal man could keep his hands off.

"I guess we told the police all we could," he said, returning to a more comfortable topic.

"Guess so."

"Thanks for coming to the zoo with me."

"I enjoyed it. Thank you for asking me."

When she smiled, her face was radiant. Even flushed from the sun with no visible makeup, she had a fresh beauty that made his heartbeat erratic and his palms damp.

He started toward the door with leaden feet. After all they'd been through, their parting called for some kind of gesture.

She moved when he did, and the friendly peck he'd aimed at her cheek landed squarely on her lips.

Bodies not quite touching, arms at their sides, their lips still collided with an impact that took his breath away. He brushed her lips with his again.

Instead of resisting, she kissed him back. Emphatically.

The chemistry between them nearly floored him, and he couldn't stop himself from wrapping his arms around her and covering her mouth with his.

He could feel a tremor in her shoulders. She wrapped her arms around his waist and moaned softly, welcoming his next kiss with parted lips.

He sensed inexperience, hesitation and white-hot need, a combination so volatile he couldn't think straight. He'd wanted her in his arms since she first walked into the wedding shop, and he was scared silly it was more than hormonal.

"We shouldn't..." she murmured.

"No," he agreed, but it wasn't in him to push her out of his arms.

"Just the excitement—chasing redheads."

She kissed him so hungrily he felt light-headed.

"Danger is a powerful turn-on."

He didn't believe it, but he'd swear the sky was red to keep her where she was.

Nick was sure of one thing. Jonathan wasn't keeping his fiancée happy. Nick should have been delighted, but he felt terrible for Stacy. He wanted to show her what passion was, but he couldn't without hurting her. Her kisses made him feel guilty. Imagine how she'd hate herself if he let this go on.

One more kiss, a memento…

Her lips were soft and swollen under his, and he had to lock his hands together behind her back to keep from touching her the way he wanted to.

Her phone rang, shrill, loud, and invasive.

"I should answer that." She slipped out of his grasp, raced for the phone, and made an heroic effort to make her voice sound normal when she picked up the receiver.

"Jonathan, I just got home."

Nick heard a harsh, barking response, but not the words.

"I am breathless," she said. "I was outside on the stairway when I heard your first ring."

If Mercer believed she could open two locks in three rings, he was an even bigger idiot than Nick thought.

"Darling, I'll need at least an hour to get ready. No, make that an hour and a half," she said.

They negotiated a time for their date, and Nick told himself he should leave.

"I can hardly wait to see you, too," Stacy cooed into the receiver.

The hell of it was, Nick believed she meant it.

She hung up, and he felt frozen to the spot.

"I'm so embarrassed." She didn't look at him.

"Don't." He tried to sound kind, but his voice was hoarse with disappointment.

"Please, never kiss me again."

He nodded. She read the promise she wanted in his silence.

"That was terrible of me—it's all my fault. I don't know what got into me. I am so sorry, Nick."

"Don't beat yourself up. Chemistry happens."

"I don't think we'd better see each other again."

"I didn't intend to see you today. It was an accidental meeting." He had to resist touching her flushed cheeks.

There was nothing accidental about the way she'd clung to him and kissed him. And kissed him. He knew foreplay when it hit him like a ton of bricks, but he wasn't sure she did.

"It was all my fault," she went on, running her hands through her mussed hair. "I'm really sorry. I've never been a tease."

She called it teasing! He called it torture. Did she think he was made of stone?

"Well, have a nice date," he said.

He wanted to say have a nice life, but he didn't have it in him to be sarcastic to Stacy. They never should've met. He wished they hadn't. But one thing was damn sure. It was time he was out of there.

STACY LIMPED into the preschool Monday morning, her ankle still wrapped from a trip to the emergency room.

The sprain wasn't serious, but her reason for stumbling was. Jonathan had been teaching her to charge the net after her tennis lesson, but her mind hadn't been on the game.

The fact that Jonathan had been so darn sweet the rest of the weekend, waiting on her and indulging her every whim, only made her feel more guilty. She couldn't count the number of times she missed the ball, or hit it out of bounds, all because she couldn't get Nick out of her mind.

"You should take the day off," Tanya, her boss and good friend at the learning center, said. "I can call Granny Beth to substitute."

"The kids run her ragged," Stacy said.

"That's true, but she's good at reading to them."

"Really, I'm fine. I want to be here."

Before Tanya could insist, she spotted a child getting into mischief.

"Randy, the vacuum cleaner isn't a toy. That's why we keep it in the supply room. Why don't you play with the fire engine?"

Tanya raced over to intercept the little boy who lived to take apart vacuums. The center's director was dark-haired, slender and sophisticated, but she had a gift with kids and taught Stacy something new every day.

Stacy loved being here, adored the kids and counted herself extremely lucky to work for Tanya. Even though her boss was nearly fifteen years older with a husband and two girls in middle school, Stacy enjoyed her company immensely. She missed their weekend junkets to flea markets and country auctions now that tennis lessons occupied her Saturdays.

"You can stay in when the kids go out," Tanya called over to her. "I need someone to count out Popsicle sticks and pom-poms for our afternoon project. Use the berry baskets in the bottom of the craft cupboard.''

A half hour later Stacy was doing shapes and colors when she was so startled she nearly fell off her little chair. She'd just gotten Kaitlin to identify a blue circle for the first time when she looked up at a pair of muscular thighs packed into faded jeans standing next to her.

''Nick!''

''Can I talk to you?''

''Not now! I'm doing shapes and colors.'' She tried to go on with the activity, holding up a piece of colored cardboard. ''Colin, can you tell me what shape and color this is?''

''I already told you it's a blue circle,'' Kaitlin said, her ponytail bobbling in annoyance.

''Of course, and you did a great job, Kaitlin. I meant to hold up this one, Colin.'' She picked up a red triangle.

''It's red.''

''What shape?''

''Kaitlin pushed me.''

''Kaitlin, do you need a time-out?'' That question belonged in a book of dumb things teachers say. The precocious four-year-old would challenge a lion tamer.

''You can see I'm busy,'' Stacy said beseechingly to Nick, exaggerating the behavioral crisis which, in fact, was business as usual.

''Are you going to kiss Miss Stacy?'' Kaitlin asked looking up wide-eyed at Nick.

''No, he is not!'' Stacy hastily assured her.

''Not that it isn't a good idea, Kaitlin.'' Nick grinned.

She'd never been so glad to hear the signal for recess. The three-year-olds were tramping into their separate room, and Debi, the youngest of the four women who worked with the four-year-olds, was energetically ringing the bell to line up for outdoor play.

"I have to go outside," Stacy told Nick.

"Don't even think of it," Tanya called over to her. "You have craft baskets to get ready."

"What happened to your ankle?" Nick asked as she limped into the supply room to get what she needed.

"I sprained it."

He was wearing a black T-shirt that made him look even sexier—and more dangerous—than usual.

"The tennis lesson?"

"Not exactly."

"Mercer's instructions on the finer points of the game?"

"Why are you here, Nick?"

"Did you play show-and-tell with your fiancé and tell him how we locked lips?"

"How can you be so—so..."

"Crass, crude, unfeeling?"

"Facetious." Darned if she'd use one of his words.

She picked up a stack of plastic berry baskets and the supplies she was supposed to count out. Carrying them to one of the low tables in the main room, she sat on one of the kid's chairs to do her job.

"About last Friday," he began, towering over her so all she saw was his knees.

She was used to little chairs, but she'd like to see him try to sit on one.

"If you must talk to me, at least get down to my level."

"Okay, I will."

He cautiously lowered his rear and managed to plant it on one of the hard plastic seats so he was facing her and the window overlooking the playground.

"Playground stuff has changed a lot since my day," he said, looking beyond her at the sturdy, bright-colored outdoor equipment.

"You didn't come here to discuss tube slides and swings," she said, having a hard time counting sticks with him watching.

"How do you sit on these chairs?" He wiggled to demonstrate how uncomfortable he was but stayed put.

"Nick, don't you ever go to work?"

"I always do—usually. I'm on my way to pick up some stuff at a building supply place."

She dumped a bag of fluffy little yellow-and-green pom-poms on the table, but her fingers wouldn't co-operate in separating them to count, not with Nick's dark, unreadable eyes scanning her every move.

"I only need to know one thing." His voice was so serious it gave her chills. "Was that some kind of prewedding test?"

"I don't know what you mean." She was afraid she did. Would this recess last forever?

"Kissing me. Were you trying to find out if you'd be missing anything by getting married?"

"I've kissed men before!" No way would she tell him how few. "Anyway, you kissed me first."

"And I deserved to have my face slapped."

"I wouldn't do that." She also couldn't look him in the eyes, which made for a very uncomfortable con-versation.

"Why kiss me back the way you did?"

He was relentless. If Kaitlin were older, they'd de-serve each other.

"I don't know."

That was at least partially true. She was too confused to understand her own motives. She'd loved Jonathan when she agreed to marry him. She was pretty sure she still did, but Nick was unlike anyone she'd ever known. She couldn't stop thinking about him.

"It wasn't just a test?" he pressed.

"No! Maybe it was the excitement. Chasing possible suspects. All the sugar in the ice cream. The aquarium."

"Can't beat a tank of electric eels for a romantic atmosphere."

"You know what I mean!"

"I still don't know if you were kissing me or just experimenting."

"I don't experiment! I haven't even done it with Jonathan!" she cried out, her temper flaring.

Oh, boy! She immediately wanted to take that back. She felt guilty enough without betraying her relationship with Jonathan.

Nick raised one eyebrow and looked so skeptical she *did* want to slap him.

"Never?"

"My fiancé is a gentleman. Our honeymoon will be so special…"

"No one, ever?"

Her face felt hot enough to singe her fingertips. She wanted to run out and hide in one of the kids' sliding tubes.

"You act like I'm a freak or something!" She was also as close to tears as she'd been in ages.

"Mercer must be made of dry ice! I'd go nuts if I couldn't make love to you—if you were my fiancée."

"I can't talk about this!"

Trouble was, she already had. Did Nick pity her? He certainly had an odd expression. Or maybe he thought she was cold and unfeeling. She didn't know which was worse.

"The children will be coming inside soon. I can't talk anymore."

"I have to get back to the site. We're finishing a new bank on Davis Road at Twenty Mile. But I don't want to leave things hanging between us."

"Nothing is hanging!"

He stood, knocking the little chair aside, and she wished she hadn't said those exact words. She couldn't let herself think about how well-hung this man appeared to be—not that she'd studied the evidence. All in all, she seemed to have foot-in-the-mouth disease.

"We can't see each other anymore," she insisted.

"We're not seeing each other now."

"You know what I mean!"

"That's the trouble! I don't. The message I got when you kissed me contradicts the happily-ever-after scenario you're planning with Mercer. Or did you use me like a cat uses a scratching pole?"

"Can't you accept a spontaneous gesture of gratitude?"

"Gratitude? Was that your idea of gratitude? I had lip burn all weekend. Gratitude is a handshake or a pat on the head."

"I don't know why you're making such a big deal of this. Don't tell me you've never been kissed!"

He sat on the edge of the table and leaned within inches of her face.

"I've never been kissed that way without ending up in bed. That's why I want to know what your game is."

"I don't have a game!" She tried to look beyond him to see if the children were ready to come inside, but there was no help there.

"No, you have a fiancé! So why so hot with me?"

"You're accusing me of being a tease, and I'm not!"

She'd asked herself the same question a thousand times since Friday, but there wasn't any answer. She wanted to marry Jonathan. He'd be a kind, loving, thoughtful husband, and she didn't doubt she loved him.

It wasn't fair that Nick made her feel the way she did at the moment. Maybe she was genetically weak, oversexed without realizing it. Or she could just be awestruck by his big muscles and aggressive masculinity.

He had saved her on the island. Add gratitude to the mix, and she couldn't help responding to him. It was only temporary insanity.

"You did kiss me first," she said, knowing it sounded like an alibi.

"I planned a peck on the cheek. You moved."

"Oh." That made her overly enthusiastic response even worse. "Well, I won't be ambiguous anymore. I'm going to marry Jonathan because I want to be his wife. I'm sorry if I made you doubt it."

She sounded uncomfortably like Aunt Lucille when she got her dander up.

"Okay."

He said it blandly, matter-of-factly, as if it didn't matter one way or the other.

"I won't be seeing you around then." He walked out without another word.

8

NICK WAS SO INTENT on installing a saw blade, he didn't even look up when Zack came into the unfinished main lobby of the new suburban bank. One thing Nick did a whole lot better than the twins was keep their tools in good shape.

"You've got company."

Nick could tell his brother was smirking without looking up.

"Send him in."

"Her. She wants you to come out."

He stood wondering if this was one of Zack's practical jokes. No, probably not, since Nick was still on the clock. Now that his brother was happily married, he took the business a lot more seriously.

"I wouldn't keep this one waiting," Zack warned, grinning as he left.

The spring mud had baked into deep furrows under the hot June sun, and Stacy picked her way carefully toward Nick the moment he came out. He froze, surprised to see her after the big brush-off she'd given him that morning.

"I bet that's your brother," she said, nodding at Zack as he retreated into the trailer that served as an on-site office. "His hair is darker, but I can see a family resemblance."

"You're imagining it. We're half brothers. I look like my dad."

He wasn't pleased to see her. It was going to be hard enough forgetting her without little surprise visits.

"Why are you here?" he asked.

He kept his distance, not trusting himself to keep his hands off her.

"We really shouldn't see each other again." She fiddled with the belt on the khaki walking shorts she'd worn that morning, and didn't meet his eyes.

"You found out where I was working and drove all the way out here to tell me again we shouldn't see each other? You have a funny way of hammering home your point."

"You mentioned you were building a bank here."

"Did I?" he said.

She blushed and avoided meeting his gaze.

"I feel bad about the way things ended this morning. I didn't intend to be cranky. I'm so grateful for the way you came to my rescue."

"Before or after I got conked with a six-pack?" he said jokingly.

"The whole time. It would have been much, much scarier without you."

He folded his arms across his chest waiting to hear where this was going.

"I didn't even ask about your head. Did you get checked by a doctor?"

"I'm fine."

"Even though we can't see each other again, I don't want you to think I didn't appreciate what you did," she said.

"You want my good opinion?" *But you don't want me,* he added to himself.

"Yes." She didn't sound very sure.

"Do you have a minute to talk?"

One of the plumbers came out of the building and gave Stacy an X-rated look. Good thing she wasn't his girlfriend. He'd have to do something about a leer like that.

"I should leave," she said.

"It took you what, half an hour to get here? I won't take much more of your time."

A couple of carpenters strolled out, their voices loud and joking until they saw Stacy.

"It's quitting time. Let's go sit in my car where it's not so public."

"Public is fine," she quickly said.

"Well, at least let's sit. You're still hobbling on that ankle."

He glanced toward the trailer but rejected it. Zack and Cole were both inside.

"Over here," he said, walking to a stack of lumber covered by a tarp. "You can sit here, but the car would be more comfortable."

"No, this is fine." She gingerly perched on the none-too-clean waterproof covering.

He'd been stewing all day about never seeing her again, but he'd rather wear a Kick Me sign than let her know it.

"Just because we got a little carried away doesn't mean we can't compromise," he said.

She was remembering their kisses. He could see it in her body language as she squirmed uncomfortably on the sharp-edged stack of two-by-fours.

"Why can't we just be friends?" he asked.

"Friends?"

Was that relief on her face?

"If we stay on friendly terms, it will be a lot less awkward if we meet by accident," he explained.

"Meet by accident?"

He knew how improbable that was in the huge metropolitan sprawl, but he wasn't ready to let her disappear from his life, not while her kisses were still branded on his mouth.

"There could be a police lineup and a trial," he said. "We'd have to meet then."

"I guess so."

"Hey, you and my mom are both brides-to-be with gimpy ankles. We met once at a wedding shop. We could do it again. Or maybe at a florist's or..." He shrugged.

Where else did brides congregate? He was pretty sure his superefficient mother had taken care of everything by now even though her wedding wasn't until fall.

"We could even meet at a party," he suggested. "My grandfather gets invited to the same places as the Mercers. He's a regular social butterfly. Sometimes I go along for kicks." Considering the situation, he forgave himself a slight distortion of the truth.

"Jonathan goes to a lot of parties, too. His law firm is giving us a prewedding party the first Saturday in July. But I don't suppose your grandfather is one of their clients."

"Could be. He's a pit bull with attitude when it comes to protecting his company's patents. He probably knows every Wayne County lawyer who's passed the bar in the last fifty years."

He was exaggerating Marsh's penchant for litigation, but at least she seemed to be giving his proposition serious thought.

Nick planted one heavy workboot on the stack of lumber and leaned close.

"Why can't men and women be friends, especially after what we went through together?"

"Friendship doesn't mean there's anything else between us," she said thoughtfully.

"I think we're already friends." He smiled, not quite believing how important another man's fiancée was to him.

"You're right. We should be friends after what we went through."

She offered her slender hand, and he took it, not even thinking about the oil from the saw.

"Sorry," he said when she pulled her hand away with a greasy black smear on the palm. "Here, wipe it on my jeans. Nothing can hurt them."

He took her hand and rubbed it on the denim covering his thigh. Bad idea! Her hand came clean at no small cost to him.

He turned his back hoping she wouldn't notice he was hot-wired and breathing hard. Part of him was elated, but being just friends would only work if they kept a mountain range between them.

"Guess I'd better go, friend," she said.

"I'll walk you to your car. Friends do that."

Friends could not hold hands, however, and they walked to her vehicle with two feet between them.

Once she was inside, he automatically checked to make sure her doors were locked.

"I'm glad you came," he said through her open window. "Silly for us not to be friends."

If he used that word one more time, he'd choke.

"You're a very nice person." She smiled with enough heat to melt glass.

"Yeah, I'm a prince," he said sourly as he watched her drive away.

No one tailed her, but he wouldn't feel easy until Percy and Harold were behind bars. He didn't for a minute doubt they'd point the finger at the brains behind the kidnapping, but how did a pair of bunglers like them avoid the police this long? Was it possible they'd never been in trouble with the law before?

The kidnapping had been a fiasco, but why grab Stacy? Sure, she was going to marry a wealthy man, but he couldn't see Percy reading the leisure section of the newspaper looking for brides-to-be with kidnapping potential. Their whole plan had been sloppy and purposeless.

He waved at Zack who was driving away in his pickup. Nick needed to talk this out with someone, and Cole was alone in the trailer.

"Pretty girl," Cole said when Nick walked in. "Isn't she the one who was kidnapped with you?"

The older of the fraternal twins by a few minutes, Cole got the best deal on looks. Once he'd been up to his ears in women, but he'd taken to marriage and fatherhood like a fish to water. Nick couldn't imagine being tied down the way both his brothers were now, but he did wonder what Cole thought about Stacy.

"Yeah, she's also the one who's going to marry Jonathan Mercer."

"We met him when you were missing, unfortunately."

"He's a colossal jerk."

"But he's not your problem, is he?"

Cole gave him a big-brother look, and Nick changed his mind about a heart-to-heart. What could he say? He didn't want to admit, even to himself, that he couldn't stop thinking about someone else's fiancée. Anyway, he already knew what Cole's advice would be: Forget her.

Now that they were friends, he wondered if Stacy's and his paths would ever cross.

By THE END of the week, he knew he had to see Stacy again even if she told him to get lost. He couldn't get her out of his mind and didn't know what to do about it. If Mercer was right for her, why all the snap, crackle and sizzle when Nick was with her?

He didn't trust Mercer to keep her safe, either. Was Nick the only one who thought there was something fishy about a couple of unarmed clowns dragging her off to a fishing shack that didn't exist on the tax rolls? According to a police buddy, whoever owned it had been a squatter on land the state owned.

Even if Stacy wasn't in danger anymore, he couldn't get her out of his mind. Too bad they didn't live in a place like Cairo where he could accidentally bump into her until he was sure there was no stopping the wedding.

He was home shuffling through his usual quota of junk mail after work on Friday when a thick square envelope slid out from between the pages of a supermarket flyer. For an awful moment he thought Stacy might be inviting him to her wedding, but it came from an old high-school buddy he hadn't seen in ages. Bachelors tended to be on a lot of lists, especially when most of the bridesmaids were unmarried.

The invitation wasn't important, but the idea it gave him was. He could accidentally bump into Stacy, even in the metropolitan area, because he knew where she'd be. Mercer's law firm was giving a big bash for the happy couple, and he knew the man who could track it down.

A couple of hours later he'd showered, shaved and put on tan dress slacks with a conservative navy knit shirt. He needed a favor, and Marsh Bailey didn't take kindly to a grandson who looked like a bum.

The big Tudor-style house in Bloomfield Hills looked inviting, but Nick knew he wasn't high on his grandfather's approval list. Now that Cole and Zack were happily married and his mother was anticipating a wedding of her own, he was Marsh's main target for reform. But tonight he wanted help more than he wanted to avoid another lecture.

Nick parked in the driveway and walked around to the back where his grandfather had a well-equipped workshop in a separate building. When he wasn't working on a project at the factory, he could usually be found puttering in his home shop. Tonight was no exception.

"Hi, Gramps."

Marsh liked to be called by his first name, but would tolerate Grandfather. Nick had long refused to use either, and he wasn't going to curry favor by changing now. He'd gone as far as he could by shaving.

"What brings you here?" Marsh didn't waste time on niceties.

"I need your help."

"Figures. Don't the twins pay you enough to make ends meet?" He slid off the stool beside a bench cluttered with electrical parts.

"Not money."

In fact, Nick tended to be frugal like his accountant father had been. He'd invested most of his pay from the ore boat for his future and had never touched his inheritance from his dad.

"Not job advice, I bet. Any new prospects?"

Talking to his grandfather was like following a familiar script.

"You've done some business with Wheaton, Miner & Greene, haven't you?"

"They've handled a couple of matters for me," he said guardedly. "You need an attorney?"

"No, I want to go to a party they're giving for one of their associates, a prewedding party."

"I see."

Nick was the only grandson Marsh hadn't tried to maneuver into marriage. So far Nick had avoided his matrimonial machinations, but his grandfather had that look.

"Marriage helps a man settle down," he pontificated. "You need a solid career to support a wife."

Cole's wife owned a successful baby store. Zack's was a popular TV personality. But this wasn't the time to explain twenty-first century marriages to a man who thought he ruled his clan.

"You know everyone in Wayne and Oakland counties. I was pretty sure you could find out about the party."

"I can."

For the next three hours Nick helped his grandfather make some modifications on the house's security system. It wasn't the worst way to spend an evening, and Marsh didn't ask any questions about his party-crashing plan.

STACY WALKED through the public part of the upscale restaurant on Jonathan's arm to the private room where his firm was holding their party, hardly seeing the candle-lit tables with gleaming tablecloths. Her thoughts were anything but happy. She wouldn't be able to eat. No one would want to talk to her. It was eight o'clock now. How long would they have to stay?

Jonathan, looking particularly lawyer-like in a navy suit and conservative blue tie, smiled at her, but she could tell he was nervous, too. Would it hurt his career if his boss didn't like her? What if she didn't fit in with his co-workers?

She returned his smile. How bad could a three or four hour party be? She wasn't walking into a torture chamber.

Taking her hand from Jonathan's arm at the wide entrance to the party room, she smoothed her black sleeveless sheath and tried not to remember Aunt Lucille's caustic remark about how appropriate a funeral dress was for this event.

"Do all these people work for your firm?" she asked, bowled over by the large crowd of expensively dressed guests. "That looks like…"

"Sonny Hayes, the weatherman. We've handled a few matters for him, mostly divorces. Quite a few of our better clients are here. After all, a law firm is only as successful as the people who consult it. Would you like to meet an automobile czar?"

"Sure."

Lordy, lordy, lordy, she thought, drawing on Aunt Lucille's picturesque use of the language in her distress. Wasn't it enough Jonathan's co-workers might grill her like a hostile witness in court? Cross-examine her? Did she have to debut in high society at the same time?

"I should've worn my green dress," she whispered,

staring at the sea of black and navy suits and peacock-colored dresses.

"You're fine, silly goose. You're easily the most beautiful woman in the room."

She strongly doubted that. She'd gladly allow that honor to go to one of the women who'd paid dearly and suffered much for a face-lift.

As edgy as she was about the party, tonight Stacy had to talk to Jonathan about her job. She was determined to keep it, and he had to understand that before their wedding plans were final. But this wasn't the moment.

Jonathan started introducing her, and she began the difficult task of trying to put names and jobs with faces. One senior partner reminded her of a bored bulldog except his eyes were never still. Another was a round-faced, beardless Santa with tiny metal-frame glasses. The big gun in tax law had coal-black hair slicked down on his long skull and a sharp pointy nose.

Red-jacketed waiters with trays of champagne circulated tirelessly, and Stacy found herself clutching the stem of a goblet of bubbly. Jonathan finished one and took another before she could stop smiling at strangers long enough to taste hers.

Somewhere she lost him—or he lost her—but people kept coming up to her, rattling off names she'd never remember. Duty done, they would move on to more engrossing conversations.

"Hi, I'm Janice Carpenter, intellectual property law. I'm sure Jonathan has told you all kinds of terrible things about me, but they're only half-true."

Stacy was absolutely sure he'd never mentioned anyone with legs like a Vegas showgirl and flaming red hair piled high on her head.

"He's always very kind when he talks about his associates," Stacy said, trying not to play whatever game this woman had in mind.

"Sly devil, but then we both knew I put my career first. Jon wants a stay-at-home wife. What is it you do?"

"I'm a preschool teacher," Stacy said proudly.

"Oh, then I'm sure you won't mind giving up your little job."

Maybe it was nerves, maybe it was the woman's grating tone.

"My little job is teaching future adults to tell the truth, share and be kind to others. If my fellow professionals do their jobs well enough, it will severely cut into your business."

"Well!" Janice turned and huffed off. Scratch one potential new friend, Stacy thought. Jon? Even his parents called him Jonathan.

For the moment, no one else wanted to check her out, so she waylaid another redcoat, got rid of her champagne, and helped herself to a cracker with shrimp. She was in the process of swallowing when she saw a guest Jonathan couldn't possibly have invited.

"Nick!" She choked on the dry appetizer and had to eject it into a cocktail napkin.

She had three choices: run for cover, find Jonathan or confront Nick. It was a no-brainer. If Nick was there because of her, she would tell him…

What? The way her heart was pounding, he could probably hear it at thirty paces. She hurried toward him hoping no one would notice, not a vain hope since the party had deteriorated into a shoptalk session that had nothing to do with her wedding.

"What are you doing here?" she whispered.

Who knew he could look this spiffy? He was wearing a charcoal suit, dove-gray shirt, paisley tie in shades of burgundy and pink, and wingtips, shiny black wingtips. He'd even had his hair tamed into trendy waves.

"Sipping champagne, scarfing down cheese puffs, the usual," he said.

"You know what I mean!"

"I'm just a friend who came to wish a friend well."

He said it so sincerely, she felt as if she'd known him forever. Maybe a day of being kidnapped together counted the way dog years did, seven times the equivalent of real time.

"But who invited you?"

"The firm represented my grandfather a couple of times. He finagled an oral invitation—sort of."

"You're crashing the party."

"Let's say, if it were a sit-down dinner, there wouldn't be a plate for me."

Waiters were hustling around a table at the far end of the large room setting up an elaborate buffet.

"You shouldn't be here," she said.

"You're in the wrong place, too. If you're going to dress for a funeral, at least show a little leg."

She instinctively looked at her hemline barely two inches above her knees. Okay, the dress was a little austere, but did he have to sound like Aunt Lucille?

"I wanted to look dignified."

She said it so primly, he laughed.

He was wearing an aftershave that teased her nostrils and made her inhale deeply. Must be her imagination, but the spicy musk made her want to rub against him like a cat in heat.

"Prewedding jitters." She said it aloud without meaning to.

"Well, one friend to another, I just wanted to wish you good luck," he said with a smile that warmed her cockles.

Why was she thinking like Aunt Lucille? Was it because she was the only one in the family who didn't like Jonathan? Whatever cockles were, she was pretty sure hers were red-hot.

He took the lumpy cocktail napkin out of her hand, discarded it along with his plate on a passing tray, and took her hand in his.

How could she have a platonic relationship with a man who made her think new and naughty things just by smiling at her? Happily, she didn't feel awkward around him, but she did feel lots of other things, attraction, desire, hot monkey love.

Where did that come from? Her mind was operating like a corn popper without a lid, spewing out all kinds of scorching ideas. From now on, she was going to do her best to concentrate on planning her wedding to Jonathan. Nick was the kind of guy she might have sighed over in high school, but now they were only friends—good friends.

She spotted her fiancé deep in conversation with a cluster of dark suits.

"Jon!"

He turned, but the surprise on his face told her he hadn't expected to see Stacy when he heard a shortened version of his name. Exactly how many women called him Jon? That was something they'd have to discuss after they settled her career future.

He was at her side instantly when he saw Nick.

She didn't know if the two men were going to speak

or spend the rest of the evening dueling with their eye-balls.

"Nick just stopped by to wish us good luck," she said.

"And represent my grandfather, Marsh Bailey. He's no stranger to your firm when it comes to patent litigation."

"Well, I hope you enjoy the party," Jonathan said with a strained smile.

"Very much. Well worth missing the ball game."

Sports was common language among men, the bond that never failed, but Jonathan wasn't going to get cozy with Nick.

"You haven't heard anything about the kidnappers, have you?" Nick asked, speaking to Jonathan but looking at her.

"No, nothing," he said. "Excuse us. I want to introduce my fiancée to a retired partner who's eager to meet her."

He steered her away, not releasing her elbow until several dozen people were between them and Nick.

"I hope you don't intend to invite him to our wedding," Jonathan said.

"I didn't invite him here. I'm grateful for the way he helped me through the kidnapping, but we're only friends."

"Men and women can't be friends," he said crossly.

The party seemed to flow around her as guests lined up at the buffet, loaded plates and found places at the round tables for ten scattered through the large room. Being lawyers, they'd probably make speeches, but for now the main business was culinary.

Jonathan drifted off again, and she found herself alone. When ignored, head for the little girls' room.

She made her way to the hallway outside the party room, looked around for the facilities, and collided with Nick.

"Leaving already?" She spoke without thinking, a little breathless from the surprise of running into him.

"I have some standards. I'll crash the appetizers, but I draw the line at the main course."

"Then your grandfather…"

"Just learned the time and place for me. Are you going to ask why?"

"Think I'd better pass on that one."

"I'm glad we're friends," he said warmly.

"Yes, so am I. Jonathan says men and women can't be friends but…"

He reached out, took her hand, and engulfed it with his. This wasn't exactly a private location, so it made her doubly uncomfortable when he caressed the sensitive side of her wrist with the ball of his thumb.

"I have to disagree with him on that. Friends are people you care about and wish well. I consider you a very good friend."

"I—you—consider, too."

She'd endured dozens of handshakes and a couple of unwanted hugs this evening, but none like this. Nick's touch radiated through her, clouding her mind and making her spine tingle. When he bent and touched his lips to her forehead, she was in big trouble. There was no way she could take it casually.

Then he was gone, leaving so abruptly she didn't have the presence of mind to call goodbye.

How could this happen to her? She was dizzy with desire, but it was Jonathan she planned to marry—wanted to marry.

"There you are, darling."

Jonathan came up behind her, shocking her back to reality. How much had he seen? Was there any way she could explain Nick?

She opted for saying nothing. Didn't all women conjure up imaginary romances with sexy hunks? It was only her libido kicking in, as well it might at the ripe old age of twenty-four.

She stood on tiptoe and planted a welcoming kiss squarely on Jonathan's lips. He looked startled, but didn't kiss her back. Of course, he wouldn't, not in sight of his whole firm.

"I'm very eager to have all this behind us and get to our wedding night," he said in an affectionate voice.

"We don't have to wait..." she began.

A woman with a face stretched taut by plastic surgery, a supershort pink suit and cherry red lipstick was bearing down on them, and Stacy never learned what Jonathan's reaction would be to her impulsive suggestion.

9

STACY WENT TO BED with Nick at night and woke up with him in the morning.

She'd always enjoyed an active fantasy life, but dreams about her island rescuer made her feel as guilty as if she'd really been unfaithful to Jonathan.

What could she do? She'd grown up daydreaming about a knight in silver armor who would carry her away on his great white stallion. Now, of course, she knew a medieval champion's personal hygiene practically guaranteed body odor and bad breath, but dreams died hard.

She had cold feet, that was the problem. She was focused on Nick, someone she hardly knew, because she had a severe case of silly-bride syndrome. Even in school, she did her most intense worrying when everything was going well. Straight A's in a class? Time to agonize over the final exam that could—but never did—spoil her perfect record.

Jonathan was kind and giving and considerate. They belonged together, and she was going to marry him if she ever decided on a wedding dress.

Today was the day, and she had an entourage to make sure she wasn't kidnapped or otherwise sidetracked in her quest for The Gown. With the wedding only six weeks away, her father had threatened to pick it out for her if she didn't make up her mind. When her easygoing sweetheart of a dad issued an ultimatum, even Aunt Lucille toed the line. She was little and tough with tight iron-gray curls and bright blue eyes. She didn't buckle under easily. Dad was probably the only one who could subdue Lucille.

So here she was in Belinda's Bridal Boutique with her mom, great-aunt and Jonathan.

"I still say it's bad luck for the groom to see the bride in her dress before the wedding," Aunt Lucille grumbled when she was momentarily alone with Stacy in the mirrored dressing room.

Stacy slithered into a bead-accented chiffon-and-crepe gown, and tried to figure out how to walk without tripping on the attached train.

"Now, I wouldn't vote that hunky hard hat off my island," the diminutive septuagenarian went on. "I knew he was good news when I saw his picture on the television."

"Shh," Stacy warned. "Jonathan will hear you, Aunt Lucille."

Given that her aunt's voice carried like a foghorn, he probably already had. It was no secret she thought Jonathan had the charm of a toad, but singing Nick's praises was one more tactic to "save" Stacy from a terrible fate.

"Do you like this one?" Stacy asked her aunt before she started itemizing the things she liked about a man she'd only seen on TV. In her aunt's opinion, Nick's number one asset was that he wasn't Jonathan.

"Too fussy." Aunt Lucille passed judgment on the wedding gown.

Stacy agreed, but she hadn't found anything as sweet and simple as the dress that had been ruined during the kidnapping.

"You're right," Stacy agreed, "but I have to wear something."

"You don't *have* to get married at all," Aunt Lucille muttered.

"Of course I do," Stacy teased. "What would you and Mom do with the thirty-dozen pink heart-shaped cream cheese mints in the freezer?"

Aunt Lucille snorted.

"How are you doing, darling?" Jonathan called from outside the dressing room.

"I'll be right out to show you," Stacy said.

"He'll like it," her aunt glumly predicted. "It's as pretentious as he is."

"Now behave!" Stacy scolded in a good-humored way.

Her aunt's animosity was no secret to Jonathan. He pretended to be amused and sometimes baited the older woman to get a reaction, but Stacy suspected he'd like to stuff her in a cage with her pet canaries.

"Your mother has a couple more picked out for you to try," he said, projecting his voice in a lawyerlike way to be sure he was heard behind the closed door.

It wasn't a bad thing to have a fiancé interested in the details of their wedding, Stacy told herself. Once Jonathan slipped the wedding band on her finger, she would forget all about Nick. They'd have a good life together. She'd always thought so, and a few last-minute jitters didn't change that.

She only wished— No, it wasn't fair to compare two men as different as Jonathan and Nick. Jon—she was trying to get used to calling him that—was restrained by their agreement not to sleep together until after the wedding, so naturally she didn't feel as close to him as she would later.

"Are you coming out, or do I have to come in?" Jonathan teased in a pseudomacho voice.

"Coming."

Aunt Lucille snorted again.

Stacy wanted to make a decision and be done with dress hunting. Jonathan was so busy at work they still hadn't had a serious conversation about her keeping her job after they were married. Right now, that was her priority.

IT WAS ANOTHER Thursday at the work site, and Stacy's wedding was three weeks from Saturday. Nick knew he didn't have one good reason to see her again, but damned if he could think about anything else.

Zack had him pushing a broom, cleaning up after the carpenters, and that was okay. He knew he was the low man in a dead-end job, but not because his brothers wouldn't welcome him into the business if he showed the slightest interest.

Hell, he enjoyed puttering around with Marsh more than he did working in the construction business. In fact, he'd dropped in on the old man at the plant a couple of evenings and helped him do some after-hours inventing. They were working on a mechanism for a plastic horse that actually walked.

Stripped to the waist in a pair of old khaki shorts, he still felt the humidity wrap around him like a blanket of steam. He bent to scoop up some chunks of wood and yelped in surprise. He'd sliced his thumb on a shard of metal discarded among the scraps.

Cole told him often enough to wear gloves, but he couldn't stand them in this heat. He examined the cut. It obviously needed a bandage to stop the bleeding.

He went to the trailer office, cranky and frustrated

because he couldn't think of one good reason to see Stacy. He could tell her there were still no leads on the kidnappers according to his old school buddy on the Elm Park police force, but no news wasn't news that justified a trip to see her.

The trailer was deserted, so he found some paper towels to wrap around his thumb. The absence of his brothers gave him an idea. He scribbled a note, thought of putting a bloody thumbprint on the paper, and decided that was overkill.

I put a piece of wood through my thumb. Went for first aid.

                                                    Nick

Who better to administer first aid than a preschool teacher?

WHEN HE GOT to Stacy's workplace, Nick pulled on the fairly fresh Red Wings T-shirt he kept in the car and stood watching her on the playground with the kids. How did she manage to chase after toddler terrorists and still look cool and fresh? He liked the short denim jumper she was wearing with a pink T-shirt. In fact, he liked everything about her except her wedding plans.

A few parents showed up to claim their kids, and Nick was content waiting unseen for the general exodus to finish. When most of her charges had left, he went inside to see Stacy.

When she saw him, she pursed her lips in a downright hostile frown, but not before he saw an instant of pure happiness on her face.

"Nick, what are you doing here?"

"I came to throw myself on your mercy."

"Bye-bye, Kitten. Don't forget to bring pictures of food tomorrow," she called out to the last departing child as she left with a curly-haired blond woman who was vaguely familiar.

"You can't drop in here any time you like," Stacy told him angrily. "That was Jonathan's sister! I met him here when he came to pick up Kitten."

"Kitten?"

"It's her baby name, short for Kristina. What are you doing here?"

"I was in the area."

Big lie. He'd fought his way across town through a million or so cars to see her.

"Like I believe that!" she protested.

"I needed someone to help me."

Small lie. He couldn't put a good bandage on his own thumb, could he? No need to mention anyone on the site could. He held it up for her sympathy.

"What is that?"

"Cut."

"I only kiss boo-boos if you're under five."

"My bad luck. You must know first aid. I was hoping you'd take care of it for me. I promise I won't cry if you hurt me."

"You want me to do it here?" She looked around at a couple of co-workers shuffling chairs and straightening toys.

"I also wanted to talk to you about something."

This was the biggest whopper of all. He didn't have a clue what he'd discuss with her.

"Oh, all right," she said, running her hand through her blond hair in frustration. "I'd rather we talked at my place than here. You can follow me home when I'm done. It's only a twenty-minute drive.''

''Thanks.''

He flashed the smile that had charmed a thousand coeds. She scowled and started stacking little chairs on the low tables.

ON THE WAY HOME, Stacy had never had a harder time keeping her mind on traffic. Nick was following her, and she didn't want to be alone with him. No, that wasn't true. She wanted it too much for her peace of mind.

When they got to her apartment, he parked in the Residents Only area. He'd be towed away if he stayed all night.

What was she thinking? He wasn't going to stay all night! She was near panic because she might not be able to say no if he really tried.

He got out of his car and waited for her with one foot on the raised curb of the walkway. He was wearing khaki shorts, and even his knees were cute! They were maybe a little bony like most men's were—well, not Jonathan's. His were rounder and plumper. But she could see herself painting happy faces on Nick's.

And where in blue blazes did that idea come from? Next she'd have fantasies about finger painting on his buns!

''How did you cut yourself?'' she asked, trying to normalize her thought processes.

''Cleaning up after the carpenters. My brothers hope I'll get tired of no-brainer jobs and try to learn the business.''

''Will you?''

''Nope.''

She unlocked the rear entrance and held it open for him.

"Go on up," she said, tossing him the keys. "I'm going to check my mailbox."

She wanted a minute to regroup her defenses, and she didn't need Nick checking out her backside as she went up the stairs. As it was, she felt as self-conscious as a nun at a stag party.

Stacy walked to the front lobby and realized she'd given Nick the box key along with the others. She pretended to unlock it to sort through a few bills and ads just to kill the amount of time it would take to really pick up her mail. Fortunately there was no one in the lobby to see her charade.

Nick was waiting in the open doorway of her apartment.

"Any mail?"

"Not today," she fibbed.

"Good thing, since I have your key."

He dangled her key ring, and she snatched it away, feeling as if she'd been caught with her hand somewhere naughty.

"I don't have many first-aid supplies," she warned, trying to pretend he was there because of a cut.

Whatever his real reason, she knew a lame excuse when she heard one.

"All women have bandages and stingy stuff."

"You've researched that?"

"Intimately."

He grinned broadly, but she refused to take the bait. Of course, Nick would have lots of experience with women, but she didn't want to know about it.

"Wash your hands at the kitchen sink. I'll get my supplies."

Actually she did have a pretty good first-aid kit, thanks to a course she took.

She heard water running and came back to find him drying his hands on a paper towel and grinning broadly.

"Can't remember the last time someone told me to wash my hands."

"You probably don't know many preschool teachers. We have the habit of command. Sit at the table, and I'll clean it."

"Do you promise to kiss it better if you hurt me?"

"Don't be silly."

She loved his silliness and his seriousness—and the sensual way he looked at her. It was enough to pop the buttons off her jumper.

Thumbs were tricky digits. They didn't lie flat, and his kept curling at the wrong angle. She really had no choice but to take his hand in hers and hold it still while she dabbed on an antiseptic.

His hands were work-roughened, but she loved his long, strong fingers and the warmth of his flesh on her palm. Touching him made it hard to remember the cut.

"If I hurt you, holler," she said, grimly tackling the bandaging job.

"You won't hurt me." He spoke in a low, seductive voice that made her hand unsteady.

"It's deep."

"So are you."

"I'm not really good at this."

"You're very good."

"If the gauze is too tight, I'll stop…"

"I never want you to stop holding my hand."

Oh… She'd never known the sunbaked scent of a man could be so disturbing.

He leaned closer to see how she was doing, and his forehead brushed hers. She could feel the tickle of his breath and sense the rhythmic pounding of his heart. Images swam in her head. She could see him stretched out naked on her sunny yellow sheets, his hair tousled and his lips swollen from...

Doing that which she'd never do with Nick!

This was not right. This was all wrong. Nick had to go home so she could marry Jonathan.

She slapped on a final strip of adhesive tape and stood up to put distance between them.

"Ouch!"

"I warned you." Her voice didn't sound quite normal.

"It's okay. You did fine. I'll bring you all my first-aid business."

"No, you won't." She tried to make her voice cold and decisive, but a little tremor betrayed her.

To her mixed dismay and delight, he leaned closer yet and brushed her lips with his.

"You shouldn't...shouldn't."

"Just a thank-you kiss."

"Please, Nick." She was trying to convince herself more than him. "If you really want to thank me, you'll leave."

"Before something happens we'll both regret?"

"Nothing is going to happen. You shouldn't have come here. You probably don't have anything important to say to me. You're confusing me, and it's not fair."

"What isn't fair? You marrying a stuffed shirt like Mercer?"

She wanted to be angry, but his face looked vulnerable, as though his strongly chiseled features had been softened by regret. The summer sun had lightened his rusty brown hair, but his eyes never seemed darker— or more compelling.

"You have no right to say that. We're very compatible."

"Compatible!" he scoffed and pursed his full, sensual lips.

"We had everything planned, our whole future, before I ever knew you." She was pacing, her running shoes thumping on the kitchen tiles.

"And now that you do know me?" He stood and blocked her nervous back-and-forth movement.

"Nothing has changed!"

Everything had changed, but she had to make Nick go before something really wrong happened. The terrible thing was, she was resisting her own impulses, not his.

"Cancel the wedding." He made it sound like an order, which made it easier to sound indignant.

"You can't say that to me!"

"As a friend, I can."

"A friend doesn't make a friend feel…"

He was so fast and so strong she didn't have to blame herself for what happened. He pulled her close and engulfed her in his arms. Before she could think of protesting, his lips came down on hers.

She closed her eyes and saw a kaleidoscope of colors. Her ears were ringing, and her toes lost contact with the floor. She clung to Nick's neck, and her mind went blank. Her breasts flattened against his muscular chest, and she could feel his arousal against her groin.

He cupped her bottom and held her tightly.

"I can't think of anything but you," he whispered

close to her ear, echoing the words floating in her own mind.

"I wish I'd met you sooner," she managed to say.

"It's not too late."

He scooped her in his arms and carried her into the bedroom. It was sunny and familiar with sunbonnets stenciled on her dresser and silhouettes of playing children on the walls, but it all seemed unreal.

"Nick! You have to put me down!"

The seriousness of what was happening came down on her in an avalanche of guilt, but the last thing she really wanted was to have him stop.

He laid her on the bed and sat on the edge, leaning toward her to fumble with the buttons on her jumper.

"They don't unbutton!"

"They're decorative."

He looked so puzzled she lost it and did the one thing that could break the spell.

She laughed.

And couldn't stop laughing.

He ran his hand up the inside of her thigh, but not even that delicious sensation could stifle her laughter.

"It's not that funny, Stacy. You're hysterical!"

"No, it's not funny at all." But she didn't stop laughing.

"You can't marry Mercer. This proves it."

"I have to! My mother bought a lace dress. The mints are in the freezer. My father insisted on taking out a second mortgage. You don't understand! Weddings can't be cancelled!"

"I do understand. You don't want to admit you were wrong to get engaged to a cold fish with an ego the size of the Grand Canyon."

He sounded so grim her eyes got teary.

"No, no, it's nothing to do with me anymore! Weddings have a life of their own. They swell up and grow. They get bigger and bigger, and there's no stopping them. My cousin is coming from Fairbanks. All the partners in Jonathan's firm will be there. The cake will use every granule of sugar in the city. I even have a wedding gown!"

The walls vibrated when Nick slammed the door on his way out.

HE'D BLOWN IT. He was so sure Mercer was bad news for Stacy, he'd tried to make her admit she'd rather be with him.

All he'd done was confuse her. She wasn't going to call off the wedding, and who could blame her? Mercer was a hotshot lawyer. If he got any splinters, they'd be in his butt from sitting around on courtroom benches pretending to earn his fees.

Nick never for a moment thought Stacy was mercenary, but all women liked security. They needed to know where their man was working and when he'd get home every night. The only thing Nick knew for sure about his future was that construction work wasn't for him, not even if he bought into his brothers' business and became a partner.

Hell, maybe he was only turned on because Stacy was off-limits. He'd never been interested in marriage, and nothing was safer than caring about a woman who was already committed to someone else.

He didn't need her. He could always find someone else. When was the last time a woman had turned him down? There'd been a brunette in the eighth grade whose parents wouldn't let her date and...

He couldn't remember any others, but he did know it was time to jump-start his social life.

The first thing he did when he got home was start making phone calls. In less than half an hour he had dates with three different women for Friday, Saturday and Sunday. And he was only warming up.

Friday night he had high hopes when he picked up Melissa, a girl he'd dated in high school. She was twenty-four now, and she'd been married and divorced twice, something he didn't know when he got her phone number from her mother. Playing the "remember when" game was fun the first five minutes, but it soon got old.

After listening to cute-kid stories about her two daughters until he started zoning out, he took her home at ten o'clock and didn't go inside for coffee.

Saturday he decided against another cozy dinner for two. Instead he took Tina, a waitress who made a point of serving him whenever he went to Ed's Diner for breakfast, to a stock car race. She didn't lack enthusiasm. She screamed herself hoarse and bounced up and down on the bleachers like a rubber beach ball.

He'd forgotten dating could be hard work. When he dropped her off at home, he didn't have enough energy left for a good-night kiss.

Anyway, she was no Stacy.

Things got worse Sunday. Ginger was a blind date. A friend set them up, and Nick owed him big time for it. A good swift kick wouldn't be payoff enough.

Ginger refused to wear a seat belt because she liked to sit close to get acquainted. Anyway, it made her panties ride up...her black lace panties.

When they drove home from a noisy time at the annual Italian festival on the waterfront, she tried to do some serious fondling. He had to drive one-handed most of the way to keep her contained.

She invited him into her place.

He declined.

Maybe he shouldn't have written the hot little number off so fast, Nick decided around 3:00 a.m. He'd been playing the lone wolf too long. Now instead of sleeping, he lay awake wide-eyed and agitated for the third night in a row. His dating spree had done nothing to get Stacy out of his head.

Somewhere he had to find a nice, available woman and do an overnight. He couldn't spend his whole life agonizing over the woman who would soon be Mrs. Stuffed Shirt.

Monday morning his eyes looked like the dark side of the moon. Zack got on his case, usually something Nick ignored, but his brother's quips were about as funny as toe fungus.

There was nothing more annoying than a reformed hell-raiser like Zack trying to sound parental and wise, unless it was a woman who wouldn't admit she was making a big mistake.

10

"MOM, I'M MOVING TO Grosse Pointe, not Australia," Stacy said on the phone, not that she could dissuade her mother from holding the big family dinner she'd scheduled for the following day. There was nothing Alice and Ray Moore liked better than rounding up all their chicks for a meal, unless it was knowing they'd have secure futures.

"Everyone's coming. It's a chance for all of us to have Sunday dinner one more time before your wedding. Three more weeks! I can hardly wait. I still can't decide whether to take up the hem on my dress an inch or so. Do you think I look good in that shade of beige?"

Stacy was leaning on her kitchen counter, phone propped up by her shoulder, working her way thought a stack of RSVPs. "Yes, you look great, Mom. Don't touch the hem. I like your dress better than mine."

This was true. She'd gone along with the consensus of her entourage rather than waste any more time shopping for a gown. Now she wasn't at all sure the lacy beaded bodice and billowing skirt were right for her.

"If you really think it's okay…"

Alice Moore usually had strong opinions and didn't need reassurance from her daughter. Unfortunately she was nervous about making a good impression on Jonathan's side of the family, but the queen of England would have a hard time upstaging Rebecca Mercer, Stacy's future mother-in-law.

"Did Kirk have any luck job hunting this week?" Stacy asked.

Better her mother should worry about a real problem instead of getting gray hair over her daughter's wedding. Her younger brother had lost his job as a fast-food manager two weeks ago and so far had no good prospects.

"He applied for a job in Saginaw. Saginaw! I'd hate to have him go so far away."

If it were up to Mom, the whole family would live on the same block.

"Maybe he'll find something closer."

They'd had the same conversation yesterday, and Stacy braced herself for the inevitable.

"I'm so happy my only daughter will be taken care of. Lawyers don't lose their jobs. You'll never have to worry about working yourself."

With five kids, Mom hadn't worked by choice. It was hard for her to understand that Stacy loved what she did. She didn't want to quit, but every time she brought the subject up, Jonathan said to wait and see.

"I like working."

Her mother chose not to hear her.

"Jonathan will make partner soon. You should be proud of him."

Was Jonathan a good lawyer? He was successful, she knew, but did he help people? Was what he did worthwhile or just profitable? Would he be offended if she asked?

"It's no fun watching every penny you spend," her mother warned.

Life with Nick would mean pinching pennies and living on hot dogs.

"Is it such a terrible thing when two people love each other?" she asked.

"You don't have to worry about that," her mother said happily. "You've made a good choice in Jonathan. Talk to you later."

Her mother hung up, and Stacy was glad her parents didn't have to worry about her future. It was under control. The last thing she wanted was to cause them distress. Still, she couldn't help but wonder what her family would think of Nick as a son-in-law. Aunt Lucille would like his directness...and his cute butt! His good humor would win over her brothers, but she doubted her parents would think of him as a good prospect. His grandfather owned Bailey Baby Products, but Nick worked as a laborer for his brothers. They wouldn't think he was steady and reliable like Jonathan.

Why was life so complicated? This was supposed to be the happiest time of her life. Tuesday her friends were giving her a big bridal shower. Friday her co-workers were taking her on a girls' night out. Her wedding was going to be perfect if only she could stop thinking about Nick.

NICK GLANCED at his watch when he got to the work site but didn't much care that he was late. His dating frenzy was taking its toll, and he wouldn't be surprised if his own brothers fired him.

So far no woman had appealed to him the way Stacy did, but he wasn't the man for her. What could he offer? He had a job he hated and no prospects of anything better.

Another couple of weeks, and she'd be married, officially off-limits. He could forget her when there was no possibility of seeing her again.

Cole was outside talking to a couple of strangers in white shirts and ties, probably inspectors or guys from the bank. Nick didn't care who they were. The complexities of getting something built were a nightmare. He was surprised the wild Bailey twins had the patience to deal with all the red tape.

"Nick, someone wants to see you in the office," Cole called over to him.

"Okay, thanks."

When the twins played good boss, bad boss, Zack always got to be the one who kicked butt. Nick ambled over to the trailer and opened the screen door, wondering if he'd finally be fired.

"Tess!" He hadn't expected his sister-in-law—make that sisters-in-law. Tess was perched on the edge of the desk with Megan behind her in the swivel chair. Zack's wife, Megan, was dressed in white jeans and a pink tank top while Tess looked ready for work at her baby store in a denim jumper and red-checkered blouse. Why were they here?

"What do you have to say for yourself?" Megan asked sternly. She flicked aside her long blond hair and scowled at him.

"What did I do?"

He could think of a whole laundry list of possibilities, but none that his brothers or their wives were likely to know about.

"For starters, you're late to work. We've been waiting nearly thirty minutes."

"Sorry."

It was the only safe word on those rare occasions

when a woman—make that women—expected him to account for himself.

"Don't tell us you're sorry. It's your brothers who rely on you to do a day's work."

His brothers had brought in their wives to read him the riot act? This surprised him. They usually took care of their own problems.

"Why are you here?" He was genuinely curious.

"I'm so disappointed in you, Nick," Tess said. "Cole and I waited for you for several hours the other evening, but you never came."

"Tess, I'm sorry. I forgot."

For this he was genuinely sorry. Tess was a sweetheart, the caring, understanding sister he'd never had. Dinner at Cole's had completely slipped his mind. He'd had a date with a Wayne State coed who was working her way through college modeling for art classes. It turned out she liked to get paid for other things, too, and he'd dumped her early on.

"You were going to help Zack install our new air conditioner," Megan reminded him.

"Your brothers didn't want to tell us what you've been up to, but we have our ways," Tess said. "You're goofing off at work and making a mess of your social life."

They were scolding him as if he were a schoolboy, but he couldn't resent their concern. He had been acting like a jerk lately. Anything he could say would sound like a weak alibi, but he hadn't enjoyed any part of his wild dating binge. Stacy made other women seem bland and dull.

"Your mother is really worried, Nick," Megan said, bringing in the heavy ammo.

This was the crux of it. His mother knew what it

was like to be young, pregnant with twins, and unmarried. She was afraid he'd cause that kind of pain in
someone else's life, but she hated to interfere. The two
furies were here to ream him over for her.

"She doesn't need to worry," he said.

"I don't like being a busybody," Tess said, "but
you blew off college and worked only part of one sea-
son on the ore boat. Now you're letting your brothers
down. They'd really like to take you into their business."

"It's not for me."

"That's your decision," Megan said, "but when you
drive our husbands nutty trying to figure you out, we
don't like it."

"Message received." He grinned sheepishly but
didn't much like himself for being the family problem.

He had one thing on his mind, and it wasn't job
related.

"I'll get out of their hair soon, I promise," he added.

He knew what he wanted to do, but it was too soon
to talk about a different job. For now, his arms ached
to hold Stacy, and the taste of her lips was as fresh as
if he'd kissed her only moments ago. He needed to tell
her how he felt, but how could he? What could he
possibly offer to compete with the shyster lawyer? She
must care about the guy. Nick knew her well enough
to be sure she'd never marry someone just for an easy
life.

THE WEDDING WATCH dragged on. After a few more
dismal dates, Nick cancelled a Saturday night and went
instead to the company lab where he expected Marsh
to be working. It was one week until Stacy's wedding,
and his crusty grandfather was the only person he felt

like seeing, a first in their relationship. Somehow Nick felt better when he could work on something challenging in the lab.

"Wondered if you'd show up," Marsh said, looking up from the well-equipped bench where he was working.

It was his way of saying, "Glad to see you."

"What are you working on?" Nick surprised himself by being really eager to know.

"This dang collapsible high chair. We can't market it until I figure out how to avoid pinched fingers. Those idiots on the payroll gave up on it."

"Let me see it." He grinned and accepted Marsh's challenge.

A few hours later Nick dashed out to a convenience store for a frozen pizza. His grandfather had been in the lab since morning and hadn't bothered with lunch. They shared a somewhat soggy pizza warmed in a microwave in the employee lounge, both in too much of a hurry to get back to work to care about what they ate.

When Nick came up with a workable way to redo the hinges, he felt better about himself than he had in a long time. It was clear Marsh couldn't have been more pleased if he'd come up with the idea himself, but it wasn't his grandfather's approval that made Nick so happy. He'd finally found work that interested him.

It was nearly midnight when he pulled into the driveway of the duplex he rented from his brothers. They'd lived there together until Cole got married, then Zack used it as his bachelor pad. It was sparsely furnished and required little upkeep, but Nick was beginning to wonder if he shouldn't move out. They charged him too little rent, and he'd had more help than he needed or wanted from his brothers.

He started toward the door, then stopped when a woman got out of a compact parked on the other side of the street where parking was legal.

Either he was hallucinating, or Stacy was crossing the street toward him. He was too surprised to do anything but watch her.

"Hi." She stopped ten feet away, her face dimly illuminated by the pinkish glow of the streetlight on the corner.

"You're out late." He was thrilled to see her, but didn't know what else to say.

"I've been waiting for you."

"What if I hadn't come home?"

"Was there any chance of that?"

Was she trying to learn whether he was seeing someone? He cared about her too much to be coy.

"None whatsoever. Want to come inside? The mosquitoes are fierce." He slapped at an imaginary bug on his arm.

"I shouldn't."

She followed him to the door, hesitated when he unlocked it, then stepped inside.

The room was dark except for the outside light over the door spilling inside. When he shut it, he could just see her standing a few steps away.

"I'll turn on a light."

"No! I mean, don't bother. It's never totally dark in the city, is it?"

"Not totally."

Having her there was unreal enough. In the glow from his sleeping computer, illuminated clock dial and answering machine, she was a vision straight from his dreams, only fully dressed in white shorts and a gauzy sleeveless top.

"I don't know why I came here."

He didn't believe that. Strange, because she usually told the whole truth and nothing but.

"Maybe you wanted to see me."

He hoped she couldn't hear the rapid beating of his heart.

"Yes, I guess so."

She sounded so unhappy he felt badly for her sake.

"I've missed you," he said.

She'd never believe how much, but the loneliness of not being with her hit him like a truckload of cement blocks.

"My wedding is one week away, six days if you count today as being over."

"It is over. It's after midnight."

Mention of her wedding made the mediocre pizza he'd eaten earlier turn to battery acid in his stomach.

"It's scary, sort of like signing my life away," she said in a hushed voice.

He had to agree. Mercer was a self-centered egotistical jerk, and she should be scared silly. But he hated hearing her sound depressed. He wanted the best life had to offer for her, but there was nothing he could give her that would compare to the security she'd have after her marriage.

He couldn't help thinking of his mother, abandoned by a guy who was too scared of Marsh to stand by her. He didn't blame her for wanting to remarry. After his father died, she'd seemed lost.

You're looking for a rock, sweetheart, and I'm a sandy beach, he thought glumly.

"I guess you have prewedding jitters," he said.

He should send her home. Whatever her reason for coming, he didn't know what to say or do to make her feel better.

"I feel as if I'm caught in an earthquake with a tornado bearing down on me!"

He laughed, and she did, too.

"Well, maybe I exaggerated a little," she admitted.

Somehow the distance between them had closed, but he didn't remember seeing her move or moving himself. Her palm was flattened against his chest, and he was sure her fingerprints would be burned through the shirt onto his skin.

If he didn't kiss her now, he might never have another chance. He bent his head, and her lips parted under his. Her mouth was the sweetest thing he'd ever tasted. When her tongue flicked against the roof of his mouth, his knees buckled. He pulled her over to the couch and collapsed on it, Stacy on his lap and their lips still locked together.

"This isn't why I came," she gasped.

"I know."

He didn't know anything, but he was at the say-anything-to-keep-her-in-his-arms stage.

"I didn't intend for this to happen," she said.

Her hand was warm and moist when she slid it under his shirt. Maybe her caresses only felt like a hot-oil massage because he was steaming.

He'd imagined touching her breasts so many times, the reality should have disappointed. It didn't. She was braless under the gauzy top, and deep contentment warred with the pressure building in his groin as he gently fondled her.

"This isn't happening. I'm only dreaming," she whispered.

He smiled at her denial and willed her to forget everyone but him. Her nipple was small and delicate under his thumb, and he longed to strip away her clothes and show her how to enjoy her body.

He longed to take her to his bed and never let her leave. At this moment, he was sure she wanted the same thing. He slid his finger under the leg of her shorts, inside the elastic of her band of her panties. She trembled under his intimate touch, and their kisses became hard and urgent.

"Why did you come here tonight?" he asked with an involuntary groan.

He pulled his hand away. Much as he dreaded her answer, he had to know.

She snuggled closer on his lap and pressed her cheek against his shoulder.

"I wanted…"

He waited.

"I needed to know…" Again the hesitation.

"If you'd be missing anything by marrying Mercer?"

"You make me sound so, so…"

She slid off his lap, but still sat beside him.

"Unsure?"

"You think I'm shallow and self-centered." She sounded close to tears.

He hated it when any woman cried, and Stacy had the power to tear him apart.

"Never! I think you're a wonderful woman."

He wanted to tell her how much he hated having her marry Mercer. He loathed the thought of the slimebag lawyer putting his hands on her.

He didn't want to accept losing her forever, but what

could he offer in place of marriage to a solid-citizen type who'd won her before they met?

Anything he said now might louse up her whole life. He'd long ago convinced himself marriage wasn't for him. He didn't know what he wanted to do with his life, but it wouldn't involve being a junior partner in his brothers' business. He couldn't offer her the security of a happily-ever-after relationship when his own future was uncertain.

"You forgot to say good friend, buddy, pal." She made it sound like a curse.

"Hey, who else has been kidnapped with you?"

"And had a bite of Elvis cake?"

"The whole thing was kind of fun," he said.

"It was once those clowns left us alone to escape."

"I'm not even mad at Percy and ol' Harold anymore."

"Do you think they'll ever be caught?" she asked.

"Maybe not for snatching you, but two crooks as dumb as they are will goof up on something else and end up in jail."

"I really came here just to talk," she said morosely.

"I know."

"But there's not much to say, is there?"

She didn't react when he covered her hand with his.

He could say a lot, but not without forcing her to make a choice between Mercer and himself, between a sure thing and a long shot.

"Guess I do have prewedding jitters. Thank you for understanding. I would have—we could have—but it wouldn't be right, would it?"

"Very wrong."

She'd hate herself if they made love. He wouldn't think much of himself, either.

He leaned over and turned on the lamp on the table beside the couch. There was nothing like a hundred watts to make them both face reality.

Her eyes were glistening, but she was fighting back the tears. She didn't succeed in erasing the crushed look from her face even though she smiled weakly and quickly averted her gaze.

He had to give her a wedding gift even if it hurt both of them.

"It never would've worked out between us," he said with false heartiness. "You deserve a home. I'd like to be my own man, have the freedom to go where I like and do as I please. Besides, I'd make you miserable. You're sweet and understanding. I'm crabby as a bear. It's my way or the highway."

"You're not *that* bossy!"

"You've only seen my good side," he assured her.

"I have a temper. Once I threw my little brother's tricycle in the trash because he got into my stuff."

"There you are. You're territorial. I own my clothes and car, and that's all I need or want. I'm living with my brothers' castoffs in their duplex. I'd make you crazy."

"I can see that." She tried to smile, but it didn't come off.

"Anyway..."

"What?"

He had to say something she couldn't dismiss, but he hated lying to her.

"I'm not sure one woman will ever be enough for me."

She looked stricken, and it was all he could do not to take it back and comfort her in his arms.

"I've known a lot of women...."

"Thank you for being honest with me."

She stood, her face pale and rigid.

"I take our friendship seriously," he said, clenching his fists to keep himself from touching her.

"I feel like a complete fool."

"No, you're anything but that. You're a warm, kind, loving woman who deserves the best in life. I'm not sure that's Mercer, but I know damn well it's not me."

"No, it's not." She moved toward the door.

"I'll walk you to your car."

"Please don't!"

He watched from the doorway until she drove away taking his heart with her. He didn't know loving someone could hurt so much.

11

THE REHEARSAL DINNER was everything Stacy had expected and worse. The Mercers wouldn't go to an ordinary restaurant and provide an edible meal. They had to show off by taking the wedding party to a snooty private club where even the doorman intimidated her.

"How is your capon, darling?" Jonathan asked, giving her knee a little squeeze under the starchy white edge of the banquet cloth.

He could see perfectly well she'd only managed to eat one tiny bite of the undersized chicken. The poultry might be delicious, but she was put off by dark, wrinkled mushrooms that looked as if they'd been left to rot on the ground, not to mention black pellets of pepper and odd little green things.

"I'm not very hungry. Too much excitement, I guess." She gave him her best imitation of a smile.

"Here, try a bite of the breast."

He leaned over and sliced a piece of hers with his knife.

"Jonathan, I don't need you to cut my meat!"

"She just has prewedding jitters," he said, smiling sheepishly across the table at a groomsman whose name she'd forgotten.

Stacy didn't know if the men in his wedding party were personal friends or business acquaintances, but she didn't need Jonathan or anyone else apologizing for her.

"Not at all," she contradicted him. "I'd just rather have pizza."

Jonathan fancied himself a gourmet, and her plebian tastes tended to annoy him. He half-turned away and started talking to her cousin, Dana, who'd flown home from Alaska to visit family and be her maid of honor.

Tonight she was willing enough to be ignored by her fiancé, but he wasn't the one who was making her miserable. He was who he was, and she'd been sure she loved him when they got engaged. That love would come back after they were married. She just had to get past her silly one-sided crush on Nick. She couldn't let an infatuation ruin her life. Nick didn't feel anything but friendship for her. She looked at her beaming parents. They were so sure their only daughter would have a wonderful life. Her heart swelled, and she knew she'd never do anything to spoil their happiness.

Maybe Jonathan was right. Men and women couldn't be friends. She didn't want Nick as a friend, and Nick didn't want her at all.

She picked at something that looked like tomato gelatin with slivers of celery in the congealed glob, then took another tiny bite of capon, more from courtesy than hunger. Jonathan didn't deserve her bad attitude. Everyone seemed to be enjoying the dinner, and the rehearsal before it had gone well even with Aunt Lucille making little tut-tut noises every few minutes. Her parents were beaming, and the senior Mercers didn't look as dour as usual.

Once the meal was over, there was nothing to keep the two rival camps together. Guests started scattering. A couple of groomsmen hovered near Jonathan waiting to whisk him away to the main event of the evening, the bachelor party.

"You can go," she said, after assuring him it had been a nice dinner. "I wouldn't want you to keep the stripper waiting."

"It won't be that kind of party."

He flushed, not unusual with his blond hair and light complexion. It was sort of cute, him not wanting her to think the party would be down and dirty.

"Just don't change your mind and elope with the lap dancer," she teased.

He made a politician's quick exit, shaking hands and slapping backs without slowing his retreat. Well, it was the first bachelor party in his honor. He had a right to be eager.

Her friends took her for a round of drinks at a tavern, where big baskets of peanuts were on the tables and the floor was covered with the shells. She forgot about Nick, but only for a few minutes.

"Here's to Stacy and Jon!" Dana said, holding up a beer glass with foam running over the side.

Her cousin had only been here from Alaska for two days, and she called him Jon. Why wouldn't it come naturally to his fiancée? Stacy smashed a peanut with her fist and winced because it hurt.

"I probably should go now," she said.

Everyone protested, even Tanya, their designated driver, who ordered another lemon-lime seltzer water and started telling a story about her wedding night.

Jonathan wouldn't do anything dumb like Tanya's husband had, locking the keys in the car with all their luggage still in the trunk. Would he be nervous? All Stacy felt tonight was resignation. Tomorrow she would get married. They weren't leaving on their honeymoon trip to Las Vegas—Jonathan's choice—until Sunday afternoon, so they'd spend their first night at his house.

What if it was a mistake for her to get married? Maybe that was why she was attracted to Nick. Had been attracted. No more. He'd squelched her infatuation.

She wanted to ask Tanya, the oldest of her attendants and the only married one, whether she'd had any last-minute doubts before her wedding. Maybe it was a phenomenon all brides experienced before the big event.

Her nine attendants—nine because Jonathan had magnanimously included her four brothers as groomsmen—banged the bottoms of their mugs on the table and chanted, "Speech, speech, speech."

"No way!"

"You don't want your bouquet to go missing."

"Or your shoes to have bubble gum on the soles."

"Bug spray instead of hair spray."

"You're completely at our mercy."

She told them the story of the Three Little Pigs, but not the version her preschoolers were used to hearing. It was only a coincidence Nick had two older brothers, too. She wasn't going to think about him anymore.

She told herself that all the way home when the party finally petered out in the wee hours.

HER ALARM rang at eight o'clock the next morning. She pushed the snooze button, remembered she was getting married that day, and pulled the sheet over her head. This was absolutely the last time she'd go to sleep and wake up thinking about Nick.

By noon she'd been processed along with all her attendants. Her hair was styled, her nails gleamed with pearly polish, and her makeup had been professionally applied at Veronica's Salon. Her face felt stiff, and her scalp itched from the hair spray, but she was officially ready.

There was nothing to do but wait for her mother to pick her up so she could dress at the church. She made toast to make up for the breakfast she'd skipped, but was afraid to eat it for fear of disturbing her lipstick.

Her mother was as excited as a kid going to a circus as they drove to the imposing stone church an earlier generation of Mercers had helped build. Stacy regretted caving on the wedding site. She got a chill just looking at the massive fortress with its medieval bell tower.

The wedding coordinator, employed by the church to oversee the marriage ceremony, met them at the side door closest to the parking area, and ushered them to a roomy lounge which served as the bride's changing room. She barked out instructions and suggestions faster than Stacy could absorb them. She hoped Mom was paying attention.

Her attendants were already milling around in their princess-style plum gowns, which were floor-length with tiny cap sleeves and modest V-necklines. Her mother looked better than any of them in regal beige lace with her naturally silver hair in a sleek pageboy.

"You look nicer than anyone here," Stacy whispered when she had a chance, hugging her affectionately.

Mom looked at her with teary eyes, and Stacy backed away. If her mother started crying, she'd probably bawl like a baby herself.

With more help than she could handle, she finally got into the bridal gown without smearing her makeup and donned the veil without ruffling her hair. It was the signal for her attendants to rave and her mother to sniff into her emergency lace hanky.

The bride-to-be walked to the full-length mirror thoughtfully provided on the back of the door.

She was in the twilight zone. The image staring back at her looked more like Wedding Barbie on clearance than Stacy Moore.

So this was how she looked as a radiant, glowing bride. Or was she still a bride-to-be? When did she become the bride? When she put on the dress or when she said, "I do"?

Suddenly there was a loud pounding on the door and the room got very quiet.

"Stacy!" *Knock, knock, knock.* "I have to see you!" *Knock, knock, knock.*

Her mother raced over to handle the wholly inappropriate summons from the groom. Or groom-to-be.

"Jonathan," she said through the smallest possible opening. "You know it's bad luck for you to see the bride before the wedding."

He mother hadn't had as much to do with planning the big event as she would've liked, but on this she was keeper of the door and upholder of traditions.

"I've seen the dress. I have to talk to Stacy."

"But...you just can't!"

Her mother was obviously groping for some reason besides an old superstition to keep him out. Maybe she was afraid he'd come to call it off.

"Please, everyone, leave us alone!" he shouted, wedging his body through the opening.

Red-faced and flustered, he waved his arms frantically, trying to shoo everyone away. One by one Stacy's plum-colored attendants slowly filed out. He mother held out for a few more seconds, then reluctantly marched out of the lounge.

"It really is bad luck," her mom solemnly warned Jonathan.

"What's wrong?" Stacy asked, more curious than alarmed.

"I have a confession to make."

He sounded penitent, humble, even sad, and she waited tensely imagining all kinds of disasters. Or maybe he had decided to elope with a lap dancer or the girl who jumped out of his cake at his bachelor party.

"Well, tell me!"

Inside the wedding-doll disguise, the real Stacy was seething with impatience. What the heck was going on?

"You're not going to like this, but please, please, darling, hear me out and try to understand."

"Are you dumping me? Now? In church on our wedding day?"

"Oh, no! I'd never do that." He paled and squeezed his hands together.

"Then what's going on?"

"One of the kidnappers has been arrested."

"That's good news! But you could have told me later instead of making my mother a nervous wreck worrying about why you're here. Which one did they catch?"

"Percy Krump."

"Percy Krump? How did they get him? Nick thought they'd commit other crimes and get caught sooner or later."

Whoops. She probably shouldn't have mentioned Nick judging by the expression on Jonathan's face.

"Something about his van. It doesn't matter how."

It did to her, but she was more curious about why Jonathan was so agitated.

"They didn't find Harold?"

"No, apparently the pair had a falling out, and Harold took off."

"Imagine, ol' Harold turned out to be the smarter one." The thought boggled her mind.

"Please, Stacy, listen. This isn't about a couple of lowlifes. I have to tell you something." He looked more miserable than she'd ever seen him.

She had a bad feeling, but only nodded.

"We seemed to be drifting apart. We were planning our wedding, but you seemed distant, not as warm and enthusiastic as you'd been."

"What do you mean?"

"You couldn't even pick out a dress to be married in. You were indifferent to our plans…"

"Your plans. And your mother's." She wanted to set the record straight on that.

"Is it too much to ask, having a wedding as nice as my parents'? Most women would be grateful for a fiancé who's hands-on."

She would have said overbearing, selfish or obnoxious, but let it pass.

"Anyway, it would be a disaster to my career if the wedding got cancelled."

She was stunned by Jonathan's admission. Was their engagement only a way to improve his image? His chance to make partner?

"Please, don't make this any harder for me. The point is, I was sure you would back out of the wedding, so I did something rash, ill-conceived, inadvisable. Something I regret more than I can possibly tell you."

"Is there someone else? That woman in your office who calls you Jon?"

"No, no, nothing like that," he snapped. "It just didn't go as planned."

"Tell me everything!" *Before I strangle you with my veil!*

"Remember, I had a panic attack..."

"So you said."

"Your kidnapping was a hoax."

"A hoax? It certainly wasn't! They threw me into the van and knocked Nick out with a six-pack when he tried to stop them. They tied me up and put nasty, horrible duct tape over my mouth. It was real, Jonathan, very, very real!"

"They weren't supposed to hurt you! How could we know that idiot would interfere?"

"We?"

She wanted to punch him for calling Nick an idiot, but the truth was slowly sinking in.

"I hired them."

She opened her mouth, but words wouldn't come out.

"I wanted to be your knight in shining armor. I wanted to rescue you so you'd never want to break up with me."

"Are you crazy? They snatched me, abducted me, kidnapped me! You had them do that? What were you thinking?"

"I was out of my head with worry, afraid you weren't going to marry me."

He was a phony knight in tarnished armor, a fraud. How could he do that to her?

"You're a manipulative creep! Everything has to be your way! How could you do something like that and still pretend to love me? Just when did you plan to 'rescue' me?"

"The next day, but by then you'd gotten away on your own."

"Thanks to Nick!"

"He ruined the plan. I was supposed to make a ransom drop, but I couldn't be expected to get cash in the middle of the night."

"The next day was Sunday! Banks are closed on Sunday. Maybe you should've waited until Monday. I would have been good and scared by then!"

"No, I could pull strings and get the money on Sunday."

"Why tell me now? We're supposed to get married in..."

She looked at her wrist, but her watch was home on her dresser. Brides didn't wear wristwatches.

"Percy asked for me as his attorney, never mind that I practice corporate law and have never taken a criminal case to court. If I can't get him off, he'll implicate me."

"He'll tell the whole sordid truth about you hiring him to kidnap your fiancée, who was wavering on her commitment to marry you."

"No one will believe him if you stand by me."

"First you want to marry me because your firm likes married attorneys. Now you want to make sure you won't be charged with kidnapping! How could you? You put me in terrible danger!"

"No, those idiots are harmless—except to me. Fortunately Harold is long gone. Somewhere up in Canada, maybe. He's too dumb to keep his mouth shut."

"I can't believe this." Her arms were trembling, and

she felt light-headed. "I just cannot believe you'd do something so nasty and horrible and criminal. To me!"

"Please, Stacy."

He dropped to his knees on the floor and reached up to capture her hands. She was so stunned by what he'd done she didn't think to pull away.

"I love you, darling. I adore you. I worship you. You're my soul mate. I'll love you through all eternity. I'll do anything if you'll only forgive me."

"Stop," she said.

Who was the real Jonathan? The conniving slimebag or this, this…

"I know you don't love me as much as I love you. You've never felt the same way I do, but you're too sweet and honest and kind to want me just for my money."

"Jonathan!"

Hadn't he hurt her enough? How could he even suggest she might…

"I only agreed to marry you because I thought I loved you."

"You still do! I'm sure of it! We were meant for each other. Darling, when we're together, really together, I'll make you happier than you've ever dreamed."

"Oh, oh…darn."

She didn't know how to feel, what to say, what to do. They were supposed to get married in less than half an hour, and she couldn't think straight.

"Please, darling, I adore you," he pleaded, still on his knees. "I'll be devastated if you won't go through with the wedding. I'll never forgive myself. I don't know how I can go on living without you."

She stared down in horror at the tears in his eyes.

Jonathan crying? He was practically crumbling in front of her.

"I did it because I was crazy in love with you."

She couldn't take this. Jonathan, a pillar of strength and emotional stability, was on his knees crying and begging. She pulled her hand away and flopped down on the closest chair.

"You're not going to cancel the wedding, are you?" he whispered.

Was she? Jonathan looked so pathetic, she didn't feel at all vengeful or mad, which was extremely odd. She wanted advice, needed it desperately, but this was a problem she had to solve alone.

Nick didn't want her.

Jonathan wanted her so much he went a little nuts—maybe a lot nuts—and had her kidnapped.

She couldn't decide now. She needed time to think.

Jonathan stood, looking pale and scared. Maybe this crisis would make him a better person. Maybe he'd learned his lesson.

Yeah, Stacy, she thought, but he isn't a four-year-old who has to learn to play fair at recess. This was her whole life, and she didn't know what to do.

Time was the one thing she didn't have.

The church was filling up, and everyone she loved would be there waiting to see her begin a wonderful new life. How could she disappoint them?

Once she'd been absolutely sure she loved Jonathan. How could she be indifferent to him now?

Her parents would be devastated if she didn't get married. She hated what Jonathan had done, but he was so guilt-stricken, she couldn't help but feel something for him.

This wasn't just about Jonathan. Nick was out of her

life forever, so Jonathan's terrible scheme didn't seem to matter much. She didn't hate him. She just felt stunned and empty.

Maybe it had been partly her fault. She'd let the Mercers take over and hadn't been honest with Jonathan about her indifference to the wedding plans. She'd genuinely wanted to be his wife.

Then she met Nick...

Someday her heart would stop aching for him. Until then, why not go through with the wedding? Her parents would go ballistic if she didn't. The guests were there, and the organist was playing. There was all the rented formal wear and the dresses her friends had bought. The church was loaded with flowers, and at the country club the chefs were cooking enough food to feed a small village for a month. The band had come across the border from Windsor, and her little neighbor was sure to be heartbroken if she didn't get to scatter the flower petals in her basket.

She couldn't march out and stop the wedding now. It had a life of its own.

"I guess we can still get married," she whispered.

Jonathan sighed so hard his bow tie popped open. He did look handsome in a black morning coat with a pearly gray cummerbund and tie. He started brushing lint from the carpet off the knees of his trousers.

"But we need to settle a few things first," she said.

She felt a foot taller. Was this what it meant to be empowered? Jonathan looked worried, but didn't say a word.

"Number one, I'm going to keep my job after we're married. I love what I do."

His eyes said no, but he nodded in agreement.

"And I want a family, at least two kids, maybe three.

Not until we have a couple of years to get used to each other, but I say when it's time. This isn't negotiable.''

"All right."

"Also I don't want to live in a house your mother decorated."

"She has very good taste." He looked stricken.

"Yes, but so do I. I don't want to live in Grosse Pointe. We should look for a home that will be both of ours. I don't care if it's a little apartment or a townhouse or…"

"I agree."

"Really?"

"Wholeheartedly."

"But do you promise?"

"I promise. An oral contract is binding if both parties enter into it in good faith."

"Okay. We'll get married."

"I'll see you in a little while, darling. You'll never regret it."

He turned and opened the door.

She felt more like herself when she had to resist an urge to give him a good hard kick under his expensively tailored tails.

12

NICK KICKED the tire of his car so hard his toe throbbed, but he hardly noticed. In his entire life, there'd never been a worse time for a car to conk out.

Where the hell was Cole? It was only a twenty-minute drive from his house to the duplex, and there was no rush-hour traffic on Saturday afternoon. He'd called him—Nick checked his watch—at least seventeen minutes ago.

Why was he wearing a suit? It was so hot standing out on the pavement, he was going to melt. He remembered his reason for trying to look his best and patted the pocket of his suit coat, not trusting the little velvet box to stay where he'd put it.

Eighteen minutes! Cole never let him down, so where was he? Using his cell phone, he punched in his brother's mobile number.

"Where are you?"

"Two blocks away. Calm down, I'm coming as fast as I can."

He should've called Zack. He lived farther away but could burn rubber with the pros.

Cole finally pulled up to the curb.

"You brought the truck!"

"Tess is coming in the car. I'll need a ride home, you know. She had to run next door and get the neighbor to baby-sit, but she can't be more than ten minutes behind me.''

"I don't have ten minutes.'' Nick didn't need to look at his watch. The seconds were ticking away in his brain. "I'll have to take the truck.''

Cole shrugged and tossed him the keys. "It's low on gas.''

"I'll buy gas. Thanks for bringing it.''

"Why don't you phone ahead? Say you'll be late.''

Nick was in the truck and didn't have time to answer. If he blew it now he might as well sign on as a deckhand again.

The tank was running on fumes, so he stopped at the first service station he saw. He pumped in ten bucks worth and threw a twenty-dollar bill on the counter without waiting his turn to pay. No time for change.

When he hit the expressway, he tried not to look at his watch every ten seconds. He wanted to go ninety, but being stopped by a cop would waste more time than he could gain by speeding.

He thought he knew where the church was. If he was wrong, he might have to ask someone. What real man stopped for directions? He'd have to make an exception this time.

He didn't let himself think about what would happen if he didn't set a crosstown speed record getting there.

BELOW THE vaulted nave of the historic old church, her mother was being seated by Kirk. Stacy's spike heels were muted by the long white aisle runner just rolled out by two other groomsmen. She couldn't hear what her brother said to make Mom laugh aloud. It was good to see her so happy, though. Kirk had a new job, better than the old one and only two suburbs away. He wouldn't have to go north to Saginaw, and in a matter of minutes, her only daughter would be Mrs. Jonathan Mercer.

Stacy was happy for her.

"I guess it's nearly our turn, dumpling," her father said, using a pet name she hadn't heard in years.

The flower girl conscientiously scattered her basket of petals, and the first of her attendants started down the aisle doing the hesitation march. Stacy had wanted them to walk normally, but Rebecca Mercer had nearly swooned at such a flagrant break from tradition. Jonathan had better like long commutes to the city because they were going to live far from her in-laws.

Their turn came, and she tucked her hand on her father's arm, surprised to feel a tremor. She was immensely proud of her tall, dignified dad, handsome in a way that wasn't affected by thinning salt-and-pepper hair or deep laugh lines by his eyes.

"I hope you'll be very happy, Stacy," he whispered.

Was that doubt in his voice? Please, no! She had enough reservations without worrying about her father's.

Just as she'd expected, Jonathan's side of the church was nearly full while her guests were huddled in the front third of the pews. Now that she'd confirmed this suspicion, it didn't matter in the least. She loved every single person who had given up a beautiful Saturday afternoon to honor her by being there. She doubted whether Jonathan even knew everyone on his side.

"I had a terrible time learning to skip when I was little," her father said under his breath when they were halfway down the aisle. "This reminds me of it."

She giggled softly, grateful to Dad for distracting

her. A bride could get downright nervous walking past all those standing and staring guests.

Then she saw Jonathan flanked by his army of groomsmen. Stained-glass windows played tricks with the light giving his pale hair a burnished effect, and she remembered their first meeting. He was nothing if not handsome. Maybe all her old feelings would come flooding back when they were man and wife.

She hoped.

The strains of the wedding march faded away as her father handed her over to the groom. She felt like the baton in a relay race, but that was only her nerves squawking.

At the rehearsal, the ceremony had promised to be short. Who knew a Santa Claus look-alike would deliver a full-blown sermon while she stood woodenly beside Jonathan unable to take in a single word. The minister had a booming voice meant to be heard at the back of the church, and the longer he talked, the more edgy she got. The hand holding her bouquet was slippery with very unbridelike sweat, and moisture was beading on her nose. Pretty soon she'd be one shiny mess, and the professional makeup job on her face would slide off.

She was about to sign away her future. Why was her mind full of mundane thoughts?

She knew the answer to that. Trivial musings kept her from thinking about Nick.

For a moment, she thought she'd spoken her thoughts aloud. But no, the minister was going into an archaic part of the ceremony that seemed as purposeless as it was dated. What possible reason could anyone have for objecting to a marriage at this point?

"Any reason why this man and this woman should not be joined...?"

"I do!"

She jerked her head around and saw Nick racing down the aisle. Nick in a suit of all things. Nick objecting to her marriage.

"Young man," the white-bearded minister said with the resignation of a man who's seen everything, "usually that line is reserved for the bride and groom."

"You asked if anyone objected!"

Nick was at the bottom of the three steps leading up to the altar railing.

"If you have a problem, maybe we could discuss it after..." Santa wasn't used to being interrupted. His frown wasn't consoling.

"After it's too late? I don't think so."

Nick bounded up the steps and put his hands on her shoulders.

"I love you, Stacy. I want you to marry me. I was a fool not to tell you when you came to my place."

"Why did you wait 'til the last minute?" Her heart was pounding. "Practically the last second!"

"My car broke down."

"Get out of here, or I'll have you thrown out!" Jonathan said in a low, furious voice.

She'd almost forgotten him in the shock of hearing Nick say he loved her and wanted to marry her.

"Stacy, tell this fool to get lost," Jonathan ordered.

She looked at her husband-to-be, not quite comprehending this sudden development. Some of the guests were commenting from the pews, including Jonathan's mother who was screeching directions to her son, the groomsmen and especially the minister.

"Oh, sit down and shut up, you old biddy!" Aunt

Lucille made herself heard to the back pew. "The girl's got a better offer!"

"Stacy! You're humiliating me in front of my firm's senior partners," Jonathan said in a venomous whisper, pulling her aside to avoid being heard by anyone. "Get rid of him before my career is a shambles."

His career? He was worried about his career?

"What would be worse, Jon? Being jilted at the altar or going to jail for kidnapping?" She spoke as softly as she could so only Jonathan could hear. This was no time for Nick to find out he was the "mastermind" behind their abduction.

She'd just called him Jon! Did that mean the last bit of her respect for him had eroded away?

"You can't do this!" Jonathan kept his voice low, but his eyes were riveted on the guests.

The church was silent now, everyone watching to see how this would play out.

"Yes, I can," she said.

"You brat! I would've dumped you a long time ago if I didn't need a nice, placid wife to make partner."

It was a cheap shot, but it erased the last iota of her hesitation.

"Talk to them!" she ordered, gesturing at the guests. "Or they'll hear the truth from me. I don't think your precious partners want kidnappers in the firm!"

With his face bright red with anger, Jonathan turned to face their guests.

"It appears," he said, stepping down to distance himself from her, "that there's been a glitch in the wedding plans. In fact, the marriage is off, but we have a lovely reception set up at the country club. I want everyone to come for one of Chef Willy's famous dinners. And please, while you're there, retrieve your gifts.

They're all on display in the Renaissance room to the right of the front entrance.''

Stacy stepped down beside him, yanked off the engagement ring she'd been wearing on her right hand to make room for his diamond-studded wedding band, and handed it over.

Nick was edging closer, but she signaled him to back off for just a minute. He looked confused, but gave her a moment with Jonathan now that it was clear the wedding was off.

''I want you to reimburse my parents for their share of the wedding,'' she whispered, turning her back to the pews in case there were any lip-readers. ''And the bridesmaids for their dresses. And my cousin Dana for her plane ticket from Alaska to watch me marry a conniving, underhanded phony. A felon who had his own fiancée kidnapped!''

''Is everything all right?'' Nick stepped up beside her and put his arm around her shoulders, speaking in the same hushed voice.

He hadn't heard the kidnapping part. She could tell by the happy look on his face.

''I'll tell you later.''

''I think my work here is done.'' Nick grinned so broadly she wanted to jump into his arms and kiss him until he was wearing all her lipstick. But the really important things in life didn't call for an army of witnesses.

He grabbed her hand, and she ran beside him down the cloth-covered aisle in three-inch heels. Her feet had wings, and her heart was bursting with happiness.

''Why were you so late?'' she gasped breathlessly outside on steps worn down by generations of Mercer feet.

"My car wouldn't start."

He gestured at the truck and grabbed her in a bear hug so long overdue she squealed with pleasure.

The first kiss exploded on their lips, and the second went on and on and on until the crowd noise inside intruded.

"Let's go," he shouted.

"To your steed, Galahad!"

"What?"

"Let's hit the road!"

He hastily boosted her into the cab of the pickup, grabbing where he could with the dress billowing out like a circus tent.

They took off before the fastest—or most curious—wedding guest could catch up with them.

For several minutes neither of them spoke. Stacy needed to digest what had happened. Until the moment Nick had yelled, "I do," she'd thought he would never be a part of her life.

"What was it you said in the church?" she asked, after he turned north on Lake Shore Drive, the Grosse Pointe name for Jefferson Avenue, and passed some of the stately old homes that auto money had built.

"It's all a blur to me." He grinned mischievously. "Something about objecting to the marriage."

"Every time I put on a wedding gown, I'm kidnapped!"

"You make a cute bride. Who could resist?"

"Is that why you came bursting into the church and…"

"Told you I love you and want me to marry you? Did I mention I can't live without you?"

"No, but it's nice to hear."

"Ahem." He pretended to clear his throat. "Is there anything you want to tell me?"

"I love you," she said shyly. "A bunch."

"And?"

"And I'll certainly think about marrying you."

"Think hard."

"Okay, I have."

"And?"

"I'll do it."

She glanced out the window and got a glimpse of Lake St. Clair. Water had never looked so blue. The sun had never seemed so bright.

"Where are we going?" she asked.

"I haven't worked out that part of my plan."

"We could…"

"Go to your place?"

"If you want to."

"Who knows you live there?"

"My family. All my friends. Point taken. Your place?"

"I didn't have time to dust."

"Be serious!"

"I am. I'm neat, organized and efficient, but I hate dusting."

"I like it, dusting, polishing, scrubbing, shining…"

"You're just what I need."

"Wish you'd figured that out a little sooner."

She didn't exactly feel guilty about running away from her own wedding considering old Jon had confessed to masterminding the kidnapping, but she was going to have a lot of explaining to do.

"I have an idea. Let's get a motel room and talk about it," he said.

"I'm not exactly prepared. No luggage, no rea
clothes, no toothbrush."

"We could pretend we just got married." H
grinned sheepishly.

She stared out the window. They'd left venerabl
Grosse Pointe Woods behind them and were passin
St. Clair Shores' public waterside park. She had no ide
why he was driving in this direction.

"First I need to ask you one question," she said.

"Okay, if I can ask one, too."

"Why didn't you tell me when I came to your place
Why say you could never settle down with only on
woman?"

"That's two questions."

"Does that mean you won't answer?"

"No, it means I want to be holding you in my arm
when I explain."

She said nothing and waited.

"Do you want to hear my question?" he asked.

"Why was I going to go through with the wed
ding?"

"Bingo." He pulled over and turned off the engine
"I've never been so miserable in my whole life tha
when I thought I'd lost you."

"You sent me packing, actually."

"What could I offer you? My brothers were close t
booting me off the job—literally so in Zack's case
How could I ask you to give up a promising future—
Well, you seemed to think it was."

"But you changed your mind," she said quietly, tak
ing his hand.

"More like I accepted what I had to do if I eve
wanted to be happy. If I wanted a chance with you,
had to feel better about myself. I'd been tinkering a

the plant with my grandfather. I figured out a hinge problem that'd stumped the design team. I finally realized what I should do with my life.''

"Marry me?"

She made lazy circles in his palm.

"It was my damn pride that held me back, but when I realized you were more important, I went to Marsh for a job. I even offered to start at the bottom sweeping floors.''

"I thought your mom was CEO."

"She is, but Gramps still runs product development. When I finally went to him, he told me he'd been saving a job there for me. So I'm not a construction bum anymore.''

"I loved you when you were."

"Why were you on the verge of marrying Jonathan?''

"When we started dating, I thought he was handsome and smart. Maybe I would have been happy with him if I'd never met you. If he hadn't had me kidnapped…''

"He had you kidnapped?" he said, clearly stunned. "*He* was the mystery man behind it?"

"Yes, he hired Percy and Harold. He thought I was cooling off. He wanted to be a hero and rescue me, but you foiled the plan. He told me just before the wedding because Percy got caught and was blackmailing Jonathan to be his lawyer and get him off. Guess I never mentioned neither of us ever saw Percy's face. His real hair is gray, by the way. He dyed it red for the job. Clever, huh?"

She kept talking because Nick sat up with a murderous expression on his face.

"That slimy, underhanded ambulance chaser. should knock him silly. He belongs in jail!"

"Yeah, well, there doesn't seem to be much poin in that. He'd probably find a way to wiggle out of i anyway."

"You were still going to marry him!"

"On my own terms! I didn't know what else to do When he told me, the church was already full of guests everything was ready. My parents would have been s disappointed— Oh, dear, I'll have some explaining t do there. Hope Aunt Lucille can convince them I di the right thing running away with you. I guess the mar riage wouldn't have lasted long, not with me crazy i love with you. You did dump me, you know! I wa pretty depressed about that, so it didn't seem to matte what I did."

"We weren't going together. I couldn't dump you.'

She leaned over and kissed his pout away.

"You certainly didn't leave me with any hope! The you nearly didn't get to the church on time!"

"That reminds me…"

He pulled his hand away from her and reached int his jacket pocket. She loved watching the materia tighten around his muscular arms so much she scarcel noticed what he took out of the pocket.

"Here's part of the reason I was late, this and m car not starting."

He handed her a blue velvet box. It could only b one thing, but the moment seemed too important t rush into opening it.

"Here." He did it for her.

It was indescribably lovely, not a rock like she' returned to what's-his-name, but a sparkling stone i an exquisite yellow-gold setting. She liked gold to look like gold. It was perfect!

"I guess this calls for a celebration," she said shyly, slipping the ring onto the appropriate finger.

"We need to start planning our wedding."

He was smiling so warmly, she melted.

"Not right now." She wrapped her arms around his neck and maneuvered herself so she was straddling him. "I'm getting tired of these stockings."

Epilogue

NICK COULDN'T STOP grinning. He woke up smiling and smirked at himself in the mirror while he shaved. Three hours later he was still beaming. Not even his brothers' off-color wedding jokes made a dent in his euphoric mood.

Rather than pick one of the twins as his best man and leave out the other, he'd asked Marsh. Gramps looked downright cheery in his brass-buttoned navy blazer, white knit shirt and tan trousers, the uniform of the day. No monkey suit and rented shoes for this groom!

The guests were waiting on folding chairs in Marsh's garden, sixty or so people Nick and Stacy really cared about. The back of the workshop was covered with climbing roses still in bloom on trellises. The noon-time sky was brilliant blue and cloudless above the rented canopy.

His mother still couldn't believe he'd managed to meet someone and arrange to marry her before her own long-planned wedding came off. She winked at him from the front row of chairs.

The musician pounded out the wedding march on a keyboard with all the gusto usually associated with massive pipe organs, and Stacy stepped into the garden on her father's arm.

Nick's grin faded, but only because he was awestruck. She was every bit a bride in pale pink lace and a hemline that stopped at midthigh. Instead of a veil, she was wearing a little crown of real flowers that matched her pink-and-white bouquet.

She'd told him her dress would be a surprise, but he hadn't been prepared for the impact. His throat swelled shut with pride, and his knees were shaky because this gorgeous woman was about to become his wife.

He must have said the right things and made the right moves during the ceremony because he heard the magic words.

"You may kiss the bride."

In the reception line, he kissed his mom, Stacy's mom, the two bridesmaids, and Aunt Lucille. Truth to tell, Aunt Lucille gave it the most oomph. Stacy kissed her father, his grandfather, her brothers and his.

"Save some of that for me," he whispered, flicking his tongue in her ear.

"Zack is some kisser," she teased.

He patted her bottom in a proprietary way and wondered how long guests stayed at a wedding luncheon.

He hadn't seen the cake, and Stacy wouldn't let the caterers bring it out to the garden until the guests had had their fill of lobster salad, cheese puffs and spinach tarts.

Zack and Cole had to help two caterers carry it out to a table festooned with pink-and-green streamers. It was a huge, flat production with maybe a square foot of cake for every guest.

Nick's jaw dropped, and he was speechless for the first time in his life. Beside him, Stacy was giggling so hard she doubled over.

A frosting Elvis stared up at him, full-length with guitar in hand and a silvery sugar jacket.

"Surprise, darling!" she said.

He lifted her off her feet and kissed her emphatically, squashing her bouquet between them.

"Hey, I have to throw this!"

"Line up, single ladies," Tanya called out in her lime-green lace bridesmaid's dress with a skirt only slightly longer than the bride's.

"You, too, Aunt Lucille!" Stacy insisted.

The spritely septuagenarian scoffed at the idea, but hustled up to join the five single women waiting for the prize.

Nick didn't know how Stacy did it, throwing with her back turned, but the colorful bunch of flowers landed squarely in Aunt Lucille's arms.

"I'll be damned!" she said.

"Now let's cut the cake," Stacy called out. "I know exactly what part of Elvis I want."

Nick knew he wanted all of her—forever.

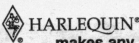

If you enjoyed what you just read,
then we've got an offer you can't resist!

Take 2 bestselling love stories FREE!

Plus get a FREE surprise gift!

Clip this page and mail it to Harlequin Reader Service®

IN U.S.A.	**IN CANADA**
3010 Walden Ave.	P.O. Box 609
P.O. Box 1867	Fort Erie, Ontario
Buffalo, N.Y. 14240-1867	L2A 5X3

YES! Please send me 2 free Harlequin Duets™ novels and my free surprise gift. After receiving them, if I don't wish to receive anymore, I can return the shipping statement marked cancel. If I don't cancel, I will receive 2 brand-new novels every month, before they're available in stores! In the U.S.A., bill me at the bargain price of $5.14 plus 50¢ shipping & handling per book and applicable sales tax, if any*. In Canada, bill me at the bargain price of $6.14 plus 50¢ shipping & handling per book and applicable taxes**. That's the complete price—what a great deal! I understand that accepting the 2 free books and gift places me under no obligation ever to buy any books. I can always return a shipment and cancel at any time. Even if I never buy another book from Harlequin, the 2 free books and gift are mine to keep forever.

111 HEN DC7P
311 HEN DC7Q

Name	(PLEASE PRINT)	
Address	Apt.#	
City	State/Prov.	Zip/Postal Code

* Terms and prices subject to change without notice. Sales tax applicable in N.Y.
** Canadian residents will be charged applicable provincial taxes and GST.
  All orders subject to approval. Offer limited to one per household and not valid to
  current Harlequin Duets™ subscribers.
® and ™ are registered trademarks of Harlequin Enterprises Limited.   DUETS01

These New York Times *bestselling* authors
have created stories to capture the hearts and minds
of women everywhere.
Here are three classic tales about the power of love—
and the wonder of discovering the place
where you belong....

FINDING HOME

DUNCAN'S BRIDE
by
LINDA HOWARD

CHAIN LIGHTNING
by
ELIZABETH LOWELL

POPCORN AND KISSES
by
KASEY MICHAELS

*Available only from Silhouette
at your favorite retail outlet.*

Silhouette®
Where love comes alive™

MONTANA
Born

From the bestselling series

MONTANA MAVERICKS

Wed in Whitehorn

Two tales that capture living and loving
beneath the Big Sky.

THE MARRIAGE MAKER by Christie Ridgway

Successful businessman Ethan Redford never proposed a deal he
couldn't close—and that included marriage to Cleo Kincaid Monroe!

AND THE WINNER...WEDS! by Robin Wells

Prim and proper Frannie Hannon yearned for Austin Parker, but
her pearls and sweater sets couldn't catch his boots and jeans—or
could they?

And don't miss

MONTANA
Bred

Featuring

JUST PRETENDING by Myrna Mackenzie

&

STORMING WHITEHORN by Christine Scott

Available in May 2002
Available only from Silhouette at your favorite retail outlet.